HER SPELL THAT BINDS ME

Luna Oblonsky

CONTENTS

PART ONE

Rivalry

1 – IONA

1801

Iona's days are spent conjuring pearls. She uses a simple spell her mother taught her that requires very little magic or skill to achieve. They sell their conjured pearls to traveling merchants and jewelers in nearby towns to use for necklaces and other adornments. Whenever they are asked how they manage to find such perfect ocean jewels year after year, they claim to have scavenged for them from clams and oysters on the beach near their cottage.

The pastoral coast of Cornwall has been their home for as long as Iona can remember. Their small white cottage sits on a cliff that overlooks the Celtic Sea. The townspeople who live nearby do find Iona and her mother to be peculiar outliers of their community but never suspect them as witches. They are known as peaceful, reclusive women with a modest trade to sustain themselves.

Iona often takes the steps down the cliffside to walk along the shore. She finds peace in the sound of the ocean and the smell of salt in the air. When it is warm enough, she swims into deeper water and floats on her back to watch the clouds pass overhead. Today, however, she wanders along the edge of the waves to distract herself from her overwhelming sense of dread.

"Iona."

Iona turns and finds her mother walking up the beach behind her. Her skin is pallid, her steps slow and labored, seeming even more ill today than she did the day before.

"Mother, you should be resting," Iona cautions.

Iona runs over to her, fearing that the trek down to the beach was too much for her to handle. Her mother's once vibrant red hair is now dull, and her skin is sallow against her sharp bones. She looks like the ghost of herself.

"Hogwash," Iona's mother says, "I would like to enjoy a stroll on the beach with my daughter."

"You are not well enough," Iona starts to say, but her mother's stern look silences her. She takes Iona's arm, and they continue walking along the shore.

"You have been well occupied," her mother says, looking over at Iona's basket which holds her small pile of shiny pearls.

Her mother pulls out her wand from the pocket sewn into her white cotton dress. She points the wand at the center of her palm.

"Pérola," her mother whispers.

She has to incantate twice more but in time, a pearl materializes in her hand. Its shape is slightly imperfect, but it reflects the sunlight beautifully. She tilts her palm to the side and lets the pearl drop into Iona's basket with the others.

"Why not have a swim today, dear? The water looks so inviting and summer is nearly over," her mother says with a warm smile.

"Maybe later," Iona says, "I would like to make enough pearls to sell in town tomorrow. We require more money for food and medicine."

Iona points her own wand in her palm and says the same incantation. A perfect pearl appears in her hand instantly. She'd only needed to say the spell once. She drops it into her basket along with the others, then says the spell again.

The town of Tintagel is only an hour's walk away and Iona plans to make the trip tomorrow to sell her wares. Normally her mother would accompany her, but her illness has kept her inside for most of the day.

Her mother makes another pearl and drops it into the basket. Iona glances at her mother's wand. It is made of ash wood and is curved downwards like a claw. Many years ago, when her mother was but seven and ten, her wand had appeared to her from within one of the final traces of remaining wildwood near York where she was raised.

As is the case for all witches and warlocks, a wand appears when its owner's magic is fully matured within them. Her mother had lived near those woods throughout her childhood and spent years traversing it in the hope of finding the instrument of her powers.

When Iona had found her wand, she had just turned four and ten. Her mother took her to a glen within a nearby forest. Iona had looked up into the thin canopy of oak trees and saw a perfect piece of wood fall from the sky to the ground in front of her.

The thin piece of oak wood was covered in smooth bark and magically petrified so it would never break or erode. When Iona picked it up, she felt her power flow into it, as if it became a part of her. Iona's mother had been astonished that Iona had found her wand at so young an age. For five years, Iona's mother had taught Iona what little magic she knew. They were common witches with no claim to formidable power or affluence. Despite this, Iona always knew that her magic was different.

For Iona's mother, it took considerable effort to conjure pearls, boil water, levitate small objects, or make plants grow. Though Iona knew very few spells, magic was like breathing. Her spells garnered instantaneous results that rarely faltered.

She hadn't thought much of it until the day her mother had explained to her that magic is generally hereditary. There were some unique exceptions but for the most part, great magic came from influential families all over the world. Iona's family did not fit that description, so her effortless power was seemingly unexplainable.

If Iona had not been the spitting image of her mother, with bright red hair, hazel eyes, and a hint of her mother's sun-kissed skin, she would have suspected that she was not related to her by blood. Iona never had the courage to ask her mother about her exorbitant magic, nor did Iona want to upset her with questions she could not or would not answer. So, she hid her power away.

"Your father used to love days like this," Iona's mother says softly.

Iona glances at her mother in surprise. She almost never spoke of Iona's father except on the one day a year when they visited his grave.

"Before he built our house, we had walked along this beach together and knew that it would be our home," Iona's mother says.

"How did you know?" Iona asks.

"It is something we felt in our bones. A sense of peace came over us and we felt we were finally free of... everything," Iona's mother says.

Iona considers this, looking back at their trail of footsteps in the sand and noticing that they have traveled quite far from the house.

"We should turn back before we get too far," Iona says.

Iona's mother nods, still lost in her memories. They turn and follow their trail of footprints back the way they came. Iona puts her basket in her other arm so her mother can lean on her.

Iona knew little about her father, only that his name was Victor Evora, he married Iona's mother when they were both young, and he was a modest warlock of common birth. He died when Iona was only five years old, and she barely remembers much more than his kind smile when they played on the beach together.

Iona notices her mother looking up into the sky, her eyes focusing on something. Iona looks up too, into the traces of blue sky almost completely covered by misty, grey clouds. She cannot see what her mother is staring at.

"I think I shall make canja de galinha for dinner tonight," her mother says.

"No, I shall make dinner," Iona says, "You must rest."

"I am not as fragile as you think," Iona's mother says, but it is difficult to believe her when she is so winded from their short walk.

"I do not mind," Iona says.

"I know," Iona's mother says, stroking Iona's cheek affectionately, "My sweet child, what did I do to deserve you."

Iona smiles and helps her mother ascend the steps back up the cliffside. It takes a while but eventually they reach their cottage with light blue shutters and a patched roof. Once inside, Iona helps her mother get back into bed. Her mother occupies herself with her weathered copy of *Othello* while Iona goes to cook dinner.

Iona sets her basket on the dining room table, glancing at the pearls that she and her mother had made. Taking her wand, she holds out her palm and whispers, "Diamante."

A flawless diamond the size of a plum appears in her hand. Iona moves it back and forth between her fingers, admiring the way the light dances off of it, then sighs heavily.

"Pérola," Iona whispers, and the diamond is transformed into a pearl. She tosses it into the basket and goes to the kitchen to get started on dinner.

When Iona gets ready for bed that night, her worries still plague her tired mind. Her mother is getting so sick, though she tries to hide it. Iona does not know how to help apart from keeping her mother in bed and feeding her well.

Her mother has always been melancholy, ever since Iona's father died, but as her frailty grows so does her disconcerting nostalgia. It makes Iona suspect that her mother knows her life is near its end. Even the strongest of magic cannot make one immortal, but Iona wishes she could find some way for her mother to live just a little while longer.

Iona looks at her reflection in the one small mirror they own and brushes her hair until all the knots are detangled. The mirror is slightly warped and has desilvered spots around the edges. Iona has asked her mother to replace it with a new, larger mirror but her mother insists that they cannot spare the expense.

Iona configures the strands of her long red hair into a braid and ties the end with a blue ribbon. She blows out her candle and crawls into bed. She squeezes her eyes shut, hoping that sleep will take her quickly, but a growing warmth in her stomach makes it impossible to drift off.

She sighs frustratedly and flips onto her back to stare at her ceiling. This persistent ache inside her only grows more insistent with time and it's a hunger that she's learned how to feed on her own.

She pulls up the skirt of her nightgown and slips a hand between her legs, sighing with relief when her fingers stroke her folds gently. She rubs her sensitive flesh in slow circles until her chest rises and falls heavily and sweat beads on her brow. Her other hand reaches beneath the loose neckline of her nightgown to squeeze her breast and play with her nipple.

Pleasure builds quickly, her wetness dripping onto her impatient fingers, then overflows in a rush. Iona covers her mouth to stifle her moan, then waits until her breathing returns to normal to bring her skirt back down and curl into her mattress.

This insatiable desire has grown exponentially over the past year, as if her body suddenly decided it was impatient with her chastity and intends to torment her until she finds a lover. She is unsure if it is normal and the idea of asking her mother about it is a mortifying prospect. She has no friends to ask about it either.

Her mother kept Iona isolated for most of her life. She finally allowed Iona to visit town when she'd turned eighteen, but only to sell wares and come straight home. Iona knows better than to ask why. The one time she did, her mother did not speak for the rest of the day until Iona apologized for her insolence. Her mother had told her that she'd done nothing wrong, and they never spoke of it again.

The closest Iona had ever gotten to making a friend her own age was when she'd met a young Cornish girl named Tamsyn when they were both sixteen. Tamsyn had wavy brown hair, coral pink lips, and even more freckles on her face than Iona does. She was beautiful and Iona needed to know her. She'd shyly introduced herself and they'd talked for a few minutes until Iona's mother came back after selling their pearls and told Iona that they were leaving.

She'd had many conversations with Tamsyn until a few months ago. Iona visited town and saw Tamsyn there with a man she hadn't seen before. Iona saw the golden ring on Tamsyn's finger and that her stomach was swollen with child. Iona's heart broke, though she'd told herself time and time again that Tamsyn would never be for her. Iona had left town swiftly before Tamsyn could see her.

The memory makes Iona bereft in her loneliness. She longs for someone to hold, to touch, to confide in. All she knows of romance comes from the many books she reads. She loves her mother so much, but she turned twenty last week. Her youth is slipping through her fingers, and she does not want to miss the chance to live her life.

Iona could never bring herself to leave her mother behind to start a new life elsewhere, especially now that she's sick. Though Iona knows her place is here, the lonely ache inside her grows more difficult to subdue.

The next day, Iona cooks breakfast for her and her mother. She sets a plate of eggs and sausages on the kitchen table. Her mother smiles up at her before picking up her fork.

"Do not forget to wear your father's ring," her mother reminds Iona when she sees her taking her blue shawl from the hook by the door.

"Of course," Iona says.

Anytime Iona left the house, her mother insisted that she wear the ring, though never explained why. Iona walks to Tintagel with her basket of pearls. She takes the long dirt path that borders the coast, wind making tendrils of her hair come lose from her bun. She hums idle tunes to herself to pass the time and spins her father's amethyst ring around her index finger, sensing the magic trapped inside the silver band.

Soon the town is visible in the distance and Iona quickens her steps. She crosses a field to enter the heart of the small town. The smell of fresh bread from the local bakery makes her stomach growl.

She passes the general store and spies Mr. Enys, a peddler who travels around the countryside to buy and distribute goods of all sorts. He befriended Iona's mother many years ago, before Iona was born.

Mr. Enys is more than happy to buy the pearls and praises Iona's uncanny ability to find such perfect delicacies, especially while there was a growing pearl shortage elsewhere.

Iona visits the general store to buy food and medicine. She notices a tiny beggar girl sitting in the dirt and holding out her hand for money. All the other townspeople pass her by without a glance. When Iona passes by the little blonde girl, she takes five coins and places them in her tiny hand.

"Thank you, miss!" the beggar girl smiles wide, then runs to the general store to spend her money. It should last her a week at least if she spends wisely.

Iona notices an old woman in black watching her from across the town square. Her clouded blue eyes are angered as she looks Iona up and down. Then she spits on the ground before her, glares at Iona with knowing eyes, and walks away. Iona pulls her shawl tighter around her shoulders and follows the quickest route out of the town.

When Iona returns to the cottage, she leaves the bags of food in the kitchen and finds the bottle of medicine. She goes to her mother's bedroom door and knocks gently.

"Mother? I have returned," Iona says.

"Come in, dear," her mother rasps, then coughs violently.

Iona opens the door and finds her mother doubled over and nearly choking on air with a handkerchief covering her mouth. Iona runs to her side and rubs her back until the coughing fit subsides. Then she gasps when her mother removes the kerchief from her mouth, and it is stained with blood. Her mother tries to hide it from Iona, but she'd seen the stark dots of red against the white fabric.

"The sickness is worsening," Iona whispers.

"I am fine," her mother insists.

"You are not fine," Iona snaps, hating that her mother insists on placating her.

Iona pours a serving of the new medicine onto a spoon and lifts it to her mother's lips. Her mother takes the medicine and avoids Iona's gaze.

"There must be some spell or potion that could help you," Iona says.

"Magic can only delay the inevitable," Iona's mother says softly.

Iona holds back tears as her helplessness overwhelms her.

"We should still try," Iona insists.

Her mother reaches for her and Iona sobs as she buries her face in her mother's chest. She strokes Iona's hair soothingly the way only a mother can.

"There is something we can do," her mother says.

"There is?" Iona asks, pulling away to look down on her.

"Please fetch my wand," her mother says.

Iona does so and hands the piece of wood to her mother. Her mother thinks for a moment, her expression tired and contemplative. Then she lifts her wand, closes her eyes, and whispers, "Nocht."

It was a spell Iona had never heard before. There is a sudden shift in the air around her. Everything looks the same, but the atmosphere has changed, as if the air was not as thin and the sunlight held more warmth.

"Convocare Samuel Lysander," her mother whispers with a wave of her wand.

"Iona, would you please make some tea?" her mother asks.

"Tea?" Iona asks.

"Yes, whatever tea we have that's best," her mother says.

"But… what spells did you cast?" Iona asks.

"I sent a message to an old friend. Please go make the tea," her mother insists.

Iona begrudgingly does as she's told. She takes out the teapot and pours water in. The tea is steeping within the boiling kettle when there is a knock on the cottage door. Iona jumps at the sound and looks to the door in surprise.

"Let him in, Iona," her mother calls from her bedroom.

Iona looks between her mother's bedroom and the front door as her apprehension grows. There is a second knock at the door, more urgently this time, and Iona goes to answer it.

When she opens the front door, she finds a tall white-haired man in a fine black suit and top hat. He looks to be similar in age to her mother, in his early sixties. When he sees Iona, he smiles and removes his hat respectfully and bows his head.

"Iona?" the man asks, looking as if he recognizes her, though they have never met.

"Yes," Iona replies cautiously.

"Your mother sent for me. May I please come in?" he asks.

Iona steps aside. The man walks in and looks around.

"Samuel, I am here," Iona's mother calls.

"Leona," Samuel says, relief in his tone.

He rushes into the bedroom, leaving Iona baffled and confused. Her mother has never spoken of this strange man before, but then again, she never speaks of her life before she settled in Cornwall.

Iona takes a few steps closer to the bedroom to try and hear what they are saying, but they converse in hushed tones. Iona slumps into a dining room chair and waits impatiently for them to finish.

About thirty minutes later, Samuel emerges from the

bedroom. His bright blue eyes are lined with red from recent tears. Iona straightens in her chair.

"Iona, I know you do not know me, but I am very happy to meet you. I wish it were under different circumstances," Samuel says.

"Who are you and how do you know my mother?" Iona asks, unwilling to let another second go by without answers.

"My name is Samuel Lysander. I am a professor of conjuration at the Lysander College for Young Witches in Austria," Samuel says.

"You own a college?" Iona asks, eyes widening.

"No, no. My ancestor founded the college," Samuel clarifies, "Your mother and I are old friends."

Iona sits, waiting for more of an explanation but none comes.

"What did she say to you?" Iona prompts.

"She wants you to come with me to college and study magic," Samuel says.

Iona stares at him in disbelief and does not know how to respond. Her head is spinning, and she is torn between getting answers from Samuel or running to her mother's bedside to speak with her.

"I cannot leave my mother here alone when she is so sick," Iona says.

Samuel nods solemnly, then gestures to Iona's mother's room.

"Please, talk to her now and she will explain," Samuel says, stepping into the kitchen to give them privacy.

Iona stands and reenters her mother's room. Iona's blood turns cold when she sees her mother's face. She looks haggard after her conversation with Samuel. She is out of breath but smiles when Iona approaches.

"Your first adventure awaits," her mother says.

"No, it does not," Iona says stubbornly, sitting on the edge of the bed, "I am not going."

"Iona, you must go. This is not... a discussion," her mother says, though her breath is labored.

"You cannot care for yourself. How could I possibly leave you here?" Iona asks.

"You are not leaving me here," her mother says, "I am leaving too."

This surprises Iona.

"Where are you going?" Iona asks.

"To the forests of Yorkshire, from my childhood. I will commune with nature, where the wildwood once stood and in whatever forests are left, and I will let its magic heal me. I have already tried potions and other healing magic, but nothing has worked. This is my final chance for magic to intervene and it is something only I can do alone," Iona's mother says.

"Could that truly work?" Iona asks.

"It very well could. And even if it does not, to spend my final days surrounded by that peaceful beauty is how a witch should leave this world," her mother says.

Iona's tears return, hating to hear her mother speak of her own death.

"Iona, meu querida, please do not weep for me," her mother says, her voice thick with emotion.

"I do not want to leave you," Iona cries, "I can live here on my own until you return."

"This was never the life you were meant to lead. It was not meant to last forever, dearest. Whatever may happen to me, you must secure your own future now. Your life is just beginning, and your power is stronger than you know. You must learn how to use it and become the witch I know you can be," her mother says, "Please promise me that you will go."

"But mother," Iona tries to say, but her mother takes her hand and grasps it firmly.

"Promise me," her mother insists.

Iona sighs, then nods reluctantly, "I will."

They embrace and weep together. Iona is gentle with her mother's frail body as she cries into her shoulder. It takes all of Iona's strength to pull away from her and leave the room.

When she remembers Samuel is still in the kitchen waiting for her, she wipes at her cheeks with embarrassment.

"There is tea on the stove," Iona says.

Then she goes to her bedroom to pack.

Samuel carries Iona's bags for her when they leave the cottage. She is still crying after saying one final goodbye to her mother. She'd insisted that her mother keep her father's ring to give her comfort throughout her journey. Iona will miss her mother terribly while she is away but hopes to see her again when she is healed. Iona would normally never cry in front of a perfect stranger, but she struggles to keep her tears at bay. Her sorrow is momentarily forgotten when she sees what Samuel had arrived in.

A hot air balloon floats on the edge of the cliff in front of them. The balloon is light blue, almost matching the sky, and is connected with rope to a wicker box.

"Have you ever traveled by hot air balloon?" Samuel asks.

Iona dabs at her eyes with a handkerchief and clears her throat.

"I have only ever traveled by foot or wagon," Iona says.

"Then you are in for a treat," Samuel says, "Though the journey will be swift."

Samuel holds out his hand for her. She takes it and steps over the edge of the cliff and into the basket. Samuel steps in too, then sets Iona's bags down in the corner of the basket and closes the compartment behind him. He pulls out his wand and points it above them.

"Pyrkagiá," Samuel says, and fire erupts from his wand and makes the balloon float upwards.

They are shot up into the air and float towards the sky. Iona watches the ground get farther and farther away. Soon the white cottage on the cliff becomes tiny in the distance until the balloon is enveloped in a white cloud. Iona looks around anxiously, unable to see anything beyond the wicker basket. Water crystals cover her hair and her light blue dress until she's soaked. She is relieved when they make it above the cloud cover and the sun shines upon them again.

"Here," Samuel says, handing Iona a warm blanket.

Iona takes it gratefully and wraps it around herself. Then silence falls as they drift through the sky. Iona wouldn't have known how fast they were going if it weren't for the clouds. They move quickly enough that Iona imagines the journey to Austria will only take a short while.

"I pushed this vessel to its very limit of speed to get to you because of the urgency of your mother's summons but on the journey back I thought a mild 400 knots per hour would be more comfortable for you," Samuel says as he wraps a second blanket around himself, "We should arrive at the college in about three hours, right before sunset."

Iona's stomach flips at hearing exactly how fast the balloon is going. She would have thought that her hair would be whipping around her, and the wind would cut her face if she felt the true force of their speed, but the balloon's enchantment seems to protect them. Iona looks out at the sky as silence falls again, then glances at Samuel.

He is looking down and fiddling with his hat nervously, "I understand that this is a very difficult time for you. I cannot imagine what you must be feeling, to leave your only home so suddenly."

"It is a bit of a shock," Iona admits.

Iona trusts this man because her mother does, but not completely. Her guard raises as the man looks at her with concern.

"Do you have any questions for me?" Samuel says.

He whispers an incantation, and two small chairs materialize near him and Iona. They both take a seat facing each other, their knees almost touching within the cramped space.

"I do not know what to ask... I wonder if you might tell me more about your college," Iona says.

"Of course. Lysander College has courses on five tenets

of magical ability. I teach conjuring, Professor Rayowa Salum teaches enchantment, Professor Corella Yun teaches phytology, Professor Talulah Pari teaches clairvoyance, and Professor Josephine Salvador teaches illusion magic," Samuel says.

Iona only had knowledge of conjuring and knew how to make a handful of simple potions, but the other magic tenets are entirely new to her. There was so much that her mother had not taught her.

Samuel says, "The college itself is enchanted in more ways than one. Many languages are spoken but we understand each other all the same."

Samuel whispers a spell that Iona cannot hear over the wind and a cup of hot chocolate appears in his hand. He hands it to Iona who takes it gratefully.

"Every witch comes to us with differing levels of arcane knowledge. Lysander College helps to expand a witch's lexicon of spells and hone the magic a witch may already know. A modest witch can become a great one. An innately gifted witch can become legendary," Samuel says.

"How long am I expected to stay at this school?" Iona asks.

"One year, two terms. Fall term begins tomorrow. You could classify it as more of a seminar given its brevity, though we cover a great deal of knowledge during that span of time. You will be a very different witch by next spring," Samuel says, "And if you decide to study further, you can attend specialized colleges in other countries depending on what kind of magic you wish to master. Some witches choose to study in every continent."

Iona supposes that a year is a commitment she could make.

"I imagine I shall be the oldest student there," Iona murmurs.

When Samuel looks at her in question, but is too polite to ask, Iona explains, "I just turned twenty last week."

"There are witches of various ages at our college," Samuel shrugs.

"Oh," Iona says, "That is a relief. I thought I was delayed."

Samuel shakes his head and smiles reassuringly, "Your mother attended Lysander College when she was two and twenty, so you are not delayed in the slightest. We have students of all ages."

"Is that where you met my mother?" Iona asks.

"No, we met in York at my family's old estate," Samuel looks down at his hat.

Iona wishes he would give her more details, but his expression makes it clear that he is not comfortable elaborating further.

A while later, the balloon descends on its own and Iona straightens in her chair. She looks over the edge of the wicker compartment as they float through the cloud cover.

When the clouds disperse, Iona gasps. Below them is an expansive mountain range with a dusting of snow on the highest peaks. Within the mountains is a hidden valley that holds a dense misty forest.

On the lefthand corner of the forest is a wide, green clearing. There sits a collection of buildings which are connected by arched corridors. The buildings are made of dark granite stone with tall, pointed spires. As the balloon floats closer, Iona can make out intricate stained-glass patterns on the lancet windows.

"Welcome to Lysander College," Samuel says.

The balloon touches down a short distance away from the college grounds. Not far from them is a two-story building that stands apart from the main structure. The air is cooler in the higher altitude and Iona shivers from the chill.

A plump old woman waits for them in the grass. She has light brown hair with strands of gray and wears a practical brown dress. Samuel takes Iona's bags and leads her to the old woman.

"Mrs. Ainsley, allow me to introduce Iona Evora. Iona, Mrs. Ainsley is the college caretaker and groundskeeper," Samuel says.

"Very nice to meet you, Iona. I hope your journey was safe and temperate," Mrs. Ainsley says with a wide smile.

"It was, indeed," Iona smiles back shyly.

"Splendid. Let's get you to your room so you can rest after your travels," Mrs. Ainsley says, "Good day, Professor Lysander."

Mrs. Ainsley takes out her wand, points it at Iona's suitcases, and says, "Kuelea."

The bags lift out of Samuel's grasp and float towards her. Iona watches the luggage hover as Mrs. Ainsley leads the way into the college grounds.

"I shall see you tomorrow for our first class," Samuel says, "Your schedule and supplies should be in your room. Mrs. Ainsley can help you with the rest."

"Thank you," Iona says, though part of her wishes that Samuel was not leaving her alone so soon.

Samuel tips his hat to her and walks away. Iona looks around in a daze. The sun is no longer visible over the acicular mountains in the west. Only faint purple and orange light paints the clouded sky overhead. In every direction, the surrounding forest has trees of various kinds and seems to be divided into haphazard sections of vegetation that would not normally coexist.

"Come along, dear," Mrs. Ainsley says.

Iona hadn't realized that she'd stopped walking. Mrs. Ainsley waits for Iona to rejoin her.

"Those are the staff apartments," Mrs. Ainsley says, pointing to the building that Samuel disappears into.

They enter one of the stone corridors, which is bordered by pointed arches with vaulted stone ceilings above. To their left, Iona can see the edge of the misty forest. To their right is a well-manicured garden filled with pink and red flowers.

"The gardens are a fine place to study when the weather is nice. Take advantage of it now, as our winters come too soon and linger far too long," Mrs. Ainsley says.

She then points to a pair of wide wooden doors across from the garden.

"The library is in the far corner, over there," Mrs. Ainsley says, pointing beyond the gardens, "And behind us is the incantation chamber where students can practice their spells."

Mrs. Ainsley continues walking at a brisk pace. They approach a substantial building that is three stories tall with countless stained-glass windows. Iona is especially taken by intricate rose windows on the higher floors that glint in the twilight.

"That is the lyceum where your classes will be held," Mrs. Ainsley says, "There will be a map included in your school things. Do not fret."

Mrs. Ainsley must have noticed Iona's nervous tension. When Iona meets her gaze, she smiles encouragingly and beckons Iona onwards. When they pass the lyceum, there is another stone plaza and three new buildings.

"Here is the central plaza. The bell tower there rings every hour and is always perfectly on time," Mrs. Ainsley boasts, pointing to the tower that is tipped with the tallest spire on campus, "The professor's offices are on the right, the dining hall to the left. You are welcome to a spot of supper after you have settled in."

Iona is relieved to see the other end of the college with two more buildings left on either side of a third courtyard of grass. At the center of the courtyard stands a statue of a witch with her wand pointed towards the belltower.

"There is the student's parlor where you can spend time with your classmates after hours," Mrs. Ainsley says, pointing to a circular building on the lefthand corner, "And on the other side of the courtyard are the dormitories."

Mrs. Ainsley walks across the grass towards the dormitories, which are almost completely covered in a layer of green ivy. They step into a lavish foyer with geometrically patterned wooden floors, columned archways that lead to sitting rooms on either side, and a wooden staircase that leads to the second floor.

Mrs. Ainsley takes Iona up the stairs and down a long hallway of doors. They pass by a blonde witch who looks Iona up and down with critical blue eyes. Iona looks away from her shyly, then almost runs straight into Mrs. Ainsley when she stops at a particular door without warning.

"Here we are," Mrs. Ainsley says, opening the door and gesturing for Iona to go inside.

The room is bigger than Iona's entire cottage. Wainscoted walls are partly covered with white wallpaper decorated with symmetrically patterned blue flowers and green leaves. There is a massive four poster bed against the lefthand wall with a white gossamer canopy and pristine white bedding. A Turkish rug of blue, gold, and hints of red covers a substantial portion of the wooden floor. Right by the door is a tall white wardrobe and on the far wall, next to a floor to ceiling window, is a wooden desk with brass filigree accents. On the desk is a collection of books, paper, pens, and glass vials.

"The washroom is behind this door," Mrs. Ainsley says, walking to the right and opening a door to reveal a bathroom with a copper bathtub, a wooden toilet, and a vanity dresser with a mirror attached.

"Make yourself comfortable. All of your school things are on your desk, along with your class schedule for the term. Samuel was kind enough to have them brought here for you," Mrs. Ainsley says, "If you need anything at all, I am just down the hall."

"Thank you," Iona says, wondering if Mrs. Ainsley meant that Samuel had bought the books for her or if they were provided by the college.

"You are very welcome here," Mrs. Ainsley says warmly.

After setting Iona's suitcases in front of her bed, the stout groundskeeper takes her leave. When Iona is alone, she looks around herself at the fine furnishings that are now hers to use. It is the richest room she has ever set foot in. She's almost scared to touch anything.

Iona looks out the window and turns the golden handle to pull it open, delighted to find that there is a small balcony framed by vines of ivy. Iona steps onto the balcony and looks out at the courtyard. She is startled when the bell tower suddenly rings out as a new hour begins. She counts seven chimes of the loud bell, then the campus goes silent once more.

Iona hears the faint sound of a page turning in a book. She looks to her left and notices another witch is sitting outside and facing in the opposite direction. She is three balconies away and has curled raven hair that is almost black. Surrounding her are bountiful arrays of multicolored flowers all in bloom. A white flower seems to be the most prominent of the many blooms, and the scent wafts to Iona on the wind, a sweet, almost creamy aroma.

The witch sitting within the botanical oasis flips another page in her book and begins to hum idly to herself with an airy, ethereal voice. It is a tune that Iona does not recognize but sounds like a complex concerto. The woman raises one hand and moves her fingers through the air, as if she were playing the pianoforte in her mind. Iona steps back inside and closes her window, not wanting to disturb the other witch from her reading.

When Iona enters the bathroom, her steps echo against the white tile floor. There is a circular window across from the bathtub that provides a beautiful view of the eastern mountains, which are made pink by the residual light of the setting sun.

Iona reaches out curiously to turn one of the two valves at the top of the bathtub and water gushes from the faucet. Where the water came from, Iona had no idea. The faucet was not connected to any water source that she could see. She reaches out to test the temperature and it is perfect.

Iona excitedly closes the bathroom door, locks it, and sheds her blue dress and underclothes. When the tub is full, she dips her hand inside and sighs at the pleasant heat. She sifts through a row of cabinets for soap, and places a bar on a small metal table near the bath. Then she steps inside the tub and sighs happily when the warm water envelopes her. She leans back against the metal, closes her eyes, and breathes in the steam.

Then she lurches in panic when she feels something moving against her back inside the tub. She feels it again and yelps. Something is in the tub with her. A sponge. More sponges materialize into the tub and run all over her body. Soap bubbles form in the water and float to the surface as the sponges scrub her vigorously. She squirms against them but finds herself watching with fascination as the tub works its magic.

The sponges scrub her arms, legs, and torso. She winces when they clean her most intimate areas with alarming thoroughness. Then she struggles and giggles when they scrub the bottoms of her feet and between her toes. She gasps when she's pulled down beneath the surface of the water and two brushes scrub her hair and scalp with shampoo. A sponge scrubs her face and behind her ears. Before she can run out of air, her head pops back out of the water. She withstands the persistent scrubbing until all of the sudden, it stops, and the bubbles disappear.

The water recedes rapidly down the drain and Iona hesitantly stands in the now empty tub. She is about to step out when a swirling rush of hot air surrounds her. The air is coming from within the tub and blows away all the water droplets from her skin and hair. Within thirty seconds, Iona's hair and body are completely dry.

Iona scrambles out of the tub and stares back at it with astonishment. Though she feels slightly violated by the tenacious bathtub, when she looks down at herself and runs her hand over her skin, it is unbelievably soft and smooth. All of her scars have disappeared, even a prominent one on her arm that she'd had since she was twelve. Her light brown freckles are all that's left.

When Iona looks at her face in the vanity mirror, she sees that any small pimples on her cheeks and chin had vanished.

Her hair shines as if she had brushed it a thousand times and her skin almost glows. All of her small insecurities have been scrubbed away, without a single blemish left behind.

"Goodness," Iona whispers to herself.

There is a knock at her bedroom door and Iona jumps. Looking around frantically, she notices a robe hanging on the back of the door. She throws it on and approaches the door. There stands a young woman with long honey blonde hair, warm amber eyes, and an elegant aquiline nose.

"Oh! Good evening," the woman says, giving Iona a once over.

"Good evening," Iona says, her cheeks going pink as she puts her arms over her chest.

"Please forgive the intrusion. I thought I'd heard a scream coming from your room and wanted to be sure nothing was amiss," the woman says, "My name is Crescentia. Crescentia Léandre."

Crescentia curtsies and Iona does as well.

"How do you do, my name is Iona Evora," Iona says.

"Are you well? You seem flushed," Crescentia says.

"Oh... um... I used the bathtub, and I did scream because I was not expecting..." Iona trails off, unable to articulate what had just happened to her.

"Oh," Crescentia giggles, "Another common witch."

Iona shrinks at the comment. Crescentia notices Iona's discomfort and quickly clarifies her meaning.

"Please do not misunderstand. I am common too! These enchanted furnishings were foreign to me when I arrived here yesterday," Crescentia says.

"Oh, I see," Iona says, her ire receding.

"You will grow accustomed to it. If I may warn you, the wardrobe is enchanted as well. It clothes you on its own, but you must picture the dress that you want to wear, or it will choose for you," Crescentia says.

Iona eyes her wardrobe warily. Did high born witches not know how to wash or dress themselves? To Iona, it seems a frivolous use of magic.

"Thank you for the warning," Iona says, "And apologies for the noise. I did not mean to alarm you."

"No apology necessary," Crescentia says, "Good night."

"Good night," Iona smiles, then closes her door.

Iona sighs and leans against the door. This day has taken everything out of her, and she can barely keep her eyes open anymore. She rummages through her suitcase for her nightdress, then sheds the robe and pulls her dress over her head.

When she sinks into her new bed and sighs happily at how comfortable it is. The mattress molds itself to the shape of her body and in no time at all, she drifts off into a dreamless sleep.

2 – IONA

The chime of the bell tower wakes Iona the next morning. The first rays of dawn shine through her window and paint the walls with golden light. Iona stretches pleasantly, in a state of complete relaxation, until she remembers what today is. She jumps out of bed and scrambles to the wooden desk in the corner. There she finds a copy of her term schedule. She had been so tired the night before that she'd forgotten to check it.

On Monday mornings, she has clairvoyance and prophecy with Professor Pari and conjuration with Samuel in the afternoon. Or perhaps she should start thinking of him as Professor Lysander, so she does not accidentally call him by his first name in class.

She rushes to her suitcase and opens it. She is taken aback when she finds it completely empty. She knew she hadn't emptied her suitcases last night. She suspects that magic had unpacked them for her, which meant only one thing.

Iona approaches the white wardrobe and reaches out to grasp one of the knobs. Iona pulls her arm back in surprise when the doors fling open, and a rotating rack of dresses and cloaks spins around inside until it lands on an amber colored dress that Iona had been thinking of wearing.

Iona gasps when her nightdress falls down her body of its own accord and a new chemise floats out of the wardrobe.

She lifts her arms up as the chemise falls onto her. Then stays fly out of the wardrobe and envelope her, tying itself snugly around her waist and chest. She is dressed in a petticoat, white stockings, and finally the amber dress with an empire silhouette and quarter length sleeves. It was one of Iona's best dresses that she normally saved for birthdays or Yule. Perhaps it was too fancy, but she wants to look her best for her first day.

The wardrobe gives her a black cloak to protect against the cold mountain air. Her hair is lifted and swirled around into a bun at the top of her head. She feels pins materialize and fix the bun to her scalp. The final detail, a pair of white lace gloves, pop from the wardrobe and into the air, floating down until Iona reaches out to catch them. These were not hers. She was sure of it. Iona glances at her desk and the books that she had been given. Had Samuel bought her new clothes as well?

Iona doesn't have time to dwell on it too long. A knock on her door startles her and she goes to open it. Behind her, the wardrobe sucks up her discarded nightgown and closes its doors.

"Good morning," Crescentia curtsies and says, "You look lovely!"

"As do you," Iona says, curtsying in turn.

Crescentia truly does look perfect in her pale pink dress. Her golden hair is pinned up with curls framing her heart shaped face.

"I thought since you did not have time to explore the campus before classes began, you could use a guide," Crescentia says.

"That would be lovely," Iona says, already feeling infinitely better.

"Gather your grimoires and let's go," Crescentia says.

Iona and Crescentia walk side by side down the stairs to the foyer. They pass other young witches as they go and Iona peers at them curiously. The students are from all sorts of far-off places. All are fair and intimidating to Iona's eyes.

Iona is struck by the genteel beauty of one woman in

particular. She is petite and prim with tanned skin, hooded brown eyes, and dark hair. The woman stands with effortless poise in her light blue dress, which is trimmed with gold thread. Iona notices a sapphire ring on the woman's right hand that sparkles beneath the lace of her glove.

"That is Samaira Dayalu" Crescentia whispers to Iona, "She is descended from a distinguished bloodline in Nepal."

"My word, she has traveled far," Iona says.

"She has indeed. Phoebe Kimball, an acquaintance of mine, came all the way from Massachusetts. And I've heard that there is a witch from Greenland as well," Crescentia says, then she pauses, "Should we wait for any of your other acquaintances to join us?"

Iona flushes, "No... in truth I have not been familiar with many witches before now, apart from my mother."

"I see. Not to worry! I shall take you under my wing," Crescentia says with a warm smile as she takes Iona's arm.

As they exit the dormitories, they cross the grass courtyard where other witches are congregating before classes begin.

Crescentia covertly gestures to a witch with caramel skin, "That is Vadoma Lovell, a Romani witch who comes from Scotland, though she has lived everywhere you can imagine. She is quite skilled in conjuration magic."

Crescentia gestures to another woman with lustrous black hair, "That is Kokuro Sato, from Japan. She brews the best potions."

Iona notices the blonde, blue eyed woman who had regarded her critically in the hall yesterday. She wears a black dress and saunters with practiced grace.

"That is Ksenia Ulanova from Moscow. She is a viper," Crescentia warns, "Pray that she never notices you."

Iona gulps and averts her eyes, "How do you know all of these women?"

"I have met them all in passing at rituals, or at some party my parents forced me to attend," Crescentia says.

"Why would they force you?" Iona asks. If she had the

opportunity to attend a grand party, she would have jumped at the chance.

"My parents like for me and my siblings to fraternize with the children of influential families as often as possible. They would die of happiness if we managed to wed one of them," Crescentia chuckles, "My parents are newly gifted with stronger magic than our ancestors had before. They hope to be the beginning of a new bloodline of powerful magic users. That is why they sent me here to learn with the very best."

A brunette woman in a white dress and blue bonnet approaches them.

"Good day, Phoebe!" Crescentia says, and all three women curtsy to each other.

"Good day, Crescentia. It has been too long," Phoebe smiles.

"May I introduce Iona Evora, from…" Crescentia trails off.

"Cornwall. In England," Iona finishes for her.

"My, you are an exotic creature, aren't you?" Phoebe says boldly, tilting her head and looking Iona up and down.

"Um… thank you. As are you," Iona says shyly.

"You are Portuguese as well," Phoebe says confidently, "and raised in Cornwall all your life."

Iona's eyebrows raise, "How did you know?"

"Her clairvoyance is unmatched," Crescentia says, "Except perhaps by me."

"We shall see about that," Phoebe says with a grin, "I have honed my skills since we last spoke."

"Phoebe!" a witch calls from across the entrance hall.

"Please excuse me," Phoebe says with a curtsy before running to greet her other friend.

"Let us not be late," Crescentia says, beckoning Iona onward.

As they cross the courtyard, Iona learns that Crescentia's family is from Lyon, France and they are distantly descended from Romans of antiquity. Her ancestors were peasants that rose higher and higher as the years passed. When she hears this, Iona is reminded that the grounds are enchanted. Crescentia is speaking to her in French but all she hears is

English. Iona marvels at the strength of the magic that lingers around them.

"Let me see your schedule," Crescentia says, holding out her hand.

Iona gives Crescentia the paper and she sighs with disappointment.

"We are on different schedules," Crescentia says, "The college is separated in two rotations to ensure the class sizes are not too large. We will only have class together on Fridays."

Iona is disappointed to hear this as well, but she supposes she can still spend time with Crescentia after class. They pass the belltower, cross the stone plaza, and approach the lyceum, the main college building.

The roof is held aloft by stone caryatids of women wearing panels of cloth that just barely cover their ample curves. Iona stares up at the women, in awe of the intricate carving that makes them appear almost real.

The interior of the lyceum is even more finely decorated than the dormitories. The stained-glass windows leave multicolored patterns of light across the marble floors and depict scenes of witches performing great feats of magic. The walls are paneled with wood and covered with rich tapestries of fae, witches, and magical creatures. Crescentia points to the largest stained-glass window that looms over the main staircase. It depicts a dark-haired woman in a deep blue dress.

"That is the college founder, Ysolde Lysander. She is descended from the Ostrogoths," Crescentia recites, "And Professor Lysander is descended from her. He teaches conjuration."

"I met him yesterday," Iona says, "He is acquainted with my mother."

"Perhaps he will give you higher marks then," Crescentia jokes.

"One can only hope," Iona grins.

They climb the staircase to the third floor and walk swiftly down the hall.

"Your class is there," Crescentia says, pointing to a door ahead of them, "We must have lunch this afternoon."

"I would be delighted," Iona says.

"Iona," Samuel calls.

Iona and Crescentia turn to see Samuel walking towards them.

"I shall see you then," Crescentia calls as she walks to her class.

Iona waits for Samuel to reach her.

"Good morning," Iona says.

"Good morning. I am glad to see you have already made a friend and found your first class. You are doing excellently for your first day," Samuel says with a smile.

"I suppose I am," Iona smiles back.

"Do not let me keep you. I only wanted to check on you, but you seem to have everything well in hand," Samuel says.

"Sir, I must ask, did you buy new clothes for me? And the books for school?" Iona asks.

Samuel scratches the back of his head sheepishly.

"No, I did not buy them, but they were conjured as gifts," Samuel admits.

Iona looks down at her white lace gloves with new appreciation and wonders when she will learn spells to make new clothes for herself. Even though she knows that the gloves were not bought with money, Iona feels awkward accepting them from a man she only just met. She takes the gloves off and tries to hand them back to Samuel.

"I appreciate your kindness, but I cannot accept them," Iona says.

"No, please, keep them. I am happy to give them to you," Samuel says.

"I do not need charity," Iona says.

"Please, consider them a gift. I have missed so many birthdays and holidays... I am happy to give these things to you. I conjured items that my daughter, Elise, also wears. I hope they are in the right style," Samuel says, "Elise is a student here as well. I am hopeful that you two can be friends."

Iona looks down at the lace gloves suspiciously.

"I have no ulterior motive in this gesture, on that I swear," Samuel says.

"Very well," Iona says, taking back the gloves, "Thank you for your generosity."

"You are most welcome," Samuel smiles, a bit relieved, "I shall see you in class this afternoon."

"Until then," Iona says.

Samuel turns and walks away toward his lecture hall. Iona turns around to go to her class as well but, in her haste, she collides into someone. Iona gasps as all of their books fall to the floor.

"I beg your pardon, I-," Iona starts to say, but the words get caught in her throat.

A pair of piercing blood red eyes bore straight into Iona's skull. The eyes belong to a tall woman with olive skin, full lips, and thick raven hair that Iona recognizes from the balcony last night. Except now, the woman's curls have been tamed and pulled back into a bun at the crown of her head. A red flower is pinned in her bun, and stray curls frame her diamond shaped face.

She wears a pristine white dress with ruffles on the hem and short puffed sleeves. On her neck sits a ruby charm necklace that matches her wideset eyes, which were initially filled with surprise when Iona bumped into her, but now are narrowed in irritation. Iona could have stood there forever transfixed by the woman's stare if it weren't for a deep frightening growl that broke Iona's daze.

Iona gasps and takes a step back when she sees that the growls are coming from a grey wolf who is baring his teeth at her. The woman seems utterly unphased by the wolf's presence and its threatening snarl. She leans over to pick her books up off the floor.

"Watch where you step!" the woman snaps at her, then bumps her shoulder against Iona's aggressively before entering the lecture hall.

Iona flushes as she picks up her grimoires and, after a moment's hesitation, enters the lecture hall. The room has three rows of raised desks that curve into a semicircle around a platform with a podium. Iona avoids the red eyed woman's gaze and finds a seat in the second row behind her.

Samaira Dayalu enters the lecture hall seconds later and takes a seat beside the red eyed woman. They greet each other as friends. Ksenia Ulanova arrives next and sits with them too. Iona watches the three young witches curiously as they whisper amongst themselves.

"Have you seen the rabble sculking through these halls?" Ksenia murmurs to the red eyed one.

"One accosted me in the hall but seconds ago," the red eyed witch says with scorn.

"Such impropriety," Ksenia sniffs, "I hope their spells are not so tactless as their manners."

"They are here to expand their knowledge of magic, the same as you or me," Samaira says.

Ksenia scoffs, her blonde curls bouncing with her movements, "Then let them learn in their hovels like they always have."

Iona cringes at the venom in Ksenia's tone. Samaira seems to resent Ksenia's words as well but when she glances at the red eyed witch, she remains silent.

"Good morning fellow witches!"

A whirlwind of curled, bouncy black hair and flowing yellow silk skirts enters the room. Iona watches the tiny, sprite-like woman bound up to the podium and drop her bag on the platform with a thump.

"My name is Talulah Pari. You may call me Professor Pari or Talulah. I have no preference really. I shall have the pleasure of teaching you the wonders of clairvoyancy, prophecy, and whatever else tickles my fancy," Pari winks, "Clairvoyancy is the interpretation of fate, that which rules over all our lives for better or worse. Our divine intuition allows us to perceive the invisible strings that pull us towards our destinies, like the ligaments of reality. It allows us to see what was, what will be, and what may be obscured. We have a great deal to cover this year so let's get to it, shall we?"

The young witches nod or give verbal approval.

"Splendid," Pari says, "First, a brief refresher for those of you who are newer to witchcraft than others."

Pari paces back and forth across the platform, orating with such passion that demands attention.

"I like to think of magic like singing. It takes technique, practice, and some natural ability. A witch requires those three elements if they want their magic to flourish. Every individual witch has a well of magic inside of them. Every well is unique and has the capacity to grow," Pari says.

The professor gestures grandly with her arms to demonstrate the size and depth of a so called well of magic.

"If you were to sing and sing for hours on end in practice, you will lose your voice and, in extreme cases, damage your vocal cords beyond repair. Likewise, if you misuse magic recklessly and overextend yourself, you can cause great harm to yourself or others. Know your limitations and if you aim to strengthen your abilities, do so with care and restraint. Learn the ways of replenishing your well of magic, through rest, meditation, communing with nature, or any other method at your disposal," Pari says.

Iona listens intently. She has never used anywhere near enough power to overextend herself but now that she would be practicing magic regularly, it is good information to have.

"Today we shall start with something simple but very useful. Our first lesson will be on auramancy, the detection and interpretation of auras," Pari says, "Auras are a way to tell the very contents of a person's mind. Occasionally a non-magic person can detect auras and decipher glimpses of a person's essence, without much detail."

Iona is reminded of the old woman in the town square who spat on the ground at the sight of her.

"Witches can see much more detailed indications of personalities, fears, desires, memories, and thoughts. They can also learn to conceal their auras from view, but they will become visible again at times of distress and intense emotion if they are not careful. Let's separate into pairs and practice," Pari says.

The professor points to two witches at a time to separate the class into partners. Pari eventually points to Iona, then points at the red-eyed witch in the first row. Iona's stomach drops.

"Once you have your partner, please try to read their aura," Pari says.

The red-eyed witch turns around in her chair to look up at Iona in the second row.

"Ariadne Zerynthos," she says.

"Iona Evora," Iona says with as much confidence as she can muster.

"Are you better at reading auras than you are at walking, Iona?" Ariadne says, raising an eyebrow.

Iona flushes and flips through her grimoire nervously.

"As common as they come," Ksenia whispers to Ariadne.

"Have you ever read an aura before?" Ariadne asks with more than a trace of condescension.

"No," Iona says stiffly.

"Well, give it a try," Ariadne says, a challenge in her eyes.

Iona scrutinizes Ariadne for any sign of her aura. She is filled with doubt as she tries to catch any glimpse of color or insight floating around Ariadne's head, but nothing emerges.

Iona's eyes glance down and notice a red mark in the shape of a single flame on the swell of Ariadne's breast, right over her heart. The mark sits just above the lace trim of her square neckline, as if Ariadne had picked her dress for the sole purpose of displaying the symbol. It would be too coincidental a shape to be a natural birthmark, but a lady like Ariadne does not seem like the sort to get a tattoo like an indigent sailor.

"Do you see it?" Ariadne asks impatiently.

Iona meets Ariadne's critical gaze and instantly regrets her lingering stare.

"Not yet," Iona says, then tries in earnest to concentrate.

"I can see yours," Ariadne boasts, "Do you want to know what I see?"

Iona did not want that at all but before she could protest, Ariadne went on.

"You are afraid of your power. I can see your well of magic," Ariadne's eyes widen slightly, "and it holds more abundance than you realize, but it does not matter. You are too faint of heart to use it."

Iona shifts uncomfortably, hating to be so dissected by a stranger.

"You know a grand total of seven spells, most of them used for housework," Ariadne smirks, "It seems you are in dire need of educating. Or perhaps you would make a fine housemaid."

Iona fumes as Ksenia and Ariadne chuckle amongst themselves.

"I would rather not continue," Iona tries to say, but Ariadne talks over her.

"You are the loneliest soul I've ever gazed upon. You've never had a real friend, and..." Ariadne squints, "as I suspected, a spinster whose virtue is still untouched."

Iona's cheeks burn red as Ksenia chuckles at her embarrassment.

"Does that sound accurate, Iona?" Ariadne asks, tilting her head to the side.

Iona wishes she could retaliate with her own insight, but Ariadne's aura still escapes her. A conceited smile spreads across Ariadne's lips.

"Any luck seeing mine?" Ariadne asks, "Do not fret if you cannot. I learned to mask my aura years ago."

Iona's frustration grows as she focuses all her energy into seeing something, anything at all.

"What more could you expect from a witch who lived in a shack by the ocean all her life?" Ariadne mutters to Ksenia, "More of a water nymph than a witch."

Iona notices a shimmer around Ariadne just then. Iona squints to try and see more. The shimmering white coruscant glow spreads until it surrounds Ariadne's entire body. She gazes at it in awe. The shimmer stretches further until it surrounds the wolf sleeping at Ariadne's feet. Iona's eyes become unfocused. The world around her blurs as Ariadne's aura becomes so clear to her that she can read its contents like a diary.

"You are very insecure," Iona says in surprise, because it was not something she would have expected from a woman who carries herself with such bold grandeur.

Ariadne's laughter stops abruptly at Iona's words.

"I beg your pardon?" Ariadne says coolly.

Iona sees clouded images of Ariadne sitting alone in her bedroom, then standing in the center of a ballroom with a crowd of finely dressed people staring at her with antipathy. Iona feels Ariadne's loneliness. It is a familiar sensation and Iona would feel sorry for her if she had not been so rude moments ago.

"You hate the way others fear you. You harbor a great deal of shame," Iona murmurs.

Iona squints, searching for anything else that she can interpret. Ariadne's mind is deeply fragmented and caliginous. Iona sees glimpses of two grim women, one middle aged and one very old, who both share Ariadne's red eyes.

"You wonder if you have peaked prematurely in life and will eventually become a disappointment to your family," Iona says, "Your grandmother's legacy weighs heavily on your shoulders."

"Watch your tongue!" Ariadne snaps.

Ariadne's words break whatever trance had fallen over Iona and the aura becomes invisible once more. As the blur over the world becomes clear again, Iona sees Ariadne's livid, offended expression, and the shocked looks of her two friends. Iona cannot help the small smile that forms on her lips.

"Does that sound accurate, Ariadne?" Iona asks.

Ariadne narrows her eyes and is about to reply when Professor Pari claps her hands and and jumps back onto the platform to lean against her podium.

"Wonderful job everyone!" Pari says. She hadn't heard the exchange between Iona and Ariadne, or if she had, she was ignoring it.

Ariadne shoots one final glare at Iona before turning around in her seat. Her friends sit silently next to her.

"Now, I will teach you how to mask your auras," Pari says, "I would like you all to calm your mind and allow your thoughts to settle."

Pari closes her eyes, and the rest of the class follows suit.

"Imagine your thoughts as ghosts. They are invisible, untouchable, except by you. Your emotions float with them too. They will slip through anyone's fingers and become a mass of spectral shadows in the confines of your mind," Pari says softly.

As Pari speaks, Iona's aura shimmers around her. She'd never been aware of its presence before. She concentrates hard and it becomes a shadow the way that Pari said.

"Very good, Iona," Pari says.

Iona smiles triumphantly. Her thoughts and emotions are only visible to her again.

"The reason I chose auramancy as our first lesson of the year is because I believe we all have a right to our own private thoughts and feelings. Knowing how to read auras is a useful skill to have but is most valuable when a person allows you to see into the very depths of their consciousness," Pari sighs dreamily, "It is the very definition of intimacy."

Pari continues describing auras and their many properties and at the end of class she announces, "Your partners here will carry over to all your other classes whenever one is required. Now off you go!"

Pari glides gracefully out of class while her students gather their grimoires to leave. As Iona makes her way to the ground floor to meet with Crescentia, she scans the courtyard curiously to see if she can detect anyone else's aura. She did not want to read them, only to see if they were accessible to her now. Indeed, she does see shimmering auras around a few of the students and the sight astounds her. She had access to this ability all this time and never knew.

Iona's newfound confidence is skewed by Ariadne's cold-blooded words. This woman she'd only just met had laid all her insecurities bare before her friends and anyone else who had been listening. Iona had returned the favor, but the exchange did not sit well with her.

After an enjoyable lunch with Crescentia, Iona had put Ariadne out of her mind. Iona thought that her next class, conjuration, might be more enjoyable. Most of the magic she did at home were conjuring spells, so she had a considerable amount of practice. She was also looking forward to watching Samuel teach.

"Conjuration is the art of manifestation. Whether it be as small as a thimble or as massive as a ship, the magic will succeed or fail based off of your mind's vision of the object," Samuel explains.

Samuel takes his wand from a pocket within his blazer and says, "We use spells to evoke these objects as accurately as possible. Spells can come from anywhere and be spoken in any language. By incanting the spells, our sheer will can reawaken the power within the words and use it to conjure or enchant."

Samuel points his wand at his desk and says, "Apfel."

A shiny red apple appears on his desk. He picks it up and takes a bite, then winks jovially at Iona as he chews. Iona smiles back.

"I conjured this apple using German because it happens to be the version of the spell my mother taught me. It is a relatively old spell, used by many before me, with magic locked into every syllable. Through practiced control of your power, you can unlock the magic of otherwise mundane words and phrases," Samuel explains, "This is also why some incantations are spoken as chants. The more you repeat the words, the more your will is conveyed as you center yourself and force your will to become tangible."

Samuel places the apple on his desk.

"I could use the French, Bolivian, or Gaelic words to conjure the exact same object, though each spell is as unique as those who made them. A different apple spell may start with the core first and build its way outward toward the skin. Or start at the bottom of the apple and work its way up to the stem," he says.

Samuel whispers the spell again, and the apple disappears.

"This is why a witch who knows many languages is very strong indeed. They have access to more incantations of all different kinds," he says, "Each culture has something to contribute, something to respect, in the magic they have uniquely cultivated. And now, as cultures become increasingly more connected, we all benefit in sharing that cumulative wisdom and use the spells of our ancestors to create wonders."

Iona is admittedly surprised, maybe even skeptical, that witches are willing to share spells despite any cultural differences they may have. Even here on campus among the small population of students, there seems to be more of an unspoken truce between them all, rather than genuine camaraderie. Iona noticed the slight but undeniable tension that lingered in the dining hall when she'd eaten with Crescentia between classes.

Samuel points his wand at his hand and says, "Light."

An amorphous entity of golden light appears in the palm of his hand that is so bright, it makes Iona squint.

"For example, the English have mastered the conjuring of light quite successfully. Their spell is powerful enough to create the equivalent of a second sun. I prefer to use this version of the spell when I am in need of illumination," Samuel says.

Samuel undoes the spell, and the outline of its shine still lingers in Iona's vision.

"The only exception for this would be nascent spells, some

of which we will learn later this term and in Spring. They are conjured using Aramaic, Greek, Arabic, Latin, or any other ancient languages we have left. Nascent spells were the very first that witches and warlocks created and shared with one another. They have been uttered for so many centuries that using the original words will always be the best method," Samuel says.

Samuel puts his wand away and looks out at his class.

"Now, I would like everyone to use any conjuring spells they are familiar with. I would like to see what level of skill each witch possesses," Samuel says.

The young witches pull out their wands and incant the strongest conjuration spells that they know of. Iona points her wand at her desk.

"Pérola," she incants, and a perfect pearl appears in front of her.

Iona stares at the pearl for a moment and frowns. She glances over at Ariadne, who sits next to her at their shared desk. Ariadne pulls out her wand, a long, thin cylindrical piece of black obsidian.

"Tímamælir," Ariadne murmurs. A bracket clock of gilded bronze and crystal appears before her. The crystal shows the brass gears ticking inside.

The complexity of the clock is undeniably impressive. Iona looks back at her simple pearl and decides she can do better and there's no sense in holding back anymore.

"Diamante," Iona says.

A flawless diamond the size of her fist appears on the table. The light from the window next to her shines onto the gem and makes rainbows dance on the ceiling. Iona hears a gasp behind her. Iona turns to see a young witch with reddish-brown hair, freckles, and blue eyes. The witch glances from the large diamond to Iona's face, then looks away.

"Impressive," Ariadne says.

Iona glances at Ariadne, who is inspecting the diamond critically. She meets Iona's eyes and slowly reaches for her. She pulls an intricately cut diamond from behind Iona's ear. Iona looks at it with surprise.

"For a magpie," Ariadne grins.

Ksenia chuckles behind them. Iona supposes that Ariadne had conjured the diamond while she wasn't looking. The rest was sleight of hand.

Ariadne places the diamond in front of Iona's on the desk. It's smaller but just as beautiful. Then Ariadne waves her wand over her diamond and says, "Duplisere."

The diamond multiplies over and over again until their desk overflows with sparkling gems. They spill onto Iona's lap and fall to the floor. Iona jumps up out of her chair and steps away from the cascading diamonds.

A second later, the spell wears off and leaves a pile of gems between Iona and Ariadne. The rest of the class goes silent as the diamonds clatter across the floor. Iona's cheeks heat as she stands there awkwardly.

"Is there a problem, Ariadne?" Professor Lysander asks in a warning tone.

"No, sir. My apologies, it was a slip of the tongue," Ariadne says with a polite smile.

Ariadne says the spell again and all the glittering diamonds fall back together until there are only two left, like before.

Ariadne points her wand to the palm of her hand and says, "Koshenya."

A ball of orange fur forms in her hand and grows until it becomes a living kitten that meows and purrs. The entire class gasps happily and gathers around Ariadne to admire the cute little animal. Iona crosses her arms under her chest and scowls.

"Iona?"

Iona turns and sees the girl with reddish-brown hair looking up at her. She is one of the only students not admiring Ariadne's new kitten.

"Yes?" Iona says.

"I thought your diamond was beautiful," she says, "My name

is Elise."

"Elise Lysander?" Iona asks.

So, this was Samuel's daughter. She could see the resemblance. Elise has her father's bright blue eyes and a splattering of freckles across her nose.

"Yes," Elise smiles politely, "I am glad to make your acquaintance after my father's unexpected trip yesterday. How are you liking the college thus far?"

"I have never seen anything like it. There is so much I did not know about magic and the possibilities are dizzying," Iona says.

"I imagine it must be overwhelming. If you would like, I could show you some conjuring tricks my father taught me," Elise says, "To help keep up with the braggarts of our class."

Elise glares behind Iona at Ariadne, who is still preoccupied with her new pet. Ariadne's wolf sniffs curiously at the kitten, making it hiss in protest.

"I would like that very much," Iona says.

Elise's expression softens at Iona's words, and she smiles. She takes out her wand, made of wood like Iona's. She waves it over her desk and says, "Bolo."

As a cupcake forms on the desk, Iona smiles at first, then frowns when it grows mold. The rotten cake sits between them. Iona looks up at Elise, but she is still staring at the cake with disdain and embarrassment.

"That normally does not happen," Elise stutters.

Iona does not know what to do but wants to make Elise feel better. She waves her wand and says the same spell. A perfect cupcake with blue icing appears next to the rotten one. Iona is happy with the result, considering it was her first attempt. Iona picks up the cupcake and splits it in half, handing one piece to Elise. Rather than taking the piece, Elise stares at it with offense.

"I could have fixed it myself," Elise says indignantly. She gets up from her chair and leaves Iona holding the two pieces of cake.

Iona sighs, not knowing how she had managed to so easily offend yet another one of her peers. She sets the pieces of cake down on the desk, no longer interested in the sugary treat.

"Another Lysander meltdown," Ariadne says, coming to stand next to Iona and taking one half of the cake for her own.

"She was just embarrassed," Iona says.

Iona watches Ariadne take a bite and lick a trace of icing from her top lip. Iona blinks and averts her eyes. She looks back at the group of witches and sees Samaira now holds the conjured kitten in her arms.

"Elise has always been too sensitive," Ariadne says callously.

"I am sure if one of your spells did not work the way you intended, it would upset you too," Iona says.

"Oh of course, those cupcake spells are rather advanced," Ariadne smirks.

Iona glowers at her, unable to fathom how so much arrogance can fit into one person.

"Elise is like many of the other witches here. Cursed with ambition but lacking the necessary skill to dominate her adversaries," Ariadne says, setting her piece of cupcake down, though there are many bites left of it.

"Dominate her adversaries? Is this college or warfare?" Iona scoffs, losing her patience, "Perhaps she would not be so easily provoked if her peers were not such obnoxious rotters."

Ariadne looks Iona up and down slowly. Iona tenses under her scrutiny. With Ariadne standing so close, Iona notices her heady scent of cloves and flowers, the same floral perfume from her balcony.

Iona watches Ariadne pull out her wand and whisper an incantation. To Iona's ears, it sounds like the spell was in Italian. A yellow flower appears between Ariadne's fingers. She holds it out towards Iona, who looks at it with suspicion. Ariadne extends the flower closer to Iona, her eyebrows raising expectantly, so Iona takes it.

"Perhaps you are not as common as you appear, nymph," Ariadne says with a smirk, "We shall see at the end of spring term, won't we?"

Iona crinkles her brow in confusion as Ariadne walks away. She notices Samuel watching her from his podium at the front of the lecture hall. He clears his throat and tells the students to take their seats so he can evaluate their creations.

Iona stares at the yellow flower in deep contemplation as she walks back to the dormitories after classes commenced for the day. Then she glimpses the edge of the misty forest beyond the border of campus and her footsteps slow. An odd sensation comes over her, as if she's being entranced by something within the trees.

"Iona!" Crescentia calls.

Iona turns her back on the forest to see Crescentia running across the courtyard to her.

"I wondered if you might like to study with me before dinner, then perhaps visit the parlor in the evening? I could introduce you to other witches in my acquaintance," Crescentia says.

"I would love to meet in the parlor later, but I had planned to take a walk in the forest this afternoon to clear my head. Would you join me?" Iona asks.

"Oh... I am afraid not," Crescentia says with wide eyes, "Those woods are far too ominous for my tastes."

"Very well, I can meet with you after I return so we can visit the parlor together," Iona says, Crescentia's words only augmenting her curiosity.

"Perfect," Crescentia says, "Anyhow, how was your first day?"

"It was fine," Iona says.

"I heard that you are Ariadne Zerynthos' newest victim, and you made Elise Lysander cry," Crescentia says.

Iona's eyebrows fly up in surprise, "Wherever did you hear that?"

"I have my sources," Crescentia grins, "Is it true?"

"Partially," Iona admits, "I do not think Elise cried but I

did upset her unintentionally. Ariadne does not like me very much... but I am not anyone's victim."

"I would die of happiness if a Zerynthos witch was threatened by my power," Crescentia says, sighing dreamily.

"No, I'm not... Ariadne isn't..." Iona stutters, "I assure you no one would be threatened by me, least of all her."

"Then how would you explain her newfound obsession with you?" Crescentia asks, waggling her eyebrows.

Iona cannot think of an answer and Crescentia says, "Zerynthos witches are known for their pride and tenacity. You should not take it personally. Ariadne is easily provoked but her bite has no teeth. Except for... well that was many years ago. She is mostly harmless, trust me."

Iona doesn't miss Crescentia's forced omission but has a more pressing question on her mind.

"She did say something rather odd to me," Iona says, "She said she would know if I was common or not at the end of Spring term. Do you know what that means?"

"The trials for the pendant are at the end of Spring term," Crescentia says matter-of-factly.

"What pendant?" Iona asks.

Crescentia gapes at her, "You do not know about the pendant? Did Professor Lysander prepare you at all?"

Iona shrugs her shoulders. Crescentia's eyes are alight with excitement as she explains it all to her.

"The pendant of Morgan Le Fay, a powerful enchantress, healer, and shapeshifter. She studied magic with Merlin and ferried King Arthur to Avalon. I assume you have heard of her?" Crescentia asks.

"I know her from old stories but haven't heard of the pendant," Iona says.

"Many accounts of her life are false, the legends being appropriated and remolded time and again," Crescentia says, "She is an honorable, formidable witch of great renown. Her pendant was one of her final contributions to magic, a way to house her power in an object that can be passed down to exceptional witches of her choosing over the centuries. The promise of enhanced spells, a longer lifespan, and an almost infinite well of magic is enough to make witches lust after its power."

"A pendant that holds Morgan's magic?" Iona breathes, "Who would be worthy of such an artifact?"

"Only the rarest and strongest of witches. When the witch who once claimed it dies, the pendant disappears and transports itself to a sacred place, like this forest. The pendant is presently housed within the college until a new witch arrives and claims it for her own by taking Morgan's trials," Crescentia explains.

"What are the trials exactly?" Iona asks.

"No one knows. Any witch who attempts them has no memory of it after they fail. There are many rumors about them that are apocryphal at best," Crescentia says, "Witches often postpone their time at college to study at home, cultivate more magic, then attend merely as a formality so they can take the trials in spring. Ariadne fits that description, as do her friends Ksenia Ulanova and Samaira Dayalu. They are already quite powerful and know a great many spells. They could easily take the trials today if they were allowed to."

"Ariadne must want it desperately," Iona muses.

"She needs it. Her grandmother, Katrin Zerynthos, was the last witch to wear the pendant and the Zerynthos family has been trying to retrieve it ever since. None of them have been successful yet, but Ariadne hopes it will be her. Her family expects it," Crescentia says, "She was a prodigy. Her wand appeared to her when she was but nine years of age. Can you imagine?"

Iona shakes her head. To have access to power that young seems irresponsible.

"And now she is a polymath of magic after years of strict instruction from her mother," Crescentia says, "Did you notice the flame mark on her chest?"

Iona nods, her cheeks turning pink at the memory.

"That is the Zerynthos symbol, her witch's mark. The mark was passed down through her sempiterna bloodline," Crescentia says.

"Sempiterna... is that Latin?" Iona asks.

"Yes, it refers to those with ancestral ties to the original magic users of antiquity," Crescentia explains.

Iona covertly glances at Crescentia for any discernable mark like the one Ariadne has but cannot see one. Perhaps the mark was somewhere that her dress was covering.

"I do not have a mark, though that only means that others underestimate me," Crescentia grins, "Anyone who has their own witch's mark is here to take the trials, not to learn magic."

"But what has that got to do with me? I did not know the pendant existed until now and I am not descended from an important bloodline," Iona says.

"If you have strong magic, Ariadne and others may consider you a threat. A wildcard if you will. In the old days, witches would be known to kill their adversaries to make the trials easier to win. Now the competition is much more civilized, with the occasional exception," Crescentia shrugs, as if such violence was commonplace.

Iona's mouth falls open in disbelief. What had Samuel allowed her to enter into? Did her mother know about this?

"Until the pendant is won, Lysander College is a field of battle more so than a school. The sabotage will only escalate with time and witches will be constantly watching each other for any signs of weakness. Be forewarned," Crescentia says.

Iona's head spins at such a prospect. She had not intended to enter in any sort of competition with her peers.

"Is that why Elise was so upset? She left in a fury when I remedied one of her spells. She must have thought that I was attempting to upstage her," Iona realizes.

"It is likely so. But to be fair, she is known to get quite frustrated with herself. Her family, the Lysanders, are as illustrious as the Zerynthos line but they have fallen out of favor of late. Elise holds herself to a standard that she may never be able to meet," Crescentia says, then shrugs, "Every so often, a family gets a dud."

"Ariadne did mention that Elise can be overly sensitive at times," Iona says.

Crescentia chuckles, "She would know. They courted for over a year."

"Ariadne and Elise?" Iona asks, "But they're so different."

"Distinguished families often try to arrange matches with their children with no regard for their compatibility. I heard it was Ariadne's mother who facilitated it," Crescentia says, "Then oddly, Elise broke off their courtship. I still have yet to find out why."

"How do you know all of this?" Iona asks.

Crescentia looks away sheepishly, "Did you learn about auras today? I saw it on many witch's minds."

"Yes, but... Wait. Are you reading auras to get this information?" Iona asks.

"It is a particular talent of mine. One that has gotten me far. And Phoebe as well," Crescentia says with a sly grin, "Though we will not be able to use this skill for long when the witches here learn how to shield their auras properly."

"Did you read my aura?" Iona asks.

"Not invasively, but yes" Crescentia admits, "When I met you yesterday, I did take a peek. But I cannot see your aura now if that is any consolation. You learned to shield it very quickly."

"I would prefer that you did not look at my aura again," Iona says, then grins, "But if you would like to tell me what you see in others, I shall not protest too much."

"I knew we would be friends," Crescentia smiles wide, then takes Iona's arm and leads her back to the dormitories.

As they walk, Iona looks down at the yellow flower again and lifts it to her nose to breathe in its scent.

"Where did you find a carnation?" Crescentia asks.

"Ariadne conjured it in Professor Lysander's class and gave it to me," Iona says, "I know not why."

"Hmm," Crescentia says.

"What?" Iona asks.

"It is intriguing that Ariadne chose that particular flower to give to you. Maybe it was only a coincidence," Crescentia says.

"Why, is it poisonous?" Iona asks.

"No, nothing as awful as that. You will learn more in phytology that all plants have meaning, both biologically and aesthetically. It is an aspect of floromancy, the divination of flowers. Knowing each flower's meaning can aid a witch in recognizing omens. A yellow carnation, for instance, signifies disappointment, hate, rejection... but she likely did not realize it when she gave it to you," Crescentia says quickly when she sees the look of disgust on Iona's face.

"What is wrong with her?" Iona scoffs, tossing the yellow carnation to the grass to wither away.

3 – ARIADNE

"Where did she come from?" Ariadne asks her friends, "A witch like that does not just sprout from the ground out of nowhere."

"Well, she did. Professor Lysander left on his trip and returned with a stray. No one knows anything about her, except Crescentia," Ksenia rolls her eyes, "The gossipmonger extraordinaire."

"And now you are stuck with her as your partner for the rest of the term," Samaira sighs, twirling a lock of her dark hair between her fingers, making her new sapphire ring sparkle in the light.

"Perhaps that is fortuitous," Ksenia says.

"How?" Ariadne asks incredulously.

"It will make it easier to keep an eye on her," Ksenia says, "Observe her and see if she is really a threat or if you are just being paranoid."

"Do you think she is powerful enough to be a true contender for the pendant?" Samaira asks warily.

"No, of course not," Ariadne says, though doubt flickers inside of her, "She is a nobody."

"Exactly, so put her out of your mind," Ksenia says.

Ariadne bursts into her dormitory and throws herself onto her bed. Ksenia and Samaira follow and find seats in the sitting area around Ariadne's fireplace.

"Aster," Ariadne calls, patting the bed beside her.

Ariadne's wolf familiar bounds up onto the bed and licks her face. Ariadne giggles and pulls away from Aster's tongue. He lays on top of her and she scratches behind his ears. Samaira is chattering with Ksenia about a rare blue comet that will soon grace the sky, but Ariadne does not care to listen.

While her friends pull out their grimoires to study, Ariadne stares up at her ceiling. She is still heated over Iona's description of her aura. Her demure hazel eyes are imprinted on Ariadne's brain.

No other witch has been able to read her aura in almost seven years, ever since she'd learned how to lock it away. Or so she'd thought. She must train harder, strengthen her mind and her magic, so no one can penetrate her defenses again. She is representing the entire Zerynthos family while she resides here, and it had been thoroughly impressed upon her the severity of such a responsibility.

Throughout her childhood, Ariadne's mother told her the stories of the Zerynthos bloodline. They are averred to be distantly descended from the goddess Hecate herself, which is why their magic has remained so prosperous for generations. Her mother also claims that it is where their red eyes originate from and why their witch's mark is in the shape of a flame, a symbol of Hecate. Her mother believes their divinity to be their merit for hegemony.

Her mother expects nothing but perfection and anytime Ariadne does not meet that impossible standard, she never lets her forget it. Zerynthos witches are not allowed to relent. They are not allowed to be weak. They must excel.

Ariadne remembers when her mother had taken her on one of their trips to the volcano on Nisyros and traversed the crater. The view was breathtaking, the ground covered in fertile volcanic soil and the rocks coated with red and yellow sulphur, but her mother was not interested in the scenery.

She had hoped that Ariadne would find her wand there one day since their ancestors were known to garner power from volcanoes. She did not expect her to find it at the ripe age of nine. The thin cylinder of pure obsidian rolled down the side of the crater and fell right into Ariadne's lap while she was meditating. She was so young but even then, she knew how significant it was for her wand to appear to her so quickly and easily.

Her mother had been overjoyed and her already lofty expectations had only risen the older Ariadne became. Now, ten years later, is her chance to make her mother proud and bring Morgan's pendant back to their family.

"We must conjure five objects that we have never conjured before for Lysander's class," Ksenia reminds Ariadne.

"I shall have to think on that. I've conjured more objects than I haven't," Ariadne says.

Ariadne turns her head to look at the two witches. Samaira is playing with the orange kitten that Ariadne had conjured in class. Ariadne had gifted it to her since Ksenia is not fond of animals.

"We already know everything about auras, so Professor Pari's assignment is useless," Ksenia sighs, "I cannot wait until Spring term when we can practice more advanced magic."

Ariadne sits up in bed, "We should take a break."

"Already?" Samaira asks.

"We only just started," Ksenia protests.

"I would like to take a stroll. If you would prefer to stay here and read about spells you learned as children, be my guest," Ariadne says, as she walks to the door.

Samaira drops her book and follows Ariadne immediately. Ksenia reluctantly follows as well. When they are outside, Aster runs in joyous circles around the courtyard, chasing red squirrels and barking at them when they climb into trees out of his reach.

They wander to the gardens, which are located in the green space between the lyceum and the library. The aster flowers are in full bloom, their purple petals bright and inviting. Aster runs over to sniff at them curiously, as if he knows that the flowers are his namesake. Ariadne finds a fallen branch in the grass. She picks it up and throws it far for Aster to run and fetch.

Ariadne stops in her tracks when she sees Iona donned in her black cloak and walking towards the forest. A gust of wind picks up and makes her red mane of hair dance around her.

When Iona sees Ariadne and her friends, she tenses warily and quickens her pace towards the trees. That is, until Aster runs up to her with the branch between his teeth. Iona yelps and backs away. Ariadne rolls her eyes and walks over to Iona. Samaira and Ksenia stay behind to watch.

"Aster will not hurt you, unless I want him to," Ariadne says.

Iona's large hazel eyes look between the docile wolf and Ariadne's face. Aster drops the branch into the grass and sniffs Iona's hand curiously, then licks it. Iona carefully scratches his head. Aster pants happily and Iona smiles. The expression transforms her demure presence into something softer.

"Is he your pet?" Iona asks.

Ariadne scoffs, "A pet? Did your parents teach you nothing about witchcraft?"

"It is a simple question," Iona says, her smile fading.

Ariadne sighs, "Aster is my familiar, a protector that will follow me throughout my life. He is tied to me and I to him."

Iona was scratching Aster's chin, but she pulls her hand away with alarm, "Can you feel..."

"No," Ariadne chuckles despite herself, "We are not tied that intrinsically or my ears would itch horribly."

Iona's smile returns and she continues petting Aster. Ariadne observes the exchange quizzically. Aster is not usually so trusting of strangers, especially with people that Ariadne does not like. The wolf had growled at Iona only hours ago but is now acting like a carefree pup. Ariadne glances at Samaira and Ksenia, who watch them with prying eyes. Ariadne looks to Iona again, but she has walked away towards the woods.

"Where are you going?" Ariadne asks.

Iona looks over her shoulder in confusion and says, "I had

intended to take a short stroll to clear my head."

"You should not walk in the woods alone so close to nightfall," Ariadne says.

"I am more than capable of traversing a forest alone," Iona says.

"There are centuries worth of magical creatures in there and opened portals to other worlds," Ariadne warns, "It is quite dangerous."

Ariadne's mother had warned her of the woods before she departed for college. Witches have been known to go missing in those woods, never to be seen again. It was safer to traverse in the daytime, but only when accompanied by other witches for safety.

Iona gazes into the woods with newfound wonder, rather than fear, and says, "I shall take my chances."

"Don't say I did not warn you," Ariadne says, walking back to her friends.

"Is she mad? That forest is no place for a common, untrained witch," Samaira says when Ariadne approaches.

"Maybe she will not come back," Ksenia says, almost hopefully.

Ariadne looks back at the edge of the woods where Iona has disappeared.

"Shall we?" Ariadne asks, and her dutiful friends follow her inside.

After studying for a couple of hours, Ariadne follows Ksenia and Samaira to the dining hall for dinner, then to the parlor to lounge for a while. The parlor is a large sitting room with many tables and chaises for students to use as they wish. The walls are painted a very light green and decorated with various paintings in golden frames. Ariadne eyes the pianoforte in the corner as she sits in a chaise lounge next to her friends.

They are soon joined by Gisela Holm and Nenet Nassry, a Danish and Egyptian witch respectively. They have been connected at the hip since Ariadne first met them years ago.

When Elise enters the parlor as well, sitting at a table in the corner to dally with her soothsaying bones, Ariadne is entirely too surrounded by past conquests to be at ease. Ariadne opens one of her favorite phytology books and attempts to block out the surrounding conversations. Then Gisela comes to sit beside Ariadne, and Nenet sits beside Gisela.

"Ariadne, have you yet gone to see Beethoven's new ballet? What was it called?" Gisela asks Nenet.

"The Creatures of Prometheus," Nenet says.

"Yes, that is the one," Gisela says.

"I haven't," Ariadne says, not looking up from her book.

"Oh, you must! We are so near Vienna that we could be there and back before anyone would notice," Gisela says.

"I do not have time for such frivolity now that college has commenced," Ariadne says dismissively.

"Oh, come now, Ari," Gisela says with a coquettish smile.

Gisela takes Ariadne's hand in both of hers, forcing her to lower her book. Ariadne tenses at the unwelcome informality. She hates when anyone other than Samaira calls her Ari.

Gisela knows that other witches in the parlor can see them. She is trying to pressure Ariadne into acknowledging an intimacy between them, to stake a claim on Ariadne so others would not attempt to proposition her, but Ariadne is in no mood tonight.

"The pendant is as good as yours. Everyone knows it. You can enjoy yourself for one night," Gisela insists.

Gisela bats her eyelashes, and it takes all of Ariadne's willpower not to resort to rudeness. She instead gently takes her hand back and smiles politely.

"Studying magic is life's greatest pleasure," Ariadne says, with slight sarcasm, "Though if it is music you crave, I am more than happy to oblige you."

Ariadne slips away from Gisela's smothering orbit and approaches the pianoforte. The American witch, Phoebe Kimball, is already playing one of Mozart's concertos, but when she sees Ariadne approach, she quickly stands and scampers off. Ariadne ignores Phoebe's fear at the sight of her and calmly sits on the bench.

Ariadne pulls out her wand and taps it against her chin as she considers what she should play, then conjures a stack of sheet music. She plays Beethoven's fifteenth sonata, one of his most recent works. Her fingers dance lightly over the keys as her thoughts drift.

Ariadne has come to regret indulging in Gisela and Nenet's all too eager affections. They have not left Ariadne alone since. Though it had been a unique and admittedly enjoyable experience to ravish two women at once, the novelty was quickly stifled by Gisela's insufferably obtrusive disposition. Ariadne prefers Nenet's polite indifference, only seeming to enjoy their carnal activities for the sake of them without any hidden motives.

What Gisela truly wants from Ariadne is the same as every woman who attempts to seduce her. The witch who could manage to court and wed Ariadne would also gain her affluent name and indomitable magic. Ariadne does not mind reveling in another woman's body when it is offered, but every witch in high society knows that she is not interested in marriage or love. Gisela Holm would not be the witch to change that fact.

"Why so glum?" Samaira asks as she comes to lean against the pianoforte.

"Gisela is relentless," Ariadne mutters, as she begins playing the Rondo portion of the sonata.

"I did warn you of her fortune seeking," Samaira smirks, "Sappho has cursed you with horrid judgement."

"Thank your lucky stars that such an affliction does not plague you," Ariadne grins, her cheeks turning pink against her will.

"I assure you, warlocks are no better," Samaira sighs.

"You have a year's impunity from such creatures, whilst I am surrounded by my vice," Ariadne says, glancing at the room filled with beautiful witches who pretend not to be observing her.

Just as Ariadne says it, Iona enters the parlor with Crescentia in tow. Ariadne averts her eyes, a bout of annoyance leading her to distraction.

"She survived the forest," Samaira says, her voice betraying her esteem.

Ariadne ignores her, focusing on the music.

"Ari..." Samaira whispers with hesitance, "Was Iona correct in her reading of your aura? Is that truly how you feel?"

Iona's aura reading repeats in Ariadne's head until her strokes on the piano keys sound more like she is accosting the instrument. She accidentally plays a discordant cord, slams her fingers on the keys with frustration, and stops playing.

"Never mind," Samaira says, walking away with a grimace.

Ariadne takes a steadying breath and notices Ksenia sitting alone across the room. Ariadne goes to her and glances at Crescentia and Iona, who are starting a game of cards at a small table beneath a stained-glass window depicting a dragon spewing fire. When Ariadne sits beside Ksenia, she glances at Ariadne, then looks back down at her novel.

"*Dangerous Liaisons* again?" Ariadne asks, noticing the title of Ksenia's well-worn book.

"My rivalries in life are not quite so compelling as yours. I must find my thrills on the page instead," Ksenia murmurs, absent-mindedly running her fingers along her witch's mark, a thin piece of rye that sits at the pulse point on her neck.

"I have no such rivalries," Ariadne protests.

"Oh please," Ksenia rolls her eyes, "Your petulant display in class today is all anyone is gossiping about. In your effort to prevent the Evora girl from outshining you, all you did was draw more attention to her."

Ksenia glances covertly at Iona and Ariadne does as well. Ariadne notices that Iona's hem is caked in mud from her walk through the forest. Such disregard for politesse is yet another sign of her lack of grace. She could have cleaned up beforehand, as Ariadne does after tending to her plants. Gisela and Nenet have approached the table and introduce themselves. Iona's smile betrays her coy disposition.

"She provoked me," Ariadne grumbles.

"When she accosted you in the hall? Or when she read your aura too accurately for comfort?" Ksenia asks.

Ariadne seethes, wishing her friends would pretend as if that had not happened. That is what she intends to do.

"Would you prefer the girl fear you like all the others?" Ksenia asks with a raised eyebrow.

"Certainly not," Ariadne says, "Though some respect would not be unwarranted. I am a Zerynthos witch, after all."

"Then show her why she should respect you," Ksenia says, "The poor girl is clearly ignorant of her proper place in this world. I am sure you and others will enlighten her soon enough."

Ariadne considers this and decides that Ksenia is right. Ariadne will prove her dignity through her magic, the way she always has. She will not allow herself to be so easily riled again.

The next day, Ariadne intends to impress beyond reproach. She enters the phytology workshop with an air of implacable determination and sits beside Iona. Ksenia was right. If an interloper was intending to make a belated claim to the pendant, she would prefer to keep them under her watchful eye.

"Good morning," Iona says timidly.

Her voice is husky and warm, as if she had breathed in bonfire smoke every day. Today she wears a mauve colored dress that compliments her hazel eyes and the same lace gloves from yesterday.

"Good morning," Ariadne says shortly, barely glancing at her, then opens her grimoire and pretends to read.

In walks a woman in her sixties. Her dark hair is fixed in a tight bun at the nape of her neck and her white dress is immaculately clean and unwrinkled. She places her bag on her desk at the front of workshop and peers out at her students.

"Good morning, students" she says, "My name is Professor

Yun. Please do not confuse me with Professor Pari. If you call me by my first name, I will be very upset."

The students shift in their seats and Ariadne suppresses a smile. She knew all about Yun, as well as every other professor at college. Her mother insisted that she learn about each professor's temperament, professional history, and a bit about their personal life for good measure.

To be in her professors' good graces would only benefit her. There may still be nuances of magic that Ariadne has not yet learned and though most of these lessons are review of her well-practiced skills, she intends to make the most of her education. Ariadne knew which professors were lenient and which were sticklers. Yun was the latter.

"Mystic Phytology incorporates botany and incantation to create powerful tonics, salves, and potions. Today we will start with a simple but useful potion. It is called by many names depending on the country but in layman's terms, it is an energy potion. Depending on the strength of the brew, it can keep a witch or warlock awake for days at a time. In extreme cases, the effects can last for weeks. Please open your grimoires to page seven and carefully read through the recipe twice. When you are ready, find the ingredients in the storeroom and the greenhouse," Professor Yun says.

Ariadne ignores her first instruction, as she has brewed many an energy potion in her life. She would drink them like water when she was an adolescent because she did not like to dream.

Ariadne gathers tea leaves, aphids, honey, cinnamon, eye of newt, and the heart of a hare. She strategically places the ingredients into her pot while Iona is still reading the recipe. Her brow is crinkled in concentration and Ariadne almost feels sorry for her. The poor thing has no idea what she's doing.

"Elinvoimaa," Ariadne incants, waving her wand over the brew.

By the time Iona has gathered her ingredients, Ariadne's finished potion is brewing mildly. She sips a tiny amount and murmurs her approval. A jolt of energy flows through her just from sipping a few drops. It is not her finest version of the potion, but it will do nicely.

"Finished already?" Professor Yun asks.

"Yes, professor," Ariadne says.

Yun appears skeptical as she picks up a fresh spoon and takes a tiny sip. Her eyes widen and she coughs in surprise as energy flows through her.

"Very impressive," Yun says, "Which Zerynthos witch graces my class this year?"

"Ariadne," she replies with a polite smile, knowing that Yun correctly identified her by her red eyes and the witch's mark on her chest.

"Please stay after class," Yun says, smiling back.

Ariadne sits back and watches Iona brew her potion. She is hesitant, the doubt Ariadne saw in her aura as clear now as it was yesterday. However, when Yun returns to taste Iona's potion, she has almost the same reaction as with Ariadne's. Ariadne sits up straighter in her chair and waits for Yun's assessment.

"Good, very good," Yun says, "What is your name?"

Ariadne notices Yun covertly checking any exposed skin on Iona's body for a witch's mark. Ariadne bristles with annoyance.

"Iona Evora," Iona says.

"I see great potential in you, Ms. Evora. I recommend adding a burn morel. Chop it finely and stir it in until it dissolves."

"Yes, professor, thank you" Iona says.

Ariadne takes solace in knowing that her potion was superior but did not like that Iona's was anywhere near as good as hers. Ariadne is lost in thought when the other students leave, and she stays behind to speak with Yun.

"Ariadne," Yun prompts.

Ariadne stands and gathers her books before approaching the front of the workshop.

"I have heard tales of your notable proclivities for magic

and potions, though it is no surprise when you come from such a distinguished line," Yun says, "I was hoping that I could interest you in an auxiliary opportunity. I am always in need of help around here. With students coming to me for cures and tonics, I am often spread too thin. Would you be interested in assisting me?"

"Of course, I would be delighted," Ariadne says, proud to be considered for a position at a professor's side.

"Wonderful," Yun says, "Come to the greenhouse in the afternoons on Tuesdays and Thursdays, starting today."

Ariadne thanks Yun for the opportunity and takes her leave. She meets Samaira and Ksenia in the dining hall. They have already started eating when she approaches their table.

"What did Yun want?" Ksenia asks.

"I have procured a sort of apprenticeship with her. She would like me to assist her in maintaining the greenhouse and the workshop, starting today," Ariadne says, smiling wide.

"I will never understand your fondness for such dirty work," Ksenia wrinkles her nose.

Ariadne's smile fades slightly as she sits.

"If I was as skilled with horticulture as Ariadne, I would surround myself with flowers like she does," Samaira says before eating a dainty spoonful of her stew.

Ariadne grins and pulls out her wand. She conjures a daffodil and hands it to Samaira, who takes it happily. Samaira smells the bloom, then lets Ariadne attach it to her hair.

After they finish their lunch, they return to the lyceum for their afternoon class. Their professor is already present at the front of the lecture hall, an austere older woman with dark skin and grey hair. She looks to be in her late seventies.

"Welcome class. I am Professor Rayowa Salum," Salum says, "Enchantment is a fickle art that some will be able to master. For others, it will escape them. Let us start with a simple spell today and see what you all are capable of."

Salum teaches them the invisibility spell and asks them to get into their pairs to practice. Ariadne sighs inwardly.

Another easy piece of magic that she'd learned as a child, to her parents' dismay.

They are all given lit candles to turn invisible, then visible again. When the candles disappear, the smoke from their flames still floats above them. Professor Salum says it is a lesson that invisibility is not perfect, so they should not depend on it entirely for their own absolution in times of trouble. Afterwards, Salum instructs them to use the invisibility spell on their assigned partners to practice using it on something larger and more complex.

Ariadne faces Iona, points her wand, and says, "Aóratos."

Iona becomes completely invisible within a millisecond. Ariadne says the spell again and it reverses. Iona is still looking down at her arms in amazement at the spell.

"Try it on me," Ariadne says.

Iona takes a deep breath and points her wand at Ariadne.

"Aóratos," Iona says.

Samaira giggles behind Ariadne and she glances at her in confusion. Then she looks down at herself and gasps. All Iona had managed to make invisible was her dress. Though she can feel the fabric on her body, all anyone else can see is her stays and chemise.

"Oh!" Iona exclaims, covering her mouth with her hand, "My deepest apologies, I-"

"Do it properly," Ariadne snaps.

Iona quickly points her wand and says the spell again. Ariadne looks down and yelps, folding into herself. Her underclothes, apart from her stockings and shoes, were made invisible. The rest of her body appears completely naked.

"Aóratos," Ariadne says, pointing her wand at herself to make her underclothes and dress visible again.

"I did not mean to," Iona tries to say but stops when she sees Ariadne's livid expression.

"You did that on purpose!" Ariadne yells.

"It was an accident, I swear!" Iona insists, her face so red that her freckles have nearly disappeared.

"Even the most incompetent witch couldn't muck up a simple invisibility spell," Ariadne scoffs.

Iona blushes furiously while the other classmates try and fail to suppress their laughter.

"Now, now. Let us not lose our heads, girls. Spells do not always work as intended," Professor Salum says, then turns to Iona and says, "It seems this spell escapes you, child. Perhaps you should continue practicing on smaller objects."

"No, let me try again," Iona says.

"Are you joking?" Ariadne says.

"Patience, please. I am sure you did not get this spell right on the first try," Professor Salum scolds, "Not all witches arrive here as skilled as you are."

Ariadne notices a flicker of defiance in Iona's eyes as she points her wand at Ariadne.

"Aóratos," Iona says, with more confidence.

Ariadne flinches but when she looks down at herself, her clothes and her body are invisible. She relaxes slightly but is still angry. Iona undoes the spell and sighs with relief.

"Much better," Professor Salum says, "Practice and you shall improve."

The professor walks away to the next pair of witches and Ariadne gathers her things. Class had only just started but she does not care. If she stays here another second, she will do or say something she'll regret.

"Ariadne, I am so sorry," Iona tries to apologize but Ariadne ignores her.

She storms out of the lecture hall, and only when she's alone does she allow her mortification to wash over her.

Ariadne had forced herself to calm down in time to assist Yun after class. The professor had her trimming herbs in the greenhouse and the verdure did help to diffuse some of her anger. However, when she left to go back to her dormitory, all her rage bubbled back to the surface.

She is infuriated that her first impression with a professor has been so permanently marred. She is certain that Iona did the invisibility spell wrong on purpose to humiliate and belittle her. When she makes it back to her room, Ksenia and Samaira are there waiting for her.

"She made you look like a fool in front of your peers and your professor," Ksenia says bluntly, "I also find it hard to believe that it was an innocent mistake."

"She is innocent of nothing," Ariadne spits. Aster growls beside her.

"What will you do to her?" Ksenia asks with a raised eyebrow.

"Why should she need to do anything?" Samaira asks.

"Should she be spineless instead?" Ksenia asks.

Samaira takes Ariadne's hand and looks up at her earnestly.

"If you attempt to harass Iona publicly, the quarrel will come to the attention of Professor Lysander. Then two professors would have a less than stellar opinion of you," Samaira points out, "Perhaps it truly was a mistake."

"It was a mistake for her to antagonize Ariadne multiple times in a row," Ksenia scoffs, "Such impertinence could hardly be seen as accidental. She clearly has ulterior motives. Look who she has befriended since she has arrived here, a social climbing gossiper and a sniveling failure of a witch who would only celebrate Ariadne's disgrace. If Iona is to be judged by her company, as well as her actions, she is not as innocuous as we once thought."

"You are making many unfair assumptions," Samaira protests, "I dare say, your view of others savors strongly of malice, not insight."

"I have to think," Ariadne sighs, rubbing her temples.

Ksenia pulls out a flask from within her dress and wiggles it side to side, "Might this help?"

Ariadne reaches for it and takes a long swig of whiskey. Then she tests the weight of the flask in her hand and asks, "Duplication spell?"

"Yes. We shall have whiskey to last us the whole year,"

Ksenia grins.

"Very clever, as always, Ksenia," Ariadne grins back.

They pass the flask around until they are giggling raucously. They started drinking in their chairs near the fireplace but eventually end up on the floor.

"I am quite sure Elise appreciated Iona's mistake," Samaira snorts, "You did string her along for a year."

"I did no such thing!" Ariadne protests through her giggles, "She knew I was only with her because my mother ordered me to. She broke it off with me!"

"Elise is even more pathetic than Iona," Ksenia says, her words slurred, "She is the worst Lysander witch in centuries. Unambiguously terrible. I would die of shame."

Samaira pushes herself up to standing, sways slightly, and walks to the window. She taps her gold wand against her chin idly.

"I love when the mountains are pink," Samaira sighs, taking another sip from her flask, then almost spits it out, "Iona is entering the woods again."

Ariadne and Ksenia scramble to their feet to look out the window. Ariadne makes it right before Iona disappears into the trees.

"She really is mad," Ksenia says, taking the flask from Samaira.

"Now is my chance," Ariadne realizes and bounds across the room to her door.

"Ariadne," Samaira says cautiously.

"I do not intend to burn her room to the ground," Ariadne scoffs, "I will do something small. A fair quid pro quo for her foolhardy trick in class."

Ariadne slips out of her room and tiptoes across the hall to Iona's door. Though in her intoxicated state, she is unsure how quiet she truly is. She hears Samaira and Ksenia gather in her doorway to watch and giggle together.

Ariadne reaches Iona's room and opens the door. She steps inside and looks around. The room is pretty but simple, without a fireplace or furnishings to make it her own. Had she not bothered to conjure any additions? Perhaps she does not know how. Ariadne closes the door behind her and pulls out her wand.

"What to do, what to do," Ariadne murmurs to herself.

She considers placing a hex on the bed, or maybe one of the textbooks on the desk, but nothing seems good enough. She almost loses her balance and giggles. Then she finds the door to the bathroom and her eyes focus on the copper bathtub. She is reminded of a hex her cousin once taught her when they were children. It is just childish enough to be harmless but bold enough to send a message.

"Vopsea rosu," she whispers, pointing her wand at the tub.

She leaves a botanical calling card behind, settling on a pink rhododendron flower, then scurries out of the room before Iona can catch her unaware. She runs back to her room and crashes into Samaira and Ksenia as they dissolve into a fit of drunken hysterics.

4 – IONA

T he woodlands surrounding the college are unlike anything Iona has ever seen before. All climates are exhibited in different sections of the woods and seem to shift at random, as if the forest were an everchanging sentient entity.

When Iona walks into the thicket today, she emerges into a dark and cold forest with coniferous evergreen trees that tower over her. Iona walks between them, drawing her cloak around herself and exhaling heavily to see her breath turn to pale mist.

When she walks far enough, the trees transition into a dense humid rainforest with a thick canopy of green leaves above. The sounds of nature change from peaceful crickets to buzzing insects and frogs. A bright green snake hangs in a twisted pile on a branch above her. It's tongue slithers out in warning and she quickly puts some distance between them. The heat causes her to open her cloak and wipe sweat off her brow. The farther she walks, the more the forest transforms around her.

She finds herself in a new evergreen forest with twinkling fireflies dancing around in the warm night air. She stops in her tracks when she hears movement and quickly hides behind a tree.

Two fauns, no taller than Iona's shoulders, walk ahead of

her. She holds her breath and watches as they stroll hand in hand. The female has light brown fur on her legs while the male's fur is black. Their ears flop downwards on either side of their smiling faces. When they look at each other, it's clear they are in love.

They go on their way, never realizing anyone was watching, and Iona leaves her hiding spot. It is her first encounter with another magical species and the discovery makes her smile so wide, it hurts her cheeks.

She continues her walk through the trees, keeping an eye out for any other unexpected beings or creatures. Her mind drifts to her classes that day and, inevitably, to Ariadne Zerynthos.

Iona doesn't understand what she did to make Ariadne assume the worst in her. She'd tried to apologize for her mistake in their enchantment class, but Ariadne had ignored every word. She must apologize again tomorrow if she could manage it. She did not want this rivalry between them to continue or become any worse.

She blushes at the memory of her botched invisibility spell. She had seen just a glimpse of Ariadne's bare breasts, dainty and fair. Iona had closed her eyes and turned her head away, but the image of Ariadne's olive skin is branded onto the back of her eyelids.

The entire college seems completely unsurprised by the behavior of witches like Ariadne. Whenever she enters a room, the air seems to change, and the other witches covertly watch her wherever she goes. Even the professors seem to treat her differently than the other students. Samuel barely reprimanded Ariadne's unnecessary duplication of the diamonds yesterday and though it does not affect Iona's opinion of him too unfavorably, she was surprised by his willingness to ignore Ariadne's behavior.

Iona did not know what to make of Samuel's generosity or his withholding of information. There were many details that Iona would have preferred to know before agreeing to attend this college. Perhaps he thought that since Iona was common and untrained, no one would ever consider her a threat the way Ariadne has. Regardless, it would have been helpful to know about the pendant at least, even if she has no chance of winning it.

It makes her wonder again how Samuel knew Iona's mother. If he was from such an important family, and the divide between magical bloodlines is so significant, how would he have gotten the opportunity to become acquainted with her mother in the first place? Perhaps if Iona befriends Elise, she could ask her what she knows of it.

Tears form in Iona's eyes when she thinks of her mother. She wonders what her mother is doing right now, whether nature is healing her or if she's suffering in pain. She wishes she could speak to her mother again, just to see how she is fairing. Though Iona cannot deny her delight at strengthening her magic, she cannot help feeling trapped within these mountains.

She's grateful to have found a friend in Crescentia, one who knows so much more about the world of witches than she does. She hopes that their friendship can grow and persist even after this year of study is behind them.

Iona surveys her surroundings as the forest shifts again and she wanders into a new rainforest. When thunder booms above her, she is snapped out of her reveries. She pulls the hood of her cloak over her head right before a torrential rain falls onto her. She runs to try and find her way out of the wood. The rain is so heavy that she can hardly see more than a few paces in front of her.

Relief fills her when she bursts through the edge of the trees and finds herself back on the college grounds. She shivers violently as the warmth of the rainforest wanes and the mountain air envelopes her. The rain from the storm has soaked straight through her clothing and the setting sun provides little warmth. She gathers her skirts, now heavy with water, and runs to the dormitories.

When she makes it back to her room, she pulls off her cloak and dress, then fumbles with the laces of her stays. It takes a while to untie them with trembling fingers but eventually she sheds her underlayers and shuffles to the bathroom. She turns on the faucet, then waits impatiently for the water to rise in the copper bath.

Only when she's fully submerged in the water does the shivering subside and she relaxes. She isn't deterred when the tub begins its process of cleaning her of its own volition, allowing the sponges to run over her body with soap and scrub any chill away. Now that she knows what to expect, the sensation is pleasant like a massage.

She rests her eyes and lays back in the tub, so her chin is touching the collection of bubbles that float up to the surface of the water. She waits for the sponges to finish their work, but they persist for quite a while longer than they did in her first bath. As they linger on, Iona tenses with suspicion.

When Iona opens her eyes, she screams just as the tub pulls her under the water. She closes her eyes and struggles until the tub finishes scrubbing her hair, and she is allowed to resurface. She coughs and sputters as she looks down at the water, which is the color of dark blood. When she looks at her arms and hands, they are dyed the same red color. As the water drains, it reveals that her entire body is stained with red. She tries to rub the color from her skin, then notices that her fingernails and toenails are red too.

Iona jumps from the tub and goes to look at herself in the mirror. She gasps when she sees that her teeth, the inside of her mouth, even the whites of her eyes are stained red. Her already red hair has been darkened as well. It does not cause her any pain, but the sight of her reflection is incredibly unnerving. She has no idea what caused it or if it may be permanent.

There is a knock at her bedroom door and Iona jumps. She runs to take her robe from the back of the bathroom door and throws it on.

"Iona?" Crescentia asks as she opens the door a crack, "Did you still desire to study tonight? I thought I saw you return from your walk."

"Uh… I am unsure if I am able to study tonight," Iona says.

"Are you alright?" Crescentia asks, noticing the distress in Iona's voice.

"Um…" Iona does not know how to describe what has happened to her, "Can you come inside please and close the door?"

Crescentia does so and when the door is closed, Iona clears her throat nervously.

"Iona, whatever is wrong?" Crescentia asks.

"Something happened to me in the bath," Iona says, opening the bathroom door and peaking her head out.

Crescentia yelps and puts her hand over her mouth in surprise.

"Oh Iona… are you bleeding?" Crescentia asks.

"No, I am just… red," Iona says.

Crescentia looks at her in disbelief, then she composes herself and takes a deep breath.

"I can fix this, I think," Crescentia says.

"You can?" Iona asks as she steps out of the bathroom.

"Let me fetch my phytology grimoire," Crescentia says.

When Crescentia returns with supplies, she scours her grimoire for a remedy and finds a potion that reverses body alterations, to be used if a witch had decided to change her appearance for a time. This potion would return that witch to their original form.

"I haven't tried this potion yet, it is a bit advanced for me, but I have brewed it with care," Crescentia says.

She takes a cup and pours the concoction into it.

"Drink up," Crescentia says.

Iona looks down at the cup filled with orange goopy sludge.

"It will not taste good," Crescentia warns, "But you must keep it down. I have water here for you."

Crescentia lifts another cup filled with water. Iona closes her eyes, tilts her head back, and gulps down the potion as fast as she can. It tastes like burnt chalk. She immediately reaches for the cup of water and drinks it gratefully.

Iona feels prickles all over her body, like when a limb has fallen asleep. She looks down at her arms and the red fades away until her warm honey complexion returns as it once was.

"It is working!" Crescentia cheers.

Iona breathes a sigh of relief and rushes to the bathroom to check her reflection in the mirror. She looks the same as before, freckles and all. The only red left is in her long, wet hair.

"That was not how I was expecting to study phytology tonight, but I dare say, I learned something all the same," Crescentia jokes.

"Thank you so very much. I do not know what I would have done," Iona says, "Explaining that to a professor would have been mortifying."

"Of course! You would do the same for me," Crescentia says, taking Iona's hand, "But now that the hex has been remedied, we must determine how it happened."

"The bath," Iona gestures to the copper bathtub, "The water turned red on its own."

Crescentia takes out her wand and points it at the bathtub.

"Kiyomeru," Crescentia says, then looks to Iona and explains, "A cleansing spell. It should reverse any hex cast upon it."

Crescentia rubs her chin in contemplation. Then she spots something behind the tub and leans down to pick up a pink flower that was left on the floor. Iona's eyes narrow as her blood boils.

"Rhododendron," Crescentia murmurs, "Did you not say that Ariadne gifted you with a flower yesterday?"

"That snake," Iona growls, "What does it mean?"

"It has a variety of meanings, but my guess is that this particular flower means beware," Crescentia says, looking at Iona with pity, "She has got her sights on you now. This was just a juvenile prank, but she is ready to do worse if you continue to irritate her."

"I already apologized for the invisibility spell! What more could she possibly want from me? A signed apology written in blood?" Iona exclaims.

"Do you think she may have hexed other items in your room too?" Crescentia asks with wide eyes.

Iona and Crescentia glance around the room warily.

"Perhaps you should stay with me in my room tonight," Crescentia suggests.

"No," Iona says, "I appreciate the offer, but I will not allow her to push me out of my own room. What was the spell you used to cleanse the bathtub?"

Crescentia teaches Iona the cleansing spell and they each go around the room casting it on everything they can think of, her bed, the wardrobe, her books, pens, hairbrush, everything. After a half hour of spells, Iona is tired but resolute.

"That should do it," Crescentia says as she puts her wand away.

Iona plops on the edge of her bed and sighs.

"Are you sure that you are alright?" Crescentia asks.

"Yes, just shaken," Iona says.

"What are you going to do?" Crescentia asks.

"I do not know," Iona says, "But this foolishness must stop."

When Crescentia leaves, after Iona promises to study with her tomorrow, Iona picks up the rhododendron by its stem. She intends to toss it in a waste basket, but when she examines the delicate cluster of pink petals, she cannot force herself to throw away such a beautiful thing. She places the flower on her bedside table instead. The flower will only live for a few days, a week at most. She can throw it away later when it has died.

Iona lets her wardrobe adorn her in a soft nightdress, then she climbs into bed with her phytology grimoire. She turns to the glossary where she finds a list of countless plants and their properties.

She reads that rhododendron is irresistible to bees and butterflies, but its toxic nectar causes the bees to create mad honey, which is known for its hallucinatory effect when ingested and can make a person sick if they eat too much. It was even used by the Romans in war to make the opposing army more vulnerable to attack. The flower is now considered an omen of danger concealed by beauty.

Iona skims through the long list of plants and herbs, each with a tiny drawing for reference, and is surprised by how much can be said by the right bloom or the wrong one.

Iona finds a flower that she does recognize, a white bloom with rounded petals and a yellow center, a gardenia. Iona had seen these flowers on Ariadne's balcony that evening when she'd arrived at college. Iona reads that white gardenias can symbolize trust, renewal, and hope.

Iona finds herself gathering all her grimoires and pouring through them voraciously, reading far ahead than was necessary for her first week of class. Her conjuration grimoire was essentially a list of multi-lingual incantations to conjure anything one could imagine, from lanterns, to silverware, flowerpots, wooden boxes, hairbrushes, ice skates, and lyres. There was an entire section dedicated to cuisine from across the globe. There is also instruction on manifestation. Conjuring a leaf is much easier than an ingot of iron because one is denser than the other and requires more energy to produce.

"Bustani," Iona recites, reading the spell from her conjuration grimoire, and a white gardenia appears in her hand.

Iona admires the flower, turning it in her hand, then lifts it to her nose. It smells like Ariadne, except without the trace of cloves. Iona quickly conjures the flower away as the scent makes her immediately nervous and irritated.

When the belltower chimes eleven, Iona reluctantly sets her grimoires aside and rubs her forehead in contemplation. When she blows out all of her candles and lays in bed, she stares at the ceiling and tries to calm her mind.

She glances at the rhododendron flower on her bedside table

until the ache inside of her reawakens, impossible for her to ignore. She lays on her side, then her stomach. She tries to count sheep, then attempts to distract herself with literally any thought other than her pulse steadily throbbing between her legs.

Finally, Iona gives in and lays on her back. She slips her hand between the sheets, pulls up her skirt, and slides her finger against her warm, slick folds. Iona almost moans at the feeling but puts her hand over her mouth in time. She circles her most sensitive flesh slowly at first, her eyes fluttering closed as she teases herself. Then her eyes pop open again when she finds herself picturing a pair of alluring red eyes.

Iona shakes the thought from her head and strokes herself in earnest. At times when Iona did picture a woman to incite her desire, it would be Tamsyn's sweet smile that came to mind. Iona tries to think of Tamsyn now but whenever she closes her eyes and lets her thoughts drift too far, she cannot stop envisioning the red flame on the swell of Ariadne's breast and her desire to press her lips upon it.

Iona whimpers as she strokes harder, her legs shifting restlessly beneath her as her muscles clench pleasantly. She finally lets her thoughts loose and allows herself to envision Ariadne looming over her, her nightdress untied and gaping open to expose her perfect breasts to Iona's gaze.

Ariadne watches her with a self-satisfied smile while her fingers drift over Iona's parted lips. Iona stifles a moan when she imagines Ariadne's head disappearing between her spread thighs and licking her sensitive flesh the way she'd read about in an obscene romance book.

Iona cries out and presses her face into her pillow when pleasure explodes from within. The sensations wash over her like a rogue wave, nearly drowning her in ecstasy. It is an impressively strong bout of sensation, but it does nothing to quell Iona's growing humiliation at what made her climax so violently. Iona brings the covers up tightly around herself and agonizes over her conflicted desires.

Iona's resolve slips when she arrives at clairvoyancy class the next morning. She must find a way to talk to Ariadne and convince her that she truly does not care about the pendant, nor is she attempting to sabotage her.

When Ariadne arrives, wearing a vibrant teal dress and matching bonnet, she glides elegantly into the room with Ksenia and Samaira at her heels. All three of them glance at each other when they notice that Iona appears normal without a hint of red on her skin. Ksenia and Ariadne giggle amongst themselves anyway and take their seats in the front row.

Iona does not want to speak to Ariadne with her friends watching and goading her on. Before she can ask to speak privately, Professor Pari enters the room, and they start a review lesson about auras. They were meant to practice shielding their aura and at the end of class, Pari makes them showcase their efforts. Iona passes with flying colors and earns praise from Pari. Ariadne does the same.

Pari then gives a short lecture on cultivating magic. Witches can draw magic from sacred days, celestial events, even from the graves of dead witches whose magic disperses into the earth when they are laid to rest. When class ends, Ariadne and her friends walk out of the class together and Iona tries to catch up with them.

"Ariadne, I would like to speak with you," Iona says.

"Why?" Ariadne says, not turning around.

"Please just stop for a moment," Iona says.

Ariadne turns to face Iona with her two friends watching over each shoulder.

"Have a nice bath?" Ariadne asks.

Iona flushes as Ariadne chuckles with Ksenia. Samaira only observes.

"Can I please speak with you alone?" Iona asks stiffly.

"We are well past the time for pointless chatter. I do not know what sort of row you are trying to start with me, but I will not waste anymore of my time on the likes of you,"

Ariadne says.

"I am not trying to start a row! That is what I am trying to tell you, but you will not listen!" Iona insists, "Why are you so convinced that I harbor such ill will towards you?"

Ksenia scoffs with skepticism and Ariadne takes two steps closer to Iona.

"This is not the first time a witch has tried to claim innocence while playing mind games with their competition. You are very unoriginal," Ariadne says, "Consider this an act of mercy. A magical artifact like the pendant would only consume a novice like you."

"If you're so sure of that, why are you making such an effort to scare me?" Iona asks.

"I would have used the word intimidate, but it is nice to know my little hex overperformed," Ariadne says, "If something as innocuous as that scares you, it is no wonder you fear your own magic."

"I do not fear my magic," Iona says, but her voice wavers.

"Consider me unconvinced of that," Ariadne says with a knowing smile.

"Then why are you still so threatened?" Iona asks, "These antics wreak of the insecurity I saw in your aura."

Ariadne's eyes go dark, and her smile disappears, "You are not capable of threatening me. You offend me. That you would think an honor from Morgan herself would ever belong to someone like you is as laughable as it is delusional. You best stay out of my way, Iona, or I will see fit to teach you a proper lesson in magic."

Ariadne is so close to Iona now that she can see her own angered expression reflected back to her in Ariadne's red eyes, the eyes that haunted her thoughts in the dead of night.

"Fine," Iona says, then turns on her heels and walks away.

She does not go to the dining hall for her midday meal. Instead, she steals away into the dormitories. When she enters her room, she takes her enchantment grimoire and flips to a spell she had noticed in passing the previous evening.

She takes the book with her to Ariadne's dormitory and slips inside. Iona had tried to resolve this rationally, but her apologies fell on deaf ears. If Ariadne wants to play games, two can play at that.

5 – ARIADNE

Ariadne screams as the water reaches her waist. She struggles and kicks at the wood that cages her, but she cannot break through. The water rises to her throat, and she sobs uncontrollably. Then she jerks awake.

Ariadne looks around frantically, then sighs with relief. No matter how many years pass, she will never grow accustomed to that wretched nightmare. Ariadne stares up at her ceiling as her erratic heartbeat returns to normal. Aster licks her face, and she kisses the top of his head.

Ariadne remembers that Iona's countenance had changed yesterday after their confrontation in the hall. In their conjuration class that afternoon, she'd seemed serene despite Professor Lysander's begrudging admittance that Ariadne's five conjured objects were the best in the class.

She'd created small complex metal automatons in the shape of a bird, a mouse, a snake, a spider, and a tree frog. They moved in the manner of their corresponding animal by twisting the keys on their backs. It was difficult, intricate magic and had taken hours to construct. Iona's other bits and bobs could not hold a candle to Ariadne's works of art. It was as it always should have been, from the start.

Ariadne gets out of bed and pulls off her nightdress to take a short bath and wash off the sweat from her nightmare. When she finishes, she is invigorated as she walks up to the wardrobe to get dressed. It opens and spins the multitude of dresses and cloaks to find the one Ariadne has pictured in her head.

She is caught completely unaware when the wardrobe swiftly wraps her in layer after layer of silk and pulls her forth into a viscera of ribbons and lace. Ariadne tries to scream but silk wraps around her mouth, muffling the sound. Ariadne is swallowed up by the wardrobe, the wooden doors slamming closed to lock her inside.

The silk of her dresses wraps around her in many stifling layers until she is swaddled within an inescapable cocoon. The inside of the wardrobe is pitch black apart from one sliver of light that peeks between the two closed doors.

No matter how violently Ariadne struggles, she cannot break free from her cloth prison. She begins to sweat, partially because of the heat from the suffocating silk, but also because of her debilitating claustrophobia. She starts to hyperventilate, pulling at her arms and legs and arching her back, but it is no use.

Ariadne falls limp and accepts that she must wait until someone finds her. She knows this must be Iona's doing and her serene expression at class yesterday takes on a new meaning. The little schemer has finally shown her true colors. Ariadne knew Iona's feigned air of innocence was but a calculated performance and this is all the proof she needs to confirm those suspicions.

Ariadne counts in her head, fights back tears, and stews in her anger as the minutes tick by. Aster barks but there is no one to hear him. Mrs. Ainsley must be out tending to other areas of the campus and the other students are in their classes by now. Aster scratches at the wood of the wardrobe doors but cannot manage to open them with his paws or teeth.

Ariadne knows that by now she has missed her morning class. Yun would not be pleased. Ariadne had hoped that Ksenia or Samaira would check on her before attending class, but perhaps they assumed she would be along shortly. They know phytology is her favorite subject and she would never skip such an important class. Ariadne waits for what feels like forever until she hears someone open her bedroom door.

"Ariadne?" Ksenia calls.

Aster barks and goes to Ksenia.

"She would never leave Aster behind," Samaira says, "She must be here."

Ariadne tries to call for aid, but her screams are still muffled. Aster scratches at the wardrobe door again until Ariadne hears someone approach. They try to open the wardrobe door, but it will not budge.

"There is something wrong with the wardrobe," Samaira says.

"Kiyomeru," Ksenia incants.

Ariadne yelps when the wardrobe doors open. She falls to the floor, still covered by the ball of silk that encases her. Ksenia's mouth falls open when she sees Ariadne tangled up within knots of fabric.

"What the blazes!" Samaira exclaims.

"Find scissors," Ksenia tells Samaira.

Ksenia kneels by Ariadne's head and tugs the fabric down so her mouth is uncovered.

"Please get me out," Ariadne begs. She's covered in sweat and has never felt so humiliated.

"Stay calm. We shall get you out," Ksenia says, "Samaira?"

Samaira runs over with a pair of scissors. Her friends cut the fabric down piece by piece until they are able to pull Ariadne out by her arms. Her friends avert their eyes from Ariadne's nakedness. Samaira quickly fetches a robe from behind the bathroom door. Ariadne takes it with shaking hands, pulling it around herself.

Ariadne tries to speak, but her breath gets caught in her throat. The stress of the past hour rushes over her as she chokes back her sobs. Samaira kneels down on the floor with her and rubs her back.

"Breathe," Samaira says, "Deep breaths."

Samaira demonstrates by taking a deep breath in and out. It

takes a few tries but eventually Ariadne is able to breathe with her. Ariadne's face burns with her embarrassment. She cannot meet Ksenia's eyes. Samaira's hand on her back soothes her until she is calm once more.

"That is a devious hex," Ksenia mutters, "How did she know about your fear of confined spaces? You do not think..."

"I doubt she knew," Samaira says.

"She could have heard the story from Crescentia or someone else," Ksenia argues.

"They would not dare speak of it," Samaira insists, "Especially Crescentia. She knows better after you spoke with her."

"Where is she," Ariadne seethes.

"Iona? She is likely in the courtyard somewhere," Ksenia says.

Ariadne forces her legs to move and pushes herself onto her feet. She only staggers slightly, rubbing the back of her hand against her forehead to wipe her sweat away.

"But Ariadne, put a dress on first," Samaira says.

"Which one?" Ariadne snaps, pointing at the pile of cut up fabric on her bedroom floor.

Ariadne grabs her wand from her desk and throws her door open as she descends down the hall in only her robe. She runs down the stairs, conjuring as she steps. She goes to the main entrance of the dormitories and pushes the doors open forcefully. Elise jumps out of the way and watches in amazement as Ariadne stomps past her without a word.

Ariadne scans the courtyard and finds Iona walking with Crescentia toward the dining hall. Ariadne intercepts them and Crescentia looks Ariadne up and down in shock.

"Ariadne, whatever is wrong?" Crescentia asks.

"Ask her," Ariadne snaps, her eyes only on Iona.

"Oh Iona, what did you do?" Crescentia whispers to Iona.

"It was only a taste of your own medicine," Iona says to Ariadne, "Since you insist that I cast the invisibility spell incorrectly on purpose, I thought you would prefer covering up."

Ariadne inspects Iona's expression for any alternative motivation for her hex but finds nothing to indicate deception. Ariadne glances at Crescentia, who imperceptibly shakes her head with wide, nervous eyes.

Iona's hex was harrowing all the same and was a gross overreaction to Ariadne's hex on the bathtub. Ariadne is not in the habit of repeating herself, her peers know that Zerynthos witches are not to be trifled with, but apparently Iona needs her special attentions to fall in line like the others.

"I will admit I underestimated your fortitude, but I will not make that mistake again," Ariadne says, her voice low, "I will not be made a fool of by you or anyone else."

"You do that well enough on your own," Iona retorts and Ariadne sees red.

She grasps Iona's hand and places a bright yellow tansy flower in her palm, forcing her fingers around the stem. Crescentia gasps at the gesture, though Iona does not seem to understand the flower's significance.

"Come now Ariadne, she did not mean," Crescentia tries to say, but Ariadne glares at her.

"I am sure you will explain to your new friend what a dangerous enemy she has made," Ariadne says to Crescentia.

With one final glance at Iona, Ariadne rushes back to the dormitories, ignoring the confused looks from the other witches in the courtyard. Crescentia will explain to Iona that a tansy flower represents a declaration of war. Though a tad overdramatic, the flower is the perfect vessel for a small but powerful hex.

With Ksenia and Samaira's help, Ariadne repaired her dresses with magic and had a quick silent lunch before their enchantments class began. Ariadne went through the motions as Professor Salum taught them the mirroring spell. It was little more than a parlor trick, making another person mirror your senses. For the less skilled witches in class, it was good practice. For Ariadne, it was tedious and did nothing to distract her from her tempestuous mood.

She was happy to continue her work with Professor Yun in the afternoon after explaining that she had felt sick that morning and could not come to class.

"If you fall ill in future, have one of your friends come find me so I can brew a tonic for you," Professor Yun says.

"Thank you, I shall," Ariadne says.

"Today, could you please cleanse all the pots and harvest the rosemary in the greenhouse? It has become terribly overgrown," Yun says.

"Of course," Ariadne says.

Ariadne begins with trimming the rosemary. The task brings peace to her troubled mind, as gardening tends to do. She knows exactly which soils and watering patterns will nurture even the most delicate of flowers. It's the only area of her life where she exhibits effortless patience.

Afterwards, she gathers the pots from all the desks and puts them in a basin in the corner. When she finishes rinsing them all, she incants a cleansing spell to remove any residual magic that might interfere with new potions that will be brewed. Aster sits by her feet and watches her work.

"Kiyomeru," Ariadne whispers.

Ariadne pauses when she sees Iona pop her head into the workshop. Iona tenses when she sees Ariadne and almost leaves the room, but Yun notices her.

"Iona, did you need something?" Yun asks.

"Um... yes I'm afraid I do," Iona says.

She approaches the front of the workshop with her hands behind her back.

"Are you sick?" Yun asks.

"Not exactly. I am not sure what happened," Iona says, bringing her hands into view.

Ariadne grimaces at the clusters of brown warts that cover Iona's hands and creep up as far as her elbows. Ariadne had perhaps been a little heavy-handed when she cast this hex, but then again, she had been livid.

"Oh dear," Yun says, approaching Iona to inspect the growths, "Were you brewing any potions or handling any animals?"

"No, I am not sure what caused it. I have never had a problem with warts before," Iona says, "I cannot even put on gloves."

"Not to worry. I have a salve that should help," Yun says, "Ariadne, could you look in the storeroom? It is in a yellow tin on the bottom shelf."

Ariadne nods and steps inside the small cupboard filled with vials. She finds the small yellow tin and returns to Yun to hand it to her.

"Perfect, now help me administer it," Yun says, "Iona, take a seat here. This will not take long."

Iona reluctantly sits in a stool and leans on her elbows against the table. Yun and Ariadne each take one of Iona's hands. They dip their fingers into the salve and rub it onto the warts.

Ariadne cannot help her small grin as she works and when she glances up at Iona, she is glaring back at her. Ariadne looks back down at Iona's hand and the places where she put the salve are already clearing up. Within a few minutes, Iona's hands and arms are smooth and soft as they were before.

Ariadne finds herself holding Iona's ungloved hand longer than necessary, when all the warts are gone. She admires the delicate bones and the blue veins visible through the thin skin, made slightly obscure by a splattering of tawny freckles. Ariadne thoughtlessly traces a finger along one of the blue veins until Iona's fingers tense. Ariadne looks up at her and releases her hand abruptly.

Iona pulls her hand away and places it in her lap, her expression guarded. Then Aster prances up to Iona and places his head in her lap. Iona smiles despite her ire and scratches his head while Professor Yun finishes with her other hand.

"There, good as new," Yun says, oblivious to Ariadne and Iona's exchange, "Such a strange outbreak... It reminds me of a hex my younger brother cast on my hairbrush when I was a child. My poor mother was horrified when I showed her my hands, and my brother got a sound lashing."

Yun chuckles to herself. Iona's eyes dart to Ariadne, who raises an eyebrow and smirks.

"Please come back and see me if the warts return," Yun says.

Iona thanks her and rises from her chair. Yun returns to the storeroom to continue her inventory. Ariadne is about to return to the pots, but Iona grabs her arm and pulls her to the other side of the room.

"What did you do?" Iona hisses.

"Whatever do you mean?" Ariadne asks, feigning innocence.

"I am not casting the cleansing spell on every one of my possessions again, Ariadne. Tell me where the hex is now," Iona says with an impressive glare.

"You may want to throw away that flower I gave you," Ariadne says nonchalantly.

"Which one?" Iona asks.

"The tansy," Ariadne says, then tilts her head to the side, "Are you keeping the flowers I give you?"

"No, of course not," Iona blushes and looks down at her now healed hands.

"If you say so," Ariadne chuckles, "Now if you will excuse me, I have work to do."

Iona shoots one final glare at Ariadne, then leaves the workshop.

Ariadne decides to take some time alone after she finishes her work with Yun. Even the company of her friends grates on her agitated nerves. She cannot look them in the eye after they found her in the wardrobe, all tied up and helpless. It was most undignified, as Iona had surely intended.

Ariadne enters the library with her grimoires cradled in her arms and Aster panting at her side. The library is two stories with massive windows that let in ample amounts of light. Candle sconces provide illumination as well, ensuring that a witch will not need to strain her eyes while reading no matter the time of day. The grey stone walls arch upwards into rib vaults in the high ceiling. Rows and rows of books border the room with a line of wooden desks in the center.

Ariadne finds a wrought iron spiral staircase and ascends to the second floor. From there, Ariadne walks past the many rows of shelves to the farthest corner of the library. The smell of old paper and dust fills her lungs. It is so quiet that Ariadne can hear her own heartbeat in her ears. It is perfect.

Ariadne takes a seat on a comfortable settee and sets her books down in her lap. She opens her clairvoyance grimoire and reads about portal magic. Portals can be created by immensely powerful magic users but more often they simply appear on their own, like the ones in the forest surrounding the college.

"Why are you all alone?"

Ariadne jumps and looks up from her book. Gisela leans against a bookshelf with her unflappable smile.

"I *was* alone," Ariadne says flippantly.

"Let us keep you company," Gisela says, undeterred by Ariadne's annoyance.

Gisela beckons Nenet over from where she waits behind the bookshelf. They both come and sit on either side of Ariadne.

"I had hoped to study in solitude this afternoon. I had a very long day," Ariadne sighs.

"Poor thing," Nenet coos, "What is troubling you?"

"Nothing of consequence," Ariadne says.

"You always work far too hard with not enough leisure," Gisela admonishes.

Ariadne glances at Gisela, who tucks a stray piece of hair behind Ariadne's ear.

"We would be happy to distract you from your troubles," Gisela says softly.

"I am not sure," Ariadne says but Gisela puts a finger against Ariadne's lips.

"Last time we were able to distract you... how many times

was it, Nenet?" Gisela asks.

"I counted six," Nenet grins and leans in closer.

"Six, that is right," Gisela grins back.

Ariadne blushes scarlet and chuckles nervously, "I do not think this is the best place..."

"No one will know," Gisela whispers.

"We are well hidden," Nenet whispers in agreement.

Ariadne's halfhearted protests slip from her mind when both witches lean in and kiss her softly on her neck, licking trails along the sensitive skin until Ariadne swallows hard.

"I think," Ariadne says, her voice breaking.

"Shhh," Gisela hushes, just as Nenet sucks on Ariadne's skin.

Ariadne finally decides to acquiesce. Perhaps she does deserve to enjoy herself for just a moment. Her studies will still be there when Gisela and Nenet are done with her. She laces her fingers into Gisela's strawberry blonde hair and guides her head back to kiss her softly. Nenet kisses lower, licking along the sloping lace neckline of Ariadne's white dress.

They kiss and fondle Ariadne over her clothes until her skin feels like it is on fire, the unforgiving grip of her stays making her shallow breaths difficult to muster. Ariadne tenses when both witches begin to lift her skirts up her legs to tease the skin just above her stockings.

"Ladies," Ariadne chuckles, "We are still in the library."

"Then you had better be quiet," Nenet giggles.

Ariadne exhales when Nenet's dexterous fingers slide up her inner thigh to tease her swollen flesh in slow, tantalizing circles. Gisela's tongue delves inside Ariadne's parted lips, and she stifles a moan.

They should not be doing this here. They should go back to the dormitories, conjure a bed big enough for the three of them, and strip themselves bare. Ariadne is about to suggest as much when she hears a small gasp of surprise. Ariadne is still kissing Gisela when she opens her eyes and sees Iona standing a few paces away with her mouth open in utter shock.

Ariadne jerks away from Gisela and Nenet, leaping to her

feet and taking a few steps back while fixing her dress. Nenet giggles at Ariadne's embarrassment while Gisela only glares at Iona.

"The grimoires for beginners are downstairs," Gisela sneers.

Iona frowns and looks to Ariadne. Ariadne steels her spine and holds Iona's disapproving gaze. She hadn't meant to betray her discomfort at being caught in such a compromising position. Iona's scorn is unmistakable, and it disarms Ariadne. She is not sure if Iona is judging her for her choice of partners or simply because she was amorous in such a public place. When Ariadne breaks eye contact to glance at Gisela, she is looking between Ariadne and Iona with suspicion.

"How silly of me. I thought the library was for studying," Iona says sarcastically, "Carry on."

Iona turns and leaves. Ariadne is relieved when Iona is gone, though internally she knows she should not care what Iona thinks of her conduct. It is none of her concern. Ariadne quickly gathers her grimoires where they are scattered across the floor.

"Do not let her ruin our fun," Gisela whines, "Let us go to the dormitories where we will not be disturbed."

"Gisela, I truly must study," Ariadne says, "I cannot be distracted by such things. This year is profoundly important to me. I should not need to explain why."

Gisela glowers at Ariadne, then stands and fixes her skirts.

"Very well," Gisela says shortly.

Gisela leaves with her nose upturned indignantly, but Nenet lingers a moment longer.

"Our doors are always open if you ever decide to reconsider," Nenet whispers, her alluring beauty almost enough to tempt Ariadne into rethinking her decision, "Or mine alone, if you would prefer to avoid Gisela's infatuation. I have no need for your name, as you well know. I simply enjoy your mouth almost as much as you enjoyed mine."

Nenet grins at whatever expression is on Ariadne's face, then turns on her heel to rejoin Gisela, as carefree as can be.

When the two witches are gone and Ariadne is alone again, she slumps onto the settee and rubs her hand on her forehead with exasperation. These women will be the death of her.

On Friday mornings, all students from both class rotations attend a collective Dreams and Illusions class with Professor Josephine Salvador in a larger auditorium. This is the subject that Ariadne is the least skilled in and though she will always have an aversion to it, she hopes that Salvador's tutelage will help her to master it. She glances at Iona, who sits across the room next to Crescentia. Iona's eyes are only on Professor Salvador as she gives her opening lecture.

Salvador is the youngest professor on campus, being only in her mid-forties, though she seems even younger. Her long jet-black hair reaches her waist, and she wears it down. With cinnamon brown eyes and a golden complexion, she commands the students' attention with a crooked smile and passionate rhetoric. Ariadne notices Iona cannot take her eyes off of the accomplished professor. Perhaps Ariadne was misinterpreting Iona's rapt absorption with the beautiful woman, but Ariadne was usually right about these sorts of things.

"Illusion magic requires a mastery of the mind and a dash of creativity. It allows you to control what a person sees and feels so they can experience what you want them to. Bending another person's mind to your will is a difficult feat. Bending the minds of many at a time is a colossal task that can sap a witch's magic if she is not careful. It's dangerous to practice and depending on how you choose to use it, dangerous for the person you are practicing it on. It requires one nascent spell that should not be used lightly," Professor Salvador says.

She waves her wand and murmurs, "Dominari Somnia."

The walls of the lecture hall melt away and are replaced by walls of water. Within the water are multicolored fish, sea turtles, and playful dolphins. The students gasp and laugh as they look around in awe.

"I can teach you how to create illusions and how to resist them. The walls of this room are still made of wood and stone. You only believe the water is there," Salvador says with a confident grin.

She waves her wand again and the water transforms into rippling fire and ash. Everything in the room turns to a shade of orange.

"The part of your mind that believes the illusion is real is the same part that creates dreams. A dream can feel very real whether it makes sense or not," Salvador says.

She waves her wand a third time and the glowing fire becomes endless sky and pink clouds.

"Please find your partners and try to create a small illusion," Salvador instructs, waving her wand a final time so the walls become wood panels again.

Ariadne approaches Iona with her wand drawn. They move to stand against the back wall, giving them plenty of room for their spells.

"Do you want to try first, or shall I?" Ariadne asks.

"You first," Iona says.

Ariadne nods and raises her wand. She knows the illusion that she wants to create, though a part of her wonders if she should reconsider.

"Dominari Somnia," Ariadne says.

Ariadne sees what Iona does, but Iona can no longer see her. She puts Iona in an art gallery with one endless wall. Iona looks around in bewilderment, then up at the collection of oil paintings in ornate golden frames. Iona walks along the wall to view the art with appreciation. There are detailed landscapes, animals in nature, and portraits of women in fine dresses and jewels.

As Iona continues walking, the paintings change. There are fewer landscapes and almost no animals left, only portraits of beautiful women looking directly at the viewer. Iona does not notice right away, but the women in the portraits are showing more skin.

Eventually, the beautiful women in the paintings are wearing no clothing at all. They are tastefully posed without being overtly sexual, but they all stare down at Iona as if daring her to gaze upon them.

Ariadne watches Iona's reaction while still being invisible to her. When she stands close enough, Ariadne can see Iona's pupils dilate and her cheeks turn pink. Ariadne smiles knowingly.

Iona's steps become hesitant, her chest rising and falling deeply, when she stops in front of a larger painting of a woman sitting on a plush red chair with a thin piece of white fabric pooling around her waist. Her breasts are round and full, her eyes are sky blue, and her long blonde hair falls down her back and shoulders.

Iona jumps in fright when the woman in the painting moves. The woman laughs at Iona's reaction and reaches out from the canvas to stroke Iona's cheek. Iona is so enthralled by her, that she seems to forget that this isn't real. The woman caresses Iona's cheek and draws her in. Iona leans forward, closing her eyes and-

The illusion suddenly becomes fragmented, and Ariadne sighs with frustration. Her illusions often did this no matter how hard she tried to concentrate. Despite her best efforts to repair the illusion, the gallery blurs, then disappears completely, and they are once again standing in a corner of the lecture hall.

Iona breathes deeply, her eyes still clouded by lust. Then she shakes her head and looks at Ariadne with a vulnerable expression. Ariadne forces a cold smile, though her mind is still reeling from what she just witnessed. It seems she has more in common with Iona than she'd previously thought.

"Ariadne, you must maintain concentration, or the illusion will shatter," Professor Salvador says from the front of the room.

Ariadne sighs. She already knows why it happened. At least the illusion was successful enough to prove her suspicions about Iona's sexual proclivities were correct. Though she does not care about Iona's sexuality in the least, it is somewhat of a comfort to know that Iona had not judged her yesterday for her sapphism, only for her impropriety. Ariadne admonishes herself for losing focus.

"My turn?" Iona asks coolly.

"Give it your best effort," Ariadne says.

Iona waves her wand and says, "Dominari Somnia."

Ariadne waits for the room to disappear and something grand to take its place but nothing changes. She looks around in confusion, then back at Iona.

"I do not see anything," Ariadne says.

"Oh… I tried to make a beach at sunset," Iona says, "Let me try again."

Iona says the incantation once more, then again, but nothing changes. Ariadne grins and crosses her arms under her chest as she watches Iona struggle.

Ariadne startles when she hears a loud bang from the hallway. All of the students stop what they're doing to listen. The door crashes inwards off its hinges and the witches scream in fright. A giant brown bear bursts into the room and roars angrily.

"Oh gods," Professor Salvador yells, "Stay back! It must have wandered in from the forest."

The bear swipes its paw against Salvador's chest, and she falls into a crumpled heap on the floor. The students screech and run to the farthest corner away from the beast. The bear swipes its large, sharp claws across the desks, turning the wood into splinters. Iona screams and cowers with the other women. Ariadne pulls out her wand and Aster barks aggressively beside her.

"Izrezati!" she yells, pointing the wand at the bear.

A cut appears across the bear's muzzle, and it roars even louder. She tries to cut the bear again and again, but instead of scaring it off like she intended, the wounds only make it crazed with anger. It bounds towards Ariadne, and she panics, backing against the wall and screaming with her eyes closed.

Ariadne puts her arms over her head in fear, expecting the bear to maul her to death, but nothing happens. She peeks out from behind her arms and is shocked to behold that the bear has disappeared.

Her heart thumps erratically in her chest as she looks around in confusion and sees Iona standing there with a triumphant smile. The other students are back where they were originally standing and gawk at Ariadne's outburst. Ariadne's cheeks burn with embarrassment when she realizes the whole event had been an illusion. Ariadne only thought Iona's first spell hadn't worked but her failed attempts had been part of the trick.

"Very good, Iona," Salvador praises, "Sometimes the simplest illusions, when cleverly manifested, can be the most effective."

"Thank you, professor," Iona says sweetly.

Ariadne straightens her dress and sulks. She should have known it wasn't real. Iona goes back to her seat without another word and Ariadne glares at her. Aster sniffs at Ariadne's hand and whines anxiously. The other students go back to their spells and whisper amongst themselves.

"What did she make you see?" Samaira asks Ariadne when class is over.

"A bear," Ariadne says.

"That is all?" Samaira asks.

"You screamed as if you saw death himself," Ksenia says, her inquisitive gaze only making Ariadne feel worse.

"The bear was charging at me, and spells were not working," Ariadne grumbles.

"That is quite clever," Samaira muses.

Ariadne's eyes shoot daggers at Samaira, and she chastens.

"But you will have many more opportunities to show her your power. This is only the first week of class," Samaira says with encouragement.

"She clearly did not heed your warnings in the slightest,"

Ksenia says.

"She will," Ariadne vows.

"Good day, Samaira," a witch calls from behind them.

Ariadne turns to see Kokuro Sato approaching with her signature mischievous smile. She is petite and fair with lustrous black locks. Kokuro curtsies briefly in her excitement and glances nervously at Ariadne, then focuses on Samaira.

"Good day, Kokuro," Samaira says, curtsying in turn.

"A group of us are having a soiree in the woods tonight to celebrate the end of our first week. I would like to invite all of you," Kokuro whispers to them, "Will you come?"

"Of course, we would not miss it," Samaira says.

"Excellent," Kokuro says with a wide smile.

"Who else have you invited?" Ksenia asks.

"Oh, the normal company and some of the newer witches as well," Kokuro says, "I am on my way to ask that new witch if she will attend. I believe her name is Iona. She truly came from out of nowhere, did she not?"

"Yes, she did," Ariadne says wryly.

"Well… I shall see you there!" Kokuro says, skipping off to invite other witches.

"Should we still go?" Samaira asks.

"Of course. In fact, I think we must. Who knows what opportunities might present themselves so far from campus," Ksenia says with a mysterious glint in her eye.

The party is held after nightfall in a dark, empyreal region of the woodlands. The trees are tall with spiked branches and the forest floor is covered with newly fallen red and orange leaves. Ariadne, Ksenia, and Samaira enter a clearing where the leaves have been raked away and a tall bonfire burns in the center. Witches stand in groups and converse while drinking from golden goblets filled with wine or mead. An enchanted pair of twin guitars play music to dance to and enjoy.

Ksenia had insisted that Ariadne wear her red velvet gown, which is decorated with embroidered silver vines on the bodice. Ariadne holds her head high, though she can tell that the other witches had been talking about Iona's illusion spell before she arrived. They glance sideways at Ariadne, and she ignores them all.

"Welcome," Kokuro says, "We have mulled wine and mead."

The convivium is full of all the usual witches that Ariadne is accustomed to socializing with, with a few stragglers from lesser-known families who seem excited to be included.

Some of the witches practice illusions to create lightshows in the sky. When Ksenia takes her turn, she makes a ballerina of light that twirls and kicks to the music of the guitars. Ariadne is so mesmerized with the iridescent strips of light now depicting a dance of fae, that she almost misses Iona and Crescentia's arrival.

When Ariadne does spot them across the clearing, her hand clenches around her goblet. Iona wears a dark green silk dress, simple but fair. Her red hair is twisted into a bun with stray strands falling around her face in long curls. Crescentia wears a white satin dress with a light pink shawl that is embroidered with tulips.

Kokuro greets them warmly and gives them each a goblet of wine. Iona looks to Ariadne only once, her expression reserved, then keeps her back towards her. A group of witches forms beside the fire that includes Iona, Crescentia, Kokuro, Gisela, and Nenet.

"Do not wear your anger so blatantly," Ksenia whispers to Ariadne.

Ariadne nods and tries to ignore Iona's presence. Samaira tells drunken jokes and enjoys the wine without a care in the world. Ariadne would happily join her if she was not so distracted. Ariadne notices Ksenia keeping an eye on Iona and silently sipping from her goblet. When Ariadne strains her ears, she can just make out Iona's conversation.

"Where is your family from?" Kokuro asks.

"York, in England. But I was raised in Cornwall" Iona says.

"Near old King Arthur's birthplace," Crescentia mentions.

"Is that so?" Kokuro asks.

"Yes, though I've never thought much of it. My mother and I rarely went into town," Iona says.

"Why is that?" Kokuro asks.

"My mother is a solitary creature," Iona says.

"How picturesque, an idyllic life by the sea," Kokuro sighs dreamily.

"I suppose," Iona says, though there is a tinge of melancholy in her smoky voice.

"It sounds a bit dull for my tastes," Gisela says, "Your parents must be proud that you are attending college."

It is a thinly veiled attempt at learning more about Iona's family but to her credit, Iona does not let it daunt her.

"My mother is very proud," Iona says.

"And your father?" Nenet prompts.

"He died when I was young. But I imagine he would be proud as well," Iona says.

"Anyhow," Crescentia says, shooting Gisela and Nenet a warning glare, "Has anyone been tracking the comet that is headed our way? I heard it will be a unique experience."

"I have!" Samaira says joyfully as she enters the conversation, "It has not graced the sky in more than a hundred years, and it's arrival happens to fall on the Autumnal equinox. It will be simply divine!"

"It is to be Iona's first ritual," Crescentia says, playfully reaching out to pinch Iona's cheek, but Iona swats her hand away.

"First ever? How odd," Gisela says.

"It will be a special one to be certain. Professor Pari informed me of a perfect moorland in the forest to the north. We will have clear visibility of the sky and room enough for a grand pyre," Samaira says.

"Brilliant," Iona smiles shyly, showing slight surprise at Samaira's amiability.

Samaira is the sort of woman who could make friends with anyone and though Ksenia does not seem pleased that Samaira is socializing with Iona, Ariadne doubts anyone could have prevented it for long.

"I still cannot fathom how you have never attended a ritual before. Did you even cast spells before you came here?" Gisela laughs, "It is a wonder you have any magic at all."

Iona flushes and looks away, then notices Ariadne watching her. Her gaze lingers for a moment, then she looks down at her goblet.

"Witches cultivate magic in all sorts of ways, Gisela," Crescentia says.

"Did you often commune with nature?" Samaira asks Iona.

"Um… Yes, I spent most days near the ocean or the forest. My mother garners power from woodlands," Iona says.

"That explains it," Samaira says, "It is what the first witches did. They evoked power from the earth, the water, and the sky, in a time long before rituals were performed. A witch with that strong of a connection to nature is rare indeed."

Gisela scoffs but does not contradict Samaira's claim. Iona smiles gratefully and sips from her goblet.

"I think I may retire for the night," Crescentia says, covering her yawn with her hand, "I studied late yesterday, and I am too tired to carry on, I'm afraid."

Crescentia looks to Iona, expecting her to follow along.

"I think I will stay a little while longer," Iona says to Ariadne's surprise.

"Yes, you must stay!" Kokuro implores, "I need a dance partner."

"If you are sure," Crescentia says.

"I will be fine," Iona says with a reassuring smile.

As Crescentia takes her leave, Kokuro pulls Iona to the open area where other witches are dancing together.

Then Ariadne notices Ksenia pull out a vial of potion from a pocket in her dress. Before Ariadne can question it, Ksenia finds Iona's goblet that she'd left on a table while she dances, pours the concoction into the wine, and swirls it around. Then she returns to Ariadne's side.

"Have you gone rogue?" Ariadne asks, a little annoyed that Ksenia did not discuss her plan with her.

"What, are you the only one allowed to have a bit of fun?" Ksenia grins.

Kokuro twirls Iona around in circles until she's laughing and swaying on her feet.

"What potion did you give her?" Ariadne asks, unable to mask her concern.

"Do not fret. I am not in a murderous mood, at least not tonight," Ksenia jokes, "Take her out into the woods before the potion takes effect."

Ariadne turns to see that Iona is already sipping her drink after dancing with Kokuro. Ariadne is about to ask for further clarification, but Ksenia walks over to Samaira. Ariadne decides to play along with Ksenia's plan, at least for now.

"Iona," Ariadne says, stepping close to her, "I would like a word."

"I am not interested in conversing with someone who refrains from listening to me," Iona says.

"We are in agreement on that point," Ariadne says wryly, "But I must insist."

"There may be bears in these woods," Iona warns, dark humor in her gaze.

"If there are, I will fight them like the first one. I'm not one to cower in the corner," Ariadne retorts.

Ariadne walks into the trees. Iona deliberates for a moment, but her curiosity wins out and she follows. Ariadne leads them deep into the forest until the sounds of the party fade away and they are completely alone.

"That is far enough," Iona says.

Ariadne turns to face Iona. Aster sits dutifully at Ariadne's feet.

"What did you want to tell me?" Iona asks, "Will you shock me with an apology for your horridly unpleasant behavior?"

Ariadne laughs, "Surely not. But if you are harboring a guilty conscience, you are more than welcome to beg for my forgiveness."

Iona scowls and Ariadne's grin subsides as she considers how best to stall.

"Why did you not leave with Crescentia?" Ariadne asks.

"I am tired of mind games, Ariadne," Iona sighs.

"It's a simple question," Ariadne says.

Iona bites her lip, then says, "I did not want Gisela and Nenet to think their questions about my family upset me. I know that everyone was listening."

"Do you know why they were?" Ariadne asks.

"I would not dare to presume their intentions," Iona says, perturbed.

"Because witches with magic like yours do not appear from thin air, no matter what Samaira implied," Ariadne says, reluctant to admit Iona's power but deciding there was no point avoiding it.

"I do not know why anyone should care either way. My father and mother were both common and I am too," Iona says.

"Are you certain?" Ariadne asks.

"Yes," Iona says, then admits, "My mother only knows simple magic. I have always been able to cast spells better than her."

"What of your father?" Ariadne asks.

Iona frowns and looks away.

"Women sometimes have… dalliances," Ariadne says.

"Do not dishonor my mother's name with your slander," Iona flares, stepping closer to look up into Ariadne's eyes, "She loved my father deeply until his death. She would never be unfaithful to him."

Ariadne's eyebrows raise at the vehemence in Iona's tone.

"I meant no offense," Ariadne says truthfully, "I only meant that family secrets can be heavily guarded."

"I do not have secrets and if I did, I would not divulge them to you," Iona snaps.

"Fair enough," Ariadne says, taking a step away.

Ariadne regards her quizzically and Iona shrinks under her

gaze until her burst of tenacity has disappeared.

"What is it?" Iona finally asks.

"There is more anger in you than you let on," Ariadne says.

"You make me angry," Iona says, "That does not signify."

Ariadne chuckles but cannot seem to let the matter rest.

"A storm then, a tempest brewing within you," Ariadne amends, "You are not as meek as you appear."

"Is that meant to be a compliment?" Iona asks.

"No, merely an observation," Ariadne says.

Another awkward silence drags on and Iona shifts restlessly.

"Is that all you wanted to say to me?" Iona asks.

"Essentially," Ariadne says, looking Iona up and down, "Though I thought it would have worked by now."

"What would have worked?" Iona asks.

Ariadne stares with anticipation, searching for any effects of Ksenia's mysterious potion. Iona looks back at her warily.

"What did you do?" Iona asks.

"I did nothing this time. Ksenia on the other hand..." Ariadne trails off.

"Tell me now or," Iona starts to say, but her words are abruptly cut off.

She drops her cup and looks down at her hands with alarm, then falls to her knees and collapses onto the cushion of leaves on the forest floor. Her eyes are open, but she cannot move. She is completely paralyzed.

"I thought it would never work," Ksenia says.

Ariadne looks up from Iona's fallen body to Ksenia as she emerges from her hiding spot in the trees. Ariadne did not know how long Ksenia had been standing there and did not like being spied on.

"Where is Samaira?" Ariadne asks.

"She is far too inebriated to help," Ksenia says with a smirk.

"At least someone is enjoying themselves tonight," Ariadne chuckles and looks back down at Iona, "What is the next step in your mysterious plan? I am not carrying her back to the dormitories."

"We should move her farther away from the party," Ksenia says.

"For what purpose?" Ariadne asks.

"We are leaving her here to spend the night beneath the stars," Ksenia says with a mischievous grin.

"Here?" Ariadne asks, "Is that wise?"

"Of course. She will not mind, will you, Iona?" Ksenia asks as she crouches next to Iona and squeezes her cheek between her fingers, "She frequents this forest every day as it is. One night will not kill her, but it will remind her not to cast such awful hexes and flaunt her magic in class at our detriment."

Ariadne is uncertain. Ksenia looks at her questioningly.

"Take her feet," Ariadne says.

Ariadne lifts Iona's limp torso off the ground while Ksenia takes Iona's legs, and they carry her deeper into the trees. When they are satisfied that they are far enough away, Ksenia drops Iona's legs unceremoniously. Ariadne more carefully places Iona onto the ground and looks down upon her.

Ariadne is surprised when a twinge of guilt runs through her at the sight of Iona lying limp and helpless. This is comparable to what Iona had done with her hex on the wardrobe. She deserves it. At least, that is what Ariadne tells herself.

This was not how she thought this night would go and again she wishes Ksenia had disclosed her plans ahead of time. Ariadne watches as Ksenia kneels down and pushes a strand of Iona's hair out of her face, almost tenderly.

"Iona, I shall say this once more, as simply as possible, while you cannot help but listen," Ksenia says with a cruel smirk, "We are superior to you in every way. We are thoroughbreds amongst nags, roses amongst weeds, or some such metaphor."

Ksenia giggles, a tad inebriated herself.

"I hope you can learn to accept this because it shall never change. When we tell you not to make a display of your primitive magic in class, you shall. If we tell you to leave college and never return, you shall. If we tell you to snap your wand in half and throw it into the sea, you shall. Ignore this final warning at your own peril," Ksenia sneers.

Ariadne shifts on her feet, wishing that Samaira were here to intervene. Or perhaps Ariadne should intervene herself.

"Consider this a brief incarceration for using such a horrible hex on Ariadne's wardrobe. I hope you enjoy enduring a similar fate, helpless to move or to call for help. I trust you shall think twice before opposing us again," Ksenia seethes, "This is tame compared to what I could do if antagonized further."

"That is enough," Ariadne finally interjects.

Iona's hex had been awful, but Ariadne does not feel as justified in this as she would have thought. Iona is unaware of Ariadne's past traumas, nor will she ever know if Ariadne has anything to say about it.

Ariadne is also unnerved by Ksenia's rhetoric. It is far too chauvinistic for Ariadne's taste, reminding her of a speech her mother would make. Perhaps that should not surprise her, considering how much her mother adores Ksenia.

"Do not lose your nerve now," Ksenia says.

"I am not," Ariadne says sharply, "Let us go, I am bored with this."

Ksenia looks Ariadne up and down critically, sniffing out a lie as she always does.

"Very well," Ksenia acquiesces, looking down at Iona again, "You are fortunate that Ariadne is far more gracious than I."

Ksenia stands and brushes leaves off of her skirts.

"She will find her way back eventually when the potion wears off tomorrow," Ksenia shrugs without concern, "Let us go back to the party. I am sure Samaira is wondering where we are."

Ariadne nods and looks down at Iona again. She pulls out her wand and conjures a red geranium flower, a symbol of folly. She lets the bloom fall onto the leaves beside Iona's head. Then she turns to follow Ksenia back towards the party.

Ariadne sighs inwardly and fidgets with her hands. Iona's

comment about bears echoes in her mind and she wonders if this is taking things too far. No matter her quarrel with Iona, she does not want to seriously hurt her. She is not that sort of witch.

Ariadne looks over at Aster, who mirrors her worried expression. With one thought, Ariadne sends the wolf back through the trees to watch over Iona's body until the potion subsides.

6 – IONA

I ona tries to will her limbs to move even an inch, but it is no use. Ksenia's potion is powerful and inescapable. The wind rustles the leaves and chills her to the bone. She's grateful for the full moon overhead. At least she is not trapped in complete darkness.

She cannot even close her eyes to sleep until it's over. She is left to sit in silence and think about all the ways she will make Ariadne pay for this. It may not have been her idea, but Ksenia had done this in her name. A few hours pass and her stomach begins to ache. It is not a sharp pain, more of a dull soreness that makes her wish she could vomit. It must be her body's bad reaction to an ingredient in the potion.

Perhaps Iona is wasting her guilt on the likes of Ariadne Zerynthos, given that she'd left her here in the forest without a second thought, but Iona cannot help feeling remorse about her hex on the wardrobe. She had been conflicted about it as soon as she'd left Ariadne's room and her anger dissipated. Iona was not able to see the hex work but based on Ariadne's distress afterwards, it was much worse than Iona had intended.

Now that Iona is the one trapped, paralyzed, and vulnerable, she understands why Ariadne had been so incensed. Though she would argue that this was even worse, being stuck in the cold forest for an entire night. If they keep going on like this, their opposition will become a blood sport.

Iona hears a rustle of leaves above her head but cannot move to look. Fear fills her as the rustle gets closer and closer. She is relieved when a fox walks into view. The fur on its back is reddish orange, similar to Iona's hair.

But rather than the usual white fur on its nose, belly, feet, and tail, the fur there is jet black. Iona read about this sort of rare animal before, a melanistic fox. Iona looks at the beautiful creature with wonder and wishes again that she was not in such a precarious position. The fox's pretty orange eyes are strikingly humanlike as it gazes down at her. It sniffs at her face with curiosity. Then it bounds off into the trees. Iona is sad to see it go and her loneliness returns.

She wonders what other creatures might lurk within the trees, watching her. She tries again to move any muscle on her body, but the potion has not subsided yet. Ksenia had mentioned that it would wear off tomorrow, but Iona hopes that was an overestimation of the potion's potency.

To Iona's surprise, the fox returns with a plant in its mouth. It sits down in front of Iona and rips off leaves with its teeth and chews. Iona thinks it must be the fox's dinner, but the fox does not swallow the paste within its jowl.

The fox hovers its mouth over top of Iona's and spits the chewed-up leaves into her mouth. She had been mid-sentence when the potion took effect, so her lips and teeth are partially ajar. She is disgusted when the mushed leaves mixed with spit touches her tongue.

The fox spins in two circles, then lays down and watches Iona. Now it seems even nature itself is laughing at Iona's thrall. But then, to her relief, she feels her body waking up again.

Iona's fingertips begin to move. She rejoices inwardly as her hands, wrists, arms, and feet are no longer paralyzed. She blinks for the first time in hours, and it feels amazing. Little by little, the potion's effect wanes until she has recovered.

Sitting up, she looks down at her body in amazement, then

over at the fox still sitting in the leaves and watching her. Then the fox opens her mouth to pant, and it seems to smile sweetly up at her.

"Are you... my familiar?" Iona asks the fox.

The fox jumps up and runs to her, licking Iona's face and making an odd barking sound. Then it looks down at the ground and sniffs. The fox takes a flower between its teeth and brings it to Iona. It is a cluster of red rounded petals. Iona takes it and sighs heavily with frustration.

Then she and the fox tense at the sound of an eerie howl not too far in the distance. Iona gazes into the dark trees but cannot see anything. She thinks she hears a faint panting sound, but it might be from the fox sitting in front of her.

"Let's go," Iona whispers to the fox.

Iona pushes herself onto her feet, making sure that she's recovered enough to walk. When she is confident that she is well enough, she walks back in the direction of the college. The orange and black fox follows by her side with a toothy grin.

Iona's next plan is tricky, but she's determined for it to work. The next morning, she waits until the dormitory hallway is empty to slip inside Ariadne's room. Then she waits patiently at the window until she sees Ariadne walking across the courtyard. The wind picks up the skirts of her white dress as she heads towards the dining hall. Iona pulls out her wand to redirect her.

"Dominari Somnia," she says, pointing at Ariadne.

Ariadne watches as Aster runs away unexpectedly. The real Aster is still by her side as normal, but Ariadne cannot see or hear him.

Ariadne gestures at the wolf to come back but the illusion of Aster does not listen. He runs to the dormitories and slips inside while someone opens the door to walk out. Ariadne runs after the wolf and disappears behind the front door. Iona turns away from the window and goes to the bedroom door to hide behind it.

"Aster, what are you doing?" Ariadne calls as she runs down the hallway, "Come back here!"

Iona sees the illusion of Aster run into the bedroom and disappear. As soon as Ariadne and the real Aster are inside the room, Iona shuts the door and locks them all in. Ariadne startles and whips around.

"Spiegel!" Iona says, pointing her wand at Ariadne.

Ariadne jumps back in surprise then looks at Iona incredulously.

"A mirror spell?" Ariadne asks.

Iona knows the spell worked when Ariadne clutches her stomach in discomfort.

"I have felt sick since last night. Can you guess why?" Iona asks bitterly, "It may have been Ksenia's potion, but she acted in your name. If I am stuck feeling ill from your friend's potion, you will feel the same until it goes away."

"You went through all that trouble just to give me a stomachache?" Ariadne laughs.

"No, I lured you here to tell you that I will not allow this foolish rivalry to continue for one more day," Iona says.

"As long as your claim to the pendant exists, we will remain rivals," Ariadne scoffs.

"Your paranoia made you see an enemy that was never there until you made me loathe you. You know that I am becoming stronger than you are and it frightens you. It's pathetic," Iona looks Ariadne up and down, "I did not want the pendant before but now, I might just take it to show you that I can."

Ariadne glares at Iona and in her rage, she slaps herself across the face. Iona gasps at the sting against her own cheek. Iona stares open mouthed at Ariadne, who has the audacity to let out a nervous laugh. On a whim, Iona slaps herself too and Ariadne flinches in pain.

They're on each other within seconds, pulling hair and ripping their dresses, slapping, and kicking until they're a screaming pile of limbs on the floor. Any blow that one of them gives is felt immediately by the other, making the fight utterly pointless and unnecessarily painful.

Ariadne's hands are boldly grabbing at Iona's waist, to what end Iona cannot imagine. Iona yanks Ariadne's hair roughly enough that it falls out of its perfect bun. Ariadne pushes Iona down onto her back on the floor and tries to pin her hands over her head. Iona bucks and kicks Ariadne in the stomach to push her off. Ariadne is propelled backwards into her desk. Her books and loose vials clatter in a mess on her desktop and onto the floor.

Before Iona can react, Ariadne points her wand and incants, "Verità."

Iona flinches but does not feel anything. She looks down at herself and tries to determine what Ariadne did but cannot see any immediate difference.

Ariadne then points her wand above Iona towards the door and incants, "Azlaj."

"What are you doing?" Iona asks.

"You are going to answer a few questions for me, nymph," Ariadne says with venom in her tone.

"No, I will not," Iona says obstinately.

"Oh, I think you will. I just cast a truth spell on you," Ariadne grins.

Iona jumps up and tries to unlock the door to flee the room. Even though she manages to unlock the physical mechanism, the door will not open no matter how hard she pulls or jiggles the handle.

"Open the door," Iona says firmly.

"Oh, so it is perfectly fine to trap me in here but now that the roles are reversed, you expect me to release you on command?" Ariadne scoffs.

Iona pulls at the door again in earnest. Then she shakes her head and remembers that she can undo the spell herself. She reaches for her wand, but it is not in her pocket. She must have dropped it in the scuffle. She looks on the floor but cannot see it anywhere. Then she glares at Ariadne, remembering her grasping for Iona's waist when they fought. She must have taken the wand from Iona's pocket when she was unaware, another sleight of hand trick.

"Where is my wand?" Iona asks.

"You can earn it back," Ariadne says nonchalantly.

"Tell me where you hid it!" Iona demands.

"Where did Samuel Lysander find you and why are you at Lysander College?" Ariadne asks.

The words spill from Iona's mouth unbidden as she replies, "He found me at home in Cornwall. I am attending Lysander College because my mother asked me to."

Ariadne nods contemplatively as she removes her white gloves and sets them on the bed next to her.

"You knew all of that already," Iona says, panic coursing through her. She must find her wand.

"Now I know for certain that it is the truth," Ariadne says, "I admittedly find you to be quite an enigma, Iona. I know most of the other young witches attending college, but not you. I intend to remedy that now, since you so kindly diverted me from my initial plans for a quiet Saturday."

Iona steps closer to Ariadne and looks for any sign of her wand.

"Reverse the spell," Iona commands, but her voice trembles embarrassingly.

"I do not think I shall," Ariadne says, "What is your weakest form of magic?"

"Enchantment," Iona says, then huffs angrily, "Though I improve every day."

"You could only improve with invisibility spells as poor as yours," Ariadne smirks when Iona grimaces.

Wisp had been sitting nervously in the corner of the room and watching the scuffle with wide, orange eyes. Now the fox cautiously steps out into the open and approaches Ariadne with her ears pressed back. Ariadne notices the animal and her eyes widen.

"Is that..." Ariadne says in disbelief.

"Did you not wonder how I made it back from the forest so

soon?" Iona asks, "Wisp cured me with herbs that she found."

"Wisp?" Ariadne asks as she reaches down to scratch behind the foxes ears.

"Yes, Wisp," Iona says.

"I would not have predicted your familiar to be a fox. I suppose I never predicted you would have one at all," Ariadne muses, "I would have guessed a cat or perhaps a rabbit."

"I would have expected your familiar to be a rat. Or perhaps a porcupine, pricking anyone who gets too close," Iona retorts.

Ariadne only laughs. Wisp sniffs at Ariadne's wand pocket and Iona suspects that her wand must be there. Wisp scuffles away and sits beside Aster in the corner.

"Perhaps I should have hoped for a bear as my familiar," Iona says, "It would frighten you away and my peace would be restored."

Ariadne seems to decide her next question in reaction to Iona's barb.

"Are you frightened of me?" Ariadne asks.

"Sometimes," Iona mumbles.

"Most witches are," Ariadne shrugs, "What scares you about me?"

"You are more skilled at magic than I am," Iona says, hating to admit it, "You are dangerous, reckless, impulsive, and beautiful."

Iona flushes and Ariadne chuckles.

"Flattery will not get you your wand back, Iona, though I appreciate the effort," Ariadne says, "I would not have taken you for a jealous creature, but I suppose it would explain your constant stares."

Iona fumes at Ariadne's misinterpretation of her admission but would not dare to correct her.

"You are arrogant as well," Iona says petulantly.

"Beauty has been known to counteract many flaws of character," Ariadne jests.

"Not well enough, it seems," Iona snaps, "How long do you intend to draw this out?"

"As long as I wish," Ariadne says, "Why? Is there a question that you hope I will not ask?"

"Yes," Iona says, grimacing at her compulsory disclosure.

Ariadne's smile widens and she taps her chin, considering what she should ask next. Iona feels the walls closing in around her.

"Do you truly want the pendant? Or did you only say you did to rile me?" Ariadne asks.

"I do want the pendant," Iona says.

Iona frowns. She has never admitted that to herself, but the idea of such a powerful artifact is undeniably enticing. If she had enhanced power, she could give herself and her mother a better life. She could help heal her mother, or at least prolong her time on earth while diminishing her pain.

"And I did say it to rile you. You are obsessed with it," Iona retorts.

"At least you can admit that you want power, same as me," Ariadne says.

"I am nothing like you," Iona says.

Ariadne's red eyes narrow as she considers her next question.

"Were you offended by the scene you happened upon in the library?" Ariadne asks, her eyes dark, "For a virtuous maid like you, I am sure it was quite a shock."

Iona's cheeks burn. She had almost forgotten that Ariadne learned of her untouched virtue from her aura. It is unfair for Ariadne to know something so deeply intimate about her.

"I was shocked by your inability to find a suitable bedroom for such debauchery," Iona scoffs.

"But not shocked by the activity itself?" Ariadne arches an eyebrow.

"No," Iona says, and she blushes so violently that she feels lightheaded.

In truth, when she'd seen Ariadne in-between Nenet and Gisela in the library, Iona had been envious, not repelled.

"Ah... this is what you hoped I would not ask about,"

Ariadne grins.

"You are mistaken," Iona stutters.

"Am I?" Ariadne asks.

"No," Iona says, then exhales angrily as Ariadne's grin widens.

Ariadne is getting far too much amusement from this. Her gaze drifts slowly over Iona's restless form.

"How old are you?" Ariadne asks.

"20," Iona says.

Ariadne whistles and Iona rolls her eyes.

"How old are you?" Iona asks.

"19," Ariadne says, "And I cannot imagine living so long without experiencing pleasure at least once."

"I have experienced..." Iona retorts, then bites her tongue, but it's too late.

Ariadne cocks her head and grins, "Well I suppose there's always that... but is your chastity due to a lack of suitable options? No maiden in your little village ever caught your eye? Your midnight fantasies must have been fueled by someone."

Iona tries to stay silent but is unable to resist Ariadne's spell.

"I did fancy one girl, Tamsyn, but she has wed recently," Iona reluctantly admits, "I do not think of her anymore."

"Why?" Ariadne asks.

"It is too painful," Iona says.

"Did you love her?" Ariadne asks.

"No, but I could have... if circumstances were different," Iona says, "I was attracted to her."

"Are you attracted to any of the women at college," Ariadne asks boldly.

"Yes," Iona says, then puts her hands over her mouth in dismay.

Ariadne chuckles at her embarrassment, her eyes flaring with curiosity. Iona's panic surges inside of her, fearful of where Ariadne's line of questioning is headed. She must remove the truth spell before she says something she will truly regret.

In an act of desperation, Iona lunges at Ariadne and tries to recover her wand from within Ariadne's skirt pocket. Ariadne laughs and manages to flip Iona onto her back on the bed. Ariadne is taller and stronger than Iona and now that the mirror spell has been removed, she finds it much easier to push Iona down and keep her there.

Iona tries to reach for her wand, but Ariadne shoves her hands away and grasps her wrists to press them down onto the mattress on either side of her head. Iona had only been able to buck Ariadne off the first time because she'd caught her by surprise. Now, with Ariadne's full weight against Iona's hips and wrists, she is completely trapped.

When Iona struggles further, Ariadne pulls out her wand and whispers a spell. Rope materializes around Iona's wrists, binding them together, and tying them to the headboard. Iona tries to pull and twist her hands free, but the rope is too strong. Ariadne places her hands on the mattress at either side of Iona's wriggling chest. Ariadne smirks down at her, her dark curls falling around her face and tickling Iona's cheeks. Iona pulls on her wrists, and she can feel the rope loosen only a fraction.

"You really do not want me to know who it is," Ariadne grins devilishly, "Perhaps I might tell them your secret once you tell me who they are."

"What interest is it of yours?" Iona asks, her heart beating faster in her chest.

"I could just make you tell me, but I think it would be more fun to guess," Ariadne chuckles.

Iona tries to kick her legs or lift her pelvis to push Ariadne off, but it is no use. Ariadne only presses her hips down harder against Iona's to keep her in place.

"I noticed you gawking at Professor Salvador yesterday. Is she who you think of at night?" Ariadne asks.

"No," Iona says flushing with embarrassment that Ariadne had noticed her admiration of the professor.

Ariadne seems legitimately surprised by this and

contemplates who else it might be.

"Is it Crescentia?" Ariadne asks.

"No, she is only a friend," Iona shakes her head.

"Ksenia? Samaira?" Ariadne asks.

"No," Iona says.

"Nenet is quite a rare beauty," Ariadne says, a small smile reaching her lips at some salacious memory she is recollecting, "I would not blame you for lusting after her."

"No," Iona says forcefully, a rush of jealousy befalling her at the lascivious look on Ariadne's face.

"Is it Gisela then?" Ariadne asks, "Certainly not Elise."

"No, please stop guessing," Iona begs.

"Who then? I forfeit," Ariadne says.

Iona grits her teeth and presses her lips together to keep the truth from spilling out. Ariadne watches her struggle, then there is a spark of realization in her eye, and she stares Iona down.

"Who is it, Iona?" Ariadne asks again.

Iona shakes her head and tries not to speak. She turns her face away and into the mattress. She pulls at her wrists, noticing that the rope is loosening more and more, but not fast enough.

"Do not try to resist the spell. It will not work," Ariadne warns.

Ariadne grasps Iona's chin and forces her to make eye contact.

"Tell me," Ariadne demands.

Iona squeezes her eyes shut and whispers, "You are who I think of."

Iona cringes as shame sets in, unable to believe what she just confessed. When she finally forces herself to look, Ariadne's eyes shine like garnets and her face is unreadable as she gazes down upon her. Iona's heart beats erratically in her chest as she waits for Ariadne to speak.

"What erotic fantasy do you have of me when your hand is between your legs," Ariadne asks, her melodic voice a gentle whisper that makes heat pool in Iona's stomach.

Iona shakes her head and rips her hands from the now loosened ropes to press them over her mouth. Ariadne sits back on her heels and simply watches Iona squirm as the spell wreaks havoc inside of her.

"I am waiting," Ariadne says, feigning boredom but Iona can sense her impatient anticipation.

Iona whimpers, removes her hands, and the words spill from her lips in a rush, "I imagine myself asleep in my bed. You sneak inside my room and pull down the sheets to wake me. Then you rip my nightdress down the middle and touch me everywhere. I know I should tell you to leave, but I cannot make myself send you away... You touch and kiss me all over and lick me between my legs. You make me fall apart over and over again... until I cannot take anymore and beg you to stop."

The only sound in the room is their ragged breathing. Ariadne looks down at Iona with unmistakable desire. Iona feels her pulse beating between her legs as Ariadne leans forward again and caresses Iona's cheek. Iona's heart stutters at the contact, then beats rapidly when Ariadne slips her fingers around her neck and stares deep into her eyes, like a succubus taking her prey.

"You want me to ravage you in such a way?" Ariadne asks, leaning even closer until their lips almost touch, "To defile you until your innocence is long forgotten? Because I could do that and so much more."

The heady scent of cloves and gardenias fills Iona's constricting lungs. She can feel the pleasant heat of Ariadne's body so close to hers and the gentle clasp of Ariadne's fingers around her throat. It would be so easy for Iona to lift her head just a fraction and press her lips to Ariadne's, abandon all decorum, and give in to her forbidden desires. Her fantasy could become a reality, if it weren't for the vain hauteur in Ariadne's eyes that embitters Iona, like a frozen wave crashing down upon her.

"No," Iona says.

Ariadne leans back slightly and looks down at her with confusion.

"But you just said," Ariadne starts, but Iona interrupts her.

"I do not wish for that in reality. How could I? You have made it your relentless endeavor to torment me from the moment I arrived here. No matter how physically attracted I may be to you," Iona flushes, "I would never give myself to someone that I hold in such low esteem."

Iona sees the flicker of hurt in Ariadne's eyes before she hides it away. Due to Ariadne's spell, they both know that Iona's words are the perfect truth. Ariadne releases Iona's throat and climbs off of her. She stands there, looking down at Iona on the bed, and chuckles darkly.

"How pitiful," Ariadne says, her eyes filled with resentment, "To be infatuated with someone who bests you at every turn. Feel free to continue dreaming of me as you have, because that is the only way you could have me. I shall be the superior witch at this school and win Morgan's pendant, as is my right. The victory will only be sweeter knowing how much you want me while I do it."

Ariadne undoes the truth spell on Iona with a flourish of her wand. She pulls Iona's wand from her pocket and tosses it to her unceremoniously. Iona takes it back with trembling fingers. Ariadne removes the locking spell on the door and departs, leaving Iona lying there on the bed; mortified, conflicted, and aroused.

7 – ARIADNE

Iona's words haunt Ariadne for the rest of the weekend. No matter how hard she tries, she cannot stop thinking about Iona's blushing face as she described what she wanted Ariadne to do to her. Or rather, what she did not want.

Ariadne had spent her entire Sunday in the incantation chamber practicing every spell she knows until her magic is entirely drained. The rooms in the chamber are filled with dummies and targets to take the brunt of her magic. By the time Ariadne was through with them, they were but scraps of cloth and straw. She'd conjured replacements and left the chamber feeling only slightly diverted.

While lying in bed on Sunday night, Ariadne touches herself as she plays out Iona's fantasy in her head; her sneaking into Iona's room and ravishing her until she faints from the pleasure. Iona had described it perfectly, somehow knowing that Ariadne enjoyed making women beg for what they want, whether it be for more pleasure or less. Iona would beg so prettily too, and Ariadne craves it so. But she shouldn't. She mustn't.

She'd never thought that Iona would be attracted to her, not after all that has happened. She'd thought it had been jealousy behind Iona's persistent demure stares, never lust. Her confession is proof that sometimes, desire ignores all common sense. It takes what it wants without regard for propriety or rationality.

When Ariadne finds her own pleasure, however brief it may be, she lays in bed and dreads the coming morning. Tomorrow she will be in class with Iona, practicing spells with her, and pretending as if she isn't picturing all that she would do to her if they were not bitter rivals.

Ariadne's goal has always been the pendant. She cannot let Iona distract her from this lifelong objective. Her family would never forgive her if she failed now. She must stay focused, no matter what it takes. Then maybe after she is victorious, and has the pendant in her possession, she might entertain an affair with Iona.

Ariadne holds fast to her ambitions while she performs her best spells and brews her best potions. Iona can barely look at her in class and Ariadne ignores her as best she can.

On occasion, during long lectures, Ariadne will find herself staring at Iona instead of the professor, letting her eyes drift down Iona's long neck, her full chest, the freckles on her arms, and her slender fingers as she nervously twirls a strand of her red hair. This is the only indulgence Ariadne will allow herself, to covertly look upon the beauty that she can never explore.

Iona does well in class too, taking up new skills as if she was Morgan herself reincarnated. Ariadne observes her education discreetly, no longer shocked when Iona exhibits another feat of magical strength. Their loud rivalry had turned into a quiet opposition, while the other young witches hold their breath and observe.

By Friday, Ariadne had grown accustomed to the tense silence between her and Iona. She sits in class and listens to Professor Salvador talk about the challenges of long-term illusions. Iona watches Professor Salvador with rapt attention. Jealousy turns Ariadne's blood to acid as she looks between the two of them. She tries to ignore it, but her intrusive thoughts are inescapable.

When class ends, Ariadne falls behind and watches as Iona

approaches the podium. Iona discusses something with the professor, putting her hand against her chest when she laughs at something Salvador says to her.

"Your illusions are quite exquisite, Iona. I have never seen a student succeed in illusion magic quite as swiftly as you have," Salvador praises.

"Thank you, professor," Iona smiles, her cheeks pink.

Ariadne lingers in her row and pretends to be having trouble gathering her grimoires. Iona notices out of the corner of her eye and immediately becomes more reserved.

"I hope you have a lovely weekend," Iona smiles.

"You as well, Iona," Salvador smiles back.

Iona leaves in a rush, her eyes down. Ariadne goes to leave as well but pauses when Salvador calls out to her.

"Ariadne, can I please speak with you for a moment?" Salvador asks.

Ariadne is reluctant to stay but approaches the podium.

"Yes, Professor?" Ariadne asks, fighting to keep her expression neutral.

"After observing you in class, I do have concerns about your illusions. They are still breaking down midway through. I know you to be a strong witch, so my instinct is that it is not a matter of strength or ability," Salvador says.

Salvador clears her throat and Ariadne fidgets with a small tear in her glove.

"Usually when a witch has trouble with illusion magic, it is because of a mental block that prevents them from maintaining their spells," Salvador says.

Salvador takes a step closer to Ariadne. Ariadne knows what the professor is about to say and steels her spine.

"I could not help being reminded of the unfortunate incident you were involved in years ago. I am wondering if any distress you experienced may be preventing your magic from performing as it should," Salvador says, the compassion in her gaze only causing Ariadne to dissociate from the conversation.

"I appreciate your concern, but I have long since dealt with the ramifications of the 'unfortunate incident' you speak of. I have no reason to believe a childhood accident is to blame for my riven illusions. It is more likely that I need practice, or better instruction," Ariadne says coolly.

"Ariadne," Salvador says, but Ariadne recklessly interrupts her.

"Or I suppose you could continue to focus your attentions on Iona. Though if her illusions are as exquisite as you claim, I must wonder at your enduring interest in her," Ariadne says.

Salvador's mouth falls open and she stutters, "I do not like what you are insinuating, Ariadne."

"Neither do I. It is most improper," Ariadne says.

"I have no interest in my students beyond their success in illusion magic," Salvador says firmly, "Perhaps if you were not so preoccupied with Iona's comings and goings, you would be able to focus on your studies long enough to improve."

Ariadne forces a cavalier smile, despite her chagrin.

"I shall take that under advisement, Professor," Ariadne says, "If that is all, I shall take my leave."

Ariadne does not wait for Salvador to reply and quickly escapes into the hallway. She sighs and rubs her temples, immediately regretting the loss of her temper.

Of course, she knows that Salvador would never indulge in improper intimacies with her students. But whenever anyone mentions the... incident, Ariadne gets into a passion that she has never been able to curb.

Ariadne's name will protect her from any disciplinary action, but she does need substantial guidance with her illusions. Alienating her professor would only hurt her progress. She is becoming more reckless than she should be. One impulsive decision after the next.

"What was that about?" Ksenia asks, making Ariadne jump.

Ariadne wasn't expecting to see Ksenia there in the hall and stutters, "Oh... uh... nothing. I had a question about the lecture."

"I see..." Ksenia says, "I am on my way to the dining hall for lunch. Would you care to join me?"

"Of course," Ariadne says quickly.

They cross the stone plaza and pass the belltower on their way to the dining hall, a circular room with many tables and chairs beneath a dome of glass. There is a kitchen for those who need it, but most witches can conjure their meals themselves.

Ariadne takes a seat between Ksenia and Samaira and decides what she would like to eat. She conjures a small bowl of avgolemono soup, a spoon, and a cup of clove tea. Samaira glances at Ariadne's sparse meal and fails to hide her disapproval.

"Is it not the perfect season for pumpkin bread?" Samaira asks with a smile, "You must try some!"

Samaira tries to offer Ariadne a piece, but she does not accept it.

"No, thank you. The soup is more than enough," Ariadne says with a tight smile.

"Gisela is staring," Ksenia gripes.

Ariadne makes the mistake of glancing about the room. She locks eyes with Gisela across the dining hall, who attempts an alluring smile. Ariadne quickly averts her gaze and sighs.

"Please tell me you haven't been skulking about with the likes of her," Ksenia says.

"No, of course not," Ariadne lies. She does not know why she bothers. Ksenia detects the lie immediately.

"Your mother would never approve of a match with her," Ksenia says, "Nor would she approve of you being led to distraction from your studies."

"You need not remind me of my mother's wishes, Ksenia. I am well aware of them," Ariadne snaps.

"Have you been practicing your illusion magic, then? Like she requested?" Ksenia asks.

Ariadne huffs angrily but does not respond. She has not been practicing, nor does she particularly desire to. Salvador's warning about a mental block only further deters her from attempting to master it. Perhaps she is no longer capable of such magic, and she should accept that about herself.

"I could help you practice, Ari," Samaira offers.

"I am no longer hungry," Ariadne sighs, conjuring away her half-eaten soup and standing.

"The ritual starts at half seven," Ksenia reminds Ariadne as she walks away.

Rituals are the highlights of every witch's year. They are performed during solstices, equinoxes, blood moons, and the occasional celestial event. The rituals serve to invigorate and strengthen a witch's magic. The more rituals you attend, the stronger you can become. This is why older witches, like Professor Salum, are exceedingly powerful and no longer require wands to cast spells. This is also what makes the pendant so attractive. What took Professor Salum decades to amass will be granted in mere seconds to the witch who passes Morgan's trials.

The students descend into the woods until they come upon the open field that Samaira spoke of at Kokuro's party. The moorland has plenty of room to build a massive bonfire at its center. Ariadne, Ksenia, and Samaira converse idly amongst themselves while they wait for all the attendees to arrive. They are only expecting fellow students to join them. The professors have their own private rituals to conduct.

Ariadne looks up into the night sky and sees the comet glow with a bright blue tail. It is an abstruse notion, that this sphere of rock and ice will not be seen again for more than a hundred years. The thought makes Ariadne feel small and insignificant in the vastness of time and space. Then Ariadne hears Crescentia explaining the ritual to Iona on the other side of the bonfire.

"It is tradition for witches to perform these rituals as nature intended. Though it is not mandatory to do so, it is a way to freely experience the ritual without any barriers. There is no shame allowed here, only joy, acceptance, and grace,"

Crescentia says.

"As nature intended?" Iona asks.

Crescentia gives Iona a meaningful look and Iona blushes.

"Oh..." Iona says.

"For humans, nudity is inherently sexual and dirty but for witches, it is sacred and beautiful. I assure you; it is only awkward at first but when the ritual is underway and you feel the magic around you, you will not think of it at all," Crescentia says, "Oh, Iona, it is like nothing else."

The other witches begin shedding their dresses and helping each other with the laces of their stays. Ariadne unbuttons her green dress and shrugs it off her shoulders. Samaira loosens her laces for her, and Ariadne does the same for her and Ksenia.

Ariadne wonders how odd it would be to attend your first ritual among witches who have been performing them since they reached adulthood. To Ariadne, this tradition is commonplace, a part of a witch's life just like spells and potions are. To an outsider, such naturism could be seen as obscene or absurd.

Ariadne watches covertly as Iona looks around with doe eyes as she decides whether to join in or bow out. Ariadne is impressed when Iona seems to steel herself and shed her clothes away. Then Crescentia teaches her the chant, "Essentia magicae lava in nobis." It is a Latin incantation which translates roughly to "The essence of magic wash over us."

Samaira starts the chanting and dances around the fire exuberantly. The other witches follow her lead and giggle amongst themselves. It is only when the pure magic begins to flow through them that the witches let go of all inhibitions and dance wildly.

A distinctive intoxication fills Ariadne with euphoria and soon she cannot stop laughing. Her limbs feel featherlight and her worries melt away, seeming so insignificant. Ariadne joins hands with Ksenia and Samaira as they circle the fire like moths dancing through the air.

The witches' voices ring out into the night as they chant. Their long hair billows in the gentle wind, their sinuous limbs and curving torsos making them seem like a single organism covered in the flickering light of the flames.

When Ariadne finds herself suddenly out of breath, she lets go of her friends' hands so they can dance on without her. She looks up at the sky again and sighs when she sees the beautiful blue comet shining brilliantly upon them, seeming brighter now than it was before. Ariadne watches the witches spin round and round the fire while she waits to catch her second wind.

Her heart stops when she sees Iona standing directly across from her on the other side of the fire. Iona stares back at her as if in a trance. Ariadne is surrounded by a crowd of naked women, but their bodies only blend into the trees, while Iona is a luminous beacon that Ariadne cannot look away from.

Ariadne gazes voraciously at Iona's shadowed form. She selfishly wishes the ritual was done in the daytime, rather than in darkness with smoke from the fire obscuring the air. What Ariadne can see is beauty beyond compare; uninterrupted skin covered in clusters of tiny brown freckles, fiery hair that reaches her lower back, and shapely curves that a goddess would leap from the heavens to caress.

Ariadne is transfixed by Iona's round breasts with nipples the color of rose quartz. The swells would fit so perfectly in Ariadne's hands and her mouth waters at the thought of taking one of those nipples between her lips, or her teeth. She longs to know what Iona's skin tastes like.

As the ritual reaches its peak, magic swirls around them and becomes fully tangible. Streams of liquid light snake their way between the women's writhing bodies. Ariadne looks down at herself and can see the orange light wrapping around her and caressing her limbs. She sighs as the new power seeps through her skin and into her very soul.

When Ariadne looks at Iona again, she is playing with the light between her fingers. She laughs with exuberant joy and throws her head back as magic fills her. The lines of her ribs become more prominent beneath her skin as she raises her arms up towards the sky, the gesture making her breasts migrate higher on her chest. Ariadne laughs too and spins around, the magic making her giddy.

Ariadne feels almost physically pulled by the magic as she makes her way around the fire to where Iona stands. It is as if the strands of light are puppet strings that urge her forward. Ariadne approaches Iona cautiously, her jubilance only slightly deterred by her uncertainty.

Iona looks up at her with dreamy eyes, her smile fading, but she does not step away or cower from Ariadne's roving gaze. Iona's own prying eyes gaze upon Ariadne's body with timid curiosity and desire. Iona's chest rises and falls slowly, her expression so vulnerable, her countenance so fair. Iona always smells of crisp, redolent ocean air and the scent is heady when mixed with smoke from the fire.

They both gasp when the magic surges even stronger than before, the light orbiting around them and luring them to be closer still. Ariadne's knees go weak as the sensation washes over her and Iona staggers forward. All the while, the other witches dance round and round, not seeming to be affected by the magic in the same way.

Ariadne is overcome with a desperate longing to kiss Iona. To forget their differences, their petty contemptible rivalry, and take what they both want. But in Iona's eyes, Ariadne can still see a flare of doubt, and it holds her back.

"Iona, come on!" Crescentia calls, taking Iona's hand and pulling her back into the circle of dancing women. Ariadne watches Iona loping away, admiring the way her curves bounce tantalizingly with every step. Then Ariadne rejoins the witches in their dance with newfound energy and resolve.

When the ritual is over, and the last traces of light have been consumed, Ariadne is exhausted. Her magic is nearly overflowing inside of her.

Ariadne wonders about the curious reverberation of magic

that seemed to be incited by her proximity to Iona. Magic has never reacted in such a strange way at any other ritual Ariadne has attended, nor has she ever heard of such a thing.

Ariadne is momentarily distracted by her thoughts when she sees Elise standing alone looking absolutely miserable. She is already almost dressed and walks back towards the college grounds with the back of her dress partly unbuttoned. Ariadne watches her go, wondering who had upset her this time. Then she decides that if Elise is in distress, she is the last person who could comfort her. Ariadne has slightly more important mysteries to unravel at present.

Ariadne had tried to find a moment to speak with Iona on Saturday or Sunday but found it difficult to do so covertly. Iona was always with Crescentia and Ariadne was always being watched by Ksenia. When Iona arrives to their clairvoyancy class on Monday morning, Ariadne pretends not to observe her. Iona sits in her usual chair beside Ariadne in the second row of desks.

It is immediate and compulsory. A distinctive frisson that makes goosebumps rise on the back of Ariadne's neck. Her hand clenches around her grimoire as she fights to keep her expression neutral. When Ariadne dares to glance to her left, she finds that Iona is not as successful at concealing her reaction. Her eyes are wide, her cheeks flushed, and her expression is one of flustered mortification.

"Iona," Ariadne whispers, leaning in closer, "The magic, do you feel it too?"

Iona's eyelids flutter and she flinches away as the sensation is amplified by their proximity. Ariadne flinches too and pulls away.

"Whatever you are doing, you had best stop it right now," Iona hisses.

"I am not doing anything," Ariadne says.

Iona scoffs. Then Professor Pari arrives, and class commences. Ariadne could not say what Pari lectured on that day when the new magic between her and Iona vibrates relentlessly. Ariadne steals looks at Iona and sees that her breath is much deeper than normal, and her blush persists on her freckled cheeks. When class ends, Ariadne follows Iona into the hallway.

"I swear, this magic is not my doing," Ariadne whispers.

"Forgive me for not believing a single word out of you," Iona whispers back, "Leave me be, or I shall tell Professor Lysander of your behavior."

Ariadne lets Iona walk ahead, unsure of how to convince her. That afternoon, Ariadne finds it only slightly easier to focus on the conjuration lecture. They learn how to conjure an assortment of household objects like pots, chairs, kettles, and mattresses. As soon as class is over, Iona practically flees from the lecture hall.

That night, Ariadne paces in her room. She is unable to study or think of anything else but this seemingly spontaneous affinity. She cannot see how she or Iona could go on without at least discussing it.

When the belltower chimes eight, Ariadne walks down the hall to Iona's room and knocks on her door. Iona, wearing only her robe and night dress, opens her door and immediately frowns.

"What do you want?" Iona asks, crossing her arms.

Even there standing in the hallway, Ariadne can feel herself being pulled closer, like Iona is her own personal gravity well.

"I swear on my grandmother's grave that I am speaking the truth. This magic is not my doing," Ariadne says firmly.

Iona looks up at her with cautious eyes.

"May I please come in?" Ariadne asks.

"No," Iona says.

Ariadne sighs, "I am sorry for what I said after the truth spell."

"No, you are not," Iona says, "You just want something from me."

"Both can be true," Ariadne says.

"What do you want, Ariadne?" Iona asks again.

"Magic does not usually react the way it did at the ritual. Do you not also want to determine its nature? Or do you thrive on ignorance?" Ariadne asks, in a lapse of patience.

Iona narrows her eyes, "Do you truly believe your taunts would convince me to trust you? Or are you so accustomed to blind acquiescence to your every whim that you cannot even feign civility to request it?"

They glare at each other. Ariadne takes a deep breath.

"What would you prefer me to say, nymph?" Ariadne asks, forcing herself to keep her composure.

Iona scrutinizes her expression, then says, "Before I could ever deign to speak to you again, you must apologize and ask for my forgiveness."

Ariadne rolls her eyes and takes a step back.

"Or I can retire, and you can play with your magic alone," Iona says.

Ariadne mulls it over and decides that she can say the words if it will get her what she wants.

"I am sorry," Ariadne says.

"For what?" Iona asks, raising her eyebrows expectantly.

"For treating you… less than kindly," Ariadne says.

Iona scoffs and goes to close the door, but Ariadne puts her hand on the wood to keep it open.

"I deeply apologize for any harm I have caused!" Ariadne says, "I may have… overreacted. I regret it now and I beg for your forgiveness. I am most contrite."

Ariadne leans against the door frame, looking down on Iona expectantly.

"Am I forgiven?" Ariadne asks.

"I shall have to think on it," Iona says.

"May I come in, while you are thinking?" Ariadne asks, putting on her best debonair smile.

Iona's frown persists but she seems to be yielding.

"No tricks?" Iona asks.

"No tricks," Ariadne says.

Iona steps aside and lets Ariadne enter her room. Aster trots in behind her and sniffs at Wisp, who is lying at the foot of Iona's bed. A chill goes down Ariadne's spine.

"It is rather cold in here," Ariadne observes.

Ariadne looks around at the sparse room. The only other time she had seen it was when she'd snuck in to place the hex on Iona's bathtub. Even then, as drunk as she had been, she had noticed that the room was not very homelike.

"I am used to the cold," Iona shrugs.

"You did not think to conjure anything for the room?" Ariadne asks.

Iona shrinks at Ariadne's comment, so meek in the face of criticism. It is an entirely unrelatable reaction to Ariadne.

"What would I need to conjure?" Iona asks, "I have everything I need."

"A fireplace for one," Ariadne says, "Bookshelves, art for the walls, plants for your balcony."

"I could always plant the many flowers you give me. My balcony would be overrun in no time at all," Iona says, crossing her arms.

"You are keeping my flowers then?" Ariadne raises an eyebrow.

Iona looks away, "What exactly did you intend to discuss with me?"

Ariadne grins but lets the subject go.

"I have never heard of this sort of magic before. I suspect that the blue comet ritual awakened... something," Ariadne says, unable to put the feeling into words.

"I do not understand," Iona says, "Was it not normal what passed between us when you stood near me?"

"Not at all. Nor were the other witches afflicted in the same manner," Ariadne says.

"But why?" Iona asks.

"I know not," Ariadne says.

Ariadne steps closer to Iona and holds out her hand. Iona looks at it warily, but she extends her own hand and lightly places it in Ariadne's. Ariadne feels a tingle in her palm that turns into a distinctive warmth. Iona feels it too, and gasps as she pulls her hand away and looks at it with astonished dismay.

"Do not look so disgusted," Ariadne protests.

"Should we tell a professor? Is there a way to reverse it?" Iona asks.

"If you would like to inform a professor that you swoon from a single touch, be my guest," Ariadne says.

"What do you suggest, then?" Iona stutters.

"We do what witches have always done," Ariadne says, "We experiment."

Iona frowns, "Experiment how?"

Ariadne holds Iona's gaze and slowly, deliberately reaches out to place her hand on Iona's stomach. Iona nervously looks down at Ariadne's hand as the same uncanny frisson occurs.

"Do you feel anything?" Ariadne asks.

"Yes, it is like... a warmth. A pleasant vibration," Iona murmurs.

Iona looks up into Ariadne's eyes, her tense composure giving way to vulnerability. Ariadne becomes hyperaware of her hand on Iona's body, and she imagines moving her hand elsewhere, caressing and exploring her. Then Iona gasps and flinches away. Ariadne pulls her hand back with alarm.

"What happened?" Ariadne asks.

"I... Do not do that again," Iona says, her cheeks flushed.

"Why, did it hurt?" Ariadne asks.

"No... the opposite," Iona says, unable to meet Ariadne's gaze.

Ariadne looks at her hand with unease. The sensation seemed to change in reaction to Ariadne's thoughts. That is... dangerous. Her thoughts were far from pure already without this hedonic magic.

"Perhaps this is a warning to keep away from each other," Iona says with uncertainty.

"Pleasure repels you?" Ariadne asks.

Iona blushes scarlet, "No, but... I do not think... I cannot..."

Ariadne's eyebrows raise at Iona's panic.

"Deep breaths," Ariadne says, as that is what Samaira tells her when she is in distress.

Iona obeys, taking a deep breath and forcing herself to calm.

"This magic is too visceral for my liking," Iona says softly.

Ariadne feels the sting upon her ego return when she observes Iona's trepidation. Ariadne's advances were rarely ever rejected. If anything, Iona's rebuff had only made Ariadne want her more, as foolish as that may be. And now, even with magic beyond their understanding, Iona is still repulsed by the thought of touching her.

"My feelings have not changed regarding..." Iona trails off.

"Going to bed with me?" Ariadne asks.

Iona nods, her blush persisting. Ariadne forces a patronizing smile and crosses her arms.

"I see. You are under the assumption that I have given your wanton confession, and subsequent reversal, a moment's thought. I assure you, I have not. If I were in need of amusement, I would simply walk down the hall and knock on Gisela and Nenet's doors to find far more eager and adept bedfellows," Ariadne lies.

Gisela and Nenet are the last two people Ariadne would indulge in now, her moment of weakness in the library aside, but Iona does not need to know that.

"Indeed, many women at college would fall on their backs if I ever so much as looked in their direction. Do not overestimate your allure, Iona," Ariadne says cruelly, "A pretty face is but a trifle to me."

Iona looks down at her hands, believing Ariadne's lies all too easily. Ariadne's composure slips for only a moment at the look of hurt on Iona's face, but she steels herself again before Iona could notice.

"With that now set aside, do you have any further objections? Or are you still convinced that I am incapable of resisting you?" Ariadne asks with heavy condescension, then grins and says, "Or perhaps you are afraid that you will not be able to abstain?"

"No, of course not," Iona snaps, "I find you more abhorrent with every passing second."

"Perfect," Ariadne says, "Come here."

Iona swallows hard and Ariadne thinks she may object, but she steps closer to Ariadne and looks up into her eyes with defiance.

Ariadne takes Iona's hand and holds it between both of her own. Iona inhales sharply but does not pull her hand away. Ariadne intends to push the boundaries of this magic and see what might happen. She focuses her thoughts on their joined hands and this time Iona's eyes flutter closed at the heightened sensations flowing between them.

Ariadne ignores the feeling as best she can and pushes the magic even farther. Iona's knees buckle and she almost collapses to the floor before Ariadne catches her and holds her up. Iona finds her footing and takes three steps away. Ariadne is surprised at Iona's acute reaction.

"Perhaps you should lay down," Ariadne says.

Iona looks between Ariadne and the bed with suspicion.

"Or you can sit. You can stand on your head if that would make you more comfortable," Ariadne says.

Iona sighs and goes to sit on the edge of her bed.

"Why do you always feel the need to disparage me like that?" Iona glares up at her.

"It is no fault of mine that you are far too sensitive," Ariadne sniffs.

"I am too sensitive?!" Iona exclaims, "If I am, then so are you."

"I do not shrivel and worry at the first sign of adversity," Ariadne retorts.

"No, you only lash out without thought or care," Iona looks down at her hands, "That is much more agreeable."

"I am not concerned with what is agreeable. Perhaps if you were not preoccupied with such things, you would not be a

HER SPELL THAT BINDS ME

perpetual victim anymore," Ariadne retorts, prickling at Iona's assessment of her, and in the process only affirming it.

Then Ariadne notices something. Her well of magic has been partially replenished, despite her magic being depleted after a long day of spells and practice.

"I am willing to test this, but you must stop if I ask. Do not take liberties," Iona says.

"I will stop immediately whenever you say," Ariadne vows.

This seems to mollify Iona as she lays down on her back across her bed. Her red hair fans out over her pillow and she fidgets with her fingers as she waits for Ariadne to continue.

Ariadne approaches the bed, reaches out her hand, and presses it on Iona's forehead. Immediately, Iona tenses and puts her hands over her mouth to stifle any sound. Ariadne is not holding back now, and she can feel Iona's magic rippling beneath her skin.

Ariadne inhales sharply when she feels a distinct trickle of magic climbing up her arm and into her chest. Except there is no comet in the sky or blood on the moon. It is all coming from Iona's body and into Ariadne's until it is as if she had not cast a single spell all day.

Then a thought crosses Ariadne's mind and, though she knows she should abstain, she cannot help herself. While Iona is so distracted by the sensations, her aura is exposed.

When Ariadne peers into the depths of Iona's soul, she finds that Iona's thoughts are only of Ariadne. Iona hates herself for her infatuation, but she cannot keep her lust at bay. Ariadne has to hold back a moan at the sight of Iona's desperate need for her and her many fantasies of how Ariadne would ravish her. Some are alarmingly accurate.

Ariadne startles when she sees tendrils of golden magic arching and warping out of Iona's body. This was not possible, not at all normal, but perhaps Ariadne should learn to expect that from Iona. Ariadne rips her hand away when the magic burns her skin. Iona remains in her enraptured state, the magic still rippling out of her like an aurora of blinding light.

"It won't stop," Iona whimpers, "Why won't it stop?"

Ariadne grimaces when Iona moans and curls into herself.

"I may have pushed the magic too far," Ariadne admits.

"Fix it!" Iona begs, "Please, I cannot take it much longer!"

Ariadne tries to touch Iona again but when she reaches out, she feels the magic creeping into her and making her knees buckle. She pulls her hand away, not wanting to get stuck with Iona in whatever prison of sensation she is now trapped in.

Ariadne does not know how to aid Iona without being able to touch her. No spells come to mind that could undo such a nebulous malady. Then Ariadne remembers Iona's harsh words after the truth spell and her resentment resurfaces.

"That is all I was curious about for the moment," Ariadne says, stepping away.

With effort, Iona pushes her torso up off the bed, then flinches when another surge of pleasure racks her body, the light rippling as it encircles her.

"Wait," Iona cries, "You cannot leave me here like this!"

"The magic shall run its course eventually," Ariadne says, feigning indifference.

"But how long will that take?" Iona asks.

"Minutes? Hours? I know not," Ariadne shrugs.

"You said no tricks. I never should have believed you," Iona whimpers.

"Perhaps not," Ariadne says with a gloating smile, "But I kept my word. I did not take liberties, like you asked."

Iona glares at Ariadne, both of them knowing that Iona truly wants the exact opposite. For a moment, Ariadne thinks Iona might ask her to stay, but instead she turns onto her side away from Ariadne, tangible magic orbiting her trembling body.

Ariadne takes out her wand and conjures a single white lily, the symbol of the virgin. She places it on Iona's bedside table. Then she silently opens the bedroom door to slip away, leaving Iona to suffer alone. Let her be reminded one final time never to cross a Zerynthos witch.

8 – IONA

Iona suffers in endless waves of devastating pleasure. It goes on and on until she thinks she might go mad. She can feel magic seeping from her pores, the light of it almost blinding her. It is as if her well of magic is overflowing to such an extent, that there is nowhere for the magic to go.

Iona had almost asked Ariadne to stay, to touch her the way she'd dreamed, and deal with her regret tomorrow. It was only Ariadne's contemptable grin that had held her back.

She sweats through her nightdress and presses her face into her pillow to stifle her moans. When she closes her eyes, all she sees is Ariadne's face, her lips lifting into an arrogant smile. She curses the day she ever met Ariadne Zerynthos.

Not long after the belltower chimes nine, Iona's eyes open again when magic finally slips away. She lays there a moment, unsure if it's truly over. She lets out a shuddering breath, pushes her hair out of her eyes, and stretches her sore muscles. She's so covered in sweat and her core is so wet that she will need another bath.

She sits up and when her eyes drift to her bedside table, her heart stops. A single white lily sits there next to her wand. Iona does not need to review her phytology grimoire to know what this lily symbolizes. Flush covers her face and chest at the memory of Ariadne standing there watching her while she convulsed on the bed. Treacherous desire fills her as her outrage is reborn.

She takes the white lily and bursts out of her room to march down the hall to Ariadne's door. She bangs on the wood angrily until Ariadne opens it with an alarmed expression. Iona pushes Ariadne inside and slams the door behind her, then throws the lily in her face.

While Ariadne is distracted by the flower, Iona points her wand at Ariadne and incants, "Verità!"

But just as Iona casts her spell, Ariadne holds up her wand and says, "Zárolt!"

Iona's truth spell is blocked by Ariadne's. Iona lifts her wand to try again, then lets her arm fall in defeat. Even if Iona was not overwhelmingly fatigued, Ariadne's magic is still more powerful than hers. Ariadne stares at Iona in shock.

"What do you want from me?" Iona cries, "Why are you so obsessed with tormenting me?"

"I do not want anything from you," Ariadne says, but her eyes betray her as they linger on Iona's body, visible through her sweat soaked chemise.

"If that is true, then prove it. Let me use the truth spell," Iona challenges.

Ariadne closes the distance between them and says, "If you do not have the ability to cast it on me, I shall not willingly let you. I am no fool."

Iona looks into Ariadne's eyes, and she cannot breathe. It's painful to be this close and not be able to touch her.

"Why did you come here, Iona? To find the truth? Or did you expect me to take you to bed despite your protests?" Ariadne asks, a challenge in her gaze.

Iona looks away, "I have not changed my mind."

"Are you sure?" Ariadne asks, "I can still see your aura, nymph. I know what you want from me."

Iona gasps and blushes deep red. She had not realized her aura was left exposed, worse than any truth spell that could be cast upon her. She fights to conceal it, but she is so exhausted that her mind does not obey her.

"The ways you imagine us entwined in your bed... they would make a harlot blush," Ariadne says in a seductive voice.

"My thoughts are not yours to take," Iona seethes.

"I see your resolve is slipping. Poor thing, you want me so badly," Ariadne grins, "I may be convinced to satisfy you, if you beg sweetly enough."

Iona pushes Ariadne away, "You arrogant miserable excuse for a-"

Iona pulls her hand back to slap Ariadne across the face, but Ariadne grabs her wrist and stops it. Iona stifles a moan from the contact, unable to fathom how one single touch could make her knees weak as they are now.

"Let's not resort to violence... again," Ariadne says, "You do remember how that ended last time."

Iona cannot tell if Ariadne is as affected by touching Iona as she is by feeling her. If she is, she conceals it much better than Iona does.

"If you want me, why not just take me and be done with it?" Iona asks.

"And you say that I am the arrogant one," Ariadne chuckles, "I never claimed to want you, Iona."

Iona is lost in Ariadne's red eyes, and she notices Ariadne's pupils dilating slightly just as her fingers squeeze tighter around Iona's wrist.

"Did I bruise your *sensitive* ego beyond repair?" Iona taunts, "Or are your sultry words merely a string of empty promises made without the necessary skill to perform them?"

Ariadne frowns and pulls Iona even closer, staring her down until her heart nearly bursts.

"I do not need to take what could be given in time," Ariadne says, "In truth I seldom take, Iona, quite the opposite in fact. How exactly did you phrase it? Until you can barely stand it and beg to stop?"

Ariadne grins at whatever expression forms on Iona's face that betrays her desire.

"Offer yourself to me. Surrender your body to me. We both

know you want to," Ariadne dares her, "I want to hear you say the words without a truth spell or aura admitting it for you."

"And what if I never offer myself to you?" Iona asks in a shaky voice, "Thoughts and actions are entirely different."

"Then I suppose we will take solace in our fantasies," Ariadne says, "What a pity that would be."

Iona pulls her wrist away, unable to think clearly with Ariadne touching her.

"Why would magic tie me to someone like you?" Iona whispers.

Ariadne has no answer for that. It takes all of Iona's willpower to step away from her and leave the room.

Iona can barely pay attention in class. Ariadne's proximity in the chair next to her is impossible to ignore. It's like their souls are calling to each other but their minds resist. Anytime Iona sees her in the hall or out in the courtyard with Aster, she remembers Ariadne taunting her, daring her to surrender to her desires. It is maddeningly distracting.

One afternoon, Crescentia convinces Iona to join her in the student's parlor to play cards. Iona was reluctant at first. She never played cards before Crescentia taught her how so their games almost always end in Crescentia winning.

Moreover, Ariadne might be in the parlor with them, and Iona would prefer to avoid her. Then Iona decides that Ariadne should not be allowed to have such power over her. She should enjoy herself and pretend as if she is not affected by her at all.

"Iona? You seem very withdrawn today," Crescentia says.

Iona had not noticed that it was her turn to play. She looks at her cards and promptly forgets all the rules of the game. She picks a card at random and places it on the table.

"Apologies, I have much on my mind," Iona says.

Crescentia places a card on the table, much more calculated in her gameplay. She is already winning.

"What is troubling you?" Crescentia asks.

Iona searches for a lie, not wanting to discuss what had

happened between her and Ariadne. The splattering of rain against the roof gives her a suitable excuse.

"It is the dreary weather affecting my mood. I miss the sunshine," Iona says.

"An Englishwoman that dislikes rain? Your childhood must have been quite arduous," Crescentia grins.

Iona chuckles at that, then notices Samaira approaching their table.

"Would you both be interested in a few rounds of whist?" Samaira asks, "I crave a diversion from my studies."

"Certainly," Crescentia says, "Though we would need four players."

Samaira looks to Ariadne, who is sitting on a chaise across the room and silently reading an advanced phytology book while petting Aster's head in her lap.

"Ari? Would you play with us? We need a fourth player," Samaira says.

Iona's stomach sinks as Ariadne looks up from her book, her eyes darting to Iona before putting on a polite smile.

"I think not. I must study," Ariadne says.

"You have already read that book twice," Samaira says, "Please?"

Ariadne sighs as she relents, shutting her book and walking over to the table. She keeps her eyes down as she comes to sit to the right of Iona while Samaira sits to the left.

Iona has only played whist once before. Last time Gisela and Nenet were the opposing team and they had won by a large margin. Iona hopes to do better this time.

Since Crescentia is sitting across the table from Iona, she is Iona's partner. Ariadne is teamed with Samaira. As Crescentia deals the cards, thirteen for each of them, Iona is hyperaware of the faint hum of magic that kindles between her and Ariadne from the moment she sits down. Ariadne seems entirely unaffected by it, which only further infuriates Iona.

Iona clears her mind as best she can, looks down at her cards, and separates them by suit. The object of the game is to play the most tricks per round. Each player sets a card down and whoever places the highest card wins, keeping in mind the special trump suit which changes for each round.

As Samaira removes her gloves, Iona spies her witch's mark on the back of her hand, across the thenar webspace between her thumb and forefinger. It is a small bird with wings unfurled. Its head and body are bright red but the long feathers in its wings are dark brown.

"It is a crimson sunbird, native to Nepal," Samaira says with a small smile.

Iona looks up at her and smiles back shyly.

"It is quite beautiful," Iona compliments, and it certainly is. Almost as beautiful as the sapphire gem on Samaira's ring.

All four witches place their first cards in the center of the table. Ariadne wins and gathers them all.

"What do you make of King George's mysterious illness?" Samaira asks Crescentia.

"Lady Monton is working tirelessly to heal him but... I heard the illness may be of the mind," Crescentia says, "In which case, there is nothing to be done."

"There may be a regency in England's future," Samaira says.

Crescentia and Samaira exchange a knowing glance. Crescentia wins a trick and takes the cards from the center of the table.

"Who is Lady Monton?" Iona asks.

"She is a close confidant of King George," Crescentia says.

"Oh... I have never heard of her," Iona says.

"Most bureaucratic figures are not so forthcoming about their occult alliances," Crescentia says.

Iona's eyes widen, "She is a witch?"

"Yes, of course," Samaira says, "Magic folk have been allies of humans for many years, like Merlin was for King Arthur."

"That is a position that many of the witches at college aspire to be in someday," Crescentia explains.

"I did not realize witches were so directly involved in human affairs," Iona says.

"We are not really," Crescentia says, "Witches and warlocks have their own politics. We are occasionally involved in significant conflicts like wars for land and power, but we are not beholden to human squabbles."

"And thank goodness for that," Samaira says.

Iona places a card and wins a trick, taking the four cards and placing them in a stack in front of her.

"Why would witches be concerned with such conquests?" Iona asks.

"Land is power. It is a rudimentary concept, Iona," Ariadne says condescendingly.

Iona glares at her but Ariadne keeps her eyes on her cards with only the ghost of a smile on her lips.

"I suppose you would know a great deal about that, Ariadne. Your grandmother's alliances were quite advantageous, were they not?" Crescentia asks.

"More advantageous than your family's anyway," Ariadne retorts.

"I doubt we will ever reach the heights of your grandmother's empire. Even we have limits to our rapacity," Crescentia says.

"How fortunate that your family's more modest aspirations happen to match their magical ability," Ariadne says.

Crescentia is about to respond but Iona interrupts, "I understand simple greed, but would it not be more favorable to use magic to help those that are harmed by empires and wars?"

Ariadne, Samaira, and Crescentia exchange glances.

"How?" Crescentia asks.

"Could a witch not stop a war from happening at all?" Iona asks, "Make men change their course with illusion magic or some other method. Encourage them to change their minds, perhaps even force them if necessary."

Ariadne raises an eyebrow, "Are you so quick to remove another's free will?"

Samaira shifts uncomfortably and glances at Crescentia, who seems more entertained than distressed.

"No... not necessarily. But if a witch could prevent harm, why would she not?" Iona asks.

"Witches should prevent harm when they can, but to take free will away from others is a rather unethical method to choose," Ariadne argues, "Even if you managed to control a significant human's mind and will, what then? Even the most powerful humans have those who they answer to. You do not have enough magic to control them all, not simultaneously. And even if you could, what a dark concept indeed. To be without autonomy is a terrible plight."

Iona is left speechless at Ariadne's impassioned soliloquy and cannot immediately reject her cynical but admittedly pragmatic logic.

"I must agree with Ariadne," Samaira says, "Witches advise, they assist, and they protect, but they do not control. That would be dark magic, no matter the intention."

"I only meant... there seem to be so many problems in this world that we could reform and improve with magic," Iona says, "There are many evil men whose plans could be thwarted by our intervention."

Samaira frowns and considers her words carefully.

"Iona, I understand your altruistic perspective but unfortunately power is not always synonymous with empathy. It may be a comfort to you that modest witches, those that live in smaller communities, tend to be the ones who help those less fortunate. Aristocratic witches endlessly squabble amongst themselves and scrounge for power, just like humans do," Samaira says with a sigh.

"That is quite a damning view of our entire class," Ariadne says, slightly offended.

"Perhaps, but it is honest," Samaira shrugs.

"We are not all so avaricious as that," Ariadne protests.

"If you win the pendant next year, how do you plan to use it?" Samaira challenges.

Ariadne opens her mouth to speak, then frowns and looks away.

"Power for the sake of power is an unfortunate waste," Samaira says.

Iona looks between Samaira and Ariadne, feeling awkward and a bit naïve. When Iona looks to Crescentia, she seems to be hiding a scandalized smile. She loves this sort of intrigue.

"Why teach us illusion magic at all if it is so unethical?" Iona asks.

"So that you may learn to control it and combat it when necessary. The magic exists and will be used whether we wish it to or not," Ariadne says with a far-off look.

The game of cards ends with Ariadne and Samaira winning the round. There is a second round to play but Ariadne excuses herself, too despondent to carry on.

"Please do not take her foul temper to heart," Samaira says once Ariadne has left the parlor.

"It is difficult not to when it is so constantly aimed at me," Iona grumbles.

"You must admit, she is in rare form of late, Samaira," Crescentia says, "I have never seen her this highly strung."

"And you know precisely why, so show some compassion," Samaira says, narrowing her eyes.

"I am not blessed with your endless supply of patience," Crescentia says, "But I shall try my best."

"Why should she deserve our compassion when she only sees fit to insult us?" Iona asks.

Samaira sighs and sets the stack of cards down in front of her.

"You met Ariadne at an inopportune time," Samaira says, "She is at war with herself, her nerves are irritated, and you have only been caught in the crossfire."

"I imagine it must be a substantial strain on her nerves to be so constantly paranoid of treasonous plots where there are none," Iona says.

"There were none this time," Samaira agrees, "But you do not know her struggles, her character, nor very much about her at all."

Iona frowns, mulling Samaira's words over in her head.

"I would never excuse her foul temper, nor would I ask you to. I only wish for you to understand that she is wrestling with many anxieties at present, in ways you or I could never fully understand," Samaira says, her loyalty made clear in her conviction.

"Are you implying that there was once a plot against Ariadne?" Iona asks.

Samaira looks away and scratches her cheek, seeming to regret her choice of words.

"Not a plot necessarily…" Samaira says cautiously, "She had a rather devastating altercation with illusion magic that has made her averse to it. Thus, she is often perturbed when the subject of illusions arises in conversation."

Iona's ears perk up at that.

"What happened?" Iona asks.

"I will not speak of it. It is not my story to tell," Samaira's eyes shoot daggers at Crescentia, "You should not tell her either. You remember what happened the last time you gossiped on the matter."

"How could I forget," Crescentia laughs nervously. She shrugs her shoulders at Iona in apology and seems to listen to Samaira's command.

Iona's curiosity is only quelled by her desire not to pry on such a personal matter. Iona should not want to know anything about Ariadne either way. She is still angry with her.

The next day, Iona decides to scour the library for any insight on the blue comet. There must be some clue as to its power and why it created such inescapable magic between her and Ariadne.

Earlier, Iona had accidentally brushed fingers with Ariadne in phytology class when picking up an ingredient for her potion. The contact made her nearly jump out of her skin. Ariadne had stifled laughter for the rest of the class and Iona's embarrassment had made her want to disappear.

There must be a way to break this spell between them and turn them back to normal. She delves into the farthest rows of the library in search of an astronomy section.

"She is clearly avoiding you," Nenet says softly, "We should choose someone else to enamor. A warlock would be much easier."

Iona freezes in the middle of her row. The whisper comes from only a few rows away.

"It is that wretched Ksenia poisoning her against us," Gisela gripes, "I still believe I could enthrall her, or perhaps you could. We should not give in so easily."

"But Gisela, she only ever entertains shallow intimacies for her own amusement. I am not against bedding her purely for our own pleasure," Iona can hear the grin in Nenet's tone, "But you must know that seducing her is a fool's errand."

"Ariadne will almost certainly win the pendant in less than a year's time and have power that rivals most anyone else's in the entire world. Such an advantageous union is more than worth the effort," Gisela says.

"I suppose," Nenet says, sounding convinced, "But I am more preoccupied with gaining power of my own, as should you be."

"I would much rather align with power than wield it myself," Gisela says dismissively.

"Then set your sights on someone that you can wrap around your little finger, just the way you like them. Beguiling one such as Ariadne is impossible, even for you," Nenet says.

"It should not be so difficult to ensnare her," Gisela sighs with frustration, "She is starved for true affection."

"And your affections are true, are they?" Nenet chuckles.

"As true as she could expect, given her bitter disposition and the simple fact that others fear the very sight of her," Gisela retorts, "Even her own family keeps her at arm's length after the tragedy in the river. I need only persist and eventually she will be lonely enough to acquiesce to my advances."

Iona flinches in disgust at Gisela's callous words, but her ears perk up at a mention of a tragedy in a river. She wonders if that could be what Samaira was referring to after the card game.

"Should we not fear her too?" Nenet asks, "She has her grandmother's temper."

There is concern in Nenet's voice, and it surprises Iona. Nenet had not seemed uneasy around Ariadne before and must have hidden her apprehension well.

"If she has her grandmother's temper, perhaps she inherited her penchant for conquest as well. There is much to be gained by such an advantageous courtship. I do not intend to let her slip away," Gisela says.

Gisela and Nenet continue their whispering as they leave the bookshelves. Iona stands there ruminating on what she had overheard. She wonders what it is that makes everyone so afraid of Ariadne. It unnerves her that she may have more to fear than this ongoing, senseless rivalry.

Iona finds a book on obscure celestial phenomena, its cover embellished with reflective silver stars. She takes it from the shelf and on her way back to the center of the library, Iona also notices a book on the many elements of fate. A creature with a woman's nude torso and a body of a spider is painted on the cover. Iona feels compelled to take that book as well, though she is unsure if it would be helpful to her.

Iona comes to sit at one of the many wooden tables in the center of the library and opens the celestial phenomena book first. There are chapters on eclipses, blood moons, and a section on comets in the back. Iona turns to it, but it is only a generalized section, nothing specific about the blue comet that had just passed.

Iona does read that comets can absorb magic from one age and transport it to the next after their journey through space. Whenever the comet returns, the same magic can be manifested in similar ways, under the right conditions.

Iona sighs and decides to peruse the book on fate instead. She flips to a chapter on omens. There she finds two paragraphs that interest her:

Fate is a strand of thread which is weaved into reality itself. For those gifted with magic, fate finds unique ways of encouraging them towards their imminent path. This may manifest as an omen of evil, a beacon of divinity, a preordained guardian, or some other vessel of kismet.

In rare cases when fate is resisted, a transmundane magnetism can occur to make one's fate near irresistible and ensure that the call of destiny is not ignored. The magic of fate is not always pellucid nor is it ever coincidental. The unexplainable may be an augury if you would only heed its call.

"Discover anything enlightening?"

Iona jumps in her chair at Ariadne's hushed voice in her ear.

"Do not sneak behind me like that!" Iona snaps, turning in her seat to glare up at Ariadne.

"Shhhh!" Ariadne hushes, gesturing to the other witches studying.

Iona flushes with embarrassment and turns back to face the table. Ariadne leans over her, one hand on the back of Iona's chair and the other bracing against the table, to look closer at the book Iona is reading. Ariadne's cheek is so close to hers, the proximity making Iona's heartbeat faster.

"Transmundane magnetism," Ariadne muses.

Ariadne's breath tickles Iona's ear. Her sultry floral scent is intoxicating and the heat from her body makes goosebumps rise on Iona's neck and back. Iona swallows hard.

"I do not require your assistance," Iona whispers, "Leave me to my research and if I find any useful knowledge, I will inform you."

"Why would you refuse the help of a witch far more skilled and knowledgeable than you?" Ariadne whispers, her lips too close to Iona's ear, "You are not having trouble concentrating, are you Iona?"

Iona slams her book shut. She pushes her chair back, almost running over Ariadne's foot in the process, and gathers the books to return them to their shelves. As Iona strides away in frustration, Ariadne follows.

"This is not funny," Iona whispers when they are deeper within the rows of shelves.

"Oh, come now," Ariadne grins, "It is a little amusing."

Iona sighs heavily and aggressively places the books back in their spots on the shelf.

"This affects me too. I should like to investigate with you," Ariadne says in a more serious tone.

"It hardly affects you at all," Iona mumbles, turning to walk away.

Ariadne grasps Iona's arm and forces her to turn and face her.

"How could you say that?" Ariadne asks.

Iona quickly pulls her arm free before the sensations grow too potent.

"I am only saying that this magic obviously tempts me more than it does you," Iona says in a low voice, checking that no one is around to overhear them, "If it affects you at all."

"Is that what you think?" Ariadne asks, "I thought you were more perceptive than that."

Iona blinks and loses part of her conviction, but she continues on.

"I am not a new toy for you to play with," Iona insists, struggling to keep her voice low, "I am hoping this outlandish... compulsion is only a passing phase that will fade with time."

"Are you truly so repulsed by it?" Ariadne asks, showing only the slightest trace of insecurity.

Iona looks up into Ariadne's red eyes, entirely unsure of her answer. Part of her thinks yes, she is repulsed. She does not want someone so capricious to have any power over her. But another part of her longs to seek it out, despite her better judgement.

"What happened at the river?" Iona asks on an impulse.

Ariadne's expression darkens within seconds. Her entire

body tenses with displeasure.

"Who told you about that?" Ariadne asks, her voice menacingly calm.

"No one told me anything. That is why I am asking you," Iona says, her voice barely a whisper.

Ariadne looks away, her expression betraying her turbulent thoughts. Iona observes her warily, now wishing she had not mentioned the river at all. Iona wrings her hands nervously.

"I barely know you," Iona whispers, "Why would I not be disturbed by your power over me, whether it be fate or simply rotten luck that caused this invasive affinity. Did you not say just yesterday that to be without autonomy is a terrible plight?"

"I have no choice in this either," Ariadne whispers.

Ariadne prowls forwards and Iona steps away until she feels a bookshelf at her back. Ariadne stands very close, her expression betraying barely controlled anger. Iona shrinks under her burning gaze.

"But do not mistake this preternatural fluke for familiarity. I do not owe you any answers, any insight into my past. Do not ever," Ariadne narrows her eyes, "ask me about the river again."

Iona nods her understanding, true fear prickling down her spine. Ariadne had only ever been petulant before, never sinister like she is now. Then the menace in Ariadne's eyes melts into desirous hunger. Iona inhales sharply when Ariadne leans in closer, hovers her lips over the skin of Iona's throat, then gently runs her nose up Iona's neck to her ear.

"Do not also mistake my austerity for indifference. I feel the magic too, in every part of me" Ariadne whispers in Iona's ear, her mouth drifting back to Iona's neck, only barely touching her, "Our arduous tantalization is being prolonged by you, not I. If you but said the word, I would strip you bare right here and ravage you on this stone floor."

Ariadne grins against the skin of Iona's neck when she swallows hard, her cheeks hot, and her hands trembling. Ariadne's mouth ghosts over Iona's jaw, then hovers but a breath away from Iona's parted lips. All Iona can see are Ariadne's red, provoking eyes.

"Perhaps that is why the magic torments you so. You are the one resisting it," Ariadne says.

Iona looks away and considers Ariadne's words. Ariadne presses her knuckle underneath Iona's chin and Iona looks up into her eyes again. Ariadne's smoldering gaze makes Iona's heart race ever faster.

"If resisting me means you are resisting fate, all I need do is wait a little while longer, nymph," Ariadne whispers, "I am endlessly patient when I desire to be."

Iona did not realize she was holding her breath until she lets it all out in a rush as Ariadne turns and walks away without another word.

"I heard a rumor," Crescentia says to Iona, her eyes alight with intrigue.

Iona's inhibitions rise in the face of her friend's playful smile. They are eating dinner together in the dining hall, the conversations of other witches loud enough to mask their own.

"A rumor?" Iona asks.

"Yes, about you and a witch with pretty red eyes," Crescentia says.

Iona cannot stop the flush that creeps up her neck. She hates how easily it manifests, preventing her from exhibiting any semblance of inscrutability.

"Oh?" Iona asks, her arenose voice going up two octaves.

"I heard that you were studying in the library when Ariadne came to speak with you in hushed tones. Then you both disappeared into the bookshelves and when Ariadne emerged, she was out of breath," Crescentia says, inspecting Iona's face intently.

"Oh... that," Iona says, aiming for nonchalance, "She was tormenting me as always, so I attempted to evade her. She followed me and we... argued."

"About what?" Crescentia asks.

"Nothing of any importance. She is still paranoid that I desire the pendant," Iona shrugs.

"You know…" Crescentia's grin persists, "You should be wary of disappearing with Ariadne in dark places. She has quite the reputation for promiscuity, and you may draw whispers about your feud becoming an affaire de coeur."

"I shall keep that in mind," Iona mumbles, picking at her food. She does not want anyone to get the wrong impression, or perhaps too accurate of one.

Crescentia shrugs, "Though you would not be the first or the last to fall for Ariadne's wiles. I heard from Nenet that she has an impressive gift for…"

"I would rather not know what Nenet thinks on the matter," Iona says, more sharply than she intended.

Crescentia's grin somehow grows even wider at Iona's reaction. Iona had never been in doubt of Ariadne's talents and does not want them described to her from the perspective of another woman.

"You would prefer to discover her dexterity for yourself? Very well, I shall not ruin your innocence. Ariadne can do that quite well enough on her own," Crescentia grins.

"No… that is not… Crescentia, can we please discuss something else?" Iona asks, feeling so hot that she is beginning to sweat.

"You are so darling," Crescentia giggles, trying to reach across the table to pinch Iona's cheeks.

"Leave off," Iona protests, unable to stifle her grin, "Nothing has transpired, I swear."

"If you say so," Crescentia says.

"It never shall, as far as I am concerned," Iona says, for good measure.

"Why is that?" Crescentia asks.

Iona gapes at her, "She has antagonized me for months. Would I not be a fool to encourage a flirtation with one so impetuous?"

"Perhaps," Crescentia says, "Though it is often said that love and hate are dual emotions. Ariadne has strong feelings for you either way."

"That is a poor excuse for her contemptible treatment of me," Iona says.

"Romances have been built on far worse," Crescentia shrugs, "Attraction is not always rational."

"It is for me," Iona says, though she is not sure if that is true.

"Perhaps I am too French for this discussion," Crescentia giggles, "All I shall say is, you are a witch, Iona, not a human. You have the freedom to indulge in whatever amorous affairs you so desire and there would be no shame in that. You do not need to love her, or even like her. If you want her, have her. It is truly that simple."

Iona's eyebrows raise as her flush returns. Crescentia winks, then conjures her plate away and leaves the table with a spring in her step.

Iona takes another bite of her mashed potatoes and puts her chin in her hand. Ariadne's words about fate come to mind. Perhaps it was futile to resist something so seemingly inevitable. But how could Iona forget all that has happened? Fate expects far too much from her.

On Friday, Iona creates her first collective illusion, a blue butterfly that floats in the air above the class. All the witches in the room can see it at once. Iona turns to Professor Salvador to accept the praise she is now accustomed to receiving, but the professor's warm demeanor is understated today.

"Good work," Professor Salvador says politely, then moves on to the next person.

Iona frowns and tries not to take the slight personally. The only other witch who is able to maintain a collective illusion is Ksenia and Professor Josephine is very complimentary to her. Iona wonders if she may be overthinking the exchange, but notices Ariadne glancing at her looking almost contrite.

After class, Iona grabs Ariadne's arm and pulls her aside

unceremoniously in the hallway.

"What did you say to her?" Iona asks, all pretenses gone between them now, "Are you involving professors in your juvenile vendetta now too?"

"I did not tell her anything that was not true," Ariadne says with defiance, pushing her raven hair behind her shoulder.

"I can divulge a truth or two to the other professors, if that is the game we're playing now," Iona threatens.

"Unlike you, I do not have improper infatuations for any of my professors," Ariadne spits.

Iona inspects Ariadne's vexed expression, resisting the distraction of their magic humming between them.

"You are jealous," Iona chuckles darkly.

"No, of course not," Ariadne says, but for once, Iona made her blush with discomfort.

In a move that is uncharacteristically bold, Iona finds herself leaning closer to Ariadne, as she whispers, "At least she would not need magic to pleasure me."

Ariadne is left speechless as Iona walks away.

When Iona goes on her evening promenade through the forest, she lingers within the trees for longer than normal. She does not want to go back to her dormitory just so she can lay awake in bed thinking of Ariadne.

Today the forest consists of dense green bamboo with narrow trails that Iona and Wisp can barely squeeze through. The air is crisp and humid. When Iona looks up, she can see monkeys with grey fur and tiny black faces hanging onto stalks of bamboo and chattering amongst themselves.

Eventually, the forest shifts into an ethereal, misty wood of moss-covered trees. In the distance, Iona can hear the sound of faint whinnying. She wonders if there may be a herd of wild horses nearby and approaches the sound as silently as she can. When she reaches the edge of a green meadow, she hides behind a tree and puts her finger against her lips when Wisp comes to sit next to her.

Standing there grazing on patches of grass are five horses with fluffy white wings on their backs, like Pegasus in Greek fables. Iona puts her hand over her mouth to muffle her breath and does not move a muscle. She is unable to believe her luck in finding such majestic creatures. Iona is most captivated by a black and white speckled stallion that canters playfully around the others who try to ignore him.

Iona suppresses a giggle when the black and white horse nips at a chestnut mare's leg to try and get her to play. The mare neighs in annoyance as the four horses move away from the stallion to try and eat in peace elsewhere. Iona's mouth falls open in horror.

Beyond where the four horses had been grazing, another winged horse lays dead in the grass, its stomach ripped open and its insides spilling out. The once beautiful mare's eyes have been gouged out. Blood stains the white hair on her side and hindquarters.

Iona finds it confounding that the horse was mutilated in such a grotesque manner. Another wild animal would not have killed the horse and left it there without consuming it, nor would they have deliberately taken the eyes. Regardless, the poor animal suffered terribly, and it breaks Iona's heart to behold such a horrible sight.

Then Iona notices that above the horse, carved into the bark of a tree, is an acicular symbol that Iona does not recognize. When Iona stares at the symbol too long, her eyes water from a sudden burning sensation that makes her look away in fright.

A twig snaps behind Iona and she whirls around. She looks but cannot see anyone. Behind her, the winged horses are disturbed by the sound and fly away.

"Hello?" Iona calls.

Silence. Iona takes out her wand and holds it tightly.

"Ariadne?" Iona calls.

Iona startles when she hears a voice far in the distance, but it is not Ariadne's. It is not the voice of anyone she knows and yet it comforts her instantly. Iona walks toward the sound and as it gets louder, its otherworldly melody makes her smile. The voice becomes many as she approaches the source of the orphic music.

Iona enters a new clearing with a crystal-clear pool surrounded by twinkling fireflies. Steam floats above the surface of the water and smooth grey stones border the edge. Iona kneels against the stones and looks down into the depths.

A woman floats up out of the water and sings her mesmerizing aria with a bewitching contralto voice. Her hair is the color of cherry blossoms and her skin glistens with tiny iridescent scales. Her large breasts are bare to Iona's admiring eyes and though she knows it is rude, Iona cannot make herself avert her gaze. The woman tips Iona's chin up to look into her roseate eyes and Iona flushes with embarrassment.

"She did not say you were so beautiful," the siren says, her voice smooth and sensuous. She reaches up to unfasten the clasp of Iona's cloak and push it off of her shoulders.

"Who?" Iona whispers, the song of many voices making gooseflesh rise all over her body.

"Your rival, Ariadne," the siren replies, a smile spreading across her cheeks, "She said you would come. She told us to call for you. She said to make it quick."

"Make what quick?" Iona asks, finding herself leaning in even closer.

"Do not worry beautiful girl. Your enemy will soon be a distant memory in the vastness of eternity. We shall make your death a pleasant one," the siren assures her.

Iona can barely register what the siren had said. The ethereal song makes her brain numb to anything but her desire. Then the siren slides a hand behind Iona's neck and pulls her down for a kiss. Iona lets go of her wand to caress the siren's face, fascinated by the feeling of her smooth, wet scales beneath her fingertips. Iona kisses her greedily as the siren slowly pulls her underwater.

The sirens' song is almost deafening inside the pool, a chorus of feminine voices that grows more insistent the deeper Iona sinks. Iona opens her mouth to let the siren slide her tongue inside and finds that she is able to breathe in as the siren exhales.

Suddenly Iona feels many sets of hands raking over her and ripping off her dress, stockings, and shoes. Sharp nails cut straight through the laces of Iona's stays, and her chemise is shredded to pieces within seconds. Then the hands are replaced by ravenous suctioning mouths on every inch of her naked body.

Iona cries out and looks around as best she can with the first siren still kissing her relentlessly. There must have been twenty sirens surrounding her, all with bright pastel hair and shimmering scales covering their voluptuous bodies. Two sirens are sucking on her breasts and nipples, one sucks voraciously between her legs, and the others take whatever skin is left.

Iona moans and laces her fingers through the pink hair of the siren that is kissing her mouth. She undulates in the warm water as the sirens have their way with her. Desire builds until Iona is trembling with need.

The sirens are all over her, licking and sucking at her curves, but their mouths are almost sloppy in their ministrations. There is an itch that they don't quite scratch, a precipice that Iona is unable to reach, though she is desperate for it. Their attentions become torturous, their teasing mouths and hands only making her hypersensitive without giving her what she wants. She squirms and writhes against them, but the sirens only giggle and hold her firmly in place, their persistent song making her dizzy.

The pink haired siren leaves Iona's mouth to trail kisses down to her neck and suck on the flesh there instead. Iona would have been more than fine with that if she could breathe underwater. As her oxygen store depletes, her limbs flail when she realizes she is going to drown. She can hear the bubbling laughter of the sirens as they continue running their hands and mouths over her mercilessly, playing with their food.

When Iona feels their teeth piercing through her skin, she kicks and struggles but she cannot free herself.

Iona barely hears the splash above her, but the sirens do. They all look up and snarl as someone they did not invite swims closer to them. Iona looks up, her vision fading, and sees that it's Ariadne in only her stays and chemise.

Ariadne points her wand at Iona and casts an imperceptible spell. Then Iona's ears no longer work at all, and she thinks it might be because she's dying.

The pink haired siren swims rapidly toward Ariadne, her sharp fangs bared, but Ariadne says a second spell. The sirens cringe and swim away in fear. Iona watches them all dive down into the dark water below. Ariadne grabs Iona's arm and pulls her up.

Iona inhales deeply when her head breaks through the surface of the pool and with effort Ariadne pulls them both out. Iona coughs up water and still cannot hear anything. Ariadne pulls urgently at Iona's arm just as the pink haired siren reaches out of the water and tries to grab her leg. Ariadne keeps hold of her and casts a spell that cuts the siren's arm. While the siren is distracted by the pain, Ariadne wrenches Iona free and pulls her away.

The siren is singing and reaching for Iona, seemingly unable to leave the water to run after them, but Iona cannot hear the song. Ariadne drags Iona along, while holding a bundle in her other arm, and they run through the trees until the pool is far behind them. It begins to drizzle, the droplets of cold water like pin pricks all over Iona's body.

After running a safe distance away from the pool, Iona doubles over, coughing and gasping from running so fast. Ariadne looks back at her, breathing heavily too, then casts a strong light spell. She tosses the sphere of light between them to illuminate the growing darkness as the sun sets behind the mountains.

Iona's sanity slowly returns to her at the same time as she remembers that all of her clothes were ripped off in the water.

She gasps and turns away from Ariadne while crossing her arms over her chest and blushing furiously. She is disturbed when she notices that her body is littered with purple bruises and shallow bite marks from the siren's mouths.

Then she reaches up to her ears in dismay. She worries that the siren's song deafened her permanently. To her relief, suddenly her hearing returns and she jumps as the sounds of the forest come back to her in a rush.

"Iona, are you hurt? Are you bleeding?" Ariadne asks, concern in her tone.

Iona cannot speak, adrenaline still coursing through her. Iona turns to look at Ariadne. Ariadne had been staring intently at Iona's back. She looks up into Iona's eyes, her anxiousness clear in her posture and expression. Iona is so confused.

Ariadne undoes the bundle in her arms, revealing it to be her dress, her shoes, Iona's wand, and Iona's cloak. Ariadne puts the cloak around Iona's shoulders to cover her and Iona wraps it tightly around herself, only now noticing that she's shivering from the cold and the rain.

"Iona," Ariadne says again, looking into her eyes, "Can you speak?"

Your rival, Ariadne, the siren had said. Ariadne had done this to her, tried to have her killed. And now she has the audacity to look concerned for Iona's wellbeing.

"Why... what did you do?" Iona asks, her teeth chattering.

Ariadne looks at her with confusion, "What?"

Iona only stares at her, still struggling to form sentences. Iona takes steps away from Ariadne, from both fear and aversion to their magic stirring between them. Iona shakes her head, trying to focus her muddled thoughts. Ariadne regards her with trepidation.

"I noticed you had not come back from your walk, and I felt that something might be amiss, so I went looking for you. When I heard the sirens, I turned off my hearing and saw Wisp running to me in distress. She led me to the pool. I looked in and I saw... I saw them all over you. I removed my dress so I could swim to you faster and jumped in, turned your hearing off, used a shrieking spell to force the sirens off of you, and pulled you out," Ariadne explains.

When Iona still does not speak, Ariadne sighs and finds Iona's wand within the bundle in her arms.

"...You're welcome!" Ariadne says, handing Iona her wand.

Iona looks at her incredulously. She cannot fathom how Ariadne could manage to lie so profusely. And what a lie it was. Ariadne has never cared about Iona's wellbeing before now, certainly not enough to traverse the woods in search of her. And even given the forest's enchantments, it would strain credulity for Ariadne to happen upon Iona or Wisp so easily without already knowing where they were. It makes no sense. It must be a lie.

Your rival, the siren had said with a cunning smile.

"Why would I thank you for saving me from your own trap?!" Iona yells, snatching her wand from Ariadne's hand.

"My trap?" Ariadne asks with raised eyebrows.

"The siren told me what you did. She said you set them on me," Iona says, "Did you have second thoughts? Were you too *fainthearted* to see it through?"

Ariadne stares at her at a loss for words. Her look of shock only makes Iona angrier.

"I knew you were obscenely ambitious, but I never would have taken you for a killer," Iona says, her rage making her skin hot despite the chill.

"I am not a killer!" Ariadne yells back so abruptly that it makes Iona jump.

"If you had waited only a moment longer, you would have been," Iona says, her eyes burning from her tears, "But do not ask me to thank you for being too weak to watch me die."

"Iona, calm down! I did not try to..." Ariadne struggles to get the words out, "Sirens do not require a reason to lure and kill their prey."

"Nor would they protest if someone handed them a meal on

a silver platter," Iona says, "Is this what you did in the river? Did you drown another poor girl to eliminate your competition?"

Ariadne closes her eyes and turns away. Her hands are shaking. From the cold or from her anger, Iona cannot tell.

"Do you deny it?" Iona yells.

"Yes! I deny it," Ariadne spits.

Iona is conflicted when she does not see any indication of deceit in Ariadne's eyes, but lying is another one of her many talents.

"Let me cast the truth spell then," Iona says, "If what you are saying is true, you should have nothing to hide."

"No," Ariadne shakes her head, "I do not owe you anything. I just rescued you from certain death. Why would I risk my life to save you if I was trying to kill you? I could have just let the sirens have their way with you. Nothing would've been left but your bones."

Iona is consumed by a roll of nausea as she realizes just how close she had been to death. She cannot bear to even look at Ariadne. Why would the siren have bothered to lie?

"Stay away from me," Iona hisses, then turns and staggers out of the woods.

9 – ARIADNE

Ariadne had not set the sirens on Iona, though no matter what she said, she could not convince Iona of her innocence. She could hardly blame her after everything they had been through since term started, but Ariadne would never agree to a truth spell when Iona could ask about more than just the sirens. Her trust in Iona was just as broken as Iona's was in her.

To see women touching Iona like that, whether they were otherworldly creatures or not, was painful for Ariadne to witness. It had sent her jumping into a siren infested pool without a second thought. Ariadne would never want Iona dead, but then who would want to kill her? And why?

Ariadne would have been more preoccupied with this question if she had not also seen something that changed the very fabric of her reality. When Iona was standing naked with her back turned towards Ariadne, she had spotted a faint purple witch's mark in the shape of a waxing crescent moon in the very center of Iona's spine just beneath her shoulder blades.

The symbol is familiar but despite her best efforts, Ariadne could not place it. She wonders for a moment if Iona knows about it already and she is keeping it a secret. But why would she do that? She would only benefit from claiming a sempiterna family name.

It would make more sense that Iona does not know. If Iona did not have a large enough mirror to spot it in, a sibling to point at it in a bath when they were children, or a lover to notice it in bed, it is possible she did not know it was there all this time. Her mother had to have known it was there though and had kept it a secret. A mark that small and in such an inconvenient spot is easily overlooked.

Ariadne would have told Iona about the mark right when she discovered it if she hadn't immediately accused her of murder. After that, she did not feel like being so forthcoming. Instead, she plans to determine what the symbol means and see if she might be able to use the information to her advantage. She won't even tell Ksenia or Samaira, at least not yet.

Iona is more closed off than ever that week. Anytime Ariadne has tried to speak to her, she walks away without even looking at her. If that was not perturbing enough, Ariadne's nightmares have plagued her almost every night since the siren attack. She tries to ignore the correlation.

One afternoon after conjuration class, Ariadne happens to overhear Iona talking to Crescentia around the corner. Ariadne slows her steps and leans against the wall. She tries to appear nonchalant as she eavesdrops.

"Are you sure the sirens were told to attack?" Crescentia asks with slight skepticism.

"I am certain. I know what I heard," Iona insists, "I might know who told them... but until I am certain I would not like to say."

"Whoever it was, they are too vile for words," Crescentia murmurs, "Do you think perhaps you should speak to Professor Lysander and ask to leave? If a witch is attempting to hurt you, and you do not feel safe, perhaps it would be prudent to go home and return another year," Crescentia suggests, "Though I would miss you terribly if you left..."

"I cannot go back," Iona says.

"But would your mother not want you to be safe?" Crescentia asks.

"I have no earthly idea what my mother would want," Iona says bitterly, "And I have no way of reaching her. No address to send a letter. For all I know, she is already dead."

Ariadne startles at that.

"It is possible that the comet aided in her healing," Crescentia says, "A celestial event like that could only help her."

"Maybe," Iona says.

"She will be okay," Crescentia says comfortingly.

"All I wanted was to study magic so I can chart my own course and make a new life for myself. It was my mother's wish, perhaps her final wish for me. But now I'm so confused. I do not know what to do," Iona says, her voice thick with her tears.

Ariadne is overcome with regret. She wishes she could turn the corner and embrace her, apologize, anything to make her stop crying. But she knows that the sight of her would only worsen Iona's despair, so she slips away and leaves her with Crescentia.

"Ari, you must focus," Samaira says.

"I am focusing," Ariadne insists.

"Try again," Samaira says calmly.

Ariadne sighs and raises her wand.

"Dominari Somnia," Ariadne incants.

Ariadne attempts to make a very simple illusion, a yellow leaf blowing in the wind around Samaira. Her mind is as scattered as ever, and her illusion keeps fragmenting. The leaf goes in and out of focus, sometimes disappearing entirely. Ariadne finally lowers her wand in defeat and the illusion fades away.

"We should take a break," Samaira says, sensing Ariadne's fatigue.

"This is pointless," Ariadne mutters.

"No," Samaira shakes her head, "I have no doubt in your

ability. Though I must admit… your illusions are usually much more elaborate. Are you alright?"

Ariadne sighs and conjures two chairs, slumping into one of them and rubbing her face with her hands.

"Perhaps speaking about your troubles will help," Samaira says, sitting in the other chair.

Ariadne does not say anything.

"Are you still having nightmares?" Samaira asks.

"I do not want to discuss that," Ariadne says stiffly.

"Fine," Samaira says, "Let's discuss the pendant then."

"What about the pendant?" Ariadne asks.

"Your obsession with it is rotting you from the inside out," Samaira says bluntly.

Ariadne cannot help the short, bitter laugh that escapes her.

"You are fortunate that your family does not care about such things. I do not have the luxury of practicing magic to amuse myself," Ariadne retorts.

"You are an adult now, Ariadne. You do not need to do everything your mother tells you," Samaira says.

"Do not patronize me," Ariadne seethes.

"The hold she has on you is unhealthy," Samaira continues, "This is their vendetta, your mother's and your grandmother's."

"I am as much a Zerynthos as they are. It is my vendetta too," Ariadne says.

"Then you plan to follow in your grandmother's footsteps? Conquer and deceive, hoard and plunder, take everything from those too weak to stand against you?" Samaira asks.

Ariadne looks away and clenches her fists in irritation.

"It will all die with you just as it did for your grandmother, slipping through her fingers when the pendant's magic faded. Such a fruitless legacy," Samaira says.

"I have more control over my own actions than you give me credit for. I should hope you would not think so lowly of me," Ariadne says, her voice trembling embarrassingly, "I shall win the pendant for my own betterment. I have no intention of becoming my grandmother, nor do I think I am capable of such a thing."

Ariadne lowers her eyes. Why should she need to be exactly like her grandmother to justify claiming the pendant? Bringing the pendant home should be enough to quell her mother's lust for power.

Samaira sighs and fiddles with her ring, "There are a great many magical artifacts in this world to covet, a few that even rival the power of the pendant. This quest is not the only way to demand respect."

"It is all that would give me the respect of my family," Ariadne points out, "Any other artifact would not hold the same value. This is what is expected of me."

"If you do claim the pendant, what will you do then? Be your mother's puppet?" Samaira says.

"So, what if I am? At least I have a purpose in life, a higher purpose than most," Ariadne says with exasperation.

"And that purpose dictates that you torment that poor Evora girl? What do you gain from that?" Samaira asks.

Ariadne glowers at Samaira, hating the shame she feels.

"Perhaps you desire the pendant for yourself and endeavor to mislead me for your own benefit," Ariadne says, though she does not believe it for a second.

"Ariadne Zerynthos," Samaira snaps, "What utter nonsense. Do not try to estrange the only one who would dare to be honest with you."

Ariadne pouts and fidgets with her wand, a flush creeping up her neck. Samaira takes a steadying breath.

"You should not be a pawn in your mother's game or Ksenia's, Gisela's, or indeed anyone's. You are worth much more than that," Samaira says, "Furthermore, I do not believe your illusion magic will work until you take control of your own mind. As long as your trauma persists and your mother still controls you, we could spend months in this room, and nothing would change."

"If you think I am so selfish and weak, why do you bother

remaining my friend at all," Ariadne mutters.

Samaira comes to kneel in front of Ariadne, taking her hand in hers and looking up at her with such kindness, it almost makes Ariadne cry.

"I know that beneath all your pretense of malignity, you feel and care more than anyone I know. You are constantly so high on the instep to harden yourself against others' misconceived fear," Samaira says.

"They should fear me," Ariadne whispers.

"No," Samaira insists, then hesitates before she says, "You tried to save her, even after..."

"I said that I did not want to speak about it," Ariadne snaps.

Samaira grimaces and rubs Ariadne's hand to soothe her. Ariadne sighs and relents.

"I am sorry... I am such a pest," Ariadne presses her fingers against her eyes to hold back her tears.

Samaira squeezes her hand and looks away, knowing that Ariadne does not like others to see her cry.

"Your refusal to speak about what happened at the river will do nothing to ease your anguish," Samaira says softly.

Ariadne's tears fall, and she wipes them away with frustration.

"Discussing it will not change what has past," Ariadne whispers.

"You do not need to change the past to heal from it," Samaira says.

Ariadne wipes away another tear with the back of her hand.

"Maybe I do not deserve to heal," Ariadne whispers.

Ariadne cannot meet Samaira's eyes.

"Of course, you deserve to heal, Ariadne," Samaira says softly, "You deserve peace after all you've endured."

Samaira reaches up to gently wipe away Ariadne's tears.

"But the pendant will not give you peace, nor will it make your mother's cruel nature disappear. Her brutal treatment of you is shameful, but you should not allow it to warp you into the broken creature she wants you to be," Samaira says.

Ariadne is not sure if she agrees, not entirely. She does agree that her mother's cruelty is as steadfast as her perpetual discontentment. However, if Ariadne finally had the pendant, with all that power at her disposal, her mother would not have a choice but to finally treat her with respect.

What's more is that if she fails, after her family's hopes have risen so high, much higher than it was for any of her older cousins, Ariadne does not know if she will have a home to go back to.

Her mother's plan, and her grandmother's before her, was to use the pendant to rebuild the ancient Greek empire. Her mother and the rest of her family will not simply let those ambitions go.

If Ariadne was to return home without the pendant, her family would promptly assume that she had not tried hard enough to succeed. To them, such a betrayal would be unforgivable.

"I shall think on what you have said," Ariadne says, "Though I cannot promise that I will change my course of action."

"That is all I ask," Samaira says with a compassionate smile, then pulls Ariadne into a warm embrace.

The next day in enchantment class, Professor Salum teaches her students about protective magic.

"Warding off the magic of an enemy is essential knowledge that every witch should know. There are two ways to go about this, using the blocking spell or enchanting an object to protect you. A protection charm can be exceedingly useful in the case of a surprise attack" Professor Salum explains, "As your magic matures, some of you may be able to cause spells to revert back onto your opponent."

Ariadne has often been capable of reflecting the spells of her attackers back onto them. It does not happen every time but when it does, it was always amusing to her and a surprise to her opponent. It is one of Ariadne's more precocious abilities that takes most witches decades to learn.

"An enchanted object will need to be recharged periodically or it will become useless again," Salum warns.

Professor Salum teaches them the blocking enchantment, then provides simple necklaces for the students to practice on. Iona casts her spell on the necklace and puts it on. Ariadne does the same.

"Test your partner's charm with harmless magic," Professor Salum instructs, with an emphasis on the word harmless.

Iona waits expectantly and Ariadne thinks of a spell to cast.

"Kuelea," Ariadne incants.

To Ariadne's surprise, her spell is not blocked by Iona's necklace, and she floats up towards the ceiling. Iona yelps and Ariadne manages to grab her ankle before she rises up to high. Ariadne quickly undoes the spell. Iona falls into Ariadne, and she catches her and sets her on her feet again. Iona immediately puts distance between them and straightens her dress while avoiding Ariadne's gaze.

"Why did it not work?" Iona mutters with irritation.

"Are you implying that every spell you try should work without any effort on your part?" Ariadne asks.

"No," Iona says indignantly, "But I cast the spell and it should have worked."

Ariadne rolls her eyes and Iona huffs with frustration. She repeats the enchantment twice more on the necklace.

"It will work this time," Iona says determinedly.

"Are you sure?" Ariadne asks.

"Do your worst," Iona says.

Ariadne raises an eyebrow and incants, "Azkura."

Iona cringes as an overwhelming itching sensation covers her entire body. She roughly scratches her arms, neck, and legs, but it does nothing to quell the prickling discomfort.

"Did it work?" Ariadne taunts.

"Reverse it, please!" Iona begs.

Ariadne undoes the spell and Iona sighs in relief as the itching subsides.

"It should have worked," Iona grumbles.

"I am happy to cast spells on you until you master it," Ariadne grins.

Iona glances at her and Ariadne watches an idea take shape within her cautious eyes.

"Enough, let's test yours," Iona says, holding up her wand.

"Sure," Ariadne says, squaring her shoulders.

"Verità," Iona says.

Ariadne gasps when the spell hits her, but it bounces off and gets thrown right back at Iona. Iona realizes her mistake and tries to undo the spell. Ariadne sees an opportunity and holds Iona's wand hand down against the table.

"Are you really a common witch?" Ariadne whispers.

"Yes, for the millionth time," Iona snaps, "Now let me go!"

Ariadne releases Iona's hand and she undoes to truth spell before Ariadne can ask another question.

"Why did you ask me that?" Iona asks with narrowed eyes.

"Why did you attempt to cast the truth spell on me?" Ariadne asks.

"You know why," Iona says, "And I would feel no remorse in casting it. You already did so to me."

"Oh, I remember," Ariadne says, letting her eyes drift brazenly over Iona's body.

Iona's blush returns like clockwork and Ariadne smirks down at her.

"See, now why ever would I want to kill you when it would rid me of that?" Ariadne whispers.

"Of what?" Iona whispers.

"That," Ariadne whispers, running her knuckle lightly over Iona's reddened cheek until she swats Ariadne's hand away, "If I wanted you dead, why would I bother saving you? Or are you cross that your first orgy was interrupted?"

Iona cringes and looks away, "Crass excuses will do nothing to absolve a conniver like you."

"Apparently simple logic cannot absolve me either," Ariadne mutters.

"Can you blame me for believing the siren's accusation?"

Iona asks.

"I can, in fact, considering how I rescued you at great risk to my own safety only for you to hurl murder accusations in my face. Can you blame me for taking offense at that?" Ariadne snaps.

Iona is chastened by Ariadne's words and bites her lip in agitation.

"Have you forgotten that every witch at this college is learning to master illusion magic? Or at least, the ones who pay attention in class," Ariadne says, smirking when Iona looks away with embarrassment, "Who can know what identity your new adversary wore when she asked the sirens to seduce you. I would not be so quick to believe the word of a feral creature."

Ariadne inspects Iona's troubled expression.

"If I were to kill you," Ariadne says with nonchalance, "I would not be so wasteful as to let sirens eat you alive."

Iona's eyes are saucers, "Whatever do you mean?"

"Virgins were once quite valuable in the old days. I am sure I could have found a use for you in some ritual or another," Ariadne jokes.

Iona fumes and Ariadne laughs at her disdain.

"It seems you have lost your chance," Iona scoffs.

Ariadne chuckles darkly, "Rutting around with a hypnotic animal is not true intimacy. You will learn the difference one day."

"Not with you," Iona retorts.

Ariadne frowns and looks away. She can see Iona's haughty grin in her periphery. Then Professor Salum approaches their desk to check their progress.

"My blocking enchantment does not seem to work," Iona admits.

"Do not despair. Practice, and you shall achieve it," Professor Salum says.

Iona nods, seeming slightly encouraged but still frustrated. She is almost as hard on herself as Ariadne is.

Professor Salum glances between the two of them and says, "The future claimant of the pendant needn't worry about this enchantment anyhow. The pendant wards off spells and never needs to be recharged. Well, it blocks all spells except dark magic. Those follow different parameters, of course."

Iona and Ariadne look at the professor, then at each other.

"And there is also Merlin's staff," Professor Salum says.

Ariadne scoffs at that and Iona looks at her questioningly.

"Merlin's staff?" Iona asks.

"It is a myth," Ariadne says.

"Some might say the same of us," Salum says with a small smile, "The staff could very well be real. It is another magical artifact similar to Morgan's pendant, imbued with Merlin's power before he passed on. No one has seen it in centuries, but it is rumored to be hidden somewhere in the woods right outside the college."

Iona seems to find the tale fascinating, but Ariadne rolls her eyes.

"Witches and warlocks have scoured those woods for countless years, and no one has found it," Ariadne points out, "If it does exist, it has been lost forever."

"Perhaps... or it may be waiting for the right witch or warlock to find it," Salum says.

"Doubtful," Ariadne says flippantly.

Professor Salum shrugs her shoulders and is about to say more but a scream startles them all. It seems Elise's necklace has not only failed to block her partner's spell, but instead has enhanced the spell it was meant to block. Professor Salum runs to Elise's aid as her hair grows rapidly and thickly until it makes her neck bend backwards. Ariadne chuckles until Iona glares at her and she chastens. Class is over then anyhow, so Iona gathers her grimoires and leaves without another word.

Ariadne stays to watch as the spell continues to grow a pile of hair. Elise has to twist her body around so her neck won't break and lets her hair fall forward so Salum can unclasp the enchanted necklace. Only then does the hair stop growing.

Ariadne jolts with surprise and walks right up to where Elise is standing to look at the back of her neck. There at the edge of her dress' neckline is Elise's witch's mark, the same crescent moon that Iona has on her back. That's why she had recognized it, she must have seen it on Elise when they were courting but hadn't thought much of it at the time.

"What are you doing?" Elise asks, unable to lift her head because of the heavy pile of hair weighing her down.

"Nothing," Ariadne says quickly and leaves Elise there to wait for Salum to reverse the spell for her.

Iona is a Lysander witch. It all makes sense. Samuel had been the one to bring her here. She'd assumed that he would never be the sort of man to be unfaithful to his wife, but anything was possible. Or maybe Iona is related to him some other way. Ariadne had no idea. But now that she knows, she must decide whether to tell Iona or leave her in the dark.

10 – IONA

In subsequent enchantments class, Iona continues to practice her blocking spell. She has become obsessed with perfecting it and will not rest until the necklace can successfully block one of Ariadne's spells.

"Iona," Samuel says behind her.

Iona turns in surprise, not realizing he had entered the room.

"Good day, Professor," Iona says.

"Please come with me," Samuel says.

Iona nods, dread filling her, and lets him lead her out of the room. Ariadne watches them go.

When they are in the hallway, Samuel turns to face Iona. She knows what he is going to say before he says the words but hopes that she might be wrong.

"My deepest condolences. Your mother passed away last night," Samuel says, clearing his throat to keep from crying.

Iona stares at him, unable to emote or move or do anything at all.

"A warlock found her while on a walk through the woods and gave her a proper burial," Samuel says softly.

Iona nods, glad that her body was not left to rot and be eaten by animals.

"She exhausted every option, but it seems even nature's magic could not keep Death at bay," Samuel says softly, "It was her time."

"Could we bring her back?" Iona asks, her voice sounding very small, "With magic?"

Samuel looks down at her with pity and shakes his head no.

"That cannot be done. It is dark magic of the worst kind," Samuel says, "It is unnatural."

"I understand," Iona says, and she does. She doesn't want a zombified, unnatural version of her mother. She only wishes that her mother wasn't gone forever.

"She was a wonderful woman," Samuel says sadly, "I am truly sorry."

Iona's eyes go unfocused, and she struggles to pay attention to what he is saying.

"I think I shall retire to my dormitory," Iona says numbly.

"I can escort you," Samuel offers, but Iona shakes her head.

"No, that will not be necessary," Iona says.

Samuel nods and lets her walk away. Iona does not know how she made it to her room, but she finds herself falling into bed and pulling the covers over herself. Wisp jumps on the bed too and curls up beside her. Tears will not come, and she feels so empty. She lays there and Wisp licks at her hand.

There is a knock on the door, but Iona ignores it, hoping whoever it is will go away. There is another more persistent knock, and Iona sighs. She pushes herself up and walks to the door. The sight of Ariadne in the doorway makes something break inside of her.

"Iona, what happened?" Ariadne asks. She is holding Iona's books, which she forgot were still on her desk when she left.

"She's gone," Iona says, then starts to cry. Her body shakes with her sobs as she sinks to the floor.

"Who is?" Ariadne asks in alarm, getting on the floor with Iona. Then she understands, "Your mother?"

Iona nods and takes the books from Ariadne.

"Just go," Iona says.

"Iona…" Ariadne says, unsure of what else to say.

"Just leave me be," Iona insists, wiping away her tears.

Ariadne regards her with pity that Iona doesn't want. It only makes her cry even harder. Ariadne closes the door, and Iona puts her face in her hands. A few minutes later, Crescentia comes to check on her and says that Ariadne had told her what happened. Crescentia hugs her close and Iona weeps into her shoulder until she cannot cry anymore.

Iona is excused from her classes for the rest of the week. She lays in bed for most of that time, with Crescentia bringing her meals to her. Samuel comes to visit her twice, and the second time he says he would like to speak to her soon when she is ready.

Iona knew in her heart that when she said goodbye to her mother, it would be for the last time. She did not want Iona to watch her die. Iona wishes they could have had more time.

But now that her mother was gone, Iona was free to make her own choices. If she wanted, she could abandon her schooling and go back home, or go anywhere she wanted. She knew more magic now than she did at the start of term. She could use what she's learned to make a new life for herself selling diamonds or any number of expensive objects that she can now conjure. At least she would never go hungry.

Iona mulls the possibilities over in her head as she dons a black velvet dress, as is customary in her mourning period. She remembers her mother told her of the custom not long ago, explaining that the mourning period depended on who had died. In the case of a parent, it is proper to mourn for six months by wearing only black and refraining from frivolous activities.

Her mother had been very clear that she did not want Iona to follow such customs too strictly. She should mourn in her own time since death means something different to witches than it does to humans. Iona had wondered what her mother meant by that but when she'd asked, her mother had changed the subject.

When Iona leaves her room for the first time in days, she

almost steps upon a bouquet of white flowers left at her door. Iona picks them up and looks for a card but there is none. Iona knows then that Ariadne must have left them there. Iona reviews her phytology grimoire to learn that Ariadne has given her a bouquet of gladioli flowers, meant to represent honor and remembrance.

Iona closes her book and sighs. She does not have the energy to interpret this uncharacteristically thoughtful gesture. She conjures a vase for the flowers, then leaves to attend clairvoyance class. When Ariadne sits beside her, she does not say a word. Professor Pari lectures on the upcoming Samhain festival and ritual.

"Samhain is a Celtic festival that holds such important significance to us as witches for a great many reasons. It is the witch's new year, when the veil between our world and the spirit world is paper thin. With a bit of magic, we can travel to that other world and converse with the dead. Communing with ghosts is one of life's greatest privileges because of the wisdom they can bestow. Lysander College holds an annual ball in celebration and the ritual is held afterwards," Pari says.

Professor Pari explains that when the ritual is performed, a witch cannot choose who they see. The vast majority of the time, one of their ancestors will appear to them, though there are rare occurrences when another ghost, one they do not know, can appear if they have something important to say.

A glimmer of hope fills Iona after days of misery. Perhaps this ritual would allow her to see her mother again.

"Today, I would like you all to use an ancestry charm to peruse your family tree. Ancestral ghosts can take offense if you do not recognize them when they visit so it is best to study at least five or six generations," Pari says, "Cast the Stamtræ spell and your family line will be revealed to you in a way that you can examine and study ahead of the ritual in a few weeks."

Iona pulls out her wand, excited to cast the spell and prepare for the ritual.

"Iona," Ariadne says.

"What?" Iona asks, unable to look her in the eye.

"Iona, wait," Ariadne says, grasping Iona's wand hand and forcing her to lower it.

"What are you doing?" Iona asks.

"I must tell you something of great importance," Ariadne says.

Iona glares up at Ariadne and she shrinks back into her chair.

"I have no tolerance left for your trickery. I had hoped that you would have a modicum of restraint while I mourn my mother," Iona hisses.

"I am not tricking you," Ariadne insists.

"Stop lying," Iona snaps, "A bouquet of flowers does not erase my hatred for you."

Ariadne sighs and looks away with a morose expression. Hatred is too strong a word and Iona regrets saying it, but she is also desperate for Ariadne to leave her be. Whatever Ariadne has to say can wait.

"Stamtræ," Iona says, waving her wand over her desk.

Grey smoke billows from her wand and settles into shapes on the dark wood of the desk. Iona can see faces and names written beneath them, with lines connecting the people to each other. The first face she recognizes is her mother's, a hint of her kind smile on her lips. Next to her mother is her father, Victor. Iona can barely recognize him from her distant memories, but his name is labeled under his face. Victor-

The world goes slow and silent around her as she reads the name. Lysander. That cannot be. His surname is Evora, not Lysander.

Iona's eyes scan the smoke for answers, and she finds Samuel Lysander, his wife Violet, and their daughter Elise. According to the spell, Samuel is Victor's brother.

Iona stands and steps away from the desk as confusion and fear make her hands shake. She drops her wand and puts her hand over her mouth.

"Iona," Ariadne says cautiously.

Ariadne reaches out tentatively to put her hand on Iona's elbow. Iona flinches away from her.

"You did this somehow. It is an illusion," Iona says.

"No, it's not," Ariadne says.

"What is it then? The spell is wrong. My father's name is Victor Evora," Iona insists.

"Oh, my stars," Samaira exclaims as she peers over at Iona's table, "She's a Lysander."

"Be quiet, Samaira," Ariadne snaps.

But it is too late. The rest of the class heard Samaira's words. They gather around the desk to look at Iona's family tree and whisper amongst themselves. Even Professor Pari looks but does not seem entirely surprised.

"It is wrong!" Iona says again, rushing to the desk and waving her hands over the smoke until it disappears.

"Spells like these do not lie," Ksenia says, "Is that correct, Professor?"

"I am afraid Ksenia is right. It is the absolute truth," Pari says softly.

Iona hurriedly gathers her things to leave, unable to look anyone in the eye. She pauses when she passes by Elise, who seems to be in a complete daze. Iona does not know what to say to her, so she runs from the room.

At first, she thinks of running into the woods and hiding where no one can find her, just so she can think, but the woods still scare her after the siren attack. So, she goes to her dormitory instead and locks the door.

Wisp sits on the bed and watches Iona pace around the room erratically. This cannot be true. It must be a mistake. The alternative would be a devastating lie that Iona cannot face.

"Iona," Ariadne calls from behind Iona's door. She knocks insistently and Iona puts her hands over her ears. "Iona, please let me in. It is important."

"No, leave me alone," Iona says. She does not want Ariadne to see her like this.

"I have further proof that you are a Lysander," Ariadne says.

Iona turns to stare at the door.

"Iona, I do not pretend to know how you are feeling in this moment but no matter what our differences have been, I am sorry this is happening to you all at once. You deserve the truth," Ariadne says.

Iona wipes away her tears.

"Please let me in," Ariadne says.

Iona composes herself and goes to the door. When she opens it, Ariadne staggers forward a step because she was leaning against the wood.

"Do not make me regret this," Iona says.

"You won't," Ariadne says, stepping inside, "Close the door."

Iona does so and crosses her arms.

"When you were naked after the sirens attacked you, I saw something," Ariadne says.

Iona blushes deep red and frowns, "I saw you looking at me. You shouldn't have."

Ariadne rolls her eyes, "Your beauty is not what I am referring to."

"What then?" Iona says, ignoring Ariadne's comment about her beauty for the moment.

"I saw a witch's mark," Ariadne says.

"What? Where?" Iona asks.

"On your back. It is small and in a place that you likely could not see," Ariadne says.

"What does it look like?" Iona asks.

"A crescent moon," Ariadne says, "The mark is the same as Elise's. Hers is higher up on the back of her neck. Look at it in the mirror."

Iona decides it cannot hurt to check. She goes to the bathroom and closes the door. She takes off her dress and stays, then she lets her chemise fall to her hips.

"Can you see it?" Ariadne calls from the bedroom.

Iona puts her back up to her vanity mirror. It takes a moment to find the right angle, but when she cranes her neck enough, she can see the faint purple crescent on her spine, no bigger than a walnut. Iona stares at the mark with a mixture of horror and fascination. It was true then. She is not who she thought she was. Her self-identity crumbles in seconds.

"Iona?" Ariadne asks from right behind the bathroom door, "Are you alright?"

Iona pulls up her chemise and goes to open the door. Ariadne looks down at her warily, unsure of what to make of her expression.

"It was there the whole time," Iona whispers in disbelief, "I never saw it. I never… and Mother knew but did not want to tell me. She lied to me all these years…"

"To keep you safe," Ariadne says.

"To keep me with her. To control me by keeping me in the dark," Iona argues, "We only had a small, warped mirror at home, and that was likely my mother's intention. She had endless opportunities to tell me."

Ariadne does not seem like she agrees but does not argue.

"Do you think otherwise?" Iona prompts.

"I do not know enough to give a proper opinion," Ariadne hedges.

"Do not let this be the one moment when you fail to speak your mind," Iona says impatiently.

"I do not want to make assumptions of your mother's intentions. All I will say is… I wish my mother had gone to such lengths to protect me from all of this," Ariadne gestures around herself, "You were able to have a normal childhood, far from this Machiavellian court of avaricious families."

Iona is surprised to hear Ariadne speak of her place in society with such a negative connotation. She'd only ever spoken of it with boastful pride.

"Why did you not tell me of the mark sooner?" Iona asks.

"You have been avoiding me since the sirens. I tried to tell you today in class, but you would not let me speak," Ariadne says.

"But why not tell me in the forest the moment you saw it?" Iona asks.

"Because you accused me of trying to kill you," Ariadne says sharply, "We were too busy arguing about that."

Iona stares into Ariadne's red eyes, searching for any truth she can decipher. Iona believes that Ariadne is being honest but doubt still plagues her. If Ariadne hadn't been the one to set the sirens on her, who had it been? The thought paralyzes her with fear. She would much rather know who was trying to attack her rather than having a hidden enemy.

"Thank you for telling me now," Iona finally says.

"You're welcome," Ariadne says.

"And... thank you for your flowers. They are beautiful," Iona says.

"Of course, it was the least I could do. Professor Yun helped me pick them," Ariadne says, averting her gaze, "They were in better bloom than the lilies."

Iona frowns, her eyebrows furrowing slightly, "You did not conjure them?"

Ariadne meets Iona's gaze again, shaking her head, "No, they are from the greenhouse."

Iona knows it might be foolish to think so, but the flowers are more valuable now knowing that they came from the earth, cultivated with care and effort.

"I must speak to Samuel," Iona finally says, leaning down to pick up her stays where she had discarded them on the bathroom floor.

Ariadne wordlessly takes Iona's laces to retighten them for her. Iona waits patiently for her to finish, surprised but grateful for the small act of care. Her hands still shake from her nerves.

Iona puts her dress back on, then she and Ariadne leave her room. They look at each other briefly, then Ariadne turns and walks away.

Samuel is in his office reviewing papers. He wears a black crepe armband on his blazer and a black cravat, signs of his mourning. Iona approaches his desk with a face of stone.

"Show me your witch's mark," Iona demands.

Samuel's eyes widen in surprise, and he says, "Iona, I do not think-"

"Show me your witch's mark now or I shall leave this place and never return," Iona says solemnly.

Samuel stares at her with contrition. Finally, he stands and takes off his blazer. He undoes the button on his right shirt sleeve and folds it upwards to his elbow. There sits Samuel's mark, the same one that Iona has on her back.

"My mother taught me that the waxing crescent symbolizes change, rebirth, and intuition," Samuel says, then looks meaningfully at Iona, "The moon has been a significant symbol in our family for generations."

"Why did you not tell me the truth?" Iona asks.

"Because your mother begged me not to," Samuel says, "I could not ignore a woman's dying wish."

Iona looks away in frustration.

"Your mother's family, the Evoras, were a family of Brazilian witches that were coming into their own, their magic growing stronger with every generation. Your grandparents came to York when your mother was a baby to consort with other powerful families. They served the Lysanders for a time, using their magic to assist with important rituals and such. My brother Victor, your mother, and I shared a childhood. She was one of my closest friends, and for my brother, she was his truest love," Samuel says.

Samuel smiles wistfully, then his expression darkens.

"Our family would never accept the match, but Victor did not care. He ran away with her, content to spend a quiet life far from his obligations and the high expectations of his family. He did not care who Leona's family was. He only wanted to be with her. He told me as much when he left. I begged him to stay, to try and reason with them, but he said this was what he wanted. I never heard from him again," Samuel says.

Samuel's eyes are filled with sadness and Iona sympathizes with him. It must have been difficult to lose a brother so abruptly.

"My family searched high and low for years, but no one could find him. I looked for him too, separately, just to see him again but never to tell my family where he was. No matter how hard we searched, they eluded us. I now know that this is because Victor and Leona used a powerful collective illusion spell to hide your home from any magic user that tried to find it," Samuel says.

"That is why my mother always wanted to stay home. Because of the spell that hid us away," Iona muses, "And my father's ring, I felt magic locked within it. I always thought it was a simple protection charm, but she had enchanted it to shield me."

"Yes, it must have taken almost all of their magic to sustain those spells. I cannot imagine the toll it would take, only leaving them with a fraction of their full power. That is how ardently they wanted to be left alone," Samuel says, "When your father died, Leona sent back his body to be buried in the family crypt with a note that said he had a daughter. My father burned the letter and told me and my mother never to tell a soul about it. They have both since passed on and I was the only Lysander left who knew that you existed."

Samuel pulls his shirt sleeve back down and buttons his cuff.

"Your mother removed the illusion after all those years and summoned me. I could not believe it. I thought perhaps she was ready to rejoin society now that my parents are gone, and you are an adult. When I found her already dying, I was devastated. I would have done anything for her, Iona. Anything she asked," Samuel says, imploring Iona to understand him, "She told me to take you here and show you how to use your magic. The illusion she had sustained for all those years made her magic too weak to teach you herself. She made me swear not to say that I was your uncle, and that when she became well again, she would tell you herself. I tried to convince her otherwise, but eventually I agreed."

Iona nods, accepting the truth though it is difficult to stomach.

"I was planning to tell you everything this Saturday. I did not want to burden you further with this sort of an incredible secret too soon. But it seems I was too late," Samuel says.

"We were learning about our ancestry in Professor Pari's class in preparation for Samhain," Iona says.

"Ah... that explains it then," Samuel says regretfully.

Then Samuel regards Iona fondly and smiles.

"You practice magic just like your father did, like a fish takes to water or a bird takes to the sky. To watch him create such wonders... it was beautiful." Samuel says, "I hated my parents for how they treated him and your mother. I regret how things transpired to this day. But now... we may have a second chance."

A bittersweet, hopeful smile spreads across Samuel's face. Though Iona's memories of her father are faint, she can now see the resemblance between them so clearly.

"I would like for Elise and me to be a part of your life now if you would have us. I hope it is not too late. Even though we never met, I loved you and always hoped you were safe wherever you were. We are family," Samuel says, "I know that what you are enduring in the wake of your mother's passing is horrible beyond what words can say, but please know that you are not alone."

Iona tries to hold back tears, but one spills down her cheek. Samuel offers her a handkerchief. Iona takes it gratefully and Samuel waits for her to collect herself.

"I understand it must have been difficult to keep this secret. I need... I need time to think. But... I am glad to know I still have family left," Iona says.

Samuel nods and says, "Please take all the time you require. I am always here for you, and Elise will be too."

Samuel's eyes widen with alarm.

"I should find Elise and discuss this with her. She must be so confused," Samuel says.

"She did seem shocked when I saw her in class," Iona says, remembering the look on her cousin's face.

"I will go to her," Samuel says, pulling his blazer back on, "We can discuss this further later. Though I wish it had come to light under different circumstances, I am so relieved for this secret to finally be out in the open."

Iona is deep in thought when she leaves Samuel's office and walks back to her dormitory. She wants to curl up in bed and sleep for a year.

"Iona."

Iona turns and sees Elise approaching her.

"Your father is looking for you," Iona says.

"Oh... I will find him, but I wanted to make sure you were alright," Elise says.

"I'm fine," Iona says.

There is an awkward silence. Elise's nervousness only further agitates Iona, and she searches to find a way to politely excuse herself.

"So, we are to be cousins then?" Elise says with a small smile.

"I regret that we both had to discover it so publicly," Iona says, "But it would be nice to have another ally in class."

"Certainly, I hope we can be friends. I've admired you since you arrived. The way you practice magic..." Elise struggles to find the words, "It is unbelievable."

"Thank you," Iona smiles wistfully.

"Where were you going just now?" Elise asks.

"I intended to go back to my dormitory. This day has been... exhausting. I just want to rest," Iona says.

"Let me accompany you," Elise says, leading the way.

They walk in step with each other. The air is becoming cooler each day and Iona wouldn't be surprised if they had snow soon. A gust of wind blows Iona and Elise's cloaks around them.

"I despise winter," Elise gripes, "I cannot wait for springtime when all the flowers will bloom again."

At the mention of flowers, Iona thinks of Ariadne. Iona

glances at Elise and hesitates, then decides it cannot hurt to ask.

"You once courted Ariadne, did you not?" Iona asks.

"In a way, yes. Though it was more of an arrangement and was very impersonal," Elise says, "Her family is obsessed with hoarding and growing their magic. They are very... unpleasant."

"Unpleasant how?" Iona asks.

Elise looks over her shoulder, then leans closer to Iona and whispers, "Last year when I was visiting the Zerynthos Manor for Yule, I was walking to the dining room when I overheard yelling. I heard Ariadne telling her mother that she did not want to court me anymore, that she never did. I was devastated, as she had not told me of her true feelings. But then midway through their arguing, Ariadne's mother slapped her across the face with such force, the sound startled me. She was vicious... She beat Ariadne until she cried, then told her that she must do what she is told."

"That's horrid," Iona says with wide eyes.

"Indeed... Ariadne attended the Yule feast not long after and pretended like nothing had happened. The only remnant of the confrontation was a cut that had split her lip almost up to her nose," Elise says, shaking her head, "I imagine it was Ariadne's small act of rebellion to leave the cut there, rather than healing it before dinner. Her mother was not pleased... I shudder to think what she does when company is not present."

Iona is overcome with sympathy. With a mother like that, it is no wonder that Ariadne is so terrified of failing the trials. Iona wonders how Ariadne does not have a scar on her lip, if it was split the way Elise had described. Then Iona remembers that the enchanted bathtubs are capable of removing scars. She did not want to know how many scars Ariadne would have if magic did not wipe them away.

"I ended the courtship with her the next day. I knew then that she did not want me so I did what she could not," Elise says.

"That is very gracious of you," Iona says.

"I will not lie; I was not gracious about it in the moment. My heart was broken. I was angry at being misled. I had hoped we could be more to each other than an obligation, but I was wrong," Elise says.

"I am sorry that she was not more candid with you," Iona says.

Elise looks to the statue of Ysolde Lysander in the courtyard and says, "I suppose that is the price we pay for having sempiterna blood. We are almost never allowed to be our own person. We inherit the cruelty and discontent of those who came before us."

"Then I suppose you are fortunate to have a father like Samuel," Iona says.

Wisp nips at Iona's hand and she looks down at the fox in question. Then she lifts the animal into her arms and scratches behind her ears to calm her.

"Quite right," Elise smiles, "Anyhow, that is nothing at all compared to what Ariadne has done to you since you arrived here. I have never seen her quite so agitated."

"Yes, well... I suppose I bring out the worst in her," Iona says, looking down at her hands.

"Then she is a fool," Elise says vehemently, "She is only jealous of your magic. Do not take it to heart."

Iona appreciates Elise's loyalty, but she is less inclined to ridicule Ariadne's temperament after hearing all that she has endured. Then they reach the dormitories and they both notice Samuel walking not far from them.

"I should go and talk to him now," Elise says, "Good day, Iona."

Iona watches as Elise approaches her father, then enters the dormitories for a well-deserved rest.

The next day, Iona sits next to Ariadne before phytology class began. There is so much unsaid between them but neither of them says a word.

Iona glances at Ariadne for only a moment, her eyes lingering on Ariadne's rosy lips where a scar may have been without magic to prevent it. Then Iona's heart stops when Ariadne notices her stare. She quickly looks away and pretends to organize the herbs on her desk. Iona is relieved when Professor Yun arrives and begins the lesson until she hears what they will be learning about.

"Today we will be studying healing potions. These brews are temperamental and difficult to cultivate. It takes years of practice to master given that the human body is so complex. What part of the body is the potion meant to heal? The brain, the lungs, the pancreas? Is it a cut, a broken bone, a tumor? Depending on the answer, the potion will need to be brewed accordingly. At times it is not apparent what exact part of a person's body is ailing them, which makes the process near impossible," Yun says, "Some witches and warlocks spend their entire lives specializing in this one type of potion and no one has truly perfected it."

Though Iona does not look, she knows that Ariadne is watching her. Iona pushes her emotions down, though it is difficult to ignore the irony. This sort of potion could have helped save her mother's life if they had been aware of what illness she'd had. They'd been to doctors in the hopes of a diagnosis, but they could not determine what was ailing her.

"Let's begin," Yun says, diverting Iona's depressing thoughts.

Iona gathers the ingredients and follows the recipe. This healing potion is meant to regrow tissue more rapidly in the case of a deep cut. Iona stirs in her moon water, feeling herself gradually dissociate.

"Put the rowan in first," Ariadne whispers to her.

Iona pauses what she's doing and double checks the recipe. She takes her rowan berries and tosses them into the pot. Then she looks to Ariadne who goes back to her own potion as if she hadn't said a word. Iona does not know what to make of it.

Iona's thoughts linger on her mother for the rest of the day. When she enters Samuel's class in the afternoon, all eyes are on her, and she hates it.

"We shall need to go outside for today's lesson," Samuel says, "Follow me."

The class leaves their desks behind and follows the professor. Iona walks near the back of the group with Elise. When they make it outside and go behind the college building, a row of targets is set up along the edge of the trees.

"Today we will be learning about elemental magic. This term we will focus on water and fire, in spring term we will learn about earth and air," Samuel says, "All four are nascent spells and are the original pieces of magic. All other magic you have learned was built off of these original building blocks of nature."

Samuel takes out his wand and says, "Neró."

A globule of water materializes before him. He manipulates the water with his wand to change its shape, making it bigger and smaller at will.

"Water is the easiest to conjure and manipulate," Samuel says, "See if you can create water with the spell."

The witches spread out across the grass and practice the water spell. Some are able to, while others struggle. Iona finds the spell very easy and creates a large mass of water. It floats around her, then she morphs it into shapes. She lifts it up toward the sky to see the sunshine through the ripples of the liquid. She spreads the water outwards like a disc, which makes the sun shimmer onto the grass.

"Wow," Elise whispers, coming to stand next to Iona and look through the water with her.

Iona looks across the grass at Ariadne who seems bored. She's lazily moving her collection of water this way and that without any rhyme or reason to it.

"I wish I could do that," Elise sighs, playing with her tiny collection of water that she can just barely manipulate.

"We could practice together later," Iona offers.

"Really?" Elise asks with an excited smile.

"Of course," Iona smiles back.

"We are ready for the second spell of the day," Samuel says.

All the witches gather around to listen.

"Fire magic is powerful but dangerous. It should be practiced with the utmost care," Samuel says.

With a wave of his wand, he says, "Pyrkagiá."

A ball of fire hovers in his hand.

"Your own fire can burn you if you are not careful," Samuel warns.

Then he throws the ball of fire into one of the targets behind him.

"Who would like to give it a try?" Samuel asks.

"I shall," Samaira says.

She stands in front of the targets and conjures multiple fireballs, throwing them into the targets with ease.

"Very good," Samuel says.

Samaira rejoins the group with a self-satisfied smile. A few other witches step up and try their hand at the fire spell. When Iona steps forward, she hears Ksenia whisper behind her, "Her magic is not so impressive anymore, now that we know where she got it from."

Iona tries to ignore her, but she is so sensitive today that Ksenia's barb cuts deep.

"Whenever you're ready, Iona," Samuel says.

Iona lifts her wand and says, "Pyrkagiá."

A ball of swirling fire hovers in her hand. She throws it at the target, and it explodes with a dazzling crash against the wooden board. Iona says the spell again, and again, each time making the fireball larger and larger. Then she doesn't bother with fireballs and simply aims her wand and speaks the spell at the targets one by one. With every blast of fire, her pent-up anger bursts from within.

"Pyrkagiá!" she screams, all of her magic leaving her in one single spell.

She creates a mass of fire so large that it consumes all three targets at once. Iona falls backwards to the ground and has the wind knocked out of her. The other witches scream and cower from the intense heat. Wisp was thrown back as well but jumps up and runs to sniff Iona's face with concern. Samuel tries to calm the witches down, then rushes to Iona's side.

"Iona, are you hurt?" Samuel asks, helping her sit up.

Iona stares at the fire still burning the targets and the surrounding trees. When she shakes her head no, Samuel leaves her side to fight the flames before they spread further into the forest.

"Neró," Samuel says, throwing water on the trees.

Iona can sense that her magic has been completely depleted. She is revolted by how helpless she feels knowing that she couldn't cast even the simplest of spells until she rests and regains her energy.

Iona looks back and sees all of the witches staring at her in fear and amazement. She had just performed an impressive feat of magic and should feel powerful, but she only feels empty and broken.

Iona runs into the forest. She sprints as fast as she can, wanting to put as much distance between herself and the mess she had just made. Branches rip at her dress and get caught in her hair until it comes undone. She doesn't stop until her lungs give out and she falls to her hands and knees in the dirt. She weeps openly as she is unable to hold in her anguish anymore.

"Iona!" Ariadne calls.

Iona doesn't respond, unable to articulate words through her sobs. Ariadne follows the sound of Iona's cries and kneels in the dirt beside her. She puts an arm around Iona's shoulder.

"Do not touch me!" Iona screams.

Ariadne cringes away. Iona looks at her, her breathing labored. Neither of them moves as they stare into each other's eyes.

Aster approaches, whimpering with his ears down, until he sits with his head in Iona's lap. She runs her hand over his soft fur. Wisp sits in front of her, and she could swear that the fox has tears in her eyes too.

Ariadne carefully shifts towards Iona again. She moves

slowly, as if Iona was a spooked animal, reaching out to tuck Iona's wild hair behind her ears to get it out of her face. Her thumb brushes against Iona's cheekbone, making her blink and look away.

"Why are you being kind to me?" Iona whispers.

"Do I require a reason?" Ariadne whispers back.

"You did not need a reason to hurt me," Iona says.

Ariadne sighs and Iona glares at her through her tears.

"Did you expect me to forget everything you did?" Iona asks.

"What about the things you did?" Ariadne retorts.

They stare at each other in silence.

"I do not need your pity," Iona mutters.

"Good, because you do not have it," Ariadne says, "I am not here because I pity you."

"Then why are you here?" Iona asks.

"I only wanted to make sure you were alright," Ariadne says, "That was a spectacular fire show you just made. I am surprised you still have your eyebrows."

Iona chuckles despite herself, "You should have seen their faces."

Iona feels another bout of tears threatening to burst from within. She tries to hold it back but her entire body shakes.

"Iona," Ariadne whispers.

Iona looks to Ariadne, not knowing what motivates her concern but deciding that right now, it doesn't matter. She lets Ariadne pull her into an embrace. She wraps her arms around Ariadne's neck and sits in her lap as she cries into her shoulder. Ariadne lightly strokes Iona's hair and does not say a word.

PART TWO

Loyalty

11 – ARIADNE

I t has been almost three weeks since that day in the forest when Ariadne held Iona while she cried. She'd ensured that Iona had solitude to process her grief, though Ksenia did not appreciate being told to leave Iona alone. Ariadne had said it was because Iona's mother had died, and that was certainly a good enough reason on its own, but by now the foolish mind games seem pointless and counterproductive.

Professor Lysander was gracious enough to claim that Iona's fireball had been an accident, though everyone knows that Iona made the fire intentionally. Their classmates, apart from Crescentia and Elise, had given Iona a wide berth since then. Iona's show of power had properly intimidated them all. Iona was the picture of lamentation in her black dresses and morose, contemplative expressions, day after day.

It was nearing the end of October, only a few days before Samhain, when Ariadne walks to the library to study and sees Iona in a black dress of bombazine silk. She walks aimlessly through the garden with Wisp beside her. The flowers and plants are long dead, the brown and yellow foliage like a cemetery of flora.

When Ariadne meets Iona's eyes, she slows her steps, then stops altogether. She hesitates, unsure if Iona would prefer isolation.

"Are you frightened of me now too?" Iona asks.

"No," Ariadne says.

Iona regards her skeptically.

"The world is made more riveting with another hysterical Lysander witch," Ariadne says with a cautious grin.

Iona's smile is brief but may as well have been a solar flare after weeks of dismal frowns. Aster runs up to Iona and licks at her hand. Iona scratches his ears as Ariadne approaches her.

"How are you?" Ariadne asks.

Iona sighs, "I am fine."

"Do not make me cast another truth spell, Iona," Ariadne raises an eyebrow.

Iona rolls her eyes, "I feel dreadful, if you must know."

Iona glances at Ariadne, then looks away, covertly wiping a tear from her cheek.

"I am sorry," Ariadne says, most sincerely.

"Thank you," Iona says.

Wisp begins chasing Aster around the garden. Iona watches them with a tiny smile. Ariadne watches Iona.

"Our familiars are an extension of us, are they not?" Iona asks.

"They are kindred souls with their own autonomy," Ariadne says.

"But they are similar to us in some manner?" Iona asks.

"Yes, I would say so," Ariadne says, wondering what Iona is getting at.

"Then why do they get along so effortlessly?" Iona asks.

They watch Wisp and Aster jump and run together, as if they were lifelong companions.

"I suppose... animals are simpler," Ariadne says, "They do not know the strife of our civilized lives and all the many complications we must navigate."

"Civilized indeed," Iona chuckles darkly.

When Iona looks at her, Ariadne gets lost in her hazel eyes. A light breeze carries the autumn chill and blows loose tendrils of Iona's hair into her eyes. Before Ariadne can think the gesture through, she reaches out and tucks a stray strand behind Iona's ear. Ariadne once again marvels at its soft texture, wishing she could lace her fingers through it.

Ariadne wants to leave her hand there, her fingers lingering on Iona's cheek, but Iona gasps when their magic stirs between them again. Ariadne quickly removes her hand and puts it behind her back.

In his excitement, Aster lifts his nose towards the sky and howls. Ariadne hushes him but he persists. Wisp watches the wolf with fascination.

"The wolf…" Iona whispers.

"Pardon?" Ariadne asks.

"After Wisp healed me of paralysis, I heard a wolf howling in the woods. It was Aster," Iona says.

"Oh… yes it was him. I asked him to stay behind," Ariadne says.

"You did?" Iona asks.

"I could not leave you there defenseless if a wild animal or some creature might try to harm you," Ariadne says, "I almost turned back to fetch you myself when Ksenia retired to her dormitory, but I heard Aster's howl and knew you were revived."

Iona seems confounded by Ariadne's words, and she regrets not mentioning this sooner. Perhaps it would have altered Iona's unfavorable opinion of her. Or perhaps that could never be undone, no matter what she might say.

"You do have a conscience, then," Iona muses, confirming Ariadne's suspicions.

"I would not go that far," Ariadne jokes, in an effort to hide her unease.

Iona falls silent, deep in contemplation. Ariadne stands awkwardly, unsure if she should leave Iona alone or stay. To distract herself, she pulls out her wand and thoughtlessly conjures an oscillating flower, unable to decide which bloom she wants. She finally settles on a deep red dahlia, its symmetrical petals reminding Ariadne of one of the college's rose windows.

Ariadne notices that Iona is watching her, then realizes that whether she had been conscious of it or not, the flower is perfect for Iona in this moment. Ariadne hands her the flower and Iona takes it.

"It is a red dahlia," Ariadne says.

"I thought dahlias were black," Iona says, lifting the flower to her nose.

"They can be many colors," Ariadne says, "Red means perseverance. Inner strength."

Iona stares at the flower with renewed understanding of its significance, twirling it gently between her fingers.

"Thank you," Iona says, "I must retire."

"Oh, of course," Ariadne says, clearing her throat, "Good day."

"Good day," Iona says, turning away and walking purposefully towards the dormitories.

The night of Samhain, Ariadne enters the forest wearing an off the shoulder dress of fine silk that is the exact same shade as her eyes. The dress has flowing sleeves that billow with every gesture she makes. The bodice is embroidered with silver starbursts, and tiny diamonds are sewn into her skirts like falling stars trickling down her body. She wears a silver circlet that is woven into her braided hair with a teardrop shaped ruby dangling in the center of her forehead. Her attire is in keeping with the medieval theme of the college's Samhain festivities.

Ariadne steps onto a stone plateau which drops off into a cliff that overlooks a breathtaking valley below where a wide river twists through the landscape. The pine needles and leaves of the forest floor transition into smooth grey stone that stretches across the cliff face, a perfect surface for dancing. An enchanted string quartet floats on the edge of the plateau and plays lively music. The moon hangs low in the sky, a waxing crescent. Golden lanterns hover in the air to illuminate the dance floor.

Ksenia and Samaira are already there, wearing a black velvet dress and a deep blue silk dress respectively. They look like feudal maidens of old as they regard Ariadne with caution, unsure of what mood she is in. Ariadne had been rather distant from them lately, so she does not fault them for their reservations. Ariadne walks directly to them.

"Good evening," Ariadne says.

"Good evening," Samaira says with a smile, "How are you?"

"I am well," Ariadne says, smiling back, "And you?"

"We're spectacular," Ksenia says, a hint of sarcasm in her voice.

"You both look lovely," Ariadne says, in an effort to keep the conversation civil.

"Thank you," Samaira says, "So do you, of course."

Ariadne takes Samaira's arm. Her loyalty has always overshadowed her ambition. Ariadne used to think of it as weakness but now, she sees that it is a virtue. Ariadne glances at Ksenia, whose ever inquisitive blue eyes inspect her every micro expression.

The professors are gathered together on the edge of the plateau, drinking wine, and laughing. Samuel Lysander looks dashing in his suit but does not seem to fully enjoy himself.

Elise arrives in a pretty light blue dress with alexandrite gemstones sewn into the trim. Ariadne watches her give shy greetings to the other witches. Ariadne had noticed that Iona found it very easy to become close with Elise since they discovered they were cousins. Ariadne would see them from her window when they practiced magic together in the courtyard. Elise had been showing some slight improvement with Iona's help and she seems to thrive off of the achievement.

Crescentia follows soon after and is wearing a white gown with intricate silver beading that sparkles in the lantern light. By now many witches have gathered in a circle to dance the La Boulangère.

"Good evening, Ariadne," Crescentia says, a knowing smile

on her lips.

"What secret are you hoarding now, Crescentia," Ariadne asks wryly.

"Oh, more than just one," Crescentia winks and walks away.

Ariadne had to respect her tenacity however irksome it may be at times. An ambitious climber like her needs her tricks. Ariadne looks out at the Lysander College class of 1802. She hasn't forgotten the siren's warning. Would Iona's new familial connection protect her or make her even more of a target? To her knowledge, no other attacks on Iona have been attempted yet but she isn't convinced the worst is over.

Ariadne appraises the crowd of women until she sees Iona emerge from the trees. She wears a flowing lavender purple silk dress that is overlayed in diaphanous Alençon lace. She has long trumpet sleeves that almost touch the ground and a purple sash tied round her waist. Two strands of her red hair are braided and joined at the back of her head, the rest falling in loose waves.

Iona finds Ariadne's gaze in seconds and approaches her, taking a goblet of mulled wine along the way. When Iona is close enough, Ariadne suppresses a gasp. Hidden in the lace pattern on Iona's dress are a variety of tiny flowers.

Upon further inspection, Ariadne recognizes five of the flowers that she had conjured and given to Iona. Iona had chosen the carnation, rhododendron, geranium, tansy, and lily. All the flowers with negative meanings, the ones that had been meant as insults, were now adorned across Iona's body. The delicate lace must have been conjured using magic and woven for many hours. Without magic, such an impossibly complex pattern would have taken countless months to weave.

"It is a fine night to commune with spirits," Iona says nonchalantly while taking a sip of wine.

Ariadne looks up from the lace and into Iona's provoking hazel eyes. The dress took Ariadne so off guard that she does not know how to respond, her lips parted but no sound coming out. Iona suppresses a smile, her eyes alight with roguery.

"It certainly is!" Samaira says, "I am hoping to see my grandfather this year. Who do you wish to see?"

Ariadne cringes as Samaira belatedly realizes her mistake.

"Oh! My apologies, I did not mean," Samaira stutters.

"It's okay," Iona says, "I hope we both see who we wish for tonight."

Samaira relaxes and smiles apologetically.

"Interesting choice of fashion," Ksenia says with narrowed eyes.

"I can make you one if you'd like," Iona says.

Ksenia cannot help but smile at Iona's boldness.

"Look who has taken so well to her new Lysander name," Ksenia says, "You have grown a backbone overnight."

"Not much in my countenance has changed. Considering this is our first true conversation, I would not expect you to know any different," Iona says, her polite smile never slipping, "But I shall forgive your ignorance."

"How magnanimous of you," Ksenia says dryly.

"What a perfect word to describe Iona," Crescentia says as she approaches and takes Iona's arm, "Shall we join the next dance?"

"Yes, we shall," Iona says.

When Iona turns away, Ariadne notices that sprigs of lavender are braided into Iona's hair, the two braids meeting at the back of Iona's skull. Lavender can represent peace, another message that Iona has embedded in her attire.

Crescentia leads Iona to the dance floor to take part in a quadrille. Partners step between the lines of dancers to take another's hand and spin before returning to their spot in line. It is clear that Iona has never danced it before, but she manages to only be a half step behind everyone else. After a while, Ksenia walks away to talk with Kokuro, but Samaira stays with Ariadne. Ariadne takes a sip of her wine, while Samaira twists her ring around and around her finger.

"She looks quite beautiful," Samaira says, observing the many dancing woman, "What color would you say her dress was?"

"Lavender," Ariadne says automatically.

Samaira grins and Ariadne flushes with regret. Samaira had never told her who she was speaking of. Ariadne assumed it was Iona and gave herself away.

"You are smitten with her," Samaira whispers impishly.

"Who?" Ariadne says, trying to feign innocence.

"Iona," Samaira says impatiently.

"No," Ariadne says but she chuckles nervously.

"After all that, all you wanted to do was bed her," Samaira shakes her head and laughs.

"Lower your voice," Ariadne hisses at her.

"She has been enamored with you since she arrived," Samaira says.

"That is not true," Ariadne says.

"How do you know?" Samaira asks.

"She told me in no uncertain terms that she does not want me," Ariadne mumbles, fidgeting with her goblet, "I have ruined any attraction she may have had for me. We may be too... volatile for one another."

"Only one so volatile could get through your thick skull," Samaira chuckles, "She could barely speak in full sentences around you at the beginning of term. Now look at her, a rare beauty indeed. And though there are many beautiful women present, she only has eyes for you."

Ariadne looks out at the dance floor again and sure enough, Iona is glancing at her as she spins gracefully between the other dancers.

"Do you think she made that dress on a lark? Whatever she may have said to you before, it seems she may be offering you a second chance," Samaira says with a knowing look, "All I am wondering now is, what are you doing standing here with me when you could be dancing with her?"

Ariadne goes to respond but Samaira only taps her cup against Ariadne's with a playful smile and says, "Many blessings."

Samaira walks away to join Ksenia and Kokuro, leaving Ariadne alone with her doubt ridden thoughts. Ariadne watches Iona, her lavender skirts flowing around her as she twirls to the music. They both went to such lengths to avoid the other's charm, all in vain it seems. Perhaps the time has finally come to find common ground and accept their fate.

"May I have the next dance?" Gisela asks as she comes to stand beside Ariadne. She is wearing an emerald-green gown that is dripping with jewels.

"I... No," Ariadne says.

Gisela's eyebrows raise in surprise, but she quickly recovers, "We could slip away and find a quiet place to be alone instead."

"Gisela," Ariadne says, making direct eye contact with her, "I must be honest with you now and only once more. Our dalliance was but a passing fancy. We are not suited for each other, though I am certain you will find someone who is, someone who deserves you."

"But," Gisela's smile falls.

"It is over, Gisela. Whatever it was, it is done. Please respect that," Ariadne says firmly.

The current dance ends and the enchanted instruments begin playing a landler. Ariadne downs the rest of her wine and sets her cup down on a nearby table.

"Please, excuse me," Ariadne says to the crestfallen Gisela.

Ariadne steels herself as she approaches the dance floor and taps Iona on the shoulder.

"Will you honor me with your hand for this dance?" Ariadne asks very formally and holds out her hand.

Iona looks down at Ariadne's outstretched hand, then up to her eyes. Other witches are observing the exchange, but Ariadne ignores them. Her heart stutters when Iona takes her hand, her soft palm sliding into hers. Ariadne pulls Iona against her and puts her other hand on Iona's waist, feeling the threadwork of the delicate lace against her fingertips.

Ariadne spins them around in time with the music and looks deeply into Iona's beguiling hazel eyes. Ariadne grins when Iona blushes under her gaze and looks away. She is hyperaware of Iona's warm ungloved hand resting on the bare skin of her shoulder. Their magic is a pleasant vibration between them but is not as distracting as times past.

"I would have given you many more flowers if I knew they would be displayed in such a way," Ariadne murmurs in Iona's ear.

"The lace is intricate enough with five," Iona says, with a shy smile, "But it was worth it to see your reaction."

Ariadne flushes and Iona giggles, the first true laugh Ariadne has heard from Iona in far too long. The sweet cadence makes it impossible for Ariadne not to giggle along with her.

"I am glad to see you wearing a color other than black," Ariadne says, then wonders if saying so is insensitive.

"I did not want to wear black to my reunion with my mother," Iona explains, "I very much hope to see her, though I know I cannot choose who will meet me."

Iona keeps glancing down at their feet as if she's scared that she will trip. Ariadne slows their movements until they merely sway at a gentle pace. The other dancers spin around them, their multicolored skirts like wings furling and unfurling with every movement.

Iona still somehow smells like the ocean breeze, though she has been living in the mountains for months now. There is also the slight hint of lavender coming from Iona's hair. Ariadne longs to lean in closer and run her nose along Iona's long neck just to hear her breath hitch in her throat like it had in the library.

"How do you know where to step?" Iona asks, breaking Ariadne's reverie.

"My father taught me how to dance when I was a girl. When my mother needed to rest at whatever ball we were hosting, he would scoop me up and spin me round with the other couples," Ariadne says, smiling at the memory.

"Are you close to your father?" Iona asks.

"Yes," Ariadne says, though even to her own ears she sounds

unsure.

Ariadne's monosyllabic answer stops any flow of conversation. Iona looks away nervously.

Ariadne clears her throat and clarifies, "My relationship with my parents is complicated."

"Why is that?" Iona asks.

"My magic made me more of a trophy than a daughter. They expect me to further our family's legacy the way my grandmother did," Ariadne explains, "They are most insistent that I do not ruin their plans."

Ariadne's tone is bitter, and Iona regards her with more compassion than she deserves.

"There are many women here with similar stories," Ariadne says, "Power has its own siren song. It compels witches and warlocks to do any number of regrettable things, though it does not excuse them."

Iona stares up at Ariadne with her inner turmoil laid bare.

"Iona, I..." Ariadne trails off, unsure how to best express her feelings.

"I have been considering leaving college," Iona says.

Ariadne stops dancing abruptly and Iona bumps into her.

"Why?" Ariadne asks incredulously.

"Keep dancing," Iona whispers anxiously, "I do not want to make a scene."

"You cannot make such a statement and expect me to continue dancing," Ariadne says, "Tell me now."

Iona sighs and glances at the other witches watching them from the edge of the dance floor.

"Not here," Iona whispers, taking Ariadne's hand and leading them back to the forest.

Ariadne follows, apprehension filling her and making her jittery. When they find a tiny meadow that is still close enough to the party to still hear the music, Ariadne paces nervously.

"You are going to let one murder attempt prevent you from finishing your studies? What of your mother's dying wish for you to learn magic?" Ariadne blurts out.

Iona gapes at her, "Is the threat of death not enough of a reason to leave?"

"It is cowardly," Ariadne says.

"That is easy for you to say when no one has tried to kill you," Iona snaps.

"Someone did, unsuccessfully," Ariadne says dismissively.

Iona was going to say something else but pauses to stare at her in disbelief. Ariadne attempts nonchalance.

"It is much more common than you would think. It has only happened to me once many years ago, but I expect it will happen again eventually," Ariadne says, "Like I said, witches are willing to go to extraordinary lengths to tip the scales in their favor. Knowing how to properly wield magic can help to protect you from them."

"When did someone try to kill you?" Iona asks with an appalled expression.

Ariadne looks down and feels her defenses raise.

"Is this to do with the river?" Iona asks with caution.

"Yes," Ariadne says stiffly.

Iona crosses her arms, "Tell me what happened."

"I am surprised that you have not yet heard the story from Crescentia or Elise," Ariadne says, attempting to avoid the question. She hates retelling this story and rarely ever does.

"I would rather hear it from you," Iona says, looking at her expectantly, "Or it shall remain an awful mystery that festers between us."

Ariadne shifts uncomfortably and averts her gaze.

"You will think less of me," Ariadne says, her voice breaking.

"Let me be the judge of that," Iona says.

Ariadne sighs and decides that she cannot keep this a secret from Iona any longer. Ariadne would prefer to tell it herself, rather than Iona hearing a sensationalized account of the worst day of her life.

"One summer in Thessaly, when I was four and ten, the eldest daughter of the Nicolo family invited me to swim with her in the river Pineios near our homes. Her name was Vivien,"

Ariadne says, "I had to sneak out of my room in the night because my mother did not often allow me to spend time with friends. She preferred that I stay home and study. I did not think she would notice I was gone."

Ariadne clears her throat and covertly pinches the skin on the back of her hand in an attempt to keep her emotions at bay. The sharp pain distracts her from her rising emotions.

"When we had waded into the water, Vivien conjured a wooden box around me and attempted to drown me inside of it. I believe she wanted it to appear like an accident, to sink the crate in the water, wait until I had drowned, then pull it back up to retrieve my body and give it to my family. I tried to conjure, blast, or kick my way out of the crate, but she kept repairing it anytime I would break through, and the water kept rising," Ariadne says, "It was pure luck that I had kept my wand in my swim costume. My mother always taught me never to part with it."

Ariadne makes the mistake of glancing at Iona, who looks at her with such astonished dismay that it almost makes her break down. Ariadne averts her gaze again and speaks quickly.

"I do not know why she did it. She may have simply been jealous. We were the same age, but my magic was already far surpassing hers, though her family is not lacking in magic of their own. She may have thought it would be easier to claim the pendant if I was dead. Or maybe her family drove her to it. I am not sure," Ariadne says.

"You did not try to ask her?" Iona asks.

Ariadne covertly wipes a tear away while pretending to scratch her cheek.

"Before the water rose too high, I created a series of illusions to scare Vivien into letting me go... in my panic, I did not hold back. I had only recently learned the illusion spell and did not know my own strength. By the time the ordeal was over, she had gone mad from the fear," Ariadne says, her voice trembling, "She fell into a catatonic state and has not spoken since. I could not ask her why she did it nor could anyone else. The mind is delicate and once it is shattered, it is nearly impossible to heal. Her family was furious but could do nothing about it. It was considered self-defense and I was only a child."

Ariadne looks away when tears pool in her eyes. The horror of that incident had nearly driven Ariadne to madness too. When she had run to her mother for help, begging for a spell or potion that could renew her friend's mind, her mother had only scoffed and said she should not want to heal someone who tried to kill her.

Her mother had been almost proud when she learned what Ariadne had done, an odd contrast to her constant criticism. Ariadne struggled with using illusion magic ever since, though her mother forced her to practice anyway.

"She was my best friend," Ariadne whispers, "Or at least I thought she was. And I destroyed her."

"Ariadne..." Iona says but is at a loss for words.

Ariadne had been careful with who she befriended since then, almost feeling more comfortable with people she knew were awful because then they could not surprise her with treachery. She has an unfortunate impulse to assume the worst in others, as Iona has inadvertently come to understand. Ariadne has never regretted this flaw more than she does now.

"And now everyone is frightened of me. They are scared that I may one day do the same to them," Ariadne says, "Though I never would, nor could I even if I desired it. My illusions have been perpetually broken since that day. Even my strongest attempts always fragment eventually."

"You did not try to explain that it was a tragic accident?" Iona asks.

"I did at first, but the rumors spread all the same," Ariadne says, then sighs, "When a room quiets whenever you enter, when witches can barely look you in the eye, except when they want something from you... I have long since abandoned the desire to change others' perception of me. It is futile, when my family are who they are, and I did what I did."

"What illusions did you make for Vivien?" Iona asks cautiously.

"That I will never say, not to anyone" Ariadne says, "I will take it to my grave."

Ariadne shudders at the mere mention of Vivien's illusions. The horror, the depravity of it, will haunt her forever. Even on pain of torture, on pain of death, she will never relive it.

"I am so sorry that happened to you. That one so young would attempt to murder you in such a way... it is unfathomable. A child could not imagine such a plot on her own. Her family should be ashamed," Iona says softly.

"They have never fully recovered," Ariadne says, "The scandal has forever marred their reputation."

"Good," Iona says firmly, then sighs, "But regardless, if my mother had known what would happen to me here, I doubt she would have told me to attend college. She would not want for me to fall prey to the same treachery."

"On the contrary, I did not know your mother, but I can guess that she sent you here because she knew your power would inevitably bring enemies to your door. Especially if they had learned you were a Lysander witch, untrained and unprotected. Having the ability to control your magic and defend yourself is the only way to ensure your own safety and autonomy," Ariadne says, "Or is your intention to lock yourself away again and waste the rest of your life alone?"

"How could you judge me for wanting to hide when you know the sort of danger I am facing?" Iona asks.

"You would not be any safer out there than you would be here. You have already come out into the light, Iona. Your existence is no longer a secret and that cannot be undone," Ariadne says, "As far as the danger, I could protect you from that, as I did with the sirens."

"Now you want to be my protector?" Iona asks skeptically.

"Yes," Ariadne says.

Iona stares at her and Ariadne waits for her to speak again. Even in the faint light of the moon, Iona's beauty is intoxicating.

"If I do see my mother tonight, I will ask her what she thinks. She and my father were able to disappear once before. It is not impossible for me to do so again," Iona says, "By the end of the night, I will have made my decision."

Ariadne nods, unhappy that Iona still might leave. She looks down at Iona's dress, decorated with Ariadne's hateful flowers. Ariadne pulls out her wand and conjures a new flower, a purple iris, and hands it to Iona. When their fingers touch, Ariadne feels a distinct flare of magic, quickly there and gone again.

"What does this mean?" Iona asks, bringing the flower up to her nose.

"Irises can symbolize new beginnings," Ariadne says.

"Is that what you want? To start over?" Iona asks.

"I do," Ariadne says, her composure slipping, "You are all I can think about."

Ariadne hadn't realized how close they had become until she felt Iona's warm breath against her lips. She wants to close the distance between them but holds back.

"You are cruel even in love," Iona whispers, "How can you make me feel this way? I ought to hate you. I wanted to hate you."

"What do you want now?" Ariadne asks.

Iona's breath deepens as her eyes glance between Ariadne's lips and her eyes. But within her stare, Iona's doubt still persists. Ariadne takes a step back.

Ariadne had confessed her deepest, darkest secret, despite every fiber of her being telling her not to. Though others cower in light of Ariadne's transgressions, Iona does not seem to fear her. Instead, Iona has only shown such compassion that none except Samaira had ever afforded her. Perhaps Iona could accept the rest of her too, however flawed and broken she may be.

"I do not understand what ties me to you, but I am tired of fighting it. If this is what you require to believe my affection is true, then I surrender my mind to you," Ariadne says.

Ariadne lifts her wand to her own forehead and says, "Verità."

Iona gasps softly, looking up at Ariadne with awe and gratitude. She understands what Ariadne is doing for her, allowing her to have perfect truth. Ariadne always thought she would be afraid while under a truth spell. She had been the last time, when Vivien's family had interrogated her after the tragedy in the river. This time, Ariadne feels oddly free knowing that she cannot amend her thoughts.

"Are you tricking me?" Iona asks.

"No," Ariadne says.

Iona relaxes a bit.

"Can I trust you?" Iona asks.

"I think so," Ariadne says, and she hates her uncertain answer even more than Iona does, "It is difficult for me to trust, but for you I am willing to try."

"It will be difficult for me too," Iona says softly.

Iona considers her next question. She seems reluctant to ask it.

"Did you set the sirens on me?" Iona finally asks.

"No, I didn't," Ariadne says vehemently, "Nor would I ever try to harm you in such a way."

Iona nods. Ariadne knows she had to ask it.

"Do you know who did?" Iona asks.

"No, but I intend to find out," Ariadne says, "Their attempt to kill you was evil enough, but to also implicate me as your attacker...They will regret their actions, that I swear to you."

"I apologize for accusing you," Iona says.

"I was... It hurt me the most that you thought I would try to drown you. Of all the ways of killing, I would never do that," Ariadne's voice trembles, "I could never... Not after Vivien tried to kill me the same way. Seeing you flailing like that, running out of air..."

Ariadne's hands start to shake. Iona takes one of them and squeezes it tightly.

"Because of you, I did not drown," Iona says, "You saved my

life."

Ariadne nods and fights to regain her composure. Iona's words mean more to her than she thought possible.

"In hindsight, I see that I was misguided. You were already so beguiled with me. Your words in the library..." Iona says with a nervous chuckle, "I should have known you had no reason to hurt me. I was only frightened and confused."

Iona looks down at Ariadne's hand in hers, tracing her finger over one of the veins like Ariadne had done to her in Yun's classroom.

"I suppose... from the very start I never understood your vehemence. Why did you hate me so easily?" Iona asks.

"I never hated you," Ariadne says, "I was... threatened by you. I was. You have a natural affinity to magic that is as strong as mine, stronger in some ways, and it made me panic."

Ariadne cringes. It's the first answer that was a bit too honest for her taste. Iona's eyebrows raise, the hint of a smile on her lips.

"Do not let it go to your head," Ariadne flushes.

"I shall make no promises," Iona's grin widens, "I suppose I can understand your folly, however misguided it was."

"You rose to the occasion quite vigorously," Ariadne retorts.

"I did try to reason with you... but I let my anger get the best of me," Iona says, "I did not think my hex would be such a reckoning. You were trembling and I could see remnants of tears on your cheeks."

Iona's smile falls at the memory.

"I have a debilitating fear of enclosed spaces," Ariadne explains.

"Oh," Iona's eyes go wide, "Because of... Oh Ariadne, how wretched of me."

"You did not know," Ariadne says, "I know it was not your intention."

"I had only meant to pester you, to show that I could not be intimidated. I did not intend to incite a fit of trauma," Iona relents, "I feel so awful..."

"We both made mistakes that we now regret," Ariadne says, "I never should have let Ksenia convince me to leave you paralyzed in the forest. The pendant is not worth such harassment."

Iona nods, then frowns. Ariadne braces herself for Iona's next question.

"It would be that much easier for you to claim the pendant if I left college. Do you truly want me to stay even if I win it instead of you?" Iona asks.

"Yes, I do," Ariadne says.

This seems to affect Iona the most and her eyes soften.

"I still want the pendant, but I cannot stand the thought of not being near you again," Ariadne admits, taking Iona's hand in hers.

Ariadne lifts Iona's hand and kisses it. Iona watches her, her chest rising and falling deeply. They get lost in each other's eyes.

"Do you want to possess me or cherish me?" Iona asks.

Ariadne thinks about this for a moment, intrigued by the question.

"Both," Ariadne says.

Iona chuckles at that. She tentatively reaches out and lets her fingers drift along Ariadne's collarbone, then dip lower to trace the red flame on the swell of her breast. Ariadne swallows hard as Iona's bold touch leaves a trail of heat in its wake.

"Do you want to control me?" Iona asks.

"No, I could not even if I wanted to," Ariadne says.

"You could," Iona argues.

"You still do not know how powerful you are," Ariadne says as she caresses Iona's cheek.

"Because I am a Lysander witch?" Iona asks.

"No," Ariadne shakes her head, "Because of who *you* are. All the magic in the world is useless to someone who is not daring and inspired like you."

Iona puts her hand over Ariadne's. In that moment, Ariadne can see that her doubt is gone at long last.

"What is your fantasy of me?" Iona whispers.

Ariadne grins and leans in even closer until she hears Iona's breath hitch, "Would you rather I tell you or show you?"

"Show me," Iona breathes.

When Iona closes the distance between them, her soft lips brushing against Ariadne's so lightly, desire spreads over her like a warm breeze. Ariadne slides her arms around Iona's waist to bring her closer and Iona melts into her, so soft and pliant. Ariadne brings one hand up to thread her fingers into Iona's silken hair, moving her mouth over Iona's until they are both breathless.

Ariadne's heart hammers in her chest as she backs Iona against a nearby tree. Her hands roam brazenly over Iona's body, feeling the texture of the delicate lace against her fingertips.

Iona moans softly when Ariadne cups her breast and squeezes the plump swell in the palm of her hand. Ariadne is more grateful than ever for the medieval theme of the Samhain ball because Iona's dress does not require stays. Her flesh moves under Ariadne's hand, her nipple hardening beneath the layers of silk. Iona arches into her touch, her cheeks and chest flushed with her growing desire.

Ariadne kisses a trail across Iona's jaw and settles in the crook of her neck to suck on her skin. Iona sighs and sneaks in a few kisses along Ariadne's bare shoulder. The haunting frisson of their magic rouses every nerve ending until their skin comes alive with luxuriant sensations.

Ariadne takes Iona's mouth again, this time licking along Iona's top lip in question. Iona timidly opens her mouth, their tongues sliding together. Iona whimpers when Ariadne sucks on her tongue. Their soft kisses turn molten and frenzied as their desire grows.

"Lift up your skirts, nymph," Ariadne says against Iona's lips.

Iona does so slowly, lifting the lavender fabric up her leg until Ariadne can see the hint of bare flesh above Iona's stocking. Ariadne grasps Iona's thigh, running her thumb along the sliver of soft, honey skin, and feeling the muscles tense beneath her touch. Ariadne wants to lick along the edge of the white lace garter, then put her tongue to better use in more sensitive places.

But before Ariadne can kneel between Iona's legs and finally learn what she tastes like, they hear Professor Pari calling for all the students to gather for the Samhain ritual. They both sigh with disappointment. It is almost painful to stop now.

"We must go," Iona says breathlessly, letting her skirts fall.

Then Iona points her wand at Ariadne and undoes the truth spell.

12 – IONA

I ona hopes she doesn't look too flushed when she and Ariadne return to the cliffside and gather with the other witches. They manage to rejoin the group without many witches noticing. Ariadne had thoroughly diverted her focus but when she listens to Professor Pari's speech about what to expect on Samhain, she remembers that she may be minutes away from seeing her mother again.

"I shall distribute talismans that have been enchanted with a strong clairvoyancy spell. I have prepared these over the course of the year to make them strong enough to invite one soul to visit each of you for a period of time. That time is determined by the ghost who answers the call. Spirits have a lifetime of wisdom to impart. Be open to their insight. One day, hopefully very far in the future, you may be one of these souls called to visit a young witch on Samhain."

Iona takes a talisman, a flat golden coin with a skull stamped into the metal. She can sense the magic trapped within, like static against her fingertips. The witches are instructed to disperse into the forest and walk until they know to stop. Iona looks to Ariadne once more. She smiles encouragingly at her, and it puts Iona at ease. There was so much they still needed to say and do to each other but for now, a ghost is waiting.

Iona enters the forest and within only a few minutes, she

steps into an immense marshland with flocks of ravens flying in circles overheard. Iona lifts her skirts high and finds a path of dry grass around the pools of dark water. She isn't sure where she is supposed to go until she notices a trail of smoke coming from the center of the marsh. Soon she can see the light from a small fire burning on an islet of grass.

When Iona reaches the fire, she looks around, but no one is there. She warms herself for a moment, wondering if she should continue walking through the marsh until she finds someone.

"Good evening, Iona."

Iona jumps and spins around. There before her is a beautiful ageless woman with long black hair that reaches her upper thighs. Her dress is black velvet with flowing sleeves and golden trim. She wears a black cloak and pulls back her hood to reveal a pair of bright green eyes. Iona has never seen this woman before but somehow, Iona knows who she is.

"Morgan Le Fay," Iona whispers.

Iona does not know whether she should bow or kneel, or if that would be too formal.

"I apologize if my presence is a disappointment. I know you were hoping to see your mother tonight, but I come to you with a dire warning," Morgan says with a silvery voice.

"A warning?" Iona asks, her wonder replaced by dread.

"A malefician has taken residence at Lysander College and their target is you," Morgan says, "She is the one who sent the sirens."

Iona flushes slightly at knowing that Morgan saw what the sirens did to her, but her fear quickly overcomes any embarrassment.

"A malefician?" Iona asks.

"A witch like you or I will use sacred nature and practiced skill to create wonders of magic, but there are limitations. A malefician bends nature to their own will without a care for balance or decency. They are sorceresses who are notoriously difficult to identify and even more difficult to defeat. You must be on your guard," Morgan says, "This malefician is ruthless and cunning. She intends to eliminate her competition, one by one, starting with you. She wants my pendant and is willing to kill for it, or worse."

Iona racks her brain for who it might be.

"That could be almost any of the witches at school. They all want the pendant and would do anything to have it," Iona points out.

"My presence here is not for me to give you all the answers," Morgan raises an eyebrow.

Iona chastens, "I am sorry, I did not intend to sound ungrateful. I just... I do not know how I am meant to find this malefician on my own. Do you not give the pendant to whomever you choose?"

Morgan shakes her head, "My pendant is not given. It is earned by skill and valor. Only one who is strong, skilled, and unburdened by doubt will claim it."

Iona does not know why Morgan is visiting her if she requires such a champion of magic. She is still only a novice with much to learn. If the malefician is as formidable as Morgan claims, Iona could not dream of opposing them.

"If the pendant was taken and desecrated by a sorceress who is enthralled with dark magic, who knows what horrors they would wreak on the world," Morgan says, "The pendant must be protected by a witch who does not lust after power or cower in the face of danger. I see that witch in you, Iona, if you are willing to rise to the challenge."

"What of Ariadne?" Iona asks.

Morgan smiles with a twinkle in her eye.

"Ariadne is a brilliant witch who could also take on this task, if that is what you desire," Morgan says.

"I do not know if I would be worthy of such power or if I am strong enough to protect it," Iona says, "Ariadne has trained her entire life for your trials. She would never let someone take the pendant from her once she possessed it."

Morgan nods with sage equanimity, "If that is what you

think is right."

"I believe so," Iona says, but she is entirely unsure.

"The malefician is after you whether you want the pendant or not," Morgan reminds her, "She only cares that you have the power to threaten her claim."

"What if I left college then? That would eliminate any doubt of my intentions and Ariadne could win the pendant herself," Iona says.

"Leaving is your right, but it is not your destiny. You were never meant to be locked away from the world forever. Power like yours often comes with a price. If you are willing to continue your studies, let go of your fear, and triumph over your adversaries, you shall find the peace you have been looking for," Morgan says, "There is more than one power in this world to covet."

Iona considers this as Morgan approaches her. She gently cups Iona's face in her hands and kisses her forehead. Then she tilts Iona's chin up to look into her emerald eyes.

"Protect the ones you love. Be careful who you trust," Morgan says, "And do not tell anyone that we spoke."

Iona gasps awake. She is lying on the forest floor with the stars twinkling faintly above her. She sits up and scans her surroundings. When she looks at her hand, the golden talisman has disappeared. She had so many other questions to ask Morgan and wishes she could have stayed longer. She wishes now more than ever that she could speak to her mother.

Wisp was sleeping in the leaves next to her. She rises and licks Iona's face until she pets her gently and stands. Morgan's words echo in Iona's mind. The siren hadn't lied. There is a witch that endeavors to harm her and she almost succeeded. Any allies she once had are now in question, all except Ariadne.

Morgan may not have meant to reinforce Ariadne's innocence, but she did so by calling her a brilliant witch. Ariadne had also proven that she did not send the sirens by casting the truth spell of her own volition. Ariadne is the only one that Iona can trust now. Perhaps this is why fate intervened with such tenacity.

Iona glances about nervously, wondering if the malefician might be watching her this very moment. Iona takes out her wand.

"Light," Iona whispers, and a sphere of light appears in her hand. She holds it up as she walks, the shadows of the trees moving and shifting ominously. Wisp follows closely next to her and is a calming presence.

Iona tenses when she sees someone in the distance. She relaxes when she recognizes Ariadne walking through the trees with Aster by her side. Iona runs over to her, then slows when she sees the look of utter shock on Ariadne's face.

"Ariadne," Iona whispers as she approaches.

Ariadne looks up at her and seems relieved that Iona is there.

"Whatever is the matter?" Iona asks.

"I cannot speak of it," Ariadne says, and her voice breaks.

Iona wonders who visited Ariadne. Had Morgan made two visits this night? Or had some other historic magical figure called upon Ariadne with cryptic warnings and demands?

"Who did you see?" Ariadne asks curiously.

"I cannot speak of it either," Iona says.

Ariadne and Iona get lost in each other's eyes again. Iona can sense Ariadne's stress. Whatever had happened to her, whoever she had just seen, had been a calamity.

"Do not leave," Ariadne implores.

Iona takes a deep breath in and out, then nods shortly, "I will stay."

Ariadne closes the distance between them and crushes her lips to Iona's with unbridled passion. As they collide, Iona lets her ball of light fall to the ground beside her and throws her arms around Ariadne's neck. They cling to each other as if any space between them would cause them agony.

Ariadne's mouth and hands are frenzied at first, groping and clawing hungrily as if she's afraid Iona will disappear.

Ariadne's touch stirs Iona's desire and overwhelms her senses. She moans when Ariadne sucks hard on her neck, enough to make her knees buckle. Iona's sex throbs impatiently as Ariadne deliberately slows down. Iona kicks off her dancing shoes and reaches behind Ariadne to pull at the laces of her gown. She does not want any barrier between them.

Ariadne makes quicker work of Iona's gown. The sloping neckline makes it possible to slide the dress over Iona's shoulders and down her body until she is only in her thin white chemise. Iona manages to loosen Ariadne's straps enough to push her dress down too just as Ariadne guides Iona onto her back on the forest floor.

Iona reaches for Ariadne, but she does not fall onto Iona right away. Instead, she kneels between Iona's spread thighs and grasps the top of Iona's chemise. She rips it all the way down the middle to expose Iona's body, just as Iona had fantasized. Their ragged breathing mixes with the sounds of the forest.

Ariadne gazes down at Iona's nakedness reverently, her burning red eyes like a caress as they roam over Iona's bare skin. Iona is tempted to cover herself, her insecurities wreaking havoc on her nerves despite knowing that Ariadne has seen her naked before. But when Ariadne's eyes meet hers again, she can see nothing but blazing hunger for her.

"I have caught a nymph," Ariadne grins, "Now what shall I do to her?"

"Ariadne," Iona blushes shyly, her skin hot beneath Ariadne's sensuous gaze.

"I like my name on your lips," Ariadne whispers.

Ariadne breaks eye contact to reach for Iona's thigh and pull at the ribbon that holds her garter in place. She does the same to the second garter, then slips her fingers beneath the white cotton fabric of her stocking. Ariadne slowly pulls it down over Iona's knee, her calf, and over her heel. The soft touch of Ariadne's fingers against Iona's skin makes her muscles tense with anticipation.

Ariadne takes her time to roll down her other stocking slowly and deliberately, then looks up at Iona. The trace of humor in her eyes indicates she is very much aware of the anticipatory havoc this is wreaking on Iona's body.

Ariadne removes the pins from her hair, setting aside her silver circlet, and pulling down her own stockings. Then finally, she pulls her own chemise over her head and discards it next to her. Iona's breath quickens when she gazes upon Ariadne's smooth olive skin, slender limbs, and round breasts tipped with nipples the color of red mulberries. Iona watches as Ariadne's long fingers push her raven curls behind her ears.

"Lust becomes you, Iona," Ariadne grins as she looms over her.

Iona looks away bashfully, but Ariadne tips her chin up to meet her eyes.

"Do not look away," Ariadne whispers, "Memorize me as I will to you."

Ariadne holds Iona's gaze as she reaches out and drifts her fingertips lightly along Iona's body from her collarbone to the valley between her breasts, over her ribs, her stomach, and down to her hip, until she gently guides Iona's thighs open wide enough for her to settle between them.

Iona inhales sharply when Ariadne's pebbled nipples brush against her own. Her heartbeat thrums between her legs. She's filled with excited nerves but has no doubt of what she wants Ariadne to take from her. Iona puts her hand behind Ariadne's neck and pulls her down for a kiss.

Ariadne rests her weight on her elbow and cups Iona's breast in her other hand. Iona moans when Ariadne teases her nipple with her thumb, then pinches it between her fingers. Iona runs her hands up and down Ariadne's smooth back, feeling her lean muscles as they shift beneath her skin. Iona moans again when Ariadne's mouth returns to her neck, then drags her lips up to suck and nip at Iona's earlobe.

With their bodies pressed together this way, the frisson of their magic is almost too much to bear. Iona wonders in the back of her mind if she should be worried about the magic reacting the way it had when they'd first experimented with it in her room, but she suspects that will not happen this time. Their desires are now in perfect harmony, not dissonant as they once were.

When Ariadne's mouth trails down to Iona's breasts, she worships them with tender kisses. Iona whimpers when Ariadne sucks one of her nipples oh so gently, her tongue darting out and flicking it as she watches Iona's reaction. Then she sucks the nipple deep into her mouth so fiercely, Iona's back arches off the ground as her core clenches with need. Iona's desire grows as Ariadne covers every inch of her skin with kisses, licking paths between the light brown freckles that cover her breasts and ribs until Iona is mewling beneath her.

Iona's nerves resurface when Ariadne follows a trail of freckles down her lower stomach until Ariadne's mouth is dangerously close to her sex. Iona watches Ariadne kiss her hip, then lick along the crease between her leg and her torso. Ariadne glances up at Iona, her garnet eyes gauging Iona's desire and noticing her hesitance.

Ariadne places a kiss on Iona's inner thigh. The skin there is even more sensitive, rivaling that of her neck and breasts. When Ariadne suctions her mouth, Iona's head falls back against the ground.

Ariadne's wicked mouth makes Iona lose all sense of where she is. Her sex throbs almost painfully, demanding attention. She gasps when Ariadne bites her thigh, not enough to draw blood but it does make her jerk in surprise. Ariadne sucks where she had bit and Iona whimpers. She can feel Ariadne's grin against her flesh and it's as infuriating as it is irresistible.

"Please," Iona whispers.

"No doubts left?" Ariadne asks, blowing air against Iona's sex and making her hips buck towards her mouth, but she pulls away again.

"No," Iona shakes her head.

"Are you sure?" Ariadne asks, then sucks hard on the flesh just adjacent to her dripping folds.

"Ariadne," Iona begs.

"Shhhh," Ariadne hushes, then licks Iona's cunt from bottom to top.

Iona moans with relief, then cries out when Ariadne licks at her pulsing bud at the top. Ariadne suckles it with the perfect amount of pressure, licks it rapidly up and down, back and forth, tracing around it, then sucks it between her lips again.

Iona's sanity is lost as soon as Ariadne's mouth is on her. She grinds her hips into Ariadne's face with abandon, desperate for release. Ariadne has to hold her hips down with her arm to keep her still. Her hand on Iona's lower stomach only further fuels her desire as magic stirs between them. Iona grasps around for something to hold onto, but her hands only find shifting leaves.

Iona looks down at Ariadne, who is watching her with a mischievous glint in her eyes. Iona almost chokes on air when Ariadne's tongue delves inside her without warning, moving against her slick walls until Iona is writhing beneath her. Iona's climax builds swiftly as she threads her fingers into Ariadne's curls.

13 – ARIADNE

Iona has never looked more beautiful than she does now. She is an exposed nerve, so responsive to Ariadne's lips and fingers. Iona's freckled stomach tenses with her intake of breath every time Ariadne touches her in a way she was not expecting. Her breasts, full and plump, move with her wanton undulations. Iona's dripping cunt is so smooth and warm against Ariadne's tongue, her soft red curls tickling Ariadne's nose as she licks her.

Ariadne moves her tongue inside Iona until she sees her lose all control, unable to hold back her desperate sighs and moans. Selfishly she would love to keep Iona here like this forever, right on the precipice of her pleasure. Ariadne has longed to touch her for so long and loves seeing the expressions on Iona's face when she tongues her in just the right spot.

"Do not look so smug," Iona gasps, and Ariadne holds back her laughter so as not to lose her rhythm.

It is difficult for Ariadne not to show how triumphant she feels. At long last, Iona is falling apart beneath her, better than any fantasy could be. Iona's pretty moans become cries and pleas for Ariadne to give her what she wants, all music to her ears. Ariadne moves her tongue languidly within her, wanting to watch her for just a moment longer. When Iona laces her fingers into Ariadne's hair and pulls on the strands, she welcomes the sting.

Ariadne circles Iona's nub with her thumb with increased pressure and speed while moving her tongue inside until Iona's back bows off the ground and she groans. Wetness drips down Ariadne's chin as Iona's climax takes her. Ariadne laps it up and licks her lips, the ambrosia of Iona's desire making her lightheaded with need. Her own cunt is throbbing below her, but she had to see Iona come apart first.

Iona's legs shake on either side of Ariadne's head. Ariadne kisses Iona's inner thigh, grinning when she sees the already forming red splotches on her honey skin.

Ariadne pushes herself up so she can look down on Iona's trembling form. Then she realizes Iona isn't only trembling from her pleasure. She's shivering.

"Are you cold?" Ariadne asks.

"I am not sure," Iona pants, "I am preoccupied with other feelings at present."

Ariadne chuckles and stands up. Iona watches her gather all their clothing and their wands, then sits up to look at her questioningly.

"Come," Ariadne says, holding out her hand.

"Where are we going?" Iona asks, still breathless.

Ariadne takes Iona's hand and pulls her along. They run through the forest, naked and free. Ariadne knows the approximate direction to run in but hopes that she doesn't accidentally get them lost. She is pleased when they find a collection of hot springs.

Ariadne puts their clothes down on the rocks and picks up her wand. She makes pieces of light and throws them around the pools. She tosses one of them inside the biggest pool to see how far it will sink. It isn't very deep, and the light makes the water glow from within. Ariadne sets aside her wand and steps into the pool. The heat is heavenly and eradicates any chill on her skin. Iona steps in after her and sighs happily as her shivers dissipate.

"How did you know this was here?" Iona asks.

"I passed by them right before you found me," Ariadne

explains, "Siren free, I promise."

Iona rolls her eyes and dips her head beneath the water to wet her hair. When she resurfaces, Ariadne takes her hand and pulls her closer. The warm water makes their skin slick to the touch. Ariadne finds a ledge against the stone wall of the spring and sits down, pulling Iona on top of her. Iona laces her fingers into Ariadne's and looks thoughtful.

"Do you remember when we experimented with the magnetism in my room?" Iona asks.

Ariadne looks down, "Vividly."

Iona tips Ariadne's chin up. There is no anger in Iona's gaze, only enduring lust. Iona's fingers drift down Ariadne's neck.

"You tested it on me, but I did not get much of a chance to test it on you," Iona says.

Iona bites her lip contemplatively and looks down. She moves her hand from Ariadne's shoulder to rest it against her lower stomach. They both look at her hand and wait.

Ariadne feels a stirring inside her that intensifies the longer Iona keeps her hand there. She inhales sharply and leans into Iona.

"Every time I'm near you, I feel your body... your magic calling to me," Iona whispers.

Iona moves her hand up to cup one of Ariadne's breasts. Her eyelids flutter when Iona plays with her nipple between her fingers.

"If we do this," Iona looks up sharply in Ariadne's eyes, "We *will* trust each other. We will protect each other. We will be loyal. And we will not talk about the pendant again until spring."

"Iona..." Ariadne trails off.

Iona rolls Ariadne's nipple between her fingers and she bites back a moan.

"If you want me, and I know you do, that is what I want," Iona says.

Ariadne is taken aback by her directness. Iona's hazel eyes pierce right through her.

"Very well. I already planned on the first three, and I agree to the fourth," Ariadne says.

Iona gives Ariadne a rewarding kiss, then draws back before Ariadne can take more.

"I also think that for the moment, it may be prudent not to tell anyone about us," Iona says, "I still do not know who might be attempting to hurt me and I do not want you to come to harm on my account."

"I can defend myself," Ariadne says, "But I agree. It is no business of anyone else's what we do together. Though in full disclosure, Samaira already knows."

"Crescentia suspects but I haven't explicitly told her," Iona admits with a sheepish grin.

"It is near impossible to lie to Ksenia, but I shall try," Ariadne grimaces, "Otherwise, our dance at the ball can be explained away and our rendezvous in the forest could have been another argument. No one need suspect a thing."

Iona nods, seemingly mollified by their agreement. She cups Ariadne's other breast in her hand and runs her thumbs over Ariadne's nipples, smiling when Ariadne moans softly and pulls her in for another kiss.

Ariadne lets Iona explore her body, enjoying how her soft hands caress her so gingerly. As their desire is reignited, Iona threads her fingers into Ariadne's hair and pulls her head back so she can kiss down her neck. Ariadne runs her hands down Iona's back until she cups her round bottom and squeezes, digging her fingers into the plump flesh. She licks a bead of water from Iona's shoulder, lightly running her nails up Iona's back until she shivers.

When Iona leans down to take one of Ariadne's nipples into her mouth, she moans almost as loudly as Ariadne does. Iona's eyebrows knit together as she suckles on the rosy bud. Her kisses are so gentle, so soft, that they are as maddening as they are sensual. Iona makes her tongue rigid, moving it up and down against Ariadne's nipple. Ariadne's pulse throbs rapidly between her legs, but she forces herself to be patient.

Iona's hand lingers against Ariadne's lower stomach. She does not mean to tease, she is only nervous, but Ariadne's core clenches all the same. Ariadne gently puts her hand over Iona's and guides her down.

When Iona's finger strokes her folds, Ariadne grits her teeth. Iona's touch leaves a trail of pleasure in its wake with one single stroke, unlike anything Ariadne has ever experienced. It's enough to make Ariadne shudder.

Iona is emboldened by Ariadne's reaction and strokes her more confidently. Ariadne clutches Iona's wrist, feeling the tendons shift as Iona's fingers circle her swollen bud with increasing pressure and speed. Iona places soft kisses on Ariadne's lips as she draws out her pleasure.

"You are so beautiful," Iona whispers, "Like a marble statue come to life, but much softer."

"I am even softer inside," Ariadne whispers against Iona's lips.

Ariadne gasps when Iona dips a finger inside of her, not needing any more encouragement than that.

"You are... like velvet," Iona whispers, probing her with her gentle finger.

Ariadne kisses her with increased abandon as Iona presses her finger in and out slowly, tantalizingly. Perhaps this exquisite torment is karma for teasing Iona so mercilessly.

"Like that?" Iona asks, her pressure and speed not nearly enough.

"Deeper," Ariadne gasps between kisses, "I will not break... Let loose your tempest."

Iona's eyes flare and Ariadne stomach flips, knowing she is in for a reckoning now. Iona kisses her with more ferocity, thrusting her finger in deep and running it against Ariadne's upper wall until she goes rigid. Ariadne's breath catches in her throat as heightened pleasure radiates through her entire body. Iona inserts a second finger and strokes Ariadne's most sensitive spot again and again, no longer holding back.

Iona presses her lips against Ariadne's breast, right over her flame mark, and sucks hard. Ariadne's core clenches around Iona's fingers, her thigh muscles tensing as her pleasure builds even higher. Iona learns Ariadne's body the same way that she learns magic, with keen intuition and nimble prowess.

Ariadne reaches for Iona's folds, needing to feel her too. Iona's eyes close and her mouth falls open as she moans. Ariadne covers Iona's mouth with hers and slides her tongue against Iona's until she whimpers. Then Iona strokes her even harder and faster, giving Ariadne no choice but to fall apart.

They reach their climax together, crying out their pleasure into the night. Iona slumps into Ariadne's embrace, her second climax exhausting her. Ariadne's fingers drift along Iona's back as she gazes fondly at the beautiful woman in her arms. She idlily traces the crescent on Iona's spine.

Then a twig snaps in the distance and Iona jolts with alarm. Iona pulls away and looks out into the darkness. Ariadne glances between the forest and Iona's frightened face.

"Iona?" Ariadne asks, "It is likely just an animal."

Iona nods distractedly but puts her arms over her breasts as if she is afraid someone is watching.

"Can we return to the college grounds?" Iona asks.

Ariadne searches Iona's eyes but her fear has been hidden away.

"Of course. Let's go," Ariadne says.

After donning their gowns, Ariadne takes Iona's hand and leads her through the trees. Aster and Wisp dart around them as they play together. Iona giggles as she watches them and her fear seems to be abated, though sometimes it is difficult to tell exactly what is going through her mind, not while her aura is masked.

Ariadne holds light to illuminate their path. She watches Iona laugh and it reenforces her mettle. She knows she made the right decision, though others may disagree. Ariadne's ghostly visit this night had been an alarming wakeup call that she chose to profoundly ignore.

When Ariadne had entered the forest holding her Samhain talisman, after walking past only a handful of trees, she'd emerged on the other side to find an immense wide-open space. The flat ground was covered by an inch of water. When Ariadne continued walking, her feet crunched into a layer of salt beneath the water. The stars were reflected almost perfectly and made it seem as if Ariadne was walking into the night sky. Her stride created ripples that blurred the reflection, so she stopped and waited for the water to settle again, not wanting to disturb the beautiful image.

"Ariadne Zerynthos," a stern, familiar voice said from behind her.

Ariadne closed her eyes and any peace she'd felt was gone.

"Look me in the eye, child," the voice snapped.

Ariadne reluctantly turned around and made sure her expression was neutral before meeting her grandmother's grim red eyes.

"Hello, grandmother," Ariadne said politely.

Katrin Zerynthos stood before her in a white tunic and blood red himation around her shoulders, an ensemble that she would normally wear on ritual nights. The traditional robes are reminiscent of ancient Greece but on her grandmother, they are timeless. Her dark hair is braided into a bun at the nape of her neck.

Ariadne's eyes lingered on her grandmother's neck where Morgan Le Fay's pendant still sat, even in death. The pendant comprises of three stones on a golden chain. Two black onyx ravens' wings frame a brilliant prismatic opal that glittered and glowed, though there was only faint starlight shining down upon them.

Her grandmother's ghost appeared to be in her late forties or early fifties. When Ariadne had known her, she had been much older, well past a century old. The pendant had given her abnormally long life and vitality, until its magic had begun to fade around the same time that Ariadne was born.

"I told your mother she was too lenient, but she would not heed my warning," her grandmother said, "I have only been dead for eleven years, and look at the state of you. A lovesick fool ready to throw away her inheritance for a pretty damsel."

Ariadne blushed scarlet but did not lower her gaze. Her grandmother would consider it weakness.

"You have lost focus. Fuck her if you must but do not let her steal your legacy from you," her grandmother said.

Ariadne had glared at her fiercely.

"I shall take your admonition under advisement," Ariadne said coolly, "If that is all you care to say to me, you may as well send me back."

Her grandmother narrowed her eyes and slowly circled Ariadne, her footsteps breaking the reflective surface of the water until it became endlessly muddled and vermiculate.

"It seems age has made you a reckless fool, not just a lovesick one. I remember a time when you could barely look at me. Now you think you are too good for your grandmother's advice?" her grandmother asked.

"I did not ask for it. You are dead. You lived your life and made your choices. Now I must make mine," Ariadne said.

Her grandmother chuckled darkly, "You insolent child. Have you forgotten what is at stake? I guarantee that your kin have not. If you fail, you shall wander this world alone with only your feral mutt as company."

"I will not be alone," Ariadne said, though her voice wavered.

Her grandmother rolled her eyes and laughed.

"The Lysander girl will bed you and leave you when she has what she wants," her grandmother said, "All relationships end eventually but the power that Morgan's pendant provides will last two lifetimes."

Her grandmother stopped circling Ariadne to stand directly in front of her.

"Does grandfather know you think so little of affection?" Ariadne asked coolly.

Her grandmother bristled at that and said, "He sends his regards and agrees with my assessment of your inadequacies. He never stood in the way of my greatness."

"It is depraved, narcissistic people like you who provoke children into drowning each other," Ariadne seethed, "I will not listen to your poisonous words a moment longer. Whether I win the pendant or not, it will never be for you or your precious legacy. I am done."

"You will never be done. You will always be a Zerynthos until your dying breath. Blood is not something you can escape," her grandmother scoffs.

"Watch me," Ariadne said, her voice low and resolute.

Her grandmother leaned forward until they were eye to eye.

"You are a disgrace. One day you will wish you had heeded my words. By then, it shall be too late," her grandmother said.

Ariadne had gasped awake violently and choked on the cold air. She'd wondered if her grandmother was smiting her from beyond the grave, but eventually air filled her lungs again and she'd sobbed with relief. Aster had whined and sniffed at her face in distress until she soothed him with kisses and pulled him onto her lap.

Ariadne had sat there in the darkness for quite a while. Though the smallest fragment of anxiety was reborn within her, she was steadfast in her choice to be with Iona. She knew in her heart that it was the right decision and she had to let go of her doubt. She will not live in fear of her family anymore.

When Iona had found her in the forest, she was still reeling from her conversation with her grandmother. She did not say which ghost had visited because she did not want Iona to lose faith in her.

Ravishing Iona on the forest floor had only solidified her resolve. To think she had almost missed her chance to experience such all-consuming pleasure. Something that felt so right, so rapturous, could never be wrong.

Once Ariadne and Iona return to the college courtyard, they run to the dormitories and out of the cold. When they make it to the hallway, Ariadne thought they had made it without being seen until Ksenia suddenly emerges from her room to peer down the hall. Ariadne quickly uses an invisibility spell on herself, but Iona is not so quick.

"Uh... good evening," Iona says awkwardly.

Ksenia only glares at her, then turns and goes back into her room without a word. Iona sighs with relief and rushes to her own door. Ariadne follows her and slips inside.

"She has been watching me like a hawk," Iona grumbles.

"She does that," Ariadne says as she undoes her invisibility spell.

"You do not think she saw us from her window, do you?" Iona asks.

"It is possible, but I imagine if she'd seen us together, she would have interrogated you," Ariadne says.

"Well... since you're here you may as well stay," Iona whispers with a shy smile.

They're on each other in seconds, ripping their gowns away and falling onto the bed. Ariadne only just manages to cast a locking spell on the door before Iona kisses her way down Ariadne's body and makes all other thoughts float away with a stroke of her tongue.

At dawn, Ariadne wakes to find Iona's naked body draped over her own. They had traded pleasure for hours last night, learning each other's bodies with avid thoroughness, before collapsing in a sweaty heap. Ariadne would have fallen right back to sleep if she had not heard raised voices from the hallway.

"I did not see her return. We must go and look for her," Ksenia says urgently.

"She may still be visiting with her ghost. It is not unheard of for visits to last the whole night, sometimes even days. Do not fret," Mrs. Ainsley says calmly.

"I will not go to class until I know she is safe," Ksenia snaps.

Ariadne tenses and, though she wishes she didn't have to,

she gently shakes Iona out of her slumber.

"Iona, wake up," Ariadne whispers.

Iona groans and curls her limbs tighter around Ariadne.

"They think I have gone missing," Ariadne whispers.

Iona's brow furrows and she yawns.

"Tell them to come back later," Iona sighs.

Ariadne grins and kisses Iona's forehead.

"The sooner we start the day, the sooner it will be over, and we can go back to bed," Ariadne coaxes.

Iona whines reluctantly but she lets Ariadne go. Ariadne pulls her gown back on as quickly as she can. Ksenia is still arguing with Mrs. Ainsley outside the door.

"Iona," Ariadne whispers urgently.

Iona reluctantly pushes herself up to a sitting position and stretches her arms over her head. Ariadne watches with greedy eyes, reminding herself that it would be unwise to pounce on Iona and let Ksenia search the forest all day if she'd like.

Iona throws on her chemise and rubs her face. Then she takes her wand from the bedside table. Ariadne reaches for her hand and tucks her hair behind her ear.

"I need you to distract them while I sneak down the hall," Ariadne says.

"Okay," Iona says.

Ariadne pulls out her wand but before she can cast the invisibility spell, Iona traps her lips with a long, sensual kiss that takes Ariadne's breath away.

"Now you may go," Iona says.

Ariadne grins and makes herself invisible as Iona opens her door.

"What is going on?" Iona asks, feigning innocence.

"What did you do to her now," Ksenia snarls.

Ariadne tip toes around Iona and down the hall towards the staircase.

"To whom?" Iona asks.

"To Ariadne, of course," Ksenia says impatiently.

"I haven't the faintest idea where she is. Could she still be in the forest?" Iona asks.

"Verità!" Ksenia says.

Ariadne's stomach drops.

"Zárolt!" Mrs. Ainsley incants in the nick of time, blocking Ksenia's spell before it hit Iona.

Ariadne lets out her breath in a panicked gasp that she hopes no one heard. Iona looks to Mrs. Ainsley gratefully.

"Do not cast spells on other students," Mrs. Ainsley snaps at Ksenia, "I am sure Ariadne will return soon."

Ariadne glances around to be sure no one is looking, undoes her invisibility spell, and turns the corner as if she had just walked back from the forest.

"Looking for me?" Ariadne asks.

"Ariadne," Ksenia says, relief in her expression.

"My great aunt kept me up all night with endless questions," Ariadne lies, yawning for affect, "I am exhausted."

"Of course, you are, dearie," Mrs. Ainsley coos, "Go on off to bed. You will feel better after getting some shuteye."

Ariadne freezes and realizes her mistake too late.

"My morning class is starting soon so I best get ready, and I can sleep in the afternoon," Ariadne says, trying to act less exhausted.

"Nonsense. Practicing magic when you are sleep deprived is dangerous. You must rest now, and your professors will excuse you," Mrs. Ainsley says.

"Oh... okay," Ariadne says, hiding her annoyance.

"There see? What did I tell you, Ksenia. You mustn't let things get you so riled up. It is bad for the digestion," Mrs. Ainsley says wisely.

Ksenia glares at her and approaches Ariadne. Iona reluctantly slips back into her room to get ready for class.

"Are you sure you are alright?" Ksenia asks.

"Yes, thank you for your concern. I am touched," Ariadne says.

"Your mother would turn my skin inside out if anything happened to you," Ksenia says dismissively, "I was sure it was

Iona again. She is such a nuisance. I do not believe a word that comes out of her mouth."

Ariadne is taken aback by the hatred overflowing from Ksenia's blue eyes.

"Iona did nothing that I did not deserve," Ariadne says.

Ksenia looks at her incredulously, but Ariadne continues.

"I misjudged her. We should lay off her now and maybe… we could be friends," Ariadne says.

Ksenia takes a step back and crosses her arms.

"You may do whatever you wish but I will never be friends with the likes of Iona, no matter whose bastard she is," Ksenia says.

"She is not a bastard. Her parents were married. She is a true born Lysander," Ariadne says.

"It matters not," Ksenia sniffs, "She was raised in filth and is still as common as they come. I do not associate with her kind, and neither should you. It is not how we were raised."

"Perhaps we have come of age to act better than our parents," Ariadne says.

Ksenia looks Ariadne up and down with contempt.

"Or perhaps you just want to bed her," Ksenia says.

Ariadne narrows her eyes, "No, of course not."

Ksenia narrows her eyes and scowls.

"Then put some salve on your neck before someone suspects otherwise," Ksenia says, then turns and walks away.

Ariadne flushes and reaches for her neck. She walks to a gilded mirror hanging in the hallway and sighs when she sees two rather noticeable purple bruises left by Iona's overzealous mouth.

Iona emerges from her room having hastily changed into a black dress with her hair arranged in a bun. Though Ariadne enjoyed seeing Iona in a medieval gown last night, the fashionable empire silhouette truly suits her best, even without color. Iona sneaks over to her.

"You must go to class without me," Ariadne whispers, "Also do not be cross but… Ksenia knows."

Iona sighs in disappointment.

"You left marks on my neck. She can put the pieces together," Ariadne says, "Lets speak on it later. You do not want to be late."

"I could stay behind and fake an illness," Iona suggests.

"That might arouse further suspicion. I will be here when you get back," Ariadne insists.

"Okay... I am sorry about the marks," Iona whispers with a guilty smile.

Ariadne shakes her head and grins.

"You will just need to learn to make them in more private places, like I did," Ariadne says.

"You did? Where did you..." Iona blushes and looks down at her body. Apparently in her haste she had not noticed the red and purple love bites that Ariadne had left on her inner thighs.

"I will show you later. Now go on," Ariadne insists.

Iona sighs and nods. She walks away to class and Ariadne goes to her room to apply some healing salve to her neck and take a long nap.

14 - IONA

I ona quickly learned what Mrs. Ainsley had meant about practicing magic without proper sleep. Her spells were muted, and her accuracy was lower than she was used to. Ksenia notices too and glares suspiciously at Iona throughout their enchantment and phytology classes. Iona tries to ignore it at first, then grows suspicious herself.

Ksenia would arguably be the exact kind of person to resort to dark magic. She's been egging Ariadne on in her rivalry against Iona, perhaps so she could eventually blame Ariadne for Iona's demise.

Iona tries to read Ksenia's aura, but she has it locked up tight. As if sensing Iona's attempt to intrude on her mind, Ksenia turns her head and glowers at Iona. Her menace is disconcerting, and Iona quickly looks back at her cauldron to continue brewing a healing potion.

"May we practice the blocking spell after class?" Elise asks behind Iona.

Iona turns to look at Elise, whose potion is bubbling precariously.

"I am afraid not," Iona says.

"Oh… why?" Elise asks.

"I am exhausted from Samhain last night. I am going straight to bed after this," Iona says truthfully.

"Who did you see?" Elise asks, her interest piqued.

Iona hesitates only for a moment, "I saw my mother. I did not want to say goodbye to her, so we stayed and talked for hours."

"I am glad you were able to speak with her," Elise says, "That must have been a great comfort to you."

"It was," Iona says. She cannot help but feel melancholy when recounting a meeting with her mother than never happened.

"We could brew an energy potion and you would feel better," Elise says, flipping to the recipe in her grimoire, "I would like to practice today before the assessment. I heard Ariadne is sleeping after staying out in the forest all night so she will not try to bother us."

"Oh… please forgive me but I really do require sleep," Iona says, "The potion would only delay my fatigue when I really should rest now. My magic is very weak."

What she truly wants is to sneak into Ariadne's room, but Elise did not need to know that. Their friendship has grown during their study sessions, and Iona does not want to ruin that if she can help it. She would tell Elise eventually, but not now.

"We could study tomorrow instead," Iona offers, "The test is not for two days anyhow."

Then Iona and Elise yelp when Elise's potion bubbles over and starts spewing black smoke. Iona coughs and jumps out of her chair to back away from the brew, scared that it might explode. Professor Yun approaches and levitates the pot, so it is no longer touching the broiler.

"Professor, I apologize. I swear, I followed the recipe exactly," Elise stutters.

"Elise," Yun sighs with frustration, "I know you tried. You may go. I will clean up here."

"I can help," Elise says.

"I have it well in hand," Yun says.

Elise's lip quivers with her frustration and embarrassment. She gathers her books and leaves without another word to Yun or Iona. Iona sighs, feeling sorry for Elise. She really is trying her best.

"Another Lysander meltdown," Ksenia says, glancing inside Iona's cauldron.

Iona glares at Ksenia, her fatigue making her temper short. Elise had heard Ksenia's comment before making it out of the room but did not look back or protest.

"Do you enjoy making people feel dreadful? Or is it an unfortunate compulsion?" Iona asks sardonically.

"Careful," Ksenia says, twirling her white marble wand between her fingers, "Picking a fight with me would only lead to permanent disfigurement. Your new name does not substitute the wealth of arcane knowledge that I have cultivated."

Iona narrows her eyes as fear prickles down her spine, "First you resented me for being common, now because I am a Lysander. It seems there is no pleasing you."

"I am not so easily impressed," Ksenia sniffs.

"And I am not so easily intimidated," Iona says, "Leave me and Elise alone or we shall see whose magic is stronger."

Ksenia looks her up and down, then smiles darkly as she walks away. Iona gathers her books, attempting to hide her shaking hands, and leaves the workshop. She forces herself not to run to the dormitories and attempts to appear as if Ksenia's threat did not scare the living daylights out of her. She takes a shortcut and walks along the side of the lyceum at the edge of the forest.

Suddenly, Iona cries out and falls on her hands and knees when she feels a spell hit her back. Wisp growls and barks aggressively. Before Iona can turn to see who is behind her, her surroundings morph and she feels so strange. The building on her right and the trees on her left stretch upwards higher and higher, as if she stepped inside a warped mirror-world.

When Iona looks down at her hands, they are shrinking. The white fabric of her dress becomes loose and heavy until she is so tiny that the dress consumes her completely. Iona wonders if she may shrink until she no longer exists at all, but to her relief the spell slows, then stops.

Iona freezes in terror as she hears Wisp's growls become more like roars. Iona cannot see her familiar through the fabric of her dress but can sense that she has transformed into something much bigger than a fox. Whoever Wisp is barking at runs away.

Iona is pressed down by the now heavy material of her dress. She uses all her strength to push the material up so she can stand. She is only able to lift it up so far before the weight is too much. The darkness makes it difficult to get her bearings, but she suspects that she is standing between a panel of her stays, with boning on either side.

Iona walks along the panel in search of an opening. When she reaches the edge of her stays, the fabric is thinner, and it lets light through. Iona runs toward the neckline of the dress and sighs with relief when she makes it out. A chill goes through her when she is exposed to the November air. Wrapping her arms around herself, she looks out at the grass that has become an endless green wilderness. She is only barely tall enough to see above the stalks if she goes on her tip toes.

When Iona looks back, her attacker is nowhere in sight. Iona stands frozen in place for a moment, entirely unsure of what to do next. Her wand is in her dress pocket, but it would be too large to pick up and use at her size. It would take hours to walk all the way back to the dormitories with legs so small. Someone might step on her if the cold did not freeze her to death first. She was only grateful that the weather had killed any bugs that she may have shared the grass with.

Wisp continues barking angrily next to her dress and sniffs at Iona's clothes in distress. Her bark is so loud and vicious that Iona has to press her hands over her ears. She did not know Wisp was capable of such a demonic noise that is unnatural for a regular fox. It was vicious enough that she did not blame her attacker for running away.

"Wisp!" Iona calls.

Wisp does not hear Iona's call over her incessant barking.

"Wisp, down here!" Iona calls.

Wisp's ears finally perk up in recognition and she sniffs around in earnest.

Wisp sniffs closer and closer to Iona until her nose bumps right into Iona's stomach and knocks her down. Iona squeals when the fox realizes who she is and starts licking her excitedly. The fox's tongue is so large that she quickly gets covered in fox drool and dirt.

"Wisp!" Iona cries, "Stop that right now!"

The fox licks her a few more times and then sniffs at her again. Iona grunts in frustration, then manages to stand up. She wipes Wisp's drool off of her mouth and spits. Wisp lays down in front of her and pants happily. Then Iona has an idea.

She runs to Wisp's side and grabs hold of her fur. With effort, she pulls herself up the side of the fox until she's settled behind Wisp's head.

"Wisp, find Ariadne!" Iona yells.

Wisp obediently stands and trots away towards the dormitories. Iona looks back at her dress and notices Crescentia is now standing over it with a look of horror and confusion. She leans down and gently picks up the dress as if looking for Iona within the fabric. Iona knows she must find some way to explain this to Crescentia later, but for now she is struggling to hang onto Wisp.

Iona leans into Wisp's orange fur as she runs through the courtyard, not wanting a witch to spot her in such a precarious position. The pins in her bun had not shrunk with her so her veil of red hair partially covers her from view. She sees Elise still looking sour faced as she practices her magic alone in the courtyard. Ksenia is nowhere in sight and that worries Iona.

It begins to rain and Iona flinches when freezing water pelts her back, but luckily Wisp is almost at the dormitories. Wisp runs inside while another witch exits the building. She bounds up the stairs and Iona almost gets thrown off but holds on for dear life.

Iona does not know how Wisp already knows which room Ariadne is in but to her relief, the fox runs right up to the correct door. Wisp scratches her nails against the wood to try and get Ariadne's attention.

15 - ARIADNE

A persistent noise wakes Ariadne from her nap. She sits up in bed and stares at her door. Picking up her wand, she cautiously approaches the door to open it. Wisp runs inside and barks happily. Ariadne looks down at the animal with confusion. Wisp would never go anywhere without her witch. Ariadne pokes her head out into the hallway to check if Iona was there.

"Ariadne!" a small voice says.

Ariadne looks around but no one is there.

"Down here!" the voice calls.

"Iona?" Ariadne calls back, but she still cannot see her.

"I am on Wisp's back!" Iona says.

Ariadne turns back to look at the fox and her eyes go wide. There on Wisp's back, camouflaged by her long red hair, is Iona. She is no more than three inches tall and completely naked.

Ariadne suppresses a giggle but cannot hold back her grin. She closes her bedroom door and walks over to Wisp.

"Did one of your spells go wrong?" Ariadne asks, a giggle escaping.

"Don't laugh," Iona protests.

Ariadne leans down and holds out her hand. Iona jumps onto it and Ariadne lifts her up slowly.

"Look at you. You're adorable!" Ariadne coos, gently poking her finger into Iona's ribs.

"This is not funny," Iona yells, her flush evident even in her tiny form.

"What happened, Thumbelina?" Ariadne asks.

"Someone attacked me from behind and made me shrink," Iona explains.

"Oh!" Ariadne says, her smile fading, "Who was it?"

"I could not see who they were. My dress collapsed on top of me and by the time I found my way out of it, they had run away. I think Wisp's barks scared them off," Iona says.

"Familiars can shapeshift when threatened. Wisp must have given your attacker quite a fright," Ariadne says.

Wisp jumps and Ariadne leans over to scratch behind the good fox's ears.

"I had hoped whoever set the sirens on you had given up, but it seems they were only waiting for another opportunity," Ariadne sighs, "I think I may enchant a necklace of yours with a blocking spell, so this will not happen again."

"I would appreciate that. My blocking enchantments still require work," Iona says, "It was also quite odd. I did not hear them say the spell out loud so I could not even try to recognize their voice."

Ariadne frowns at this, "I think we ought to tell one of the professors what happened."

"No, we cannot," Iona says.

"Why?" Ariadne says.

Iona hesitates and bites her lip. Ariadne walks over to her desk and tilts her hand so Iona plops onto the wood.

"What of all your talk of trust?" Ariadne asks, "Were those just empty words?"

"No, of course not, but I was told I cannot tell anyone," Iona says, standing up and putting her arms over her chest.

"By whom?" Ariadne asks.

"The ghost who visited me on Samhain," Iona says.

Ariadne considers this, now doubly curious.

"I am not inclined to help those who keep secrets from me. I hope you enjoy being that size. Perhaps I can lend you my old doll's clothes," Ariadne says, hoping Iona will believe her bluff.

"You would not leave me like this," Iona says, but her voice wavers.

"I'll take you to class in my pocket and play with you when I'm bored," Ariadne says, grinning and shrugging her shoulders, "Who has not once dreamed of having a living doll? I can braid your hair and feed you crumbs."

Iona sighs with exasperation, "I will just have Wisp take me to Crescentia instead. Or Elise."

"Will you now?" Ariadne asks.

Before Iona can scurry off, Ariadne scoops her up and playfully hangs her upside down by her ankle. Iona yelps and tries to struggle but she's stuck dangling there.

"Let me go!" Iona growls.

"You are in no position to make demands, nymph," Ariadne says.

"Are you truly asking me to break my word with a powerful ghost?" Iona says.

"What promise did you make exactly?" Ariadne asks.

"I was told not to tell anyone that we'd spoken and be careful who I trust," Iona says.

"Then you can tell me what you spoke about. You just cannot tell me who told you," Ariadne says, "That is if you do trust me as you claim."

Iona considers this, "I suppose you're right."

"Out with it then," Ariadne demands.

"Ariadne... I do not want to involve you in this unnecessarily. It could be dangerous," Iona protests.

"Now that I think of it, it may be too difficult for a young student like me to unshrink you. We ought to consult a professor for assistance, maybe Salvador?" Ariadne taps her chin.

"Fine! Fine," Iona relents, "I was warned that there is a malefician somewhere in the college. They are targeting me because they want the pendant, and they think I am their competition."

Ariadne almost drops Iona as cold dread fills her. She gently places Iona back into the palm of her hand, so she is no longer dangling upside down.

"A malefician?" Ariadne whispers.

"That is what I was told," Iona says.

"Why did you wait to tell me this? Do you know what sort of danger you are in?" Ariadne snaps, "That shrinking spell could have been infinitely worse. If Wisp had not been there and they had managed to capture you in a jar or a cage, you would have been completely trapped with no magic. They could have done any number of things to hurt you."

Ariadne puts her hand over her mouth as the terrible possibilities flood her mind. This was more sinister than she could have ever imagined.

"Ariadne," Iona says, "It is okay. I am fine. Just please unshrink me. I am so discombobulated, and it is very cold."

"Of course," Ariadne says, "I would never leave you like that."

Ariadne sets Iona back on the desk and opens her phytology grimoire. She remembers reading of a potion that can undo sizing spells. She flips a page, and the wind knocks Iona down onto the desk.

"Sorry!" Ariadne cringes.

"Being this small is horrid. I do not know how anyone could stand it," Iona grumbles.

"If I am unable to set you to rights, perhaps a colony of pixies would adopt you," Ariadne chuckles, then remembers, "Wait, where did you say your clothes were?"

"Outside in the grass to the right of the lyceum," Iona says.

"I should go and fetch them before anyone sees and wonders where you are," Ariadne says.

"Crescentia already found them right when I'd left on Wisp," Iona says, "Hopefully she did not tell anyone."

"You can explain later," Ariadne says, frowning, "I shall return shortly. Do not move or fall until then."

Ariadne leaves Aster behind as a guard and conjures an umbrella before stepping outside. She runs through the rain to the lyceum until she finds Iona's discarded clothes in the mud. She looks around to see if anyone is lurking about, then leans over to gather the dress in her arms. She is relieved to feel Iona's wand is still in her pocket.

When Ariadne makes it back to her room, Iona is curiously inspecting her inner thighs and running her fingers along the purple bruises Ariadne had made. Iona quickly closes her legs and pretends that she was only standing there silently. Ariadne suppresses a smile as she tosses the dress onto her bed and returns to her grimoire. She finds the potion she was searching for and gathers the ingredients from her kit.

"Can you not just undo the spell?" Iona asks.

"If I knew the exact spell she'd cast, I could undo it, but there are many different versions. Saying the spell in the wrong language or using a different version of the spell altogether, might just make you shrink even smaller until I cannot see you," Ariadne says, "A potion is a much safer option even if it takes longer. I would rather not take any chances."

"Very well," Iona says, leaning her elbow on her knee and cradling her head in her hand.

"Serves you right for thinking you could discover and face a malefician on your own," Ariadne scoffs.

"I was told it would be dangerous. I did not want to involve anyone else," Iona says.

"Do you truly understand how dangerous this is?" Ariadne asks, "Did your ghost tell you?"

"They told me that a malefician ignores the balance of nature, and they are difficult to identify," Iona says, "What more should I know?"

Ariadne stirs her potion as it brews and collects her thoughts. She does not want to frighten Iona, but it would be worse for Iona to be ignorant of her predicament. Iona sits back on her feet and looks up at her with apprehension.

"I do not have extensive knowledge on the subject. I only know what my mother told me and what I've read in books," Ariadne says, "They are called by many names, malefician, maléfique, maleficiare... They are evil witches who practice magic with the sole purpose of harming another."

Ariadne breaks off pieces of rosemary and stirs it into her brew.

"Dark magic, also called maleficium or goetia, is inordinately powerful. The tradeoff is that it poisons the user the more they practice it and can make them go mad," Ariadne explains, "Hubris convinces the witch that they can handle it until it is too late, and they've lost all control. This witch appears to be new to using maleficium... though it seems they are strong enough not to require their wand to cast spells. That makes them much more dangerous. They can attack silently, and you will not know what magic they throw at you until you are already affected by it."

Ariadne sighs with frustration, wishing again that Iona had told her of this sooner.

"They are starting with detached, simple spells so far but in time, they may become vicious and bloodthirsty. Soon they will not be casting shrinking spells to trap you. They may try a leeching curse or a wraith curse or something equally dreadful," Ariadne says.

"What spells are those?" Iona asks.

"The leeching curse allows a malefician to devour another witch's magic. It can leave a witch without any magic left for the rest of their life," Ariadne says, "A wraith curse takes control of a person's soul and forces them to obey the caster's every whim. They become a phantom, forever tied to the malefician, and cursed to perform magic on their behalf as they wither away but can never die."

Iona's face goes pale with fear, "That is terrifying."

"I cannot even make you a protection amulet now. Maleficium can break right through that sort of enchantment," Ariadne sighs.

"Blocking spells will not work?" Iona asks incredulously.

"The spell works part of the time, depending on the strength of the witch casting it. Blocking enchantments on objects are easily broken. The magic is not as strong," Ariadne says, "It can take entire covens of witches to take down just one malefician, especially if they have been practicing dark magic for years. Your best chance of taking down a malefician is to catch them by surprise and attack before they do."

Iona seems to understand now what she is up against and looks completely downtrodden.

"But do not fret. Now that I know, I will help you find the witch and we can defeat her together before she becomes too strong," Ariadne says.

She puts her finger under Iona's tiny chin and makes her look up.

"I will not let anything happen to you," Ariadne vows.

"If I had known how dangerous this was, I never would have told you," Iona says, her voice trembling.

"Do not worry about me," Ariadne says, then goes back to her potion, "Is there anyone who you suspect?"

Iona thinks for a moment and reluctantly says, "Ksenia has been increasingly antagonistic towards me. She threatened me in phytology class today right before I was attacked. I stood up to her but that may have gotten me shrunk."

Ariadne blinks in surprise.

"But I told her to leave you be," Ariadne says.

"Ksenia has only doubled her efforts to bully me and Elise. I know she is your friend but... she frightens me," Iona says.

"I shall talk to her," Ariadne says, her voice hard.

"No, I do not want to tempt her to attack again in earnest. I think we ought to observe those we suspect and see what we can uncover," Iona says, "Perhaps if we determine who the malefician is, gather evidence, and present it to a professor, they can handle it for us. For now, we have no proof."

Ariadne stirs her potions and says, "I do not blame you for thinking of Ksenia first. She would be an obvious suspect given her low opinion of you. However, you should not rule out anyone who may be pretending to be kind. A malefician can be very skilled at concealing themselves in plain sight. If the witch is trying to attack and get away with it, they may not be obvious about their hatred for you. It could be Kokuro or Phoebe. Gisela does not appear deft enough to attempt this, but it is not impossible. Perhaps Nenet... but she always seems to rise above such things. It could be Elise, but her magic is so impotent. Samaira detests dark magic, so I would not easily suspect her. It could very well be Crescentia."

"Crescentia would never," Iona says.

"You said she found your dress, but she has not alerted anyone of your disappearance. Why would she stay silent? Why was she walking around the side of the building in the first place?" Ariadne asks.

"Possibly for the same reason I was, taking a shortcut," Iona says.

"Possibly," Ariadne says.

Iona looks away with a frown. Ariadne finishes her potion and stirs it until she is satisfied with the consistency. Then she doublechecks the instructions.

"For this potion to work, you need to be completely coated in it," Ariadne says.

"I cannot just drink it?" Iona whines.

"No, it needs to sink into your skin," Ariadne says.

Iona sighs heavily and stands up.

"Thank you, Ariadne, for making me my normal size again," Ariadne says as she scoops Iona up.

"Thank you," Iona mumbles.

"You're welcome," Ariadne says with a grin.

She takes her cauldron by the handle and goes to the bathroom. Then she carefully sets Iona on the tiled floor and puts the cauldron next to her.

"Ready?" Ariadne asks.

When Iona nods, Ariadne uses a ladle to pour the green potion all over Iona. When she is completely smothered in it, Ariadne takes a step back. Iona grows taller and taller until she is her normal size once more.

"Ugh... this is revolting," Iona whines, holding her potion

coated arms away from her body.

"Use the bath to wash off the excess," Ariadne says.

Iona turns on the tap and waits for the bath to fill up. Meanwhile, Ariadne admires the shape of Iona's bottom and feels her desire stir again.

"I can feel your stare," Iona says, looking over her shoulder at Ariadne with a coquettish grin.

"If you were not covered in potion slime, I would be touching you too," Ariadne says.

Iona chuckles shyly and looks back at the bath. She quickly reaches for the faucet before the tub overflows. Then she steps inside and dips her head under the water. Bubbles rise to the surface as the tub begins scrubbing her. Iona's head pops back up and she already looks cleaner.

"I do not know if I will ever get used to these bathtubs," Iona says.

"What do you mean? It's a normal bath," Ariadne says, walking over to her. She sits next to the tub, leans her arm against the edge, and rests her chin against her arm.

"I did not grow up with magical bathtubs. We simply cleaned ourselves," Iona says, then giggles sharply and tries to pull her foot away from the sponge.

"Oh, I see. I always had one," Ariadne grins.

"Lucky you," Iona says wryly, then giggles again and sighs angrily, "I would never willingly have one of these in my home. Especially after your hex. It ruined the experience for me."

"It was not that bad... was it?" Ariadne winces.

"Even the whites of my eyes were red! The shock of it was almost worse than being shrunk," Iona gripes.

"Would it be any excuse to mention that I was drunk when I cast it?" Ariadne chuckles with embarrassment.

"I should have known. Only someone quite belligerent would have thought of such a bizarre hex," Iona giggles.

"I would use the word creative," Ariadne grins.

It is so difficult to believe that they had bullied each other not long ago. It seems so foolish and melodramatic now.

The bath finishes cleaning Iona, and the bubbles subside. The water filtered itself out and is crystal clear. Iona sighs contentedly and leans back. Then she looks at Ariadne with contrition.

"Are you still angry with me?" Iona asks in a small voice.

"I am not angry," Ariadne says.

"Do not make me cast another truth spell," Iona raises an eyebrow.

Ariadne chuckles and looks down at the tiled floor, "I was upset... I shudder to think what could have happened. If I had known, I would have insisted on accompanying you to class no matter what Ainsley said."

"I am sorry... I should have told you," Iona says.

Iona reaches out and caresses Ariadne's cheek.

"I am glad that I do not have to face this all alone," Iona whispers.

Ariadne turns her head to kiss the center of Iona's palm, then kisses up Iona's arm, before kissing her lips. She stands and pulls off her nightdress.

"Lean forward," Ariadne instructs.

Ariadne points her wand at the tub and says, "Megálo,"

The bath grows in size until it is big enough to fit both of them. Ariadne steps in behind Iona and sits in the water. Ariadne coaxes Iona backwards so she leans against Ariadne's chest and tilts her head to kiss her softly.

Ariadne looks down at Iona's body, deciding what she wants to do to her first. The surface of the water just barely touches Iona's pink nipples, and her legs are pressed together in anticipation. Ariadne kisses along Iona's neck until she sighs and relaxes.

Ariadne reaches around Iona to palm her breasts. She rolls both nipples between her fingers, plucking and teasing them until Iona's breathing deepens. Her fingers dance over Iona's ribs and stomach without going much lower than her navel. Iona's hips rise up impatiently, searching for Ariadne's fingers.

Ariadne moves her hands back up to Iona's breasts and she

sighs in disappointment. Ariadne grins and plants soft kisses on her cheek, neck, and shoulder. She plays with Iona's breasts until her legs fall wide open and she is ready for her.

Ariadne traces the purple splotches on Iona's inner thighs playfully, enjoying how Iona squirms at her light touches.

"I could give you a healing salve to remove these marks," Ariadne says.

Iona considers for a moment, then says, "No, I like them."

Ariadne grins and kisses Iona's cheek, "I like them, too."

When Ariadne does slide her hand down to stroke between Iona's opened thighs, she ghosts her middle and ring finger along her folds, circling the nub at the top. She gradually increases the pressure until Iona is moaning her name and arching her back, so her hard nipples point towards the ceiling.

"I'd like to try something," Ariadne whispers in Iona's ear.

"Like what?" Iona breathes.

Ariadne moves her fingers down to circle Iona's entrance. She tenses and Ariadne kisses her shoulder soothingly.

"I've never," Iona says.

"I know. I will go slow," Ariadne whispers, "until you beg me to go faster."

"I won't beg," Iona grumbles, then inhales sharply when Ariadne nips at her neck, then sucks where she'd bitten until Iona whimpers.

"Sure, you won't, nymph," Ariadne chuckles.

Ariadne's fingers circle Iona's hole again, teasing her patiently. Then she presses her finger inside only barely. Iona clenches her muscles and Ariadne sucks on her neck until she relaxes again. Ariadne presses her finger in a little more, and a little more, until she's able to stroke her gently. She moves slowly, deliberately, so Iona can grow accustomed to the feeling. In time, Iona's muscles relax, letting Ariadne delve in deeper.

Ariadne finds a particularly sensitive spot inside Iona that makes her tense in surprise, then moan as Ariadne strokes lazily in the same spot over and over. Iona's core stretches and compresses around her finger as her hips grind against Ariadne's hand of their own accord. Ariadne forces herself to hold back, not wanting this to end so soon. Iona whimpers, but Ariadne keeps her pace and adds the slightest bit of pressure.

"Does it feel good?" Ariadne asks.

"Yes," Iona sighs.

"Would you like me to go faster?" Ariadne asks.

Iona only nods, her eyes squeezed shut and her mouth falling open to gasp for air.

"Beg," Ariadne whispers.

"No, you arrogant lout," Iona growls.

Iona whimpers when Ariadne removes her fingers and circles her nub ever so softly. That combined with the mysterious magic between them makes Iona's breathing stutter.

"You are so irritating," Iona groans.

Ariadne pushes a finger back inside and Iona gasps.

"I could play with your pretty cunt for hours and never get enough. I think I shall, just to see how desperate I can make you," Ariadne whispers in her ear.

Iona's core clenches at Ariadne's words. Ariadne grins against the skin of her neck. Iona's legs press together when Ariadne's finger strokes harder for just a moment, then slows down again.

"Beg, darling," Ariadne whispers again, "Ask me nicely to give you what you want."

Ariadne tries inserting her ring finger too and Iona whimpers at the feeling of being stretched. She strokes Iona until she's quivering and clutching the sides of the bathtub.

"Ariadne," Iona whines.

"Iona?" Ariadne grins, pressing a gentle kiss on her pulse point.

"Please," Iona whimpers.

"Please what?" Ariadne asks.

"Please give me what I want. I need you, please," Iona says in a small, needy voice.

Ariadne thrusts her fingers in and out, no longer holding back, and Iona moans in relief. Ariadne puts her spare hand over Iona's throat and squeezes slightly while moving deep inside of her.

Iona's hips undulate so brazenly that water spills from the tub and onto the tile floor. Ariadne does not stop until Iona is crying out her pleasure. She moves her hand from Iona's throat to her mouth to stifle her scream.

Ariadne gently removes her fingers from Iona's constricting channel and drifts her hands up and down her body as she recovers.

"I told you you'd beg," Ariadne whispers in Iona's ear.

"I swear Ariadne..." Iona sighs, "You take everything as a bloody challenge."

"And I always win," Ariadne grins.

Iona turns around to straddle Ariadne's lap. She leans in and licks at Ariadne's bottom lip while placing both her hands on Ariadne's breasts.

When they kiss, Iona presses their sensitive nubs together and circles her hips like Ariadne had taught her last night. Ariadne moans into Iona's mouth, not expecting the intense jolt of pleasure that runs through her. She snakes a hand behind Iona's neck, her other hand on Iona's hip, gripping her as she grinds her hips round and round. Iona braces one hand on the edge of the tub and her other hand on Ariadne's shoulder.

Ariadne thrusts against her from below until Iona cries out. She throws her head back and moans. Ariadne takes the opportunity to suck one of her nipples deep into her mouth. The water splashes around them as their hips move faster and their pleasure builds until their desperate cries create salacious harmonies that echo off the bathroom walls.

Ariadne gazes up at Iona as she falls apart before her. Her full breasts bouncing with every thrust, her eyes squeezed shut, her lips parted, and her fiery hair falling in wet tendrils over her shoulders and chest.

Ariadne climaxes soon after and Iona slumps against her, out of breath and satiated. The tub senses that they are done and drains on its own. Hot air envelopes them to dry them off. Iona buries her face in Ariadne's neck until it's over. Her breathing slows until Ariadne thinks she may have drifted off. Then Ariadne coaxes Iona up and leads her to the bed where they curl up together in peaceful sleep.

Ariadne gasps awake from another nightmare. The sound of rushing water and creaking wood still rings in her ears. Her entire body trembles from fear.

"Whatever is wrong?" Iona asks, having been jostled awake.

Ariadne swallows hard and forces her breathing to slow.

"Nothing, go back to sleep," Ariadne whispers.

Iona rests her head back on Ariadne's chest.

"Your heart is racing," Iona says, "Did you have a nightmare?"

"Yes, but I am fine," Ariadne says.

Iona lifts her head again to look down on Ariadne.

"What was the dream about?" Iona asks.

"I'd rather not discuss it," Ariadne says, a little sharper than she intended.

"Alright," Iona says, lowering her head back down.

Ariadne looks up at the ceiling, then she closes her eyes and fights back tears.

"Ariadne," Iona says softly, feeling how tense Ariadne has become.

Ariadne presses her fingers into her eyes to try and stop the tears from coming. Iona pulls her hand away and looks up at her with concern.

"I have had the same nightmare since I was fourteen. Trapped and drowning," Ariadne whispers.

Ariadne takes a shuddering breath to try and calm herself.

"The worst part is the screaming, mine and hers," Ariadne whispers.

Iona reaches up to caress Ariadne's cheek. She does not have words, only compassion in her eyes. Ariadne's instinct is to turn to stone when someone looks at her in such a way but after all these years, she just wants to be comforted. She lets Iona shift their bodies, so Ariadne's head is resting on Iona's soft chest.

Iona presses kisses to her forehead, whispering to her that the dream is over and there is nothing to fear. Ariadne's fingertips trace idle patterns along Iona's breasts and stomach until her eyelids get heavier. Iona strokes Ariadne's hair until she is lulled back to sleep.

Professor Pari has invited her students to a special night class in the courtyard. She explains the wisdom of the stars above them and how to read the constellations.

"Stars are able to give you hints of the future if you are able to speak their language. Knowing the stars by name and the patterns they follow can help to unlock their secrets," Professor Pari says, "There are star maps in your grimoires that you can reference. Take this hour to look up at the sky and see what the stars would like to say to you."

Ariadne and Iona lay down in the grass side by side. The other witches are spread out across the courtyard, some in pairs and others by themselves. The college has extinguished all the lamps and candles for the duration of the class so the stars can be fully visible and easily read.

"What did you decide to tell Crescentia?" Ariadne asks.

"I told her that I'd tried a shrinking spell for the first time, but I'd botched it and had to run to Elise for help. She laughed for ten minutes straight," Iona rolls her eyes and grins, "She'd left my dress there in case I came back for it. I caught her right before she told a professor I was missing. She was worried sick."

"She believed that Elise could undo the spell properly?" Ariadne asks dubiously.

"Now, now, Elise has been improving lately. Everyone should show her more compassion," Iona says, "It is awful to be so constantly discredited by your peers. Trust me."

Ariadne concedes and they both go silent as they gaze at the night sky above them. Iona has her grimoire open to compare the sky with the charts.

"What do you see?" Iona asks.

"Jupiter and Venus are very close together," Ariadne says, pointing at the two twinkling planets directly above them.

"What does that mean?" Iona asks.

"It can mean harmony and peace. It may be easier to recognize beauty in life," Ariadne says, "What is your astrological sign?"

"Libra," Iona says.

"Interesting…" Ariadne says.

"Interesting how?" Iona prompts.

"Venus is in Libra. Jupiter is in Aries, which is my sign. For them to conjunct like that, it is interesting," Ariadne says.

"The stars know we are together?" Iona asks in awe.

"I do not put a lot of stock in astrology but at times it can reflect life in surprising ways," Ariadne says.

"Is it rare for Venus and Jupiter to align?" Iona asks.

"No, it happens every few years. A rarer conjunction is Jupiter and Saturn. It only happens once every twenty years and is said to mark a new period of history," Ariadne says.

"When will that happen?" Iona asks.

Ariadne lifts her grimoire up to read the charts. She creates a small marble of light and holds it up to the page.

"It is happening next year in May, or maybe June," Ariadne says.

They both glance sideways at each other but do not say a word. Ariadne had been careful to follow Iona's rule and not mention the pendant around her. They did not need to say the words to acknowledge the significance of this celestial event.

"Our planets have literally aligned," Iona whispers, "That is so romantic."

Ariadne chuckles and says, "You should learn more about the stars if they impress you that much."

"I think I shall," Iona grins.

Ariadne looks over at Iona as she admires the light of Venus and Jupiter.

"What else do you see?" Iona asks.

Ariadne scans the heavens for anything she may have missed.

"Lupus and Vulpecula are mirroring each other," Ariadne says.

She traces the Lupus constellation for Iona and says, "That is Lupus, the wolf."

She traces the Vulpecula constellation and says, "That is Vulpecula, the fox."

"Aster and Wisp," Iona grins.

"That is unusual. Normally those constellations are not so visible in November," Ariadne says.

Iona inches her hand closer to Ariadne's, then entwines their fingers. Ariadne looks down at their joined hands and lets out a stressful sigh.

"What is wrong?" Iona asks.

"Nothing," Ariadne says, looking back at the stars.

"You can tell me," Iona says.

"It is nothing, I am just… anxious. I feel like I cannot let you out of my sight or you will be attacked again," Ariadne admits, "From now on, you should not be isolated for too long. Stay with Elise or Crescentia whenever I am otherwise engaged. Do not go on walks in the woods alone anymore. And we should stay in the same room every night in case someone attempts to sneak in while you're asleep."

Iona grins, "That is only an excuse to share a bed with me every night."

"For protection," Ariadne reiterates but she mirrors Iona's grin.

"Whatever you say," Iona shrugs, "You shall hear no complaints from me."

16 – ARIADNE

A riadne curls her fingers into Iona just as she sucks hard on her pulsing bud. Iona moans and throws her arms over her head, grinding herself into Ariadne's face. Ariadne reaches up with her free hand to squeeze Iona's breast and pinch her nipple. Iona puts her hand over Ariadne's and moans again from deep in her chest.

Ariadne had been sure to cast enchantments on both her and Iona's rooms to mute any sounds from within. Iona's impassioned cries would have woken the entire campus otherwise. They had found it quite easy to share the same room every night but found it difficult to actually sleep.

"Ariadne," Iona moans, knowing how much Ariadne loves hearing her name on Iona's lips.

Ariadne rewards her by inserting a third finger and stroking her faster. Iona almost weeps as her pleasure overflows and her walls compress around Ariadne's fingers. Then Ariadne slowly crawls up Iona's body and steals a final kiss. She lays on her back and lets Iona catch her breath.

Iona's room is much warmer now that Ariadne had conjured a fireplace. The flickering flames make dancing shadows on the walls. Ariadne's thoughts drift and Iona sighs.

"What are you thinking of?" Iona murmurs.

"The malefician. They've gone quiet again and I do not like it," Ariadne says.

"You'd rather they continue attacking me?" Iona asks.

"No, of course not, but whenever they pause in their attacks, they are likely performing rituals to strengthen their magic. Mutilating animals, bathing in their blood, meditating on forbidden spells... the next time you face them they may be stronger," Ariadne warns.

Iona tenses beside Ariadne. When Ariadne turns to look at her, Iona's brows are furrowed as she struggles to remember something important.

"I saw a dead winged horse just moments before the sirens attacked me," Iona whispers, "Its stomach was ripped open, and its eyes were gouged out."

Ariadne looks down at Iona incredulously, "You did?"

"I almost forgot about the wretched creature. The sirens sang to me right after I discovered it and my thoughts were no longer lucid," Iona says, "There was a symbol written above it in the bark of a tree, but I could not gaze upon it."

Iona shivers at the memory. Ariadne immediately draws Iona closer until she is nestled against her chest. Iona sighs with renewed contentment.

"That is... ghastly. The malefician must have used the animal for a ritual to grow her power. I wonder if perhaps she used the magic that she'd gained to force the sirens to seek you out and kill you," Ariadne says.

"I think so too," Iona whispers, "Have you been observing Ksenia and Samaira?"

"Yes. They are not showing any signs, but it is difficult to tell. Have you checked on Crescentia and Elise?" Ariadne asks.

"Yes, and I do not see how or why they would do something like this. I am wondering if it could be a witch we are not as closely acquainted with," Iona says.

"It's possible. It would be easier to torment someone you do not know," Ariadne says.

"Are there any witches that you think could be capable of it?" Iona asks.

"I have wondered if Gisela would be capable of this, or

Nenet for that matter" Ariadne muses, "Though the more I consider it, the more I am unsure. They are both clever, Nenet especially."

Iona worries at her bottom lip in contemplation.

"There is a Peruvian witch, Yoselin, who was rumored to have tried to maim her older sister because she was worried that she would claim the p-," Ariadne almost says but stops herself, "She was worried her older sister would attend Lysander College before her and she would lose her chance at taking the trials. It turned out she should not have worried because her sister failed in her attempt, but it has ruined their relationship irreparably."

"That's awful…" Iona says.

"A witch from Greenland, Yuka, tried to summon a monster but lost control of it," Ariadne says, "Kokuro accidentally poisoned her cousin with a new potion she formulated but some have speculated that it was purposeful. Fortunately, her cousin survived but can no longer see out of her left eye."

"This is impossible," Iona grumbles, "It could be anyone."

"We will find them. It's only a matter of time before they make a mistake or grow too impatient. We shall be ready," Ariadne says.

The next day, Ariadne was glad to be distracted by her studies. Professor Lysander had asked them to gather in the courtyard for a special lesson on flight. When his students gather around him, he has taken his blazer off and has it folded in the grass in front of him.

"Can we not use brooms to fly?" Vadoma asks.

"Certainly, but there will be times when you need to travel quickly and do not have a broom handy. In the event of that happening, I have a conjuration trick," Samuel says, "There is always more than one method or spell to solve a problem."

Samuel points his wand at his back and incants, "Sciathháin."

A pair of fluffy white wings grow from his back until they are each at least ten feet long. They rip through his white shirt, but he is undeterred.

"Do not fret about your dresses. We will repair them when we descend," Samuel says, "Morgan herself used wings to fly. Her fae magic made her a natural shapeshifter. We can emulate her preferred method of travel by using this spell."

Samuel folds his wings against his back so he can walk around and help the witches create their own. Ariadne casts the spell and slumps forward from the heaviness of the massive white wings. She reaches out to stroke the soft feathers. Iona casts the spell too and her wings sprout in seconds.

Ariadne noticed their powers were growing substantially stronger, especially Iona's. This was partly because they were learning and practicing magic by day, but by night their transmundane magnetism is creating so much excess energy that even complex spells seem like mere trifles.

When all the witches have their wings, Samuel has them spread far apart and practice stretching and tilting the wings with the newly constructed muscles in their shoulders. Then Samuel allows them to test their wings but only to float above the ground.

"Alright, I believe we are ready to take flight. I would like you to please not stray too far and practice caution. You have all the time in the world to perform daredevil maneuvers but today, we will be safe above all else," Samuel says sternly.

He flaps his wings steadily and vigorously and he encourages the other witches to follow. Ariadne flaps and breaks a sweat as she leaves the ground behind. Samuel pulls out his wand.

"Ánemos!" he yells, and a gust of wind propels them upwards into the clouds.

Ariadne laughs as she glides through the air. The afternoon sun lights up the cumulonimbus clouds in pretty oranges and yellows. The air is cool and thin but the effort it takes to flap her wings makes her body warm up on its own. Below them, the mountain peaks are covered in blankets of snow.

In the vastness of the open sky, all the witches disperse and find their own area to explore. Ariadne squints to try and spot Iona. She finds her to the east, twirling and gliding as if she had been flying all her life. Her black dress contrasts with the orange cloud behind her. Ariadne glides over to her and when she is close enough, she can hear Iona's laughter ringing over the sound of wind.

"This is incredible!" she yells, twirling downwards only to flap her way back up and fall downwards again.

Ariadne grabs her hand and falls through the air with her. Ariadne points her wand toward the ground and yells, "Ánemos!"

Iona screams and laughs when a gust of wind propels them back up.

"Do that again!" Iona yells.

"You try it!" Ariadne calls over the rush of air.

"We are not supposed to practice the air spell until Spring," Iona says, "You already know how it works."

"You are strong enough to try," Ariadne says, "Unless you are too scared."

Iona scrunches her eyebrows and looks down at the ground. She pulls out her wand and points it below them.

"Ánemos!" Iona yells.

They both scream when an impressive gust of wind propels them up and away from each other. Ariadne laughs and with effort she rights herself and glides on her wings. She looks around to see where Iona had ended up. Her heart stops when she sees Iona still spiraling down towards earth.

"Iona!" Ariadne screams, angling her wings to dive towards her.

"Help!" Iona cries. She is trying to stretch her wings and stop her descent but anytime she tries, the air spins her about and she gets confused again.

They fall below the clouds and Ariadne's fear is heightened as the mountain range gets closer and closer. She slams into Iona and uses her wings to stop her out of control spinning.

Then when she has her bearings, she stretches out her wings right before they plummet into the peak of a snow-covered mountain.

Iona wraps her arms tightly around Ariadne's neck as she cradles Iona's body against her chest. Iona is speechless and trembling with fear. Ariadne flies around the mountain and with effort she carries them both back up into the clouds.

"That was close," Ariadne says nervously, "Are you alright?"

"Uh huh," Iona says.

Ariadne holds back a nervous laugh.

"Are you laughing?" Iona asks incredulously, "You almost killed me!"

"You almost killed yourself. It was your spell," Ariadne argues.

"A spell you convinced me to attempt in the middle of the sky," Iona points out.

"You could use some practice," Ariadne says and laughs when Iona shoves her shoulder, "Are you well enough to fly again?"

Iona nods tentatively. Ariadne holds Iona's hand to steady her as she stretches her wings and glides beside her. They fly in tandem, and Iona does not let go of Ariadne's hand. They look like angels flying in and out of clouds.

By the end of class, Iona seems reluctant to return to campus. Ariadne is relieved that she hasn't inadvertently ruined the experience of flying for her.

"Tomorrow after class, I am going to practice with Elise in the incantation chamber. Would you like to join us?" Iona mumbles.

She lays limp across Ariadne's chest after having quite a violent climax that left her boneless.

"Sure," Ariadne says.

"It will not be awkward for you?" Iona asks.

"No. Not for me. I am sure when we eventually tell her about us, it will be awkward for a while," Ariadne says.

"I worry about that at times," Iona sighs, "I do not want her to feel betrayed by my actions."

"You cannot control how she reacts," Ariadne says.

"That is true... but I do not want to ruin our new friendship. I never had a cousin before," Iona says.

"The fortunate thing about family, and at times the most unfortunate; the bonds are not so easily broken," Ariadne says ruefully, "Whatever happens, it can be fixed with time."

"I supposed you are right," Iona says, curling in closer to Ariadne.

"Now sleep and do not worry," Ariadne whispers, pressing a kiss to Iona's forehead.

They both drift off within minutes. Ariadne dreams of running through the forest with Iona. What they are running from, she does not know. Iona trips and Ariadne pulls her back onto her feet to keep running. They both fall into a small glade where the grass is soft and littered with red wildflowers. Beams of moonlight break through the canopy of leaves and shine down onto them.

Ariadne jerks awake. She sighs with relief when she sees her familiar wallpaper and furnishings. She lets her breath slow as she stares at the ceiling. Then she looks down at herself again and sits straight up in bed. Iona is not there with her. The space beside her is empty and cold.

"Iona," Ariadne whispers.

No one answers. She jumps out of bed and though the bathroom door is open, she checks inside just in case. She quickly pulls on a nightdress, throws her bedroom door open, and looks up and down the empty hall. She runs back into her room to find a cloak and a pair of boots from her wardrobe. She takes her wand from her bedside table and notices that Iona's wand is still there. Then she checks the floor and sees that Wisp is gone. Aster looks up at her and whines. Ariadne rushes down the hall with Aster close behind.

When she makes it outside, she looks around the courtyard and calls, "Iona!"

Not a sound. The first snowflakes of winter flurry around her as she searches for any sign of Iona.

A blood curdling screech cuts through the silence and makes Ariadne flinch. The distant sound is coming from deep within the forest.

"Ariadne!" Iona screams.

"Iona!" Ariadne calls.

Ariadne sprints at full speed into the trees with her wand drawn. Iona's screams reverberate through the trees and though Ariadne's limbs scream at her in protest, she runs even faster toward the sound.

The ground turns from dirt to shifting stones as she breaks through the trees. A wide river stretches out before her, the water dark and murky. About forty paces from the riverbank is a wooden box bobbing precariously in the water. Ariadne's blood turns to ice when she hears someone pounding against the wood.

"Ariadne!" Iona cries, her voice muted by her wooden cage that is filling with water.

"No!" Ariadne screams. She runs into the water, ignoring its frozen sting on her legs as she wades deeper towards the box. Aster remains by the shore and barks savagely.

"Izrezati!" Ariadne yells.

The cutting spell makes a gash in the wood but does not break all the way through.

"Izrezati!" Ariadne yells again, tears falling down her cheeks.

The spell only barely makes a slice through the wood. This cannot be happening again.

"Ariadne, please help! She is here!" Iona screams.

Ariadne racks her brain for any spell that might work.

"Kuelea!" Ariadne yells.

The box stops sinking and floats in place. Ariadne sighs with relief.

"I have to cut through," Ariadne yells, "Go against the far wall. I do not want to hurt you."

Ariadne sees the box shift backwards as Iona moves.

"Please get me out," Iona sobs.

"I will, just stay calm!" Ariadne says.

She throws the cutting spell at the box over and over until the wood splinters and she makes a hole big enough for Iona to squeeze through.

"Can you crawl out?" Ariadne asks, about to poke her head into the hole.

Iona grabs Ariadne violently, pulling her inside the box. Ariadne screams and tries to pull away, but Iona is inhumanly strong. Her eyes are black orbs, and her teeth are pointed. Her sharp nails dig into Ariadne's arms as she pulls her into the box. The hole is patched up behind her and the box starts sinking again.

"No, no, no!" Ariadne cries, scratching and kicking at the box as the water level rises to her waist.

The wraith of Iona has disappeared, leaving Ariadne alone in her watery grave. Aster's distant barking abruptly stops, followed by a high-pitched yelp of pain, then silence.

"Izrezati!" Ariadne yells, pointing her wand at the box.

It has no affect at all.

"Fuck!" Ariadne sobs, banging on the side of the box, "Help! Please!"

Ariadne hyperventilates as the water reaches her neck. She throws every spell she can think of, but her magic stopped working.

When the water completely fills the box, Ariadne tries to punch and kick the wood, but nothing works. She feels her air running out and screams.

Suddenly the bottom of the box gives way and Ariadne falls out with all the water. She gasps and wheezes, her lungs burning with every breath she takes in. She looks around and sees that she's in the forest again. She does not know why or how. She pushes herself up to her feet and points her wand out as she spins in a panicked circle.

"Come out and face me, coward!" Ariadne screams, then coughs and doubles over.

"Ariadne," Iona gasps.

Ariadne points her wand and spins to see Iona running toward her. She no longer has black eyes and sharp teeth.

"We must run," Iona says, grabbing Ariadne's hand.

"No, wait," Ariadne says, pulling her arm back.

"She used illusion magic on both of us but the spell broke. We have to run, or she will trap us again," Iona insists, taking Ariadne's arm and pulling her along.

Ariadne lets Iona pull her through the trees, "Did you see her?"

"No, did you?" Iona asks.

"No," Ariadne says.

They run out of the trees and onto the stone cliff where the Samhain Ball was held. There is no moon in the sky and barely any stars.

"It's a dead end!" Iona cries.

"We should make wings and fly from here," Ariadne says.

"My magic is not working," Iona says.

They both test a few spells, but nothing happens.

"Can maleficians do that?" Iona asks.

"I do not know," Ariadne says, "But we should keep running. We cannot stay in one spot, or she will trap us."

The air picks up around them and Iona runs into Ariadne's arms. A gale builds steadily until they are both pushed and pulled by the force of the wind. Ariadne tries to keep them steady, but the weather is too strong. They fall onto the stone and are pushed out towards the edge. They scream and claw at the stone but there is nothing to grab onto. They slide back until they're dangling off the cliff.

Iona screams when she looks down at the jagged rocks beneath them. Ariadne tries to reach out and hold her up, but a gust of wind hits them, and Iona loses her grip. She screams as she falls all the way down. Ariadne turns her head away and closes her eyes, not wanting to see the impact, but she hears the crunch of bone as Iona's body hits the rocks.

Ariadne sobs and almost loses her grip on the cliffside. She screams angrily as the wind continues to push her backwards. The trees at the edge of the forest sway turbulently, leaves and pine needles flying everywhere. Trees fall and crash into each other, the splinters of wood cutting Ariadne's cheeks as they ricochet through the air. Ariadne cries when she feels her arms slipping. She thinks of Iona's mangled body below and wonders if she should just let go. She should let go. Let go. Let go.

"Ariadne!" an echoing voice calls, "Hold on!"

Ariadne closes her eyes, not wanting to endure another cruel deception.

"Dominari somnia!"

The wind stops in an instant. Ariadne's eyes open in shock. She is still clinging to the cliffside, but Iona is not dead below her. She is running towards her and is led by Wisp and Aster.

"No, no, it is another trick," Ariadne sobs.

"Ariadne, this is real. You must believe me," Iona says, "Do not let go or you will die!"

"You are already dead," Ariadne cries.

"I'm not," Iona says as she lays against the stone and crawls towards her, "Grab onto me so I can pull you up."

"You will just push me off," Ariadne says.

"No, I would never do that," Iona says, eyes wide.

Ariadne whimpers and looks down. The drop seems even higher than it was before.

"I am pulling you up," Iona says.

She wraps her arms around Ariadne and pulls. Ariadne reluctantly lets the cliffside go and grabs onto Iona. To her relief, Iona does pull her up like she promised. It is a struggle but with their combined strength, Ariadne makes it back onto solid ground.

Ariadne pulls out her wand and immediately points it at Iona. Iona puts her hands up in surprise.

"Throw your wand away," Ariadne says.

"Ariadne," Iona starts to say.

"Throw away your wand now!" Ariadne screams.

Iona does what she's told, the wood clattering against the stone. Wisp growls next to Iona and Aster's ears go back in distress.

"What was the flower I gave you in the woods on Samhain," Ariadne asks.

"An iris," Iona says.

"What color," Ariadne asks.

"Purple," Iona says.

Ariadne's wand arm goes limp, and she breaks down into sobs. Iona runs to her and holds her as she collapses on her knees.

"It's okay. I am here," Iona whispers.

"You died," Ariadne whispers, her voice trembling terribly, "I heard your bones cracking."

"It was not real. It was…" Iona trails off.

Iona tenses and Ariadne pulls away to look at her.

"She knows," Iona says, "She knows about us, and she used me to entrap you."

Ariadne nods and wipes away her tears.

"Did you tell anyone else?" Ariadne asks.

"Not a soul. Did you?" Iona asks.

"No…" Ariadne says, "But another witch could have been closely observing us and discovered it on their own."

"I suppose that is possible…" Iona says, "What did you see?"

Ariadne describes the illusion in detail, holding back her tears as best she can. Iona is horrified by it all, especially when Ariadne tells her about almost drowning in the river.

"Who have you told about Vivien?" Iona asks.

"Not many people," Ariadne says, "But it is not exactly a secret. They are all frightened of me because of what I did."

Ariadne breaks down in tears again and Iona caresses her cheek.

"I should have drowned in that river," Ariadne cries.

"No, Ariadne do not say that. You were a child," Iona says her own tears pooling in her eyes.

"I did to Vivien what a malefician almost did to me! What

does that make me?" Ariadne cries.

Iona takes Ariadne's face in her hands and looks her in the eye.

"You are nothing like her," Iona says fiercely.

"I do not want to be," Ariadne whispers.

"Then you won't," Iona says.

Iona holds her close, and Ariadne feels safe for the moment. She glances at the edge of the awful cliff. The malefician knew exactly how to break her. She knew exactly how to trigger Ariadne's panic. It made Ariadne's blood boil to think of the evil witch laughing at her while she suffered. Whatever comfort Iona's embrace gives her, Ariadne knows she will not get any sleep tonight.

17 – IONA

"**Y**ou are courting Ariadne Zerynthos?" Crescentia gasps, her face alight with excitement and curiosity.

"I am not sure if the entire college heard you. You might want to scream it a bit louder," Iona hisses as she blushes deep red.

"I must say I had my suspicions but... goodness me," Crescentia says, at a loss for words, "I only thought you were sneaking off together, not having a torrid romance!"

Iona and Ariadne had a long talk last night about what to do next. Ariadne thought that since the malefician already knows about their relationship, there was no use in hiding it anymore. Today, they will tell all their friends that they are officially courting and will gauge their reactions.

Ariadne had told Ksenia and Samaira about their courtship unceremoniously in the dormitory hallway. Samaira had been overjoyed and Ksenia was predictably sullen. They both reacted as expected, as did Crescentia. Iona despises the need to be so suspicious of their friends but understands why it is necessary.

"Is that why you have been so tired lately?" Crescentia whispers and giggles when Iona's blush deepens, "We have so much to talk about."

Iona giggles with Crescentia. She cannot imagine someone

as vibrant and good-natured as her doing something so evil to Ariadne just hours ago. She must believe their friendship is true, no matter how new it may be.

"I miss my beau," Crescentia sighs, "His name is Erik. I am expecting a proposal from him when I return to France."

"How romantic! How long have you known each other?" Iona asks.

"A few years now. You would love him, I think. You simply must meet him when the year is over," Crescentia says.

"I would like that very much," Iona smiles.

Crescentia takes her arm, then hesitates.

"Will Ariadne smite me if I take your arm like this? She seems like the jealous sort," Crescentia says warily.

"I will fend her off," Iona grins.

When Iona arrives in the lecture hall for illusion class, she sits next to Ariadne, who smiles at her, but it does not reach her eyes. She has been in a lachrymose state all morning and it pains Iona to see it. She takes Ariadne's hand and holds it tight.

Iona was worried when she'd found Ariadne in the forest that she would catch hypothermia. Ariadne had only been wearing her thin nightdress, no shoes or cloak. She was shivering violently when Iona held her. It did not help that the falling snow turned to sleet, soaking both their clothes until they were both frozen.

Their long trek through the woods back to campus was one of the scariest hikes of Iona's life. She was not sure if the malefician was still out there watching them or if they had fled the scene.

Along the way, they'd found a bear whose head had been severed, its eyes gouged, and stomach ripped apart. It was a truly gruesome sight and Iona had gagged at the smell. There was a new symbol written in blood on the face of a boulder that stood behind the bear's carcass, like a tombstone. It burned Iona's eyes and she'd told Ariadne not to look at it for too long. Ariadne hadn't recognized the symbol but said that this was clearly a maleficium ritual site.

When they'd made it back to the relative safety of the college, Iona had rushed Ariadne to her room and followed her instructions to make a warming potion. It seemed to do the trick because Ariadne appears to be physically alright. The night left a scar on their newfound harmony. They may have finally set aside their own mistaken grievances, but they are facing a very real danger now.

As class is about to begin, Professor Salvador enters the room and notices Iona and Ariadne's joined hands. A small knowing smile reaches her lips before she starts a lesson on controlling dreams. If one learns how to control dreams while they're happening, the same trick can be used on illusions, once you're able to determine that you are in one. If a witch is strong enough, they can manipulate the illusion and take back control of their mind. Ariadne grows tense in her chair. Iona runs her thumb over the back of Ariadne's hand to soothe her.

"I encourage you to try and control your dreams this weekend with the tricks I gave you. See how drastically you are able to manipulate your dream before you wake up. And as always, continue practicing your illusions," Professor Salvador says.

Ariadne and Iona walk silently across the stone plaza together, the belltower chiming loudly ahead of them. When Iona sees Elise practicing spells in the courtyard, she pauses.

"I ought to tell Elise," Iona says, "Before I lose my nerve."

"Go. I must speak with Professor Salvador," Ariadne says, scanning the courtyard cautiously.

"About what?" Iona asks.

"I owe her an apology," Ariadne grimaces, "It should only take a moment."

"Very well," Iona smiles encouragingly, "I shall meet you at the belltower."

Iona approaches Elise, who finishes her water spell and smiles at her.

"Good day," Elise says.

"Good day. How are you?" Iona asks.

"I am very well actually. I believe I'm close to mastering the water spell. I never thought I would be able to, but I have been practicing," Elise smiles.

"That's wonderful, Elise, really," Iona says.

"Why is Ariadne watching us?" Elise asks, looking over Iona's shoulder.

Iona turns and sees Ariadne give them one final glance before she turns to walk back to the lyceum.

"I have something I must tell you," Iona says, "I do not want it to come between us, Elise. I value your friendship immensely."

Elise's brow furrows in confusion, "What is it, Iona?"

"Ariadne and I are courting. We have been since Samhain. I want to be entirely honest with you because I respect you and greatly value your friendship. You courted her too and I do not want this to be awkward or unpleasant for anyone," Iona says in a nervous rush.

"Oh, I see" Elise says, "That is... surprising."

Elise furrows her brow as she gathers her thoughts.

"I did wonder if your rivalry had ended when you danced together at Samhain, but I couldn't have predicted this," Elise says with a nervous chuckle.

"I am overwhelmed with guilt," Iona admits, her anxious thoughts spilling out of her, "I know you were deeply hurt when you learned that Ariadne had been lying to you on her mother's order. It was horrid unpleasant what her family did to you, and you did not deserve any of it. I refused Ariadne's affections at first partly because of what she'd done to you and-"

"Iona, please do not fret over me," Elise says.

"But I am ever so sorry," Iona says.

"I am not," Elise says.

"Really?" Iona asks.

"I am happy for you," Elise insists, "With time I was able to accept that Ariadne is not who deserves my anger. I have no quarrel with her anymore. It is in the past."

Iona's shoulders slump with relief.

"Are you certain?" Iona asks.

"Yes, I swear. Poor thing, you were so nervous to tell me," Elise giggles, "If this is what you want, then I wish you both every happiness."

Iona embraces her cousin and for the moment, everything seems to be okay. She was most worried about Elise's reaction and was not expecting her to be so gracious.

Over the weekend, the news of their courtship spread across campus like wildfire. Iona is relieved not to keep it a secret anymore, though her paranoia only grows with every day that passes without another attack.

Iona looks up at the statue of Ysolde Lysander that stands on a pedestal in the center of the courtyard. The stone statue depicts a tall witch in a flowing cloak, with the hood raised, and a simple medieval dress beneath. The statue's expression is what Iona focuses on most. It is one of pure determination and confidence, with only a trace of warmth.

Iona is promenading around the courtyard while Ariadne does her work in the greenhouse with Professor Yun. Whenever Iona is alone, and one of her friends cannot be with her, she passes the time in a public space rather than being alone in her room where the malefician could attack without witnesses. Normally that public space would be the library or the parlor, but Iona desired some fresh air this afternoon. Wisp runs in circles in the dead grass, happy as a fox can be.

"I can see the resemblance," Ariadne says.

Iona looks to her left as Ariadne approaches in a long-sleeved crimson dress and a black velvet cloak. Ariadne walks up to Iona and pleasantly surprises her with a sweet kiss in full view of any passersby. Their lips linger softly, until Iona finally pulls away, her cheeks pink.

"I do not know if I look much like her," Iona says, squinting up at the stone statue.

"You share that same expression of defiance when someone

says you cannot do something," Ariadne says, pointing to the statue's expression of certitude.

Iona inspects Ysolde's face more intently as Ariadne chuckles to herself. Iona welcomes the sound.

"You seem refreshed," Iona observes.

"Do I?" Ariadne smiles ruefully, "I suppose my work in the greenhouse helped to calm my nerves. It usually has that effect."

"I am glad for it," Iona says as she takes Ariadne's arm.

Wisp and Aster run in wide circles around the courtyard, only pausing in their play to be pet by Vadoma and Yoselin where they sit in the grass.

"Shall we spend an hour or two in the parlor? It is far too cold to stay out of doors," Ariadne says.

Iona notices Ariadne glancing at the woods, unable to hide her unease.

"I couldn't agree more," Iona says, snuggling closer to Ariadne for warmth.

At the student's parlor, Ariadne takes residence at the pianoforte and plays song after beautiful song. Iona sits nearby and reads from an astronomy book that she had borrowed from the library. She is in the midst of a chapter on meteor showers when she notices Elise sitting at a table with a deck of tarot cards. Deciding that she could use a short break from reading, Iona leaves her book on the chaise and approaches Elise.

"May I join you?" Iona asks.

"Certainly," Elise smiles wide.

Iona sits and notices Elise shuffling her cards with practiced skill.

"Have you ever had your tarot read?" Elise asks.

"No, never," Iona asks.

"Would you like to?" Elise asks.

"I would be delighted," Iona says, "How does it work?"

"That depends on what you would like answered," Elise says, "There are different configurations of the cards. The

Celtic cross, a simple three card spread, spreads for birthdays, dreams, past lives, love. Is there a specific question that you have been considering lately?"

Iona's mind immediately goes to the malefician, but she cannot speak of that. She would be curious to ask about love, but that might be inappropriate given Elise's previous courtship with Ariadne. She has no immediate interest in dreams or past lives, nor does she know what the Celtic cross spread would mean.

"Perhaps for your first reading, we can start with something simple. Three cards for your past, present, and future," Elise suggests.

"That sounds grand," Iona agrees.

Elise shuffles the cards a few times, cuts the deck in half and recombines the stack, then sets three cards faced down in the center of the table. Elise flips the first card, which has a golden chalice held aloft by a floating hand. Five spouts of water fall from the chalice and a white bird is flying above it.

"The ace of cups," Elise says, "The first card tells of your past. The ace of cups represents new beginnings, new insights, renewal of all sorts. You learned new information about yourself that gave you a fresh start with abundant potential. It can also indicate that you had someone new enter into your life, a new love, or a new friend."

Iona glances at Ariadne, who seems oblivious to their conversation as she continues playing her music. Elise flips the second card; a woman wearing robes and a headdress with a crescent moon at her feet and two pillars on either side. The card is flipped upside down, facing Elise instead of Iona.

"The high priestess," Elise says, "Intriguing... this second card is your present. The high priestess represents secrets and intuition, but the card is in reverse. This can mean that there is a secret, an eminent mystery, but to uncover the secret, you must not let others' opinions sway your own intuition and you should not let doubt hinder you. There may be a betrayal of some kind. Realign yourself and you will uncover what is hidden."

Iona is thoroughly engrossed in the reading now. This must be referring to the malefician, and their identity being shrouded in secrecy.

Elise flips the final card and Iona's heart sinks. On the card is a skeleton in full armor riding a white horse. The skeleton holds a flag adorned with a rose and the roman numeral for thirteen. At the horse's feet are people on their knees, a priest with his hands clasped in prayer, and a king lying dead with his crown on the ground beside him.

"Death," Elise says softly, "Though this does not always represent dying in a literal sense. It can also represent transformation or intense change. You must sometimes die to be reborn. Your future will bring this sort of change, for better or worse."

Iona is overcome with a sense of foreboding as she gazes upon the chilling skeleton. Iona looks up at Elise who studies her inquisitively. Her freckles mirror Iona's, a light dusting across the bridge of her nose. Elise pushes a strand of her brown hair behind her ear, then collects the three cards and returns them to her deck.

"You are quite adept at this. How did you learn?" Iona asks.

"My grandmother taught me," Elise says nonchalantly.

"Oh, what was she like?" Iona asks.

Elise smiles wistfully, "She was lovely. Very doting and refined. She was skilled in soothsaying as well, due to our Gothic pagan roots. She taught me all of her tricks."

Iona cannot help feeling envious of Elise. Their grandmother saw fit to dote on Elise but not on her simply because of who her mother had been. But of course, that is not Elise's fault.

"What have we here? A family reunion?" Gisela asks as she approaches the table, "Elise, you surprise me. Are you already resorting to telling fortunes? I suppose that is just as well, since all other magic escapes you."

"Leave her alone, Gisela," Iona says with a glare.

"It must be so terribly awkward for you both, knowing that Ariadne has a fetish for Lysander women," Gisela asks, narrowing her eyes at Iona and smiling cruelly.

Elise shifts uncomfortably in her chair and Iona blushes scarlet.

"Is it terribly awkward for you, knowing that you practically whored yourself to Ariadne and still she did not want you?" Elise asks Gisela.

Iona's eyebrows raise in surprise, and she coughs to hide her laugh. Iona did not think Elise had it in her. Gisela tries and fails to conceal her embarrassment.

"I can hear all of you," Ariadne calls with annoyance from behind the pianoforte, not bothering to look up from her hands as she continues playing a nocturne.

"Take care in how you speak to me, Elise," Gisela hisses, "There is more power in my future than you have in your little finger. You can be sure of that."

Gisela huffs with anger, shoots one final glare at Elise, then leaves the parlor in a rush. Nenet follows behind her but seems to be stifling a grin.

"I do not need to read cards to know there is nothing good in her future, no matter who she may try to seduce," Elise mutters.

"She was kind to me during fall term," Iona frowns, "I suppose she is cross with me now that I am courting Ariadne."

"That is almost certainly part of it," Elise agrees, "Though now that you are a Lysander, you will be more of a target for hostility."

"Why?" Iona's eyes widen.

"Power invites enemies," Elise shrugs, "Nevertheless, I thank you for defending me from unkind words."

"Of course, though you clearly did not need defending," Iona grins.

Elise smiles back, then packs up her cards.

"I should be going. I have reading to do," Elise says, "Have a pleasant evening."

"You as well," Iona says.

Iona stands and glances at her astronomy book, then decides to approach Ariadne at the pianoforte instead. Ariadne begins playing a new song and Iona listens with appreciation.

"What song are you playing?" Iona asks, finding the melody to be quite enchanting and almost cyclical.

"Les Barricades Mystérieuses," Ariadne says in perfect French, "By François Couperin."

Iona leans against the top board of the pianoforte to listen. When Iona inspects Ariadne's face, there is barely masked displeasure in the lines of her furrowed brow.

"Do you enjoy being the most eligible bachelorette on campus?" Iona asks with mock seriousness.

"What do you think?" Ariadne glances up at Iona with a brooding expression, until she notices that Iona is only joking. Ariadne cracks a smile and looks back down at her hands.

Iona walks around the instrument to sit on the bench next to Ariadne and watch her play. Her talented fingers look like agile spiders as they strike each chord with precision.

"I have dreaded being trapped in the mountains with all these buzzards for a year," Ariadne mutters, "It is bad enough to consort with them at the occasional party or ritual. At least then I can leave and go home when I desire it."

"Your beauty is your burden," Iona says, still attempting to make Ariadne laugh. She is successful, though the sound has a trace of melancholy.

"My name is my burden," Ariadne corrects.

"I am beginning to understand that now," Iona says, "It is disconcerting... having so much attached to me simply because of my name. A centuries long history that I am barely privy to."

Ariadne glances at Iona with empathy.

"The preconceptions can be stifling," Ariadne says, "After a while, I did not bother to correct them, opting to embrace them instead. I thought it would be preferable, but in hindsight it only made me feel worse."

"I did wonder…" Iona says.

"What?" Ariadne asks, ending one song and starting the next without a pause.

"If the women are this persistent, how bad were the men?" Iona stifles a giggle.

Ariadne lets out a heavy sigh, "They were insufferable."

"Oh dear," Iona winces, "I can only imagine."

"Oh… the idiotic comments about my witch's mark. They thought they were so clever, using it as an excuse to leer at my breasts," Ariadne rolls her eyes, "At least you only looked once when we met."

Iona blushes at that and Ariadne grins.

"Many of them were determined to convert me," Ariadne says, her past frustration coming back, "I knew very early in life that I was only interested in women. Some more honorable warlocks did not press the issue while others were still unconvinced."

Ariadne's fingers falter on the keys, and Iona notices. An uncharacteristically bashful smile spreads across Ariadne's lips.

"So, I took matters into my own hands," Ariadne says.

"I am scared to ask how," Iona says.

"There was this beautiful witch, Euphemia, from Sweden. She is a few years older than me and has hair like spun gold," Ariadne smiles at the memory, "Her parents would not stop pestering her about marriage, but she wanted to wait for a love match, so I proposed a plan. We spent some time unchaperoned at a party and intentionally got caught together in a rather compromising position."

Iona stifles a rush of jealousy, not wanting to distract Ariadne from her story. Ariadne glances at her, then clears her throat and continues, a pink flush creeping up her cheeks.

"The news spread like we'd intended, only amongst the younger coterie, until it was common knowledge that I was rather actively sapphic, without ambiguity. Euphemia is not sapphic, unfortunately for me at the time, but when men thought she and I were, many of them moved on to other conquests. She could find a match in her own time, while her parents were in the dark about her sudden lack of suitors. She told me that it was easier to know if a man was truly kind while being his friend first without any expectations for romance. I haven't met her husband yet, but I imagine he was smug thinking he managed to change her proclivities. She just had a child recently, a little boy," Ariadne grins.

Iona laughs, "I suppose that is one way to solve a problem. But was Euphemia not worried about scandal?"

"There are some who think affairs with women do not count in the same way, as ignorant as that might be," Ariadne shrugs, "She was willing to take the chance. A man who would shame her for such a thing is no man at all."

"Were you not worried about scandal?" Iona asks, scrutinizing Ariadne's expression.

"No, I welcomed it," Ariadne says.

"Why?" Iona asks, at a loss.

Ariadne sighs, picking her words carefully.

"If there must be gossip about me, I would rather it be about my penchant for beautiful women, rather than the fear of my magic being too strong," Ariadne's expression darkens, "My mother was not pleased when she learned of the many rumors about me, many of them untrue but it mattered not. I had earned a reputation for being..."

Ariadne searches for a polite word.

"A rake?" Iona says with a teasing grin.

"Promiscuous," Ariadne amends with a wry smile, "That is why my mother forced me to court Elise. She thought it would dispel the rumors, while also being a beneficial match for me and the family."

"Should I be concerned about ulterior motives?" Iona asks, raising an eyebrow.

"You have many more attractive qualities than your name, Iona," Ariadne grins, "I would be happy to remind you of them tonight."

Ariadne chuckles when Iona flushes and looks down at her hands. Then Crescentia bursts into the parlor and when she spots Iona at the piano, she rushes over.

"Did Elise just call Gisela a whore?" Crescentia asks Iona with rapt excitement.

Iona grins despite herself, "That she did. It was rather impressive."

"Of course, such a spectacle would occur when I happen to be studying," Crescentia pouts.

Soon November turns to December. During the last week of fall term, Iona is somewhat reluctant for it to be over. Partially because, apart from the melodrama with Ariadne and the malefician attacks, she takes great joy from learning about magic.

She is also nervous because this means the campus will be empty apart from Professor Salum, who will be staying behind. Iona has nowhere to go. Technically she has a house in Cornwall, but spending Yuletide there is the last thing she desires. She misses the sea, but not the house she'd been trapped in for so long. Instead, she will stay on campus alone while everyone goes home to their families.

Iona lays on Ariadne's chest in bed and listens to her steady heartbeat. The one constant in her life now is Ariadne and she will be leaving with everyone else to go back to her family's manor in Greece. Iona's bed will feel so empty without her.

"I have been thinking," Ariadne says, her fingers drifting up and down Iona's back, "What if I did not go home for Yule."

Iona pushes herself up on her elbow and looks down at Ariadne.

"But your family is expecting you," Iona says.

"I can send them a letter," Ariadne shrugs.

"You should not miss celebrating Yule to stay here with me. You would miss out on all the food and festivities," Iona says.

"I would rather be almost anywhere than at home with my parents," Ariadne insists, "Their idea of festivities is to invite all their pompous friends to dine with them, and my mother would not allow me to eat much of the food anyhow. She does not like when I overindulge. If I was with you, I could enjoy myself."

Iona softens at that but is still uncertain.

"It is no grand sacrifice. I promise you that," Ariadne says.

"Very well, if you are sure," Iona says curling back up against Ariadne.

"I am," Ariadne says, taking Iona's hand and kissing it.

"I would love to escape far from college for a while, even if it was only for a day. I feel the walls closing in on me. I do not feel safe here, even with all the other students leaving," Iona whispers.

Ariadne considers this and says, "I shall see what I can do."

On the last day before winter break begins, Samuel asks Iona to meet him in his office. He wears a sprig of holly in his lapel and seems much more at peace than the last time they'd spoken privately. Iona sits in a chair across from his wooden desk.

"I wanted to meet with you again before the holidays. You have been performing spectacularly in class," Samuel praises, "And Elise tells me that you have a new courtship as well?"

"Yes, with Ariadne Zerynthos," Iona says.

"Oh. I thought you despised each other," Samuel says.

"Uh… It is a bit of a long story," Iona flushes.

"I see," Samuel chuckles.

"She is not who others believe her to be," Iona reassures him.

"I trust your judgement," Samuel says, "Just… be careful."

"I shall, I promise," Iona says.

"Very good," Samuel says.

Samuel laces his fingers together on his desk.

"The reason I asked to speak with you was to inquire if you had any plans for the holidays. If you did not, I would like to extend an invitation to spend Yule with me, my wife Violet, and Elise at our home in Vienna. We would love to have you,"

Samuel says.

"Oh… I have made plans to spend Yule with Ariadne. She already sent a letter to her family that she will be staying behind. I wish I had known," Iona grimaces, wishing she could be in two places at once.

"I see. Not to worry! I always leave such things until the last minute when I know I ought not to," Samuel shakes his head, "The invitation is extended to you for all holidays henceforth. In fact, if you wanted to spend the summer with us next year, once college has ended, we would be delighted to host you."

"I would love to spend summer with you all. That sounds lovely," Iona says, relieved to have an alternative way to spend time with her new family members.

"Perfect! Elise will be so excited to hear it," Samuel says, "She has grown quite fond of you. I am so glad you have become friends. I always hoped you would be someday."

"I am grateful for her friendship too," Iona says.

"Where will you and Ariadne be staying for the holiday?" Samuel asks.

"I am not sure yet. She wants it to be a surprise," Iona smiles, "But I hope it's someplace warm."

Ariadne waits for Iona outside Samuel's office. When Iona exits the room, Ariadne takes her hand, and they pull up the hoods of their cloaks as they step outside into the snow. Mrs. Ainsley had cleared paths in the courtyard for the students to walk down. The forest looks magical with a dusting of snow on the evergreen trees. Iona almost wishes she could explore, but it's too dangerous.

Iona looks over at Ariadne and cannot help noticing the prominent dark circles under her eyes. Ariadne has been having trouble sleeping since that night in the forest. She is afraid that she will wake up and Iona will be missing again. Her nightmares have been plaguing her twice as frequently. They are so visceral that sometimes Ariadne wakes up and bursts into tears until Iona can calm her down.

Ariadne enchanted both of their rooms with a protection

spell in the hope that it would deter anyone from trying to break in. It did seem to help Ariadne fall sleep a bit faster but did nothing for the nightmares. It makes Iona wonder if there is something she could do with magic to help give Ariadne some peace while she sleeps.

The first morning of winter break, the witches are all packed and ready to leave. Iona says goodbye to Crescentia, who tells her that when she returns, she expects to hear all the sordid details of Iona's trip with Ariadne.

Ariadne says goodbye to Ksenia and Samaira as they leave for their vacation. Iona notices Ksenia glare at her before flying away on her broom with a handful of other witches. Iona would not miss her one bit and already feels safer with her gone.

Iona watches Elise and Samuel float away on their hot air balloon. They have a relatively short trip back to their manor in Vienna. Elise had been slightly disappointed when she'd learned that Iona could not visit for Yule, but she had been mollified by the plan for Iona to visit in the summer.

When all the other witches have gone, Iona and Ariadne have a quick lunch in the dining hall before going to their rooms to gather their bags. Iona is brimming with excitement. She still does not know where Ariadne plans to take them, which had made packing complicated. She supposes that whatever she does not bring, she or Ariadne could always conjure later.

"Ready?" Ariadne asks.

"Yes, I believe so," Iona says, scanning her room for anything she may have forgotten.

They carry their bags through the snow and into the forest. Iona had been reluctant at first, but Ariadne swore that it was safe with all the other witches gone. The forest changes quickly, and the snow disappears as they enter a tropical jungle. A blanket of humidity falls upon them, and they take off their cloaks.

Ariadne leads them to a tree with orange blossoms. At the base of the trunk is an oval mirror. When Iona looks harder, she decides it cannot be a mirror. The reflection is not the same as what is directly across from it. Iona and Ariadne stand in front of it, and they are not in the reflection either.

"Remember when I told you that there were portals in these woods?" Ariadne asks.

Iona nods.

"This is one. The jungle around us came from the portal when the forest assimilated to it. All the ever-changing forests in these woods come from these doorways," Ariadne says, pointing to the curious oval before them.

"Where do they go?" Iona asks.

"They lead to other worlds with strong ties to nature and magic. I explored a few others, and they were ghastly, filled with unfriendly creatures or dangerous landscapes. This one, however, is perfect for a vacation and is completely safe," Ariadne says.

"You went into the woods alone?" Iona asks, glaring sideways at her.

"No, Samaira came with me. We were swift and careful," Ariadne assures her.

"Oh. Good," Iona says, "Where does this portal lead?"

Ariadne holds out her hand and says, "Let's find out."

Iona takes her hand, and they step through the portal.

18 - IONA

The humidity intensifies until Iona feels almost as if she's breathing water. The air smells sweet and unique bird calls echo around them. Iona feels a bug against her cheek and goes to swat it away. Then she gasps when she almost slaps a pixie right in the face but stops her hand just in time.

The pixie's orange wings are shaped like a butterfly's and her dress is a similar color. She is quite tiny, no more than an inch tall, with black curly hair. The pixie looks at her curiously, then smiles at her. Iona smiles back and the pixie flies away into the jungle toward a massive flower the size of a small tree. The sweet smell in the air is coming from its giant pink petals that flop outwards around itself like a daffodil.

Ariadne beckons Iona along. She pushes leaves and branches of trees out of Iona's way until Iona's ears perk up. The sound of waves crashing in the distance has Iona running through the trees ahead of Ariadne.

Iona breaks through the edge of the jungle and onto a beach with pink sand. The water is so clear, you can see straight down to the ocean floor. A sun that is twice the size of Earth's and two small moons hang low in the sky, casting bright light onto the glistening water.

"The sun is enormous," Iona says, pointing at the sky.

Ariadne gives her an odd look, then seems to remember

something.

"Α, παραλίγο να ξεχάσω τα κολιέ," Ariadne says, then leans over her bag to rummage through it.

For a split second, Iona wonders if she is having a stroke, then realizes that the college's magic must not reach this other world. Iona and Ariadne's speech will not be translated automatically, and Iona does not understand Greek.

"Ορίστε, φόρεσε αυτό, νύμφη," Ariadne says, handing Iona a simple gold chain necklace.

Iona takes it and Ariadne motions for her to put it on. Ariadne has her own and fastens it to her neck.

"I almost forgot. We must wear these while we're here so we can understand each other. I cast an enchantment on them that is similar to the one on the college grounds. We will need enchant them once per day," Ariadne says.

"That is quite a relief, though it was fascinating to hear you speak in your own language," Iona says.

Ariadne stands next to her, and they watch the gentle waves.

"Do you like it?" Ariadne asks, "You said you missed the ocean."

"I love it," Iona says with a wide smile, "It's perfect."

Ariadne grins triumphantly and pulls out her wand. She walks back up the beach until she is almost in the jungle again.

"Fau fale," Ariadne says.

The spell conjures a small wooden house that is raised off of the sand and has one floor. There is a deck with two chairs at the front and two glass windows facing the water.

They bring their bags inside and Iona looks around at their temporary home. There is a small kitchen on the far wall with a dining table and a wood stove. A large white bed sits against the righthand wall, a sitting area with a bookcase is on the lefthand wall, and a bathroom next to the kitchen. Iona sets her bag down near the bed and cannot stop smiling.

Ariadne watches Iona's expression to make sure that she is happy. Then she practically skips back outside, and Iona follows. Ariadne stands on the dock and starts taking off her dress. Iona checks that no one is watching but the beach is entirely deserted. For all she knew, there were no humans on this entire planet.

"Care for a swim?" Ariadne grins as she unlaces her stays.

Iona undoes her own black dress and watches as Ariadne runs naked into the waves. Iona pulls impatiently at her laces, then throws her stays down on the deck in frustration, glad to be rid of them. She runs into the waves and directly into Ariadne's outstretched arms. They giggle and splash at each other, then wade into deeper water.

Swimming in the ocean again feels like coming home. Iona floats on her back and the water against her ears blocks out any sound but the waves. She closes her eyes and drifts to and fro.

Arms wrap around Iona's waist from below and she yelps as Ariadne pulls her underwater. Ariadne pulls them back to the surface and laughs when Iona splashes her. They wrestle playfully until Iona wraps her arms around Ariadne and kisses her. They float together, Iona's arms around Ariadne's neck and her legs wrapped around Ariadne's waist. Their touches grow more insistent as the sun sets behind them and the two moons stay visible within the blue clouds.

Ariadne carries Iona up the beach to the bath where they wash off all the sand and tease each other with soft, stirring touches. When Ariadne lays Iona down on the big bed and looks down upon her, spread wide and desperate for her, Ariadne's red eyes almost glow.

Iona and Ariadne explore the beach and jungle over the course of that first week. Iona missed the ability to commune with nature without the fear of someone lurking in the shadows. They spy odd blue birds with curved feathers in the trees and a pack of small hogs that live in a cave nearby.

They often curl up in the sand and gaze at the stars, though they are unable to read them because it is a new sky. They swim in the ocean for hours at a time until Ariadne practically drags Iona from the water at the end of each day. They play fetch with Aster and Wisp and take them on long walks along the shore. Other times they sit on their deck and read next to each other in comfortable silence.

Ariadne uses magic to catch fish. She casts the floating spell on them to lift them above the waves and into her net. Iona cooks the fish in their small kitchen. She tries to teach Ariadne but when she accidentally burns a fish to a charred crisp, Iona demotes Ariadne to chopping vegetables. They scavenge for greens and find an equivalent of potatoes growing in the jungle. They can also conjure whatever food they crave if they ever want a break from the island's food.

When they are deemed trustworthy, the orange pixies lead them to the large pink flowers scattered across the jungle which are filled with tart nectar. From then on, Iona and Ariadne drink a cup of the nectar for dessert each night.

On Friday night, Iona lays in bed and waits for Ariadne to finish brushing her hair. She is so relaxed that she might just float away.

"I have never met or heard of gingers that can tan like you can. Usually, they are all pale and allergic to the sun," Ariadne comments, her eyes roaming over Iona's exposed skin which is more golden than usual due to her many hours in the sun.

"I did not know I could either, until now," Iona smiles gleefully as she admires her tanned arms, "Perhaps it is a Brazilian trait. I did not know my mother was from there until Samuel told me. I thought she was from Portugal."

"Really?" Ariadne says as she climbs into bed beside Iona.

"Mmhmm," Iona says, nestling against Ariadne, "I look just like her, except my mother's skin was a tad darker than mine."

"Did she have freckles too?" Ariadne asks, drifting her fingers over the light brown dots on Iona's back.

"No," Iona says, "I believe those came from my father."

"Such eclectic features," Ariadne grins.

"You are one to talk," Iona says, "How many women with red eyes are you acquainted with?"

Ariadne looks away and Iona wishes she had phrased the question differently.

"My mother claims we have red eyes because we are distantly descended from Hecate," Ariadne says.

Iona's eyes go wide, "Is that true?"

"That is what she says," Ariadne shrugs.

"So, I am sleeping with someone who is part goddess?" Iona asks.

"Was that not always apparent?" Ariadne grins.

Iona rolls her eyes, reaching up to trace the flame on Ariadne's breast again.

"I think I saw something quite large swimming in the water when I caught the fish this afternoon," Ariadne says.

"Did it seem dangerous?" Iona asks.

"I am not sure. It did not surface. It swam back down to deeper water," Ariadne says.

"As long as it is not a siren," Iona jokes.

"No, sirens are not that big," Ariadne says stiffly.

Iona looks up at Ariadne, then grins and buries her face in her neck.

"What?" Ariadne asks.

"You have no reason to be jealous of a scaly creature," Iona says.

"More than just one," Ariadne grumbles, "It was a shock to see you like that, with their hands all over you."

"And mouths," Iona says cheekily.

Ariadne digs her fingers into Iona's ribs, making her squeal and squirm as Ariadne climbs on top of her and pins her hands over her head.

"You did enjoy it, didn't you? Having so many women touching you that you cannot keep track of them," Ariadne asks, raising an eyebrow.

Iona flushes and says, "I would be lying if I said it was not enjoyable, apart from the drowning bit. I imagine there are worse ways to die."

Iona can sense Ariadne mulling over a plan in her head. She

297

gulps as Ariadne grins at her and takes her wand from the bedside table.

"What are you doing?" Iona asks.

"Not to worry," Ariadne says, "I am only practicing my illusion magic."

"To do what?" Iona asks, heat pooling in her stomach as she holds Ariadne's sensual gaze.

Ariadne only smiles at her and whispers, "Dominari somnia."

Three naked Ariadnes appear before them. They smile at Iona as they crawl onto the bed with them.

"Uh…" Iona stutters.

"I could make twenty if you'd prefer, though by my reckoning, four of us will be plenty," the real Ariadne says. Or is she the real one? Iona is not quite sure anymore.

They pull down the covers and take Iona's arms to lift her up onto her knees. Four sets of hands explore her body, caressing her breasts, fondling her bottom and thighs, sliding up and down her back. One of them captures her mouth while another leans down to suck a nipple between her lips. Iona moans when one strokes between her legs. She's already overstimulated, and they've barely touched her.

"Which one of you is the real one?" Iona whispers.

The Ariadnes look at each other, then point to the one Iona is kissing.

"Lay down on the bed," Iona says.

Ariadne considers whether she will obey, then nods and lays down, spreading her legs wide. Iona buries her face in Ariadne's soft curls and licks her fervently. Ariadne moans and laces her fingers in Iona's hair.

The other Ariadnes touch Iona purposefully, trying their best to divert Iona's attention however they can. They coax her hips down onto one of their faces and Iona moans into Ariadne's cunt as they suck on her tender flesh. The Ariadne above her chuckles darkly at Iona's reaction.

Iona licks and sucks at Ariadne's slick folds, delving her

tongue inside, and fighting to maintain concentration when three other sets of hands are all over her. She is almost relieved when Ariadne cries out above her as pleasure overtakes her.

Iona leans back, wipes her mouth with the back of her hand, and grinds her pelvis into the other Ariadne's face. Iona glances at the three illusions of Ariadne, impressed that Ariadne had been able to keep them intact despite being in the throes of passion. Her practicing is paying off, or perhaps she was simply motivated more than usual. When the real Ariadne has caught her breath, she takes her wand and points it at Iona.

"Once is enough for me tonight," Ariadne says, "Halat."

Rope materializes and wraps around Iona's wrists. Her arms are pulled up, so her elbows are pointed towards the ceiling. Her arms are crossed behind her head, and her hands are resting on each adjacent shoulder. The rope twists itself around her arms and into a tight knot, leaving her at Ariadne's mercy.

The real Ariadne sits back and watches the three illusory Ariadnes descend upon Iona in full force until she is a trembling mess of whimpers and gasps. They take full advantage of Iona's incapacitation, moving, restraining, and folding her in varied positions whenever they like. Then the real Ariadne joins in by sliding two fingers into Iona and stroking her with an unforgiving rhythm.

It is entirely different from the sirens. They had only ravaged Iona, their mouths sloppy and animalistic. Ariadne knows Iona's body as well as her own. She knows how to make Iona come undone effortlessly when there is only one of her. Four of them at once is overwhelming as Iona's climaxes begin to blend into one another.

The Ariadnes take turns whispering in Iona's ear with little taunts and infuriating teases. They coo and soothe her, only to double their efforts just to hear Iona scream their name as she climaxes yet again.

"It's too much," Iona whimpers, her body covered in a sheen of sweat.

"I know, sweet Iona."

Iona's breasts are fondled a bit rougher, one of them taking a tender nipple between their teeth.

"But you can take just a little bit more, can't you?"

Iona gasps as a tongue slips deep inside of her again. She curls into herself, clenching her fists and closing her eyes.

"Do not try to hide your face, let me see you."

Hands fist Iona's hair to position her head back, ensuring that her face is clearly visible. A finger traces her parted lips, her cheekbone, and the line of her jaw. Then one of them sucks hard on her swollen flesh and she lets out an animalistic groan, pulling at the rope that restrains her.

"I can taste the sun on your skin."

Tongues roam over Iona's curves, licking the sweat off her skin, teasing her until she is trembling with desire.

"Ariadne," Iona moans.

"If you moan my name in such a way, how can you expect me to stop?"

Iona's legs tense as fingers thrust inside her again. Her walls constrict and her legs shake, barely able to hold herself up anymore. Iona's voice is nearly hoarse from her cries. She climaxes again and it is violent, making her entire body spasm and fall limp, until they catch her and prop her up.

"I am going to ruin you with my tongue."

"You already have," Iona whimpers, but the women only chuckle.

They rearrange Iona's rope, so her forearms are tied together flat against the middle of her back. One Ariadne is leaning against the headboard with Iona lying against her warm chest. The Ariadne at her back has her hand around Iona's throat, pressing soft kisses on her shoulder, her other hand playing with Iona's over sensitive nipples.

Two Ariadnes lay prostrate between Iona's thighs, licking and sucking at her cunt simultaneously, their tongues sliding together along her wetness as they each hold one of her legs open wide. The fourth Ariadne hovers over Iona and kisses her relentlessly, not allowing her to come up for air, and swallowing every moan.

"My speckled beauty," Ariadne whispers in Iona's ear, "You cannot know how you have captivated me. I dreamed of you, wished for you, ached for only you, perhaps even more than you did for me. Every second in your presence was exquisite torture. You must know how much power you have over me, then and now."

"Ariadne," Iona moans, having lost track of the real one again.

The Ariadne behind her tips her chin back and presses a gentle kiss to Iona's lips just as the two licking her cunt suddenly increase their ministrations until Iona cannot take it anymore and breaks. Iona moans into Ariadne's mouth, her pleasure like molten fire all over her trembling body.

Iona begins to think it may never end but the real Ariadne, the one at her back, reaches for her wand and undoes the illusion at last. Ariadne shifts them so Iona slumps into the mattress, completely boneless and rubbed raw. Ariadne turns her over to untie her arms and plants kisses over Iona's back, tracing her witch's mark with her tongue. Then Ariadne puts her wand back on the bedside table and gathers the languishing Iona into her arms. It takes Iona a moment to be capable of speech.

"Sirens... should be... embarrassed.... by their lackluster... abilities," Iona pants.

"I could not agree more," Ariadne says and though Iona's eyelids are too heavy to lift, Iona knows she is smiling triumphantly.

"I must... present such challenges... to you more often," Iona grins, "Then I will never... need to leave our.... bed again."

"I will only be a challenge to myself now, as I am the only one allowed to touch you," Ariadne growls, tipping Iona's chin to gently kiss her swollen lips.

Iona giggles and rests her tired head on Ariadne's soft chest, her breath returning to normal.

"The illusion was perfect," Iona mumbles as her eyelids grow heavy, "The best you've made so far."

Ariadne is silent for a moment, then kisses Iona's forehead and says, "Thank you, nymph."

"I have another idea," Ariadne says as she gazes out at the ocean the next day.

"I do not know if I can survive another one of your great ideas. I need time to recover," Iona says, her voice still hoarse from last night.

Ariadne smirks at her and says, "Not that sort of idea."

"Oh, what then?" Iona asks.

"Take off your chemise," Ariadne says.

"Ariadne," Iona says, a warning in her tone.

"This is not sexual, I swear," Ariadne says as she pulls her chemise over her head and steps into the shallows of the water.

Iona joins her and Ariadne points her wand at herself.

"Havfrue," Ariadne incants.

Ariadne's legs fuse together, and red scales grow over her skin from her feet to just below her belly button. She falls backwards as the tail grows until it is four feet long with a wide, flowing caudal fin. Gills form along her neck.

"Unbelievable," Iona breathes.

"Havfrue," Ariadne says again, pointing her wand at Iona.

Ariadne hesitates, then throws her wand on top of her discarded chemise in the sand and pushes herself backwards until she is fully submerged beneath the waves. Iona collapses onto the wet sand and watches in awe as her legs transform into a long tail with shiny blue scales.

Iona would have gasped but she chokes on air when her gills form. She pushes herself deeper into the water where she finds Ariadne waiting for her. Ariadne takes Iona's hands and twirls them both around in circles.

Iona giggles, her air creating bubbles that float to the surface. Iona flaps her tail experimentally, learning how to maneuver it and finding it surprisingly intuitive. The push and pull of the cool water against her bare torso are like a constant caress, making her long hair float around her like a crimson halo.

Ariadne takes Iona's hand, and they swim into open sea. The unfathomable depth of the water is mesmerizing. The light only reaches so far until darkness collects on the ocean floor. For some, the endless void might be frightening but to Iona, it is mystifying.

They find a magnificent, multi-layered coral reef not far from shore. Near it, a school of thin purple fish swim in circles like a shimmering tornado. Within a piece of beige coral that is shaped like a brain, tiny fish poke their heads out and observe the sea life around them. A wave of red fish swims with no discernable pattern around the reef. Sharks swim lazily back and forth, the smaller prey disappearing into the coral until the predators are gone.

Iona and Ariadne float a safe distance away, so they do not scare the fish into hiding. Ariadne swims behind Iona, puts her arms around her waist, and rests her head on Iona's shoulder. Their sensitive fins brush against each other as their tails flow idly and Iona tries to ignore the brush of Ariadne's pebbled nipples against the bare skin of her back. Iona expels a mouthful of bubbles when Ariadne presses a kiss to Iona's neck.

Then Iona looks to her right and tenses. Ariadne senses her distress and looks around for what she sees. Iona points to a colossal sea serpent that is swimming in the distance, not far beyond the reef. Its face looks like a dragon's and its green snakelike body is covered in dorsal fins and scales.

Ariadne takes Iona's hand and pulls her towards the coral to hide behind it. Iona follows but cannot look away from the creature. Then she pulls at Ariadne to stop her and points again. A baby sea serpent, only a fraction of the size of its mother, swims in playful loops. The sea serpent nuzzles its baby, then continues swimming away, uninterested in the two mermaids watching her. Iona admires the behemoth animals as they swim into the distance.

Iona turns to Ariadne and smiles wide. She throws her arms around Ariadne's neck, unable to say how grateful she is for this experience. Instead, she kisses her, and she knows Ariadne will understand. A school of blue fish swarm from below and curve around them towards the sun. Iona and Ariadne linger there for hours, admiring the fish and the multi-colored coral, until they make their way back to the island before nightfall.

The day of the Winter Solstice, Ariadne and Iona prepare a Yule feast. They have been celebrating in smaller ways all week, but the Solstice is always special.

They assemble a collection of dishes from both of their countries. Iona conjures a goose, mutton, turtle soup, mince pies, and plum pudding. Ariadne conjures roasted lamb shanks, sweet bread, braised chestnuts, kourambiethes cookies, and baklava. They conjure a little extra to give to the pixies and when they are done eating their fill, they walk through the jungle to the flower the pixies call home.

"I think the mince pie was my favorite," Ariadne says.

"The lamb was divine," Iona sighs, rubbing her full stomach, "I hope the pixies can enjoy it too. I am not sure what they eat apart from the nectar."

They follow the sweet air to the large pink flower. Pixies flit overhead and glow orange as dusk falls upon them. They fly down to Iona and Ariadne, who place the plates of food down for them to eat. The pixies seem to understand the food is for them and gather to take their fill.

"I think they like it," Ariadne smiles.

There is a fallen tree nearby. Ariadne takes Iona's hand and leads her to the log to sit down. Iona rests her head on Ariadne's shoulder.

Though their voices are too faint for a witch's ear to discern, the pixies hum their happiness as they eat the food crumb by crumb. When they clear the plates, they disperse into the air again in a sort of dance. The orange glow of their wings makes streaks of light across the sky.

"I wish we could stay here forever," Iona says, "I wish we could forget about college and the malefician and just live in peace."

"That would be simpler... but hiding from problems does not make them disappear," Ariadne says softly.

"My mother and father hid. They left everything behind to be together," Iona says.

"Did that make them happy?" Ariadne asks.

Iona frowns and contemplates the question.

"My mother barely spoke of my father after he died. It pained her to remember him. When I was a child, I worried that it was because he caused her harm or betrayed her in some way. When I grew older, I knew it was because she loved him dearly. Even when she was happy, there was always a sadness in her that never faded. Though their time together may have been cut short, I have to believe that they were happy if she was so devastated when he was gone," Iona says, "Though I am sure they had moments where they wished things could be different."

"I admire their bravery to leave. Especially in your father's case. As the eldest son, he had the weight of many responsibilities and expectations on his back. To walk away from that was not an easy feat," Ariadne says, seeming to empathize with his predicament, "However, if I am to be with you, I would like it to be in the light of day. We should not have to hide. We deserve peace on our own terms."

Iona lifts her head to look at Ariadne. They seldom ever talk of the future and to hear Ariadne speak of her in such a way makes her heart soar.

"We should make a fire," Ariadne says.

Iona nods and they stand to leave, waving at the dancing pixies as they go. They gather wood for a bonfire in the sand to use for their winter solstice ritual. Once they've disrobed, they join hands and chant together, laughing and dancing around the flames. Soon magic swirls around them again, the incandescent strands of light wafting through the air, into their hair and brushing against their bare skin.

Ariadne takes Iona's face in her hands and kisses her softly, the way Iona wished they had at her first ritual. The simple kiss is almost orgasmic when pure magic flows between them like lightening. They hold each other close until the light of magic vanishes. Then Ariadne pulls away and leans her forehead against Iona's until their breathing slows.

"Come inside. I have something to give you," Ariadne says.

Iona's eyebrows rise with curiosity as she lets Ariadne take her to the house. They put on their nightdresses and Ariadne tells Iona to take a seat on the bed.

Ariadne opens a drawer in the nearby cabinet and pulls out a present wrapped in blue paper and silver ribbon. She grins when she turns to see that Iona has a present wrapped in golden paper already in her lap.

"I have something for you, too," Iona says.

"Nothing too extravagant I hope," Ariadne says.

Iona shakes her head no and Ariadne sits on the bed next to her. They exchange presents and rip the paper simultaneously.

Iona opens her box first and she smiles when she finds a stem with a collection of white gardenias in full bloom. Upon further inspection, Iona notices that each of the petals is perfect.

"Those are different from the other flowers I gave you," Ariadne says, "They are petrified, like our wands, so they will never wither away. And if you ever decided to plant it in the earth, it will bloom into a gardenia bush that will never die and will always be in bloom regardless of the season."

"Undying flowers," Iona says, lifting them to her nose and inhaling the sweet scent, the same smell of Ariadne's skin and hair, "I love them!"

Ariadne opens her gift and pulls out a necklace. It has a sturdy golden chain with a charm made of selenite.

"Is this..." Ariadne looks at it closer.

"A dream talisman," Iona says, "It allows the person who

crafted it and the person wearing it to share dreams. If you were to wear it tonight, you could call my name and I will appear in your dream with you as long as I am also asleep at the time. At least, that is what I read in my grimoire."

Ariadne looks down at the talisman with an unreadable expression.

"I read ahead in my enchantment grimoire and found the spell to make it. I cast it almost fifty times to make sure it will work," Iona admits.

Ariadne is still silent, and Iona becomes nervous.

"You do not need to wear it every night. Or ever. I only thought... the next time you have a nightmare you could call for me and I could help you wake up or change the dream," Iona says.

A bittersweet smile spreads across Ariadne's lips as she holds back her tears. Iona shifts closer and puts her arms around her.

"This is extraordinarily thoughtful, thank you," Ariadne says.

"Many blessings," Iona smiles.

"Many blessings, nymph," Ariadne smiles wide.

They kiss and set their gifts aside as they crawl into bed, quickly shedding their nightdresses that they needn't have bothered putting on in the first place. Ariadne settles between Iona's thighs and kisses her with abandon. After they've finished drawing every drop of pleasure from their bodies, Ariadne was sure to fasten the dream talisman to her neck before collapsing in Iona's arms.

The second week of their tropical vacation is mostly spent lazing about. They turn themselves into mermaids twice more to explore the ocean and they visit the pixies at least once per day with treats to amuse them. They lay in the sand and watch the sunset each evening while eating their dinner, then fall into bed and lose themselves in each other.

One night that week, Ariadne did have a nightmare. Iona

had been dreaming about walking through the forest when she is suddenly implanted in Ariadne's mind. By the light slipping through the thin slats in the wooden boards, Iona sees a fourteen-year-old Ariadne screaming and clawing at the small box they're trapped in. Iona can also hear the blood curdling scream of another girl on the outside.

"Ariadne," Iona says.

The young Ariadne turns to look at Iona with wide terrified eyes.

"It's just a dream," Iona says, "I know it is frightening but I am here with you."

"The water," Young Ariadne cries, "It's rising."

"It is not real," Iona says clearly.

Iona holds out her arms and Ariadne falls into them. Iona squeezes her tight as the cold water rises. Vivien's bloodcurdling screams are deafening.

"You are safe. You are safe. It's not real," Iona says over and over, "You are safe in my arms. I will not let go."

Then Iona pulls back to see that Ariadne is her normal age again. Vivien's screams abruptly stop as their surroundings shift and blur like clouds moving against the wind. The box and the water disappear, and they find themselves in a glade with soft grass and red wildflowers.

"It worked," Iona smiles and looks around at the beautiful clearing.

"I've never been able to do that before," Ariadne marvels.

"What is this place?" Iona asks.

"I do not know. I started dreaming of this glade only recently, but I have never been here," Ariadne says.

They sit silently in the grass and feel the breeze in their hair until the dream fades away and their eyes open.

"Last chance to turn back," Ariadne jokes.

"Do not tempt me," Iona says.

They carry their bags through the massive green leaves in search of the portal. They'd said goodbye to the pixies along the way. Iona would miss their tiny, sweet faces.

"We can always come back to visit," Ariadne says.

Iona nods but she knows that she would never feel safe enough to traverse the woods once the other witches return, and the malefician with them.

They eventually find the portal. Iona eyes the other side warily, knowing she must go back but wishing they could have just one more day. Ariadne takes Iona's hand and lifts it to her lips.

"Whatever happens, we will face it together," Ariadne says.

Iona and Ariadne step through the portal and back into the cold.

PART THREE

Ascendancy

19 – IONA

"**A** new term brings with it more advanced magic than before. You will be refining the spells you learned last term as well so that in five months' time, you will be prepared for Morgan's trials if you choose to partake in them," Samuel says.

Iona and Ariadne sit together at the front of the class. Their new term schedule put Conjuration and Phytology on Mondays and Wednesdays, Enchantment and Clairvoyance on Tuesdays and Thursdays, with Dreams and Illusions still on Friday mornings. Some students were also shifted around so now Crescentia is in their class rotation. Iona is glad for it so they can spend more time together.

"A new term also necessitates new partners. I shall divvy you all into pairings now," Samuel says.

Iona braces herself for a much more difficult term when she is paired with Ksenia. Iona is jealous of Ariadne, who gets paired with Crescentia. She wishes they could switch but it is not allowed. Ariadne gives Iona a sympathetic smile, then shoots Ksenia a warning look before moving seats to sit with Crescentia. Ksenia primly sits beside Iona and puts her grimoires on the desk in front of her.

"I think I will find a way to make this amusing for me," Ksenia says with a wicked smile.

"Or we could choose maturity and refrain from unnecessary

unpleasantness," Iona says half-heartedly.

"Why? This is our opportunity to see 'whose magic is stronger'," Ksenia says, quoting Iona from last term.

Then Samuel begins the lesson and Iona bites back her retort. They are learning about healing spells today. Kokuro raises her hand.

"Could we not use a potion to heal someone?" Kokuro asks.

"If you happen to have a healing potion on your person, that is always a safe option. But what happens if you do not and there is no cauldron nearby? Healing potions take time to brew, and a wounded person may not have time to wait. This is an alternative method to heal, though it is complicated, as all healing magic is," Samuel says.

He takes out a knife and winces as he slices a shallow cut in his palm.

"Healing spells can be difficult because you will be conjuring tissue, blood, bones, even organs, depending on the severity of the injury. Just as with other conjuring spells, you must picture what you are creating in your mind in order for it to manifest. Conjuring pieces of the human body, if done incorrectly, could result in killing the person accidentally. And if you do not know what part of the body is ailing them, like with potions, the spell cannot properly heal them," Samuel says.

He pulls out his wand and before any blood can spill onto the podium, he incants, "Philisa."

The cut heals itself, the flesh binding back together until there is not even a scar left behind.

"Shallow cuts like this one are more easily fixed and should not necessitate a potion to heal. More serious injuries should only be attempted by skilled healers who have trained specifically in this type of magic."

Samuel pulls his handkerchief from his blazer pocket and wipes the blood from his hand.

"The only injury that cannot be healed with this spell, or any potion yet created, are injuries of the brain. We simply do not yet understand the many complexities of the human mind and as long as that is the case, those injuries are permanent even for us," Samuel says.

Iona glances at Ariadne, then quickly looks away.

"Today I would like to start with healing shallow cuts," Samuel says.

Ksenia conjures a particularly jagged knife and grabs Iona's hand. Iona gasps when Ksenia presses in the blade far too forcefully and makes a deep cut across her palm.

"Oops," Ksenia says.

Iona's blood drips onto her dress and her hand trembles from the pain. Wisp growls from underneath the table.

"You brute! You cut straight through to the bone," Iona cries.

"Hush hush," Ksenia says, "No need for dramatics. It is only a cut."

"Ksenia," Ariadne snaps from the next table over.

Ksenia glances at Ariadne and purses her lips. Then she lifts her wand and says, "Philisa."

Iona sighs with relief as the cut slowly closes, the flesh meshing back together until it and the pain are gone. Ksenia seems pleased that her spell works, then hands Iona the blade. Iona takes it and Ksenia's hand. She does not cut as deeply as Ksenia did but does not hold back either.

"Philisa," Iona incants.

The cut heals so quickly, it is almost instantaneous. Iona blinks in surprise at how swift the magic worked. Ksenia sniffs indignantly.

"What were you saying about stronger magic?" Iona asks with a small smile.

"Strong witches do not require guard dogs," Ksenia seethes, glancing over Iona's shoulder at Ariadne.

"They should not need to bully their way to power either," Iona retorts.

"They should fuck their way to it instead?" Ksenia asks.

Iona flushes angrily, "My magic was strong long before courting Ariadne, as you well know."

"And now that you have Ariadne in your pocket, the pendant is that much closer to being yours," Ksenia says, "Though if you did somehow manage to claim it, Ariadne's family will exile her, and she will always resent you for it."

Iona opens her mouth to dispute her, but words escape her. Ksenia grins.

"When she inevitably becomes bored with you like she does all the pretty little things she plays with, you will go back to being the lowly beach flea that you are," Ksenia says.

"I am not ashamed of where I come from," Iona says, "Nor am I required to engage in such vitriol with you. Your ambition is unbecoming."

Ksenia's glare turns sinister.

"Unlike you, I am willing to do what is necessary to win," Ksenia says, "That is a strength of its own."

Iona stares deeply in Ksenia's eyes, trying to unlock her aura or see any hint of corruption in her. Ksenia sneers and faces forward in her seat with her arms crossed.

"What did she say to you?" Ariadne asks when they walk to the dining hall for lunch.

"Nothing," Iona says but even to her own ears she does not sound convincing.

In phytology class that afternoon, Iona ignored Ksenia completely. Professor Yun gave a lecture on human ingredients in potions. Locks of hair, nail clippings, saliva, and tears all have their own unique properties, whether you are using your own or another person's. Crescentia raises her hand.

"What about blood?" Crescentia asks.

Professor Yun narrows her eyes slightly, "We will not be using blood in this class."

"Why?" Crescentia asks, chastened by Yun's cold response.

Yun considers her answer carefully, then finally says, "Blood is the most powerful natural element in our bodies. It can be used in potions to make them stronger, but I cannot in good conscience advise that. Blood magic is a rather gray area of witchcraft, neither good nor bad. It can be considered unethical at best and the darkest of magic at worst."

"What makes it unethical?" Kokuro asks.

"Blood can be used in rituals to control and manipulate another witch's mind and body from anywhere in the world without needing any proximity to them. It is unethical because of how anonymous the magic is, quite cowardly, sneaky, and invasive. That is why dark magic users tend to be the only ones who use such magic. Unlike illusions, you cannot learn to resist blood magic. It is nearly unbreakable. You should never give your blood to anyone unless you trust them implicitly, like in the case of bonded pairs," Yun says, "Just like with all magic, how you choose to implement it can make it noble or vile."

"I shall meet you in my room in an hour, when the belltower chimes five" Ariadne says, giving Iona a quick kiss goodbye, "Stay with Crescentia or wait in the library until I am back."

"Yes, ma'am," Iona says.

Ariadne grins as she and Aster reenter Professor Yun's class.

Iona scans the courtyard for Crescentia but does not see her. She decides to check if Crescentia is in her dormitory. She walks along the shoveled paths in the snow with Wisp running ahead of her.

"Iona!" Crescentia calls.

Iona looks but does not see Crescentia. Iona covertly pulls out her wand and continues walking as her heartbeat quickens in her chest.

"Iona, wait," Crescentia says as she runs out of the forest and lingers at the edge.

Iona looks at Crescentia warily through the stone archways that border the courtyard.

"Are you well?" Crescentia asks, "You look like you've seen a ghost."

"I am fine," Iona says as her suspicion wains, "What were you doing in the forest?"

"I was gathering ingredients for a potion I am brewing,"

Crescentia says, "But I think I heard someone sculking around. I called out but they would not answer."

Iona steps into the snow to approach Crescentia.

"It is not safe in the forest at present," Iona says.

"But you go on walks in the woods frequently," Crescentia says.

"I know but… I do not anymore," Iona says.

"Could you not walk with me just this once?" Crescentia asks, "I left my bag with all my herbs in the woods, and I do not want to retrieve it alone."

"I do not know," Iona says, looking back towards the lyceum where Ariadne is still working.

"Please? It will only take a moment," Crescentia says as she takes Iona's hand.

"We should wait until Ariadne can accompany us," Iona says.

"Do not be silly! We do not need her," Crescentia says.

Iona is still apprehensive and tries to take her hand back, but Crescentia pulls her deeper into the trees with an iron grip.

"Crescentia, I would like to go back," Iona says.

"Only a little farther," Crescentia insists.

"Crescentia, why are you not listening to me?" Iona snaps.

"This is almost too easy now," Crescentia says, but her voice is distorted.

"What?" Iona asks.

Then everything goes black.

20 – ARIADNE

A ster runs ahead of Ariadne when they leave the lyceum. Yun had gifted her some fresh wing of bat to use in her potions and she carries the bundle on top of her books. The belltower chimes five as Ariadne enters the courtyard and walks through the paths in the snow toward the dormitories.

"Aster do not run too far," Ariadne says.

Aster looks back at her and whines.

"You have been a terror all afternoon," Ariadne scolds, scratching behind the wolf's ears when she is able to catch up with him.

She frowns when she senses Aster's growing distress. Something is wrong. Then it begins to rain, a sudden downpour that makes all the witches walking across the courtyard run to the safety of buildings nearby.

Ariadne runs to the dormitories and rushes to her room. Her stomach drops when she finds that it is empty. Ariadne tosses her books onto the bed and runs back out into the hallway with her wand drawn. Ariadne goes in the direction of the staircase, but Aster runs further down the hallway in the opposite direction and scratches at Iona's door. Ariadne follows Aster and knocks on the door.

"Iona? Are you there?" Ariadne asks.

"Come in," Iona says.

Ariadne opens the door and sees Iona sitting on her bed with Wisp's head in her lap. The undying gardenias that Ariadne had gifted to Iona are planted in a metal pot on her bedside table.

"Why are you in your room?" Ariadne asks.

Iona looks over at Ariadne and tilts her head to the side.

"Why would I not be?" Iona asks.

"We planned to meet in my room," Ariadne says.

"No, we did not," Iona says, shaking her head.

"Do you not remember?" Ariadne asks.

Iona furrows her brow and seems to be concentrating heavily.

"Are you well?" Ariadne asks.

Aster walks up to Iona and sniffs at her hand. Ariadne approaches and gently takes Iona's wrist. When she turns Iona's hand around, there is a cut across her palm that is still seeping blood. There is a dark stain on the skirt of her black dress where her hand had been resting.

"How did you get this cut?" Ariadne asks.

Iona looks at the cut in confusion and does not say anything.

"Iona?" Ariadne asks, tilting her chin up so she can look in her eyes.

"I do not know," Iona whispers, her eyes distant.

Ariadne pulls out her wand and heals the cut, then sits down on the bed next to Iona.

"What is the last thing you remember?" Ariadne asks.

Iona concentrates again, then says, "I was looking for Crescentia in the snow. She called to me from the woods. I told her I did not want to go in, but she took my hand and pulled me inside. Then she said... this is almost too easy now."

"Then what happened?" Ariadne asks.

"I... I do not know," Iona says, "Everything went black. Then you came through the door."

"A lethe spell," Ariadne mutters.

She is kicking herself for letting Iona out of her sight. She thought Iona could be safe inside for one hour but that was all it took.

"What is a lethe spell?" Iona asks.

"It takes memories from your mind. It is a rather advanced spell. She is getting stronger," Ariadne says.

Iona rubs her fingers against her forehead anxiously. Ariadne looks down at Iona's feet and notices that the hem of her dress is caked in mud and looks singed.

"It's been Crescentia all along," Ariadne says.

"No…" Iona shakes her head.

"Iona, I know it must be difficult to accept but," Ariadne starts but Iona interrupts her.

"It is not her," Iona says.

"But you just said she pulled you into the woods," Ariadne says.

"I do not believe it was really her," Iona says, "Where is she?"

Iona gets up and Ariadne takes Iona's hand to hold her back.

"Where are you going?" Ariadne asks.

"To Crescentia's room to see if she is there," Iona says.

"Are you mad?" Ariadne says, "If a malefician is next door, we ought to be running in the opposite direction."

"But if she was in her room while I was in the woods, then the person I saw was an illusion," Iona says.

"If she is the malefician, then she would just tell you what you want to hear," Ariadne says.

Iona frowns, then says, "Then why did she not erase my memory of her taking me into the woods if she still desires to conceal her identity?"

That stumps Ariadne and she racks her brain for an explanation.

"You forgot our agreement to meet in my room?" Ariadne asks.

"Yes, I did…" Iona says with a frown, "I do not remember how I got here either."

"Crescentia is of middling talent. She may be stronger now with maleficium but apparently not strong enough yet to take a substantial portion of memory from you. She only took bits and pieces, some memories she meant to take and others she did not need to, like our plans to meet in my room. She may not even realize how much you still remember," Ariadne says.

"Or the real witch only wants us to think it is Crescentia, so we do not suspect the real person," Iona insists.

"It seems you've already made up your mind then," Ariadne snaps, her frustration bubbling inside her.

"And so have you, though your intuition is not the most reliable," Iona retorts, "You have never been the best judge of character."

Ariadne flinches and looks away. Iona's anger recedes the moment the words pass her lips, and she reaches for Ariadne's hand.

"I am sorry," Iona relents, "I just... We cannot make assumptions in this quandary. I believed the siren's lie when they accused you of treachery. I do not want to make the same mistake again. The truth may not be so easily deciphered when we cannot trust what we see."

Ariadne takes a deep breath and meets Iona's big hazel eyes. The regret in them is enough to quell Ariadne's indignation.

"Take me to the last place you remember," Ariadne says.

They walk to the forest, both of them scared of what they may find. The persistent rain is like drops of ice against their backs, their cloaks only barely able to shield them from the foul weather. Iona shows Ariadne exactly where Crescentia had appeared to her, and they enter the woods cautiously. At first the forest appears normal, the evergreen trees dusted with white snow, until Iona steps into water.

"It is flooded," Iona says.

Ariadne conjures rainboots for them. They put the boots on, tie up their skirts so they don't drag in the water, and leave their shoes and familiars behind on stable ground. The forest becomes more of a swamp with six inches of dirty water. They wade deeper into the trees until they reach a small recently made clearing.

They see the aftermath of a brutal duel of water and fire.

The trees are scorched and splintered, some of them reduced to jagged stumps. Iona reaches out to touch a blackened tree with trembling fingers.

"What happened here?" Iona whispers.

"You did," Ariadne says with admiration.

"No... that is not possible," Iona says, wiping the ash off her hand.

Ariadne almost falls into a crater of deeper water, but Iona pulls her back before she can sink into it.

"They underestimated you," Ariadne says, "They attacked you, but you were too evenly matched. When they knew they could not defeat you, they panicked and took your memory so that rather than failing today, they can bide their time a little while longer to build their strength."

"They seem quite strong to me," Iona says, gesturing to the destruction around them.

"Now that you are here, are you able to remember anything more? A voice, a face, anything?" Ariadne asks.

Iona shakes her head no. Ariadne takes Iona's hands.

"Center yourself and concentrate," Ariadne says, "If the memory spell was done in haste, and without the necessary skill, you may be able to recollect more if you try."

Iona takes a deep breath in and out, then closes her eyes. Ariadne waits patiently. Then Iona's eyebrows furrow as a memory emerges.

"I see fire," Iona says, "My fire. I was angry. I felt betrayed."

"Can you see her face?" Ariadne asks, then waits for Iona to search her mind.

"No," Iona says, opening her eyes in defeat.

Ariadne pulls Iona into her arms and holds her close.

"Do you think you would have felt betrayed if it was Ksenia who attacked you?" Ariadne asked.

"...No, I would have expected it to be her," Iona says.

"Crescentia would stand to benefit the most if she gained more power, eliminated competition, and won the pendant. Her entire family wants their influence and magic to grow,"

Ariadne says.

"I am still not convinced it was her," Iona says, "This witch could take many shapes. She could have kept the illusion of Crescentia's form while she fought me. She could have made herself look like anyone, Crescentia, my mother, or you. And that sort of cruelty, to use a face I trust, is something Ksenia would do."

Ariadne pulls back and sees Iona is crying, her tears mixing with the rain on her cheeks.

"If you truly do not believe it was Crescentia, I trust your instincts. However, I do think we should be cautious around her from now on, as a precaution," Ariadne says.

Iona nods reluctantly, sniffling and wiping her tears away.

"I also think we are past the point of handling this ourselves," Ariadne says.

Iona tries to protest but Ariadne will not let her.

"Look around us, Iona. You could have died, and I cannot be with you every second of every day. Even if I could, I cannot always protect you," Ariadne says, though she hates admitting it, "This witch has grown too strong and too bold. We should not underestimate her the way she did to you."

Iona looks down at her hands and Ariadne tucks a strand of hair behind her ear.

"I am so proud of you for fighting this well," Ariadne says, gesturing to the burned trees.

"Does it count if I do not remember it," Iona asks with a tired smile.

"Yes," Ariadne says, smiling back.

"The ghost told me that I had to be careful who I trusted," Iona says.

"But there is someone you trust who could help," Ariadne says, "Let's talk to him together."

Professor Lysander's face is grave as he inspects the aftermath of Iona's forgotten duel. Iona clutches Ariadne's hand so tightly that it's almost painful, but she would never let go.

Iona agreed to tell her uncle about the malefician, but only if Ariadne promised not to tell him about Crescentia. A wrongful accusation would ruin her life and Iona does not want that for her. Ariadne only hopes that Iona is right. Lysander inspects the scene with keen eyes.

"I am glad you told me about this," Lysander says, "And I am sorry you both had to shoulder the burden of this scourge alone. Please know that I will do everything in my power to help you."

"Thank you, Samuel," Iona says.

"I agree with Ariadne that you must be careful and should not be left alone, at least until the trials in May. Whenever Ariadne cannot be with you, you should stay with me or Elise," Lysander says, "I will be on my guard as well to see if I catch any odd goings on."

Lysander waves his wand and whispers, "Meydana çıkarmak."

He sees something in the air. Ariadne squints and notices very faint vapors of magic, but instead of the orange and yellow lights that form at rituals, the magic is dark blue and black that seems to absorb any light surrounding it. Samuel follows the traces of maleficium in the air, with Ariadne and Iona close behind. Thunder booms above them.

"The rain... another sign of dark magic," Samuel murmurs.

The rain had dissipated into a light drizzle. Iona looks up at the sky in surprise.

"I would not have thought rain would be linked with darkness," Iona says.

"It is a reaction to the darkness. The rain is washing the corruption away until the earth is cleansed of evil," Samuel says.

The traces of magic lead them to a cave that seems to curve down into the earth. The mouth of the cave is a black ominous abyss.

"Wait here," Lysander says.

He enters the cave with his wand raised. The seconds tick by as they wait for him to reemerge. Eventually he does, looking aghast.

"The cave is empty, but she was here," Lysander says solemnly.

He beckons them inside and they use light spells to see in the darkness. Unlit candles are scattered in haphazard clusters about the edges of the cave. In the center are crude drawings of symbols written in ash, new ones that Ariadne has never seen before. They still burn if she looks at them for too long, as if they are offended by any scrutiny. In the center of the symbols is a partially decomposed rabbit that has been mutilated. Its insides are spilling from its stomach and its eyes have been gouged out, just like the bear.

"These are maleficium runes," Samuel says, pointing at the symbols that surround the rabbit.

"What do they mean?" Iona asks.

"I do not know exactly," Samuel says, "You would need a maleficium grimoire to interpret the symbols."

Iona turns her face away from the symbols and rubs her eyes.

"I have only seen this sort of ritual site once before," Samuel says, "When I was a young man, I lived in a prosperous community of witches and warlocks in Tibet. There was a malefician among us, and they were leeching magic. Two witches had already been attacked. Their power was stolen away permanently, and their memories were erased. With each well of magic that the malefician consumed, they grew three times stronger."

Samuel sprinkles dirt onto the awful symbols on the ground and the burning in their eyes dissipates.

"There was a period when we all pointed fingers, our paranoia leading to dissension that only served to divide us in our search. We did not know at the time that maleficians have the uncanny ability to be in multiple places at once, projecting their perfect likeness so no one will notice their absence while they practice their dark rituals far away," Samuel says.

Ariadne's head spins with that tidbit of information. They truly could not trust their senses at all.

"No one would admit it was them and truth spells would not work on a malefician that powerful, but luckily for us they made a mistake. We discovered a ritual site, very similar to this one, and found a glove. It was properly identified the next morning at breakfast when one of the witches lied and said she'd found the glove in the garden. The malefician said she had been looking for the glove for ages and took it back," Samuel says.

"How did you defeat her?" Ariadne asks.

"We did not. A warlock in our company waited until she was asleep and slit her throat," Lysander said.

"Goodness," Iona whispers.

"She would have picked us off one by one until she had all our magic for her own. To attack her directly when she was already so strong would have been suicide. I do not condone murder, of course, but to this day I do not see any alternative," Samuel says.

A grim silence lingers among them. Ariadne looks to Iona, and she is pale as a sheet.

"Could one of us wait here for the malefician to return?" Ariadne asks.

Samuel shakes his head no, "Maleficium ritual sites are not reused. Maleficians know that they could get caught if they made a lair. Their anonymity is their greatest weapon. See the rabbit is almost fully decayed? This site was used quite a while ago and was potentially one of her first. She did not even bother to clear her mess away. Such is the hubris of a malefician. She wants us to confront her, to discover her identity, but only when it suits her. She will toy with us while we struggle and ensure that she has ample time to cultivate her magic until she is certain that we will stand no chance against her."

Samuel grimaces. Ariadne glowers angrily, then feels Iona

shiver beside her.

"We should return to the college grounds before dark," Ariadne says, taking Iona's arm and leading her from the cave.

"Of course," Lysander says.

He whispers a spell. The desecrated rabbit sinks until it is buried in the earth.

A week later, Ariadne has another nightmare. She calls for Iona and in seconds she is there to help her. As the familiar scene at the river disappears, they find themselves transported to a beach at sunset. Iona leans her head against Ariadne's shoulder and sighs.

"This is quite pleasant," Iona says.

They listen to the gentle waves as adrenaline leaves Ariadne's system. Before Ariadne can call for Iona to help her, she has to first realize that she is in a dream. By the time she comes to that conclusion, she has already heard Vivien's screams for quite a while.

As they sit and watch the gentle waves, Ariadne's thoughts drift to the pile of letters from her mother that sit unopened on her desk. She used to write to her mother at least once a week but recently, she has not been able to put pen to paper.

Ariadne cannot tell her mother about her new courtship, or her newly conflicted feelings about the pendant. She cannot confide in her mother about anything at all. She dreads the day when she will have to tell her parents about everything that has happened, perhaps at the same time that she tells them that she did not claim the pendant like she'd promised. She can picture their angered expressions so clearly.

The idea barely crosses her mind before the beach fades away and is replaced by Thessaly. They are now sitting on the face of a cliff where her family's manor stands tall and imposing before them. The manor is two stories of beige stone with a terra cotta roof. A familiar view of a valley with luscious green trees is bordered by tall mountains. Iona stands and looks around in confusion.

"Where are we?" Iona asks.

"Thessaly. This is my family's manor," Ariadne says.

"Oh," Iona says, gazing out at the valley of black pine trees, then up at the manor in front of them, "It is beautiful."

"I only thought of it briefly, and it appeared. I shall try to bring back the beach," Ariadne says as she stands.

"We do not need to leave," Iona says, "Give me a tour."

Ariadne hesitates but Iona offers her hand. Ariadne takes it and they ascend the stone steps to the front door. Ariadne opens it for Iona and observes her amazement.

They enter into a small courtyard with hallways that are open to the air with painted columns of marble holding them aloft. In the center is a tiered fountain and against the far wall is a staircase to the second floor. There is also an altar with a triple goddess carved into the stone, a depiction of Hecate.

"This is where you live?" Iona asks in astonishment.

"Yes, for most of the year," Ariadne says.

"Most?" Iona asks, "Where do you go when you are not here?"

Ariadne hesitates, not wanting to sound boastful, "My family also has manors in Constantinople and Rome."

"Oh, I see," Iona says, unable to hide her confoundment.

"This manor is where my mother taught me magic throughout most of the year. It is remote, far from any distractions," Ariadne says, "Would you like to see more?"

Iona nods, so Ariadne opens a door for her, and they enter a large sitting room. A painting of Ariadne and her parents hangs on the lefthand wall. Ariadne and her mother sit while her father stands behind them. Her grandmother's portrait is on the righthand wall. She looks down on them with displeasure, dressed in the same red robes that she wore when she visited Ariadne on Samhain. Morgan's pendant lies against her chest. Iona glances at the painting of Ariadne's grandmother, then walks up to the family portrait to examine it.

"How old are you in this?" Iona asks.

"Seventeen," Ariadne says, grimacing at the ostentatious painting.

"You look beautiful... but sad," Iona says.

"An astute observation made by the painter," Ariadne says wryly, "Though it escaped my mother's notice. She adores this painting."

"I must admit your brooding has a certain allure, though I prefer your smile," Iona says.

Iona briefly caresses Ariadne's cheek before strolling off to explore more of the house.

"Has your family lived here for very long?" Iona asks.

"No, only for a generation. My parents wanted a house that would exhibit architecture from both of their cultures in a neutral setting," Ariadne says, "They often entertained here on ritual nights."

Iona leaves the sitting room and enters the library next door. She walks down the rows of dark wooden shelves filled with books. She eyes a copy of *Evelina* and takes it from the shelf but when she opens it, she is disappointed to see that it is a Greek translation.

"If your father is Italian, does that mean you speak it?" Iona asks.

"I speak Italian, Greek, Arabic, Latin, and a bit of French," Ariadne says, "And English soon too, I expect."

Iona grins and puts the book back.

"Or I could learn Italian to speak to you after college. Crescentia speaks it too," Iona says.

Ariadne considers this, then sneaks behind Iona.

"L'italiano suonerebbe peccaminoso sulle tue labbra, ninfa," Ariadne whispers in Iona's ear.

"What did you say?" Iona whispers back.

Ariadne only grins and runs back into the courtyard before Iona could grab her. They run around the fountain until Iona gives up on trying to catch her. Then she looks about, deciding which room to enter next.

"Do you speak any other languages?" Ariadne asks.

"Only a bit of Portuguese. My mother spoke it fluently but rarely used it around me," Iona says, "I think it made her sad to speak it and know that she could never return home."

They enter the dining room. At its center is a long table with wooden benches on either side and two golden candelabra at each end. There are also klines against the wall, which could be used to recline and eat instead.

"Do you have siblings?" Iona asks.

"No," Ariadne says, "My mother could barely stand to have one child in the house, let alone two or three."

"Then why have such a large dining table? Did you sit in a different chair each day?" Iona asks, gesturing to the many seats available.

"My family holds rituals every solstice and equinox. They invite their many friends to feast beforehand," Ariadne explains.

"Such frivolity is foreign to me. My mother never had visitors," Iona says.

"Never?" Ariadne asks.

"She preferred solitude. Or at least, I thought it was a preference but now I know it was because she was hiding me away," Iona sighs.

Then Iona frowns as she realizes something, "If your grandmother is a Zerynthos, and your mother is too, how are you also a Zerynthos? Do witches not pass down the name of men?"

"They do if the man has the stronger tie to sempiterna blood," Ariadne says, "Whoever has the more prestigious name will have it passed down. It is better for the child, in theory, to have the more distinguished surname. None of the Zerynthos women have married men more powerful than them."

"So then if we had a child, they would be named Lysander?" Iona asks with a grin.

Ariadne's mouth falls open, "I beg to differ. It would be Zerynthos."

"I suppose I could humor you," Iona shrugs.

"How very considerate," Ariadne rolls her eyes and Iona giggles.

As Iona wanders back into the courtyard, Ariadne considers the implications of Iona's jest. She knows that passing down the Zerynthos name is expected of her but never considered it in a serious manner. Ariadne sets the thought aside for the moment when Iona glances at the staircase.

"Is your room upstairs?" Iona asks.

"Yes, would you like to see it?" Ariadne asks.

When Iona nods, Ariadne leads her there and holds the door open for her. In fact, she has two rooms of her own, a sitting room and her bedroom. She took Iona to her sitting room first, which has two klines facing each other, a fireplace, and a wooden desk covered in books and papers. Ariadne would invite Samaira and Ksenia to tea here when their parents allowed them to travel. The ceiling is painted with blue clouds and stars, and there is a balcony that faces the valley below, but Ariadne rarely uses it anymore as it overlooks the Pineios River.

Iona gasps when she notices the glass doors that lead to Ariadne's bedroom. Iona eagerly pulls the doors open and steps inside. The room has two glass walls and a glass domed ceiling. Littering the walls and the floor are copious species of plants; roses, ferns, gardenias, orchids, poppies, too many to count. Some plants have their own pots that sit on the many shelves along the walls, while others grow from the floor itself, with the help of some carefully placed charms on the floorboards.

The air is warm and humid, and the scent is a heady combination of herbs and florals. Wisteria flowers are growing from the ceiling too and have purple blooms that hang like a canopy overhead. They partially block the sun's rays but still allow for all the other plants to have ample sunshine. It was Ariadne's compromise when her mother refused to allow her to have a greenhouse. She'd made her own instead and lived amongst the flourishing greenery.

"It's beautiful," Iona whispers.

Iona finds a lavender plant and leans forward to smell it. Ariadne picks a red tulip and hands it to Iona. She smiles and lifts it to her nose, then approaches Ariadne's bed, which is up against the lefthand wall.

"This is where the child prodigy slept?" Iona asks, approaching the canopied bed.

"I wish you would not call me that," Ariadne says with a nervous laugh.

Iona looks back at her and tilts her head.

"Would you prefer genius?" Iona grins.

Ariadne smiles back but it is forced.

"I do not feel much like a genius lately, being so often outwitted," Ariadne says.

Iona's eyes soften as she approaches Ariadne and puts her finger under her chin.

"If it is any consolation, I never thought you were a genius," Iona says solemnly with humor in her gaze.

Ariadne laughs, then sighs, "Perhaps that is why you are so gracious of my many flaws. You do not expect perfection like so many others do."

Iona chastens and says, "You do not ever need to be perfect around me."

Ariadne runs her hand along Iona's cheek, and the skin turns pink beneath her fingertips. Ariadne grins, loving how a single touch could elicit such a reaction, even in a dream.

"Shall we continue the tour?" Iona asks breathlessly.

"We shall," Ariadne says, taking Iona's arm and leading her out of her chambers.

Ariadne takes Iona downstairs to the ballroom, which is built in the Italian style. Gilded mirrors and paintings hang from the walls and a pianoforte sits in the corner. The maple floor creaks as they walk. Ariadne looks up at the crystal chandeliers and the candles light in an instant.

"You have a ballroom in your house?" Iona asks, twirling around and looking up at the ceiling painted with nymphs and fauns.

"A home would never be complete without one," Ariadne says with a shrug.

"I have only read about rooms like these in books," Iona says.

Ariadne goes to sit at the pianoforte and begins to play Bach's Italian Concerto in F major. The song echoes prettily in the empty ballroom. Iona comes to sit beside her, and Ariadne sits straighter in her chair, not wanting to play a false note.

"You have such beautiful hands," Iona says casually.

Ariadne blushes and her fingers falter for a moment before she recovers. Iona notices and grins.

"And lips, and eyes, and breasts," Iona whispers, leaning in and kissing Ariadne's neck until she squirms away, still attempting to continue her piece.

"Your sordid compliments will not distract me," Ariadne chuckles, "I am attempting to serenade you with music and all you can think of is my body."

"How rude of me. Please continue," Iona giggles, leaning her head on Ariadne shoulder and watching her play.

Ariadne's fingers roam across the keys and she cannot shake a persisting thought in her mind.

"What are you thinking of so seriously," Iona asks, putting a hand on Ariadne's lap.

"I feel..." Ariadne pauses, arranging her thoughts, "You make me feel... safe."

Iona lifts her head to look up at Ariadne.

"You are safe with me," Iona says softly.

"Do you feel safe with me?" Ariadne asks.

"Yes," Iona says.

Ariadne frowns, still riddled with doubt. Then she says what she truly meant to say, letting go of any pretense.

"I still feel guilt for the beginning of fall term," Ariadne admits, "I was wrong to do those things, and say those things. I am so sorry."

"I know you are. I am sorry, too," Iona says, gently cupping Ariadne's cheek and guiding her face to look at her, "We let ourselves go a little mad, didn't we?"

Ariadne looks to Iona and her hands slow on the keys until they stop completely.

"If only the aura lesson had not been on our first day," Ariadne chuckles nervously, "Then perhaps we could have been more cordially introduced without feeling attacked by secrets we were not yet ready to share."

"That certainly would have helped, though I am still skeptical that we would have been able to harmonize without clashing first" Iona says with a wry smile.

"Probably not," Ariadne winces.

"I believe that is why the blue comet's magic ensorcelled us the way it did. Fate bound us to each other despite our many differences," Iona moves her hand from Ariadne's cheek and places it against Ariadne's heart, "Fate knew our hearts better than we did and tempted us relentlessly to ensure that we would not miss… this."

Iona closes her eyes and leans her forehead against Ariadne's. They breathe as one, in perfect sync.

"I cannot imagine why I would deserve such intervention by fate," Ariadne whispers.

Ariadne closes the distance between them and kisses Iona so softly, their lips barely touching.

"Whatever is to thank for our affinity, I will never let you go. Not now," Ariadne vows.

Iona smiles brilliantly and it makes Ariadne's heart constrict. Ariadne kisses Iona once more, letting their lips linger gently, then takes Iona's hand and guides her to the center of the ballroom floor.

Ariadne imagines an 18th century gown, a robe a l'Anglaise retroussée, in light blue with ruffled sleeves and roses embroidered in the skirt and bodice. The gown appears on Iona, and she looks down at herself with delight. Ariadne dons a mauve dress in a similar fashion as Iona's and curtsies low. Iona curtsies shyly too, then jumps when the piano begins playing on its own.

"May I have the honor of a dance, signorina?" Ariadne asks.

Ariadne does not wait for an answer, taking Iona's hand and pulling her into her arms. Iona laughs and throws her head back when Ariadne dips her low. Ariadne kisses along Iona's neck and the swells of her breasts which have been pushed obscenely upwards by her corset.

"Ariadne Zerynthos," Iona gasps, putting the back of her hand against her forehead dramatically, "You dare to take such liberties with an honorable maiden?"

"Honorable you may be, but maiden you certainly are not," Ariadne declares loudly, "I saw to that myself."

Iona giggles when Ariadne pulls her back up and twirls them around the room. They never grow tired as the piano plays one song after another, but eventually Ariadne slows their pace until they are merely swaying back and forth. Iona leans her head against Ariadne's shoulder.

"I feel like a princess," Iona sighs happily.

"A queen," Ariadne says, kissing Iona's neck softly.

Iona leans back to look up at Ariadne. Iona lifts herself onto her tiptoes to kiss Ariadne sweetly, barely able to hold back her smile to pucker her lips.

Then Ariadne awakens and looks over at Iona, who groans sleepily beside her. Ariadne kisses her forehead, both of her eyelids, her nose, cheek, and finally her lips.

21 – ARIADNE

Ariadne's desk is too far away to hear what Ksenia is saying but judging by Iona's glum expression, it was something very unpleasant. Enchantments have never been Iona's strongest suit but with Ksenia badgering her, she struggles even more. Ksenia's sharp tongue used to amuse Ariadne but now it only vexes her.

"Poor Iona. She got the worst partner possible…" Crescentia says.

Ariadne glances at Crescentia sitting next to her. Despite Iona's insistence that Crescentia is not the malefician, Ariadne is still very suspicious of her. In light of that, she would argue that she got the worst partner. She remains polite with Crescentia, out of respect for Iona, but it takes every ounce of her self-control to do so.

"Apologies, I forgot Ksenia is your friend," Crescentia says, misinterpreting Ariadne's glare.

Ariadne looks back at Ksenia and wonders if that is true anymore. They have barely spoken since Ariadne told her about courting Iona.

"Excuse me," Ariadne says as she stands and walks over to Iona's table.

Ksenia stops speaking midsentence when she sees Ariadne approaching. Iona looks relieved to see her.

"Ksenia, may we please speak in the hallway for a moment?"

Ariadne asks.

"Ariadne," Iona says nervously.

"Everything is fine. I would just like a word with my oldest friend," Ariadne says.

"Of course, lead the way," Ksenia says, with a saccharine smile.

They leave the lecture hall and Ariadne takes them to a discreet corner of the corridor. A stained-glass image of a witch casting a fire spell shines orange light down upon them.

"Ksenia, I thought I had made myself clear months ago but evidently you did not hear me. Iona is with me now and if I ever see you harassing her again," Ariadne says, but Ksenia interrupts her.

"You will what, Ariadne? What will you do?" Ksenia asks, looking her up and down with contempt.

Ariadne is taken aback by Ksenia's bellicose reaction. Normally her friends would listen to her without a second thought. Now Ksenia acts as if Ariadne is barely worth her time.

"I did not think I needed to do anything for my friend to heed my words. I would never dream of treating a beau of yours with such disrespect," Ariadne says.

"Friend," Ksenia scoffs, "Is that what I am?"

"I thought so but now I am unsure," Ariadne says.

"We only became friends because you broke your last one," Ksenia says.

Ariadne blinks and takes a step back as if Ksenia's words were a physical blow.

"What do you know of me, really? You never cared to ask, and I never cared to tell you. We were allies, adolescents with similar ambitions, but we were only delaying our inevitable opposition," Ksenia says, "You were so preoccupied with Iona that you never realized your true adversary. It suited me just fine to watch your petty feud with her. You were always so impulsive; it took barely any encouragement on my part to turn you against her."

Ariadne flushes with anger at Ksenia and herself.

"I will win the pendant. It will choose me. Why would it choose someone like you? A traumatized, spoiled Zerynthos girl who is so easily manipulated. You do not deserve it. You never did," Ksenia says.

A chill goes down Ariadne's spine when Ksenia's deep blue eyes stare back at her with such icy indifference. Was Iona right in thinking Ksenia is capable of maleficium? Ariadne hadn't thought so, but in that moment, she believes it could be true.

"What is the matter?" Samaira asks as she rushes over to them.

"Go back to your desk, Samaira," Ksenia snaps.

Samaira looks between Ariadne and Ksenia with apprehension.

"Please let us not fight. We should not let blind ambition ruin our friendship," Samaira says.

"Your naïveté is not needed in this conversation, Samaira. Run along," Ksenia sighs.

"Stop treating me like I am beneath your dignity!" Samaira says, "I understand what is at stake, but this is a pointless argument. Only Morgan knows who she will give the pendant to. We have no control over such things."

"You may not, but I do," Ksenia insists.

"Do you truly believe that Morgan will be impressed by your foul temperament?" Samaira asks.

"More impressed than she would be of your inferior breeding," Ksenia spits.

Samaira steps away, hurt but not surprised by Ksenia's condemnable view of her.

"Leave her be, Ksenia," Ariadne says, standing between Ksenia and Samaira.

Ksenia looks between Ariadne and Samaira and crosses her arms.

"Your mother writes to me, you know. She asks after you because she knows what I always have," Ksenia says to Ariadne,

"You are weak. Every show of strength, every brash word, it was all an act. Your heart was never in it. You do not have what it takes to be truly great."

"We have very different views of what greatness looks like," Ariadne seethes.

"And that is why I shall win the pendant instead of you," Ksenia says, flipping her blonde locks over her shoulder.

"Fine," Ariadne snaps, "Take it. I do not want it anymore."

Ksenia's mask slips to reveal her shock. Samaira seems shocked as well, but it is mixed with pride.

"But..." Ksenia says, "You have always wanted it."

"As you said, it was all an act. My family wants the pendant, not I. If you mean to intimidate your competition, then you are confronting the wrong witch," Ariadne says, "Though if you even so much as look in Iona's direction again, you will have me to answer to."

"Oh Ariadne," Ksenia smiles coolly, "You have never scared me."

Then she turns on her heels and walks away. Ariadne has a feeling of foreboding deep in her gut that will not abate. Samaira sighs unhappily and Ariadne turns to check on her.

"Are you alright?" Ariadne asks.

"Yes... Ksenia has become unbearably cruel. Not that she was ever a paragon of benevolence, but normally her bigotry is not quite so blatant," Samaira says.

"Has she taken frequent walks in the forest of late?" Ariadne asks, attempting nonchalance.

"Not that I have seen but we have not been socializing as often as we once did, not for months," Samaira says, "You were all we had in common."

Samaira furrows her brow and fidgets with her ring.

"Something feels wrong," Samaira muses, "A darkness in the air that I cannot explain. Do you feel it?"

Ariadne nods cautiously, "We should all take care until the trials are behind us."

Samaira nods and shakes off her uneasiness.

"She should not have said that about Vivien," Samaira says softly.

Ariadne nods and is frustrated when her vision blurs from unwanted tears. She'd hoped that Samaira had not overheard that part of the conversation.

"I have had terrible luck with friends," Ariadne chuckles darkly, "Except for you. I still do not know why you bother with me at all."

"Ariadne," Samaira sighs, "You have had a very difficult life. I do not expect you to be unaffected by your pain. I know you were raised by horrid people who equate blood with sublimity, but you never fully assimilated into their ways of thinking, even when it would have been easier for you to. I hoped you would find your way eventually and since you began courting Iona, I have seen such change in you that makes me proud to be your friend."

Samaira pulls Ariadne into a warm hug. Ariadne squeezes her tightly, so grateful for her gracious, generous view of her.

"You should come and study with me and Iona sometime soon," Ariadne says when she pulls away.

"I would like that very much," Samaira says.

When Ariadne and Samaira reenter the lecture hall, Professor Salum eyes them sternly. Ariadne goes to sit by Crescentia again but remembers that Iona is now without a partner. She is incanting over a ring but seems to be losing patience. Ariadne walks to Iona's table instead and sits next to her.

"You were gone for quite a while," Iona says, glancing over at her.

"I will tell you what happened later," Ariadne says, "Which spell are you practicing?"

"I am still stuck on the blocking enchantment. No matter what I try, it does not work," Iona sighs.

"You will get it eventually," Ariadne encourages.

"How do you do it?" Iona asks.

Ariadne searches for a way to describe something so

inscrutable. Her protection spells have always been her strongest forms of magic. She had practiced the spell fervently in her youth, primarily because she never wanted to be vulnerable to another witch's magic again. Ariadne is still surprised that Iona struggles with this particular enchantment but knows that she is capable of it.

"I feel magic coming from within me and into the object. It's a faint sensation but it's there," Ariadne says, "You must be entirely confident that your magic is strong enough to withstand another witch's spell. You cannot doubt whether the spell will protect. Otherwise, it will not work. It is all about intention."

Iona stares determinedly at the ring in front of her and takes a deep breath.

"Zárolt," Iona says.

Iona picks up the ring and puts it on her middle finger.

"Test it," Iona says.

Ariadne points her wand at Iona and says, "Aóratos."

Iona turns invisible and sighs. Ariadne undoes the spell. Iona takes off the ring and flings it back on the desk with frustration.

"Try again," Ariadne says.

"It will not work," Iona protests, tossing her wand onto the table.

"I will cast spells on you until you try again," Ariadne warns.

"Professor Salum would have something to say about that," Iona rolls her eyes.

"Oh, not here. On our walks to class, during dinner, while you're sleeping," Ariadne counts on her fingers, "You will learn how to block them eventually, but I will have fun in the meantime."

Iona rubs her hands over her face and groans. Then she picks up her wand and glares down at the ring. Ariadne suspects that this time it might work because when Iona dons that expression, nothing can withstand her will.

"Zárolt," Iona incants forcefully.

Iona puts the ring back on and faces Ariadne again.

"Aóratos," Ariadne says.

Iona does not turn invisible. The spell has no effect. It is not strong enough to reflect the spell back on Ariadne, but it works just as well. Ariadne grins and glances down at Iona's body. Iona looks down at herself and her smile is radiant.

"It worked!" Iona exclaims.

Iona throws her arms around Ariadne and squeals happily. The rest of the class pauses their conversation to look at them and Iona sits back in her chair and smooths out her skirt. Ariadne coughs to hide her laugh.

"Apologies," Iona says, looking around in embarrassment.

Iona gives Ariadne one more smile before gathering her grimoires to leave class. Ariadne's humor fades when an image crosses her mind of Iona as a wraith, from the illusion that the malefician had implanted in her mind. Ariadne has found herself remembering the wraith more and more. It is a reminder of what could happen to Iona if Ariadne should fail to protect her.

With every touch, every smile, every wound that Iona heals in her, Ariadne dreads the thought of losing her. She knows she loves Iona, though they haven't yet spoken the words to each other. Ariadne is afraid to love someone who is facing such peril. As Iona becomes stronger and masters a new spell, the malefician does the same somewhere in the forest.

Ariadne peers into the trees as she skates across the courtyard. Elise had made a sheet of ice in the middle of the grass that is large enough to skate on and perfectly smooth. Iona had never skated before, and she clutches Ariadne's arm so tightly that she is losing circulation.

"Push your feet to the side and back," Ariadne says.

"How are you balancing so easily," Iona asks, then almost falls backwards but Ariadne pulls her back up.

"May I join you?" Crescentia calls.

Iona looks over at her, then back at Ariadne, who nods.

"Only if you promise not to let me fall," Iona calls back, then wobbles over to Crescentia at the edge of the ice. Crescentia just finishes tying on her skates when Iona makes it to her, and she takes Crescentia's arm to hold her up. Ariadne skates on her own as Iona tells Crescentia that she is learning Italian. Then Elise skates up to Ariadne.

"Perhaps I ought to have made the ice longer so more people would fit," Elise muses.

"We still can if others ask to join us," Ariadne says, "The ice is perfect."

"Thank you," Elise smiles with pride, then her eyebrows furrow in contemplation, "I had initially intended to skate on a pond I had found in the forest on Samhain, but when I mentioned the idea to my father, he told me not to go into the woods because they are not safe at present. It was so strange... I am not sure what has scared him, but I thought I would relay the message, since I have seen you and Iona enter the woods on occasion."

Ariadne fights to keep her expression neutral.

"Oh... that is odd. Thank you for the warning. Iona will be disappointed. She loves those woods," Ariadne says.

"As do I. They are a marvel," Elise smiles wistfully.

"I am sure that if your father believes the woods are unsafe, he has a good reason," Ariadne says.

Ariadne hopes Elise does heed her father's warning. It would be awful if she, or indeed any of the other witches at college, were inadvertently attacked by the malefician lurking in the wood.

Iona and Crescentia laugh at something, and both fall onto the ice in a giggling heap. Ariadne chuckles.

"Crescentia has come far since we met her," Elise says, "What was it, the spring equinox ritual at your manor... three years ago?"

"That sounds correct," Ariadne says.

"It feels like a lifetime ago," Elise murmurs, "I remember her parents were so nervous."

"They were," Ariadne says, "Though can you blame them?

They were the only new family present."

"I heard Professor Salum say that soon the new witches at college will outnumber witches from established families. Such a change will certainly ruffle feathers," Elise says.

"Perhaps it is a good thing. All of our families began modestly at some point in history. If we have more of them, it would only strengthen the presence of magic in the world," Ariadne says.

Elise glances at Ariadne in surprise, "Do not let your mother hear you speak in such a way."

"She never listens to what I say regardless," Ariadne mutters.

Elise looks at Ariadne with an unreadable expression.

"What?" Ariadne asks.

"You have changed a great deal," Elise says.

"I suppose I have," Ariadne says, a little self-conscious, "I have gained perspective on matters. A better perspective."

"How refreshing. Iona has had a good influence on you," Elise grins.

"And on you as well, I hear. Your magic is much improved," Ariadne says.

"All credit to Iona. She is very patient with me," Elise says, looking back at Iona.

Iona lets go of Crescentia and skates over to Ariadne, almost falling again but Ariadne catches her. Elise skates ahead of them and twirls around in circles.

"Flying is simpler than this," Iona gripes.

"I had to catch you then too," Ariadne grins.

Ariadne takes Iona's arms and puts them around her waist so she can pull Iona across the ice. Iona holds on as Ariadne increases their speed. She whips them around the corners of the ice to make Iona laugh. Then Ariadne runs out of breath and slows down.

"No, do not slow down!" Iona protests.

"I need... a moment..." Ariadne pants.

Ariadne skates forward at a crawl and Iona holds on and

waits for her to catch her second wind. Then Iona moves one of her hands from Ariadne's waist and shifts it to her lower stomach. Ariadne grits her teeth when Iona's magic courses through her and makes her core clench. She takes Iona's hand and returns it to her waist.

"Behave," Ariadne chuckles darkly.

"I am so very cold. Shall we retire to the dormitories so you can warm me up," Iona whispers in Ariadne's ear.

Ariadne takes Iona's hand and spins her around, then dips her low. Unable to balance on her skates alone, Iona yelps and clings to Ariadne, who leans close until their lips almost touch.

"Iona Lysander, are you attempting to seduce me?" Ariadne asks.

"Yes…" Iona's says bashfully, "Rather successfully I'd wager."

Ariadne's retort is silenced by Iona soft, warm lips. Ariadne pulls Iona back to standing and cups her cheek as they wrap their arms around each other and sink into a deep kiss.

"No fornicating on the ice!" Crescentia calls, then whistles raucously.

Iona pulls away from the kiss and giggles, her cheeks already pink from the winter chill. Ariadne kisses her once more on her cheek, then helps her back to solid ground. They say goodbye to Elise and Crescentia, who stay on the ice a while longer.

Iona is ripping Ariadne's clothes off as soon as her bedroom door is shut. They make knots of each other's laces in their haste but eventually Ariadne has Iona naked and laid out on the bed, looking up at her with ravenous lust. Iona's glistening sex is spread wide, and her fingers slide through her wetness to tease them both.

Ariadne crawls onto the bed and kneels between Iona's spread thighs. Iona lifts her hips up excitedly, expecting Ariadne to lick her, but Ariadne has other plans. She lifts one of Iona's legs up until her knee is in line with Ariadne's shoulder. Then Ariadne straddles Iona's other leg, so their folds are aligned.

Iona watches her until Ariadne grinds her cunt into Iona's. Their swollen buds circle and rub together until Iona's eyes roll into the back of her head as she moans at the delicious friction. Ariadne grasps Iona's waist as Iona digs her nails into Ariadne's thigh. Their combined wetness makes lewd sounds as Ariadne rolls her hips.

Their magnetism intensifies the pleasure until Iona is a woman possessed. She shifts so she is laying more on her side and buries her face in the mattress, clinging to the sheets for dear life. Ariadne rolls her hips into her again and again while gripping Iona's raised leg, never letting up as she watches what she does to the beautiful woman beneath her.

"Please, please," Iona sobs. It is all she can manage to say.

Ariadne whimpers and grinds harder. She can barely stand it when Iona sounds so desperate for her. She kisses the soft skin next to Iona's knee. Iona reaches out and Ariadne grabs her hand and uses it as leverage.

When Iona reaches her climax, magic explodes from her, and Ariadne cries out as she is pushed over the edge too. Ariadne's hips stop as their tender flesh becomes far too sensitive. Ariadne trembles as she pushes her hair from her face and gasps for air.

"Ariadne," Iona says, weakly reaching for her.

Ariadne gingerly disentangles their legs. She lays down onto the bed and pulls Iona on top of her. They lay there for a while, exhausted but sated. Iona traces the flame on Ariadne's breast until her fingers stop moving. Ariadne notices and looks down at her. Iona's face is serene in sleep. Ariadne drifts a finger from Iona's forehead to her cheek and wonders how this lovely, insatiable creature could be fated for her.

Ariadne lays her head back and looks up at the ceiling. It is only barely sunset, so she is not tired enough to sleep but does not want to move and risk waking Iona. She drifts her fingers along Iona's smooth back and lets her thoughts wander.

Iona stirs and Ariadne tenses, hoping she did not wake her accidentally. Then Iona lifts herself from the bed without a word and walks away.

"Iona?" Ariadne says.

Iona walks to her pile of clothes on the floor and kneels next to it to find something. Ariadne watches her with a feeling of unease. A crack of lightening makes Ariadne jump, then rain pelts the window, the wind howling as thunder booms.

"Iona, are you well?" Ariadne asks.

Iona pulls out her wand from her dress pocket and holds it firmly in her hand. When she turns around, Ariadne gasps as a flash of lightening illuminates the room. Iona's eyes are white, with no iris or pupil. Her expression is flat and lifeless as she lifts her wand towards Ariadne.

Ariadne pushes herself off the bed and hides as Iona throws spells at her. She does not speak or emote, only waves her wand as she attacks. Ariadne's wand is still in her dress pocket where Iona is standing, but even if she had it, she did not know what she would do. She would rather be attacked by Iona than hurt her.

"Iona," Ariadne yells, then tries to lift her head over the edge of the bed, but Iona tries to throw another spell.

Aster and Wisp cower in the corner of the room, not seeming to understand what was happening. Iona walks slowly toward the other side of the bed, throwing spells along the way.

"Aster, my wand!" Ariadne orders.

Aster runs around Iona and dodges her spells. Iona does not seem to notice him, only focusing on Ariadne. The wolf takes Ariadne's dress between his teeth and runs back to where Ariadne is hiding. Her wolf has earned a bloody steak for his bravery, but for now she takes the dress from him and pulls out her wand. Ariadne takes a chance and lifts her head. Iona throws a spell at her.

"Zárolt," Ariadne yells.

She blocks the spell successfully and continues to block them as she steps closer to Iona. She tries to pry Iona's fingers open to take her wand, but Iona holds fast.

"Iona, let go," Ariadne begs.

Iona suddenly pushes Ariadne to the ground and straddles her. Ariadne tries to hit her with a shrinking spell, but she dodges it, rips Ariadne's wand from her hand and throws it across the room. Then she wraps her hands around Ariadne's throat and squeezes.

"Iona," Ariadne chokes, clawing at Iona's hands.

Aster growls and barks at Iona while Wisp still cowers in the corner.

"Aster, do not attack!" Ariadne orders, before Iona squeezes so hard that she can no longer speak.

Ariadne's legs kick and she tries to buck Iona off, but it is no use. Iona's white eyes are vacant and impassive as she watches Ariadne struggle. It is torture for Ariadne to watch someone so gentle as Iona commit such a heinous act.

Ariadne reaches up to grasp at Iona's face, using the only magic she has left. She closes her eyes and tries to call upon their affinity to wake Iona up. She does not know if it will work, but she must try. As she puts the last traces of her remaining energy through her fingertips, she can see Iona's magic stirring and spilling from her pores the way it had when they experimented in her dormitory.

Ariadne feels her consciousness waning as Iona's hands press down on her throat. Aster's barks grow faint as Ariadne's vision blurs. Ariadne thinks of lying down in the sand with Iona beside her, looking deeply into her hazel eyes until she blushes and smiles shyly. The hands choking Ariadne's throat relax, then fall away completely.

"Ariadne?" Iona cries, "Oh no, oh no!"

Ariadne opens her eyes and coughs, gasping for air with wheezing breaths. Iona's hazel irises have returned, and they convey her shock.

"I am alright," Ariadne manages to say, before another coughing fit makes it impossible to speak.

"How did I... What happened? I was asleep and when I woke up, I was..." Iona weeps.

Ariadne takes her hand and though she feels Iona pulling away, she coaxes her into an embrace. Iona sinks into her and sobs.

"It was not you," Ariadne rasps, when she is able to speak again.

"But I had my hands on your throat," Iona cries.

"It was blood magic," Ariadne says, "Your eyes were white. You did not speak or show any emotion."

Iona trembles with fear and Ariadne holds her tightly. The rain has become a tempest, so blustering that Ariadne worries that the windows might break. Then Ariadne tenses as a realization strikes her.

"The duel in the forest. When I found you in your room there was a cut on your hand," Ariadne remembers, "I had thought it was a wound from the fight, but they were harvesting your blood."

Iona pulls back and looks at Ariadne with horror.

"What do we do?" Iona asks.

Ariadne racks her brain for anything that could be done. Iona shuffles away from her until her back is against the bedframe and she is hugging her legs against her chest.

"As long as they have your blood, there is nothing we can do. Unless we find the malefician but... they still elude us," Ariadne says, "They will eventually run out of your blood if they continue to use it for spells but there is no way to know how much blood they stole."

Tears stream down Iona's cheeks and Ariadne reaches for her again. Iona flinches away and shakes her head.

"I could hurt you again," Iona whispers.

"It is okay. I know it was not really you," Ariadne rasps, "I broke the spell with our magnetism. If I need to, I can do it again."

"But if you were only seconds too late, I would have killed you. They could cast their spell again at any moment," Iona says, "You cannot be alone with me."

Iona stands and searches for her chemise in the pile of

clothes on the floor.

"What are you suggesting? That I should leave you here alone?" Ariadne asks, pushing herself up and rubbing her throat tenderly, "That is what the malefician would want, so they could attack you more easily."

"We should discuss this with Samuel tomorrow to see if anything can be done, but otherwise I do not see any recourse. I will not be responsible for injuring you... or worse," Iona says.

"I will not leave you alone when you need me the most," Ariadne says.

Iona tries to argue but Ariadne takes both of her hands and holds them tightly.

"I will not let her take you away from me! Do not ask me to abandon you because I never will," Ariadne says obstinately.

Ariadne coughs again from the strain on her voice. Iona looks down at Ariadne's neck and her tears are renewed. Ariadne can only imagine the kinds of bruises that are forming on her skin, and she is too scared to check in a mirror.

"This is nothing. I will brew a healing potion and it will disappear," Ariadne says, gesturing to her neck.

Iona only cries and Ariadne holds her. Ariadne lets her go to find her own chemise, then coaxes Iona back into bed. Ariadne holds Iona against her until her sobs dissipate. Then they lay there silently, neither of them able to sleep.

22 – IONA

Iona feels violated. She cannot sleep and struggles to eat. Now that the malefician has her blood, they could do virtually anything to her body whenever they so desire. They could make her find a knife and slit her own throat. They could make her do the same to Ariadne or one of her friends. To lose her own autonomy is unbearable, but to be a threat to everyone around her is unforgivable.

Ariadne's healing potion worked as all her potions do, but Iona will never forget the bruises in the shape of her handprints. She keeps imagining herself waking up and looking down at Ariadne's lifeless body. Ariadne has told her multiple times that she can protect herself, but the truth is they are both defenseless. It makes Iona's paranoia nearly debilitating but Ariadne refuses to let her out of her sight.

Ariadne had also brewed energy potions for both of them to help with the exhaustion. It is not as renewing as true sleep, but it was the only way Iona could make it through a conversation with Samuel about blood magic. Ariadne and Iona visited him in his office before classes began for the day. When they told him what had happened, he turned ghostly pale.

He confirmed what they already knew. Once a witch has your blood, there is almost nothing that can counteract the spell. It was a miracle that Iona had not killed Ariadne last night. Samuel tells them that he will do research and let them know if he finds anything that might help, but he does not seem optimistic.

Nights go by tortuously. Iona fears shutting her eyes and losing control before she can wake up. All that comforts her are Ariadne's arms around her, her fingers in her hair and her lips against her forehead. Ariadne stays awake with her all night, sometimes reading to her to pass the time or humming concertos and nocturnes with her ataractic soprano voice.

Classes feel utterly pointless in light of everything that is going on, but Samuel is adamant that they must pretend as if everything is fine. If an all-out witch hunt occurred, the mass hysteria would make it that much more difficult to find the true culprit. A malefician would only use the chaos to their own advantage.

In conjuration class, they are learning the air and earth spells. Iona pays attention as best she can despite her overwhelming fatigue and debilitating stress. It is apparently not enough attention for Ksenia because Iona is knocked out of her reverie by a splash of mud. Ksenia had used an earth spell to throw a rock that landed at Iona's feet, spraying her with wet dirt all over her dress.

"Am I boring you, Lysander?" Ksenia asks.

"No more than usual," Iona grumbles.

Ksenia narrows her eyes and frowns.

"Gíinos," Iona uses the earth spell to remove the dirt from her black dress so only wet spots are left behind.

"You seem strained. Do you have something on your mind?" Ksenia sneers.

Iona glares at Ksenia and her hands tremble. Iona does not know why Ksenia would phrase her question in such a way if she did not know about the blood magic.

"Gíinos," Ksenia says, lifting a larger rock so it hovers next to her.

Iona clenches her fist around her wand. They are meant to be tossing rocks between each other to practice the earth spell, but all Iona wants is to create an avalanche in Ksenia's direction.

Ksenia tosses the rock to Iona, and she stops it in midair, then throws it back at Ksenia. It hits her square in the chest and knocks her down.

"Ánemos!" Iona screams throwing air at Ksenia to keep her down on the ground, "Neró!"

Ksenia is drenched with water, and she screams from the cold. Iona is overcome with the urgent desire to force a confession from Ksenia. She cannot stand another of Ksenia's taunting remarks. Before Iona can cast another spell, Ariadne tackles Iona to the ground and takes her wand away.

"Are you mad?" Ksenia screams as she wipes the water from her eyes.

The other witches in class murmur amongst themselves and Samuel runs over to them.

"Is anyone hurt?" Samuel asks.

"I am fine," Ksenia says petulantly.

"Iona, calm yourself," Ariadne says.

"Why did you stop me," Iona whispers so only Ariadne can hear. She only looks down at Iona with concern.

"I did not know if it was you or another blood spell," Ariadne admits.

"Iona, in my office, now!" Samuel yells.

Iona closes her eyes and fights back her tears. Ksenia stomps away muttering to herself about crazy Lysander witches. Ariadne helps Iona up off the ground but does not give back her wand.

They walk in silence. When they make it to Samuel's office, Iona slumps into a chair and covers her face with her hands.

"Iona, I understand that you were unnerved by the blood magic, and we are all upset by the predicament we are in, but that does not give you the right to attack other students without cause," Samuel says.

"I was certain it was her. Who else could it be? She hates me. She is blindly ambitious. She wants the pendant at any cost.

What more is there?" Iona yells.

Samuel and Ariadne exchanged a worried look.

"This is not the time to be reckless. The witch is getting stronger by the day. You cannot force her to reveal herself by cornering her. Provoking her while she still has your blood is suicide," Samuel says.

"You only showed the malefician, whoever she is, that her attacks are unraveling you the way she'd hoped," Ariadne says.

"I do not know what to do," Iona laments, "We are no closer to finding her than we were months ago. I cannot sit idle and wait for the next time they use my blood to hurt someone I care about."

Ariadne kneels before Iona and takes her hands.

"I wish I could commune with the ghost one more time to beg for their wisdom," Iona says.

"The ghost you met on Samhain?" Samuel asks.

Iona nods, knowing before Samuel speaks that such a thing is impossible.

"By the next Samhain, the trials would have already happened. We cannot wait that long," Samuel says.

Iona notices that Ariadne is deep in contemplation. She has an idea. When she meets Iona's eyes, she signals that she does not want to speak of it yet.

"Did you find any information on blood magic that could help us?" Iona asks Samuel.

"Not as of yet, but I shall keep looking. There may be something but... I would rather search for a less drastic alternative," Samuel says rather vaguely.

"Very well," Iona says.

Samuel tells them to claim that he punished Iona severely for her outburst. He warns them that if either of them attacks a student again without proper proof, he will discipline them accordingly.

"What did you think of?" Iona asks Ariadne as they walk across the courtyard.

"I may have a way for you to see your ghost," Ariadne says,

"But it is in the forest."

Aster and Wisp lead Ariadne and Iona through the trees. They both have their wands drawn, ready for anything or anyone who might attack. They approach an old, dead tree with grey bark and limbs that bend crookedly and reach up towards the sky. Iona feels a chill run down her spine.

"This tree is a witch's grave, a sacred sepulcher. No one remembers her name, only that she was powerful and lived a long life," Ariadne says.

"Why did you bring us here?" Iona asks.

"Normally we would need to wait for Samhain when magic is strong enough to fuel our trip to the land of the dead. Since it is not Samhain, we need to create that magic another way. This tree is connected to the dead witch and has magic locked within. We must unlock it," Ariadne says.

"How do we do that?" Iona asks.

"We perform a ritual and ask the witch if she will help us," Ariadne says, "My mother does this at my grandmother's grave when she desires an audience with her. It takes a considerable amount of energy, but I am hoping the connection we share may be enough to sustain it."

"I suppose it is worth a try," Iona says.

Ariadne approaches the tree and Iona feels the ground tremble the closer Ariadne gets.

"Izrezati," Ariadne says, cutting a limb from the tree.

The limb falls with a thump. Ariadne cuts two more limbs off, then arranges the limbs together, and uses a fire spell to set them ablaze. Iona watches as the tree regrows the limbs that Ariadne had cut off, like a lizard grows a tail. Then Ariadne kisses Iona's neck from behind and she jumps slightly.

"Frightened of a tree, darling?" Ariadne jokes in an attempt to lighten the mood.

"Why would I be frightened of a haunted tree that shakes the ground?" Iona asks sarcastically.

Ariadne chuckles as she undoes the buttons of Iona's dress.

"How did you survive a childhood filled with this weirdness?" Iona asks, shaking her head.

"By the skin of my teeth," Ariadne says as she undoes Iona's laces, "And with a keen sense of humor."

Iona helps Ariadne out of her dress until they are both ready for their ritual. Iona is grateful for the heat of the bonfire that keeps the winter chill at bay.

"We should chant the spell used to make the Samhain talismans," Ariadne says, "Mortuus loqui cum magis."

"Mortuus loqui cum magis," Iona repeats.

They join hands and repeat the spell. Iona does not feel much like dancing, but Ariadne pulls Iona along, poking her in the ribs when she falls to far behind. Iona giggles, evades Ariadne's playful jabs, and chants the spell in earnest.

Iona knows the spell is working when she sees magic in green fragments slithering between their bodies. The serpentine magic extends from the tips of the dead branches until the magic almost looks like leaves bringing the tree back to life.

Iona gasps when the magic constricts itself around her arms, legs, and torso, sliding across her skin as it tightens its grip. It does the same to Ariadne and pulls them towards each other. Ariadne takes advantage of their proximity and steals a kiss. Iona moans into Ariadne's mouth with the magic crawls around them, tying them together inescapably.

Ariadne's kisses make Iona's knees weak, her wicked tongue exploring Iona's mouth eagerly. Iona tightens her arms around Ariadne's neck just as Ariadne slides her hands down to squeeze Iona's bottom.

Ariadne groans as she reluctantly pulls away from Iona to look at the tree, which is glowing greener by the second. She takes Iona's hand and leads her to the trunk, placing Iona's hand on its bark. Iona's blissful intoxication is abruptly lost when her fingertips touch the rough bark. She cries out as she feels all of her magic sapped from within her and into the tree. Ariadne holds onto Iona as she crumples from the desolation of her power.

"Do not give in!" Ariadne says, placing her hand over Iona's.

Iona screams as she feels her magic waning. Then everything goes black.

The sound of waves in the distance makes Iona open her eyes. She looks up to a cloudy sky and takes a deep breath of salty air that reminds her of home. She sits up and looks around. She is on an island with green and red grass.

Iona tries not to despair because this is not where Morgan had met her on Samhain. Another ghost is waiting somewhere on the island for Iona to find them. Iona stands and notices that she is wearing a blue dress that shimmers gold in the light. Iona turns around and inhales sharply.

A house made of opaque glass stands on the very top of the hill. It reflects the light of the sun and makes rainbows that stretch out in every direction. Beside the glass house stands a single oak tree.

Iona approaches the structure and holds her hand up to shield her eyes from the brilliant glare. Then a man with a long brown beard comes out from behind the oak tree and startles Iona. He is wearing a billowing blue robe and holds an oak wood staff with a labradorite stone the size of Iona's fist housed within a cage of branches at the top. Iona hesitantly approaches the man, who smiles kindly at her.

"You are disappointed," the man says.

"No, sir," Iona lies.

The man smiles knowingly but does not seem offended.

"Morgan is a much lovelier visitor to be sure, but you will have to resort to my company instead," the man says.

Iona is surprised that the man knows about her visit with Morgan. He must be a very powerful warlock. Then Iona inspects the man's staff closer, and her eyes widen.

"You are Merlin," Iona says.

"Yes, I am he," Merlin says, "Morgan has informed me of the malefician that is plaguing you."

"Are you able to help me? Morgan would not tell me who the malefician is because she says it is my destiny to find them myself, but they continue to evade us," Iona says.

"Morgan is correct. It is your destiny to unravel the mystery, as it is the malefician's destiny to descend into darkness. Fate has decided that you are not yet ready to know the identity of your attacker, but you will not need to wait much longer. I cannot tell you who they are, but there may be another matter that I can advise on," Merlin says.

"Please, sir, is there nothing you can do to help me?" Iona begs, "I do not know who else to turn to."

Merlin averts his eyes and Iona worries that she may have offended him.

"The only clue I can provide is that the malefician is no stranger to you. They are one who wishes to gain power and respect, but you are in the way of that in more ways than one," Merlin says.

Iona is disheartened by this. The malefician is one of her friends. Or at least, someone she knows well. Iona is reminded of Ariadne's ordeal at the river. Her closest friend had been the one to betray her. Iona hates to consider it, but maybe it could be Crescentia after all.

Iona remembers that Crescentia had asked about blood magic during phytology class. Had her question been less innocent than she'd thought? Crescentia was also quick to encourage Iona to leave school after the siren attack. Iona had thought it had been out of concern for her, but perhaps Crescentia had tried to get rid of Iona that way since the sirens had not finished the job. Iona had been so sure that the version of Crescentia who lured her into the forest was an illusion to deceive her, but maybe she was wrong.

"The malefician stole my blood. It is imperative that I find them soon. They grow stronger every day," Iona says.

Merlin's expression darkens, "Blood magic is perilous indeed. It would be catastrophic for one so sinister as this sorceress to take control of you."

Merlin strokes his beard in contemplation. A falcon flies up from the other side of the hill and lands on Merlin's outstretched arm. He pets the bird as he thinks.

"There is only one way to counteract the malefician's spell," Merlin finally says, "It requires complete and permanent trust. This ritual must never be performed lightly. "

"What is it?" Iona asks warily.

"Do you have someone in your life who owns your heart implicitly? Someone you could trust with the very essence of your mind and soul?" Merlin asks.

"Yes," Iona says, immediately thinking of Ariadne, who has risked her own life for Iona's on multiple occasions now.

"Are you absolutely certain of this?" Merlin asks.

"I am," Iona says, then blinks away tears, "I love her."

Merlin nods solemnly.

"You must give her your blood," Merlin says.

"But I was told never to give anyone my blood," Iona says.

"Normally yes, except in the case of one ritual as ancient as magic itself," Merlin says, "A ritual that would bind you to her for the rest of your mortal lives and into eternity. A blood bond spell."

Iona considers the weight of this prospect. To be tied to someone even after death is an everlasting affinity.

"How would that help to combat the malefician's spell?" Iona asks.

"If your beloved is blood bound to you, she can counteract any blood attack with protection magic. By incanting protective charms over you each day, it would negate any blood spell the malefician would try to cast," Merlin says, "Normally this ritual would be conducted between longstanding partners after many years of courtship and meditation on their bond, but in this extreme case, you could be in grave danger without it."

"I will do it," Iona says, "If Ariadne agrees to perform it, I will."

"I must implore you, do not take this spell lightly. It can

be the most sacred connection between loving souls but can easily become a wretched subjugation if the love goes sour. It is bloody difficult to reverse and to do so would rip your souls apart. Very nasty business," Merlin warns, "Your very mind will be Ariadne's to penetrate when she sees fit. She will feel your emotions as if they are her own, see with your eyes, feel with your skin. Only do this if you believe that Ariadne's love is true."

Iona nods, her head swimming with the ramifications of this spell.

"Follow your heart, Iona, but do not let it blind you," Merlin says.

Iona gasps awake. She is no longer standing, nor is the tree glowing with green magic. She is curled up in Ariadne's lap, still naked and trembling from the effects of the debilitating ritual.

"Are you alright?" Ariadne asks as she strokes Iona's cheek gently.

"I saw Merlin," Iona says, breathing heavily.

Ariadne stares at her in disbelief, "Merlin? The Merlin?"

"Yes," Iona says, too exhausted to point out that they only know of one Merlin.

"What did he say?" Ariadne asks, unable to hide her excitement.

"One moment, please. I am... so tired," Iona says, her eyelids drooping.

Ariadne holds Iona closer and kisses her forehead. When Iona catches her breath, she recounts what Merlin had told her. When Iona mentions the blood bond spell, Ariadne keeps her expression neutral, but Iona can tell she is shaken by the prospect.

"He said that normally a couple as young as we are would not perform such a ritual, but we do not have the luxury of time. He said that if I truly trust you with my soul, I should perform the ritual to protect myself from the malefician," Iona says.

"And do you? Do you trust me that completely?" Ariadne asks, unable to mask her incredulity.

"Yes, I do," Iona says without doubt, "You have protected me from harm from the very first time the witch tried to kill me. We are already tied to each other uniquely."

"This would be a much stronger tie," Ariadne argues, "Near permanent and unavoidable. If you ever decided... that you did not want me anymore..."

Ariadne swallows hard, the idea making her visibly upset.

"If you ever decided to leave, you would only need to refrain from touching me again to avoid our current connection. If you were blood bound to me, I would see your thoughts, feel everything you felt, no matter where in the world you were," Ariadne says.

"I know," Iona says.

"And you truly believe I am worthy of such trust?" Ariadne asks with a trace of frustration.

Iona cups Ariadne's face in her hands and holds her gaze.

"I love you, Ariadne Zerynthos," Iona says.

Ariadne's expression is a mixture of disbelief and vulnerability.

"You may love me now, but what about when we leave school? What happens when I make a mistake or," Ariadne stutters, but Iona cuts her off.

"You were willing to face death to be by my side, even when I told you to go," Iona reminds her, "You have shown me such loyalty and devotion in ways that I do not deserve."

"You deserve much more than me," Ariadne says, tears forming in her eyes.

"I love you," Iona says again, leaning her forehead against Ariadne's.

"I love you, too, but..." Ariadne does not know what to say.

"I love you," Iona whispers, kissing Ariadne softly.

"You shouldn't," Ariadne says, tears falling down her cheeks.

"I do," Iona says.

Ariadne takes a deep, shuddering breath and strokes Iona's cheek.

"Will you do this for me?" Iona asks.

Ariadne stares at her with a vulnerable expression.

"Only if you take my blood as well," Ariadne says.

"But that is not necessary. The malefician does not have your blood. I only need to be bonded to you," Iona says.

"I will only do this if it is reciprocal. A soul for a soul," Ariadne says.

Iona sighs but knows better than to argue once Ariadne has made up her mind.

"Very well," Iona says.

Ariadne helps Iona back to her feet and Iona pulls Ariadne into her arms. Ariadne kisses her fiercely and Iona can taste Ariadne's tears on her lips. When Ariadne pulls away, Iona leans in to take another kiss and Ariadne chuckles.

"We will have more than enough time for that after the ritual, an eternity in fact," Ariadne says.

Iona looks up at her with wide eyes. The enormity of eternity with Ariadne is too vast for her to envision.

"How is the ritual performed?" Iona asks.

"We need a knife," Ariadne says, finding her dress in the dirt and taking her wand from her pocket.

Ariadne conjures a dagger with a golden hilt. Iona and Ariadne kneel facing each other. Ariadne gently takes Iona's hand and runs the blade across her palm. Iona winces at the pain and Ariadne glances up at her sympathetically. Then she takes Iona's other hand and makes a similar cut. Ariadne cuts her palms as well, then takes Iona's hands. Iona notices then that both of their hands are shaking.

"Cup your hands like this," Ariadne says, demonstrating by putting her hands together.

Iona mirrors Ariadne, who places her cupped hands adjacent to Iona's. Then Ariadne closes her eyes.

"Meum semel et futurum amorem," Ariadne says.

"Meum semel et futurum amorem," Iona says along with

her.

They repeat the incantation as one. Iona stutters when her blood collects in her hands, coming from the cuts in her palms, until she is holding a pool of red. Ariadne's blood collects in her hands too until it crosses over into Iona's hands. Their blood blends together, some of it overflowing onto the forest floor.

Then the blood begins to float as it swirls with increasing speed until it glows bright red. The liquid turns to auroral light that bathes the small clearing with crimson. The ball of light suddenly explodes outwards and Iona flinches away in surprise.

Tiny sparkling particles dance in the air until they float down and slip back through the cuts in Iona and Ariadne's palms. Iona watches open mouthed as the glittering magic travels up her veins and spreads through her entire body from head to toe.

She feels the exact moment when the magic reaches her heart, and her entire body trembles as her pulse races. Then the magic goes up her neck through her spine and coats her brain. Iona closes her eyes and gasps, unable to fathom the sensations until suddenly, it stops.

Iona's eyelids flutter open as her mind expands within her skull. She hears Ariadne's thoughts within her head as if they were her own.

She may regret this one day, but I would rather live an eternity of misery with her than to lose her forever to that dreadful witch, Ariadne thinks.

Iona flinches when she sees an image in Ariadne's mind of Iona as an infernal wraith. The image comes from the illusion that the malefician gave to Ariadne. Ariadne had never described what a wraith looks like and now Iona knows why. Ariadne did not want to scare her. Iona is horrified by the image of her with sharp teeth, sallow skin, and black orbs for eyes. Iona can feel Ariadne's dread. She would die to prevent Iona from becoming the malefician's slave.

"Philisa," Ariadne says to heal the cuts on Iona's hands, then does the same to herself.

"Ariadne," Iona whispers, reaching out to cup her cheek.

She is mine. Mine forever. I will never be alone again. I do not deserve her, Ariadne thinks.

"You do deserve me," Iona says.

Ariadne's eyes widen, then she grins sheepishly.

"I will need to grow accustomed to that," Ariadne says.

Iona grins and tucks Ariadne's hair behind her ear. She inhales sharply when she feels her own fingertips touching Ariadne's cheek. She hesitantly runs her fingertips along Ariadne's jaw, then over her parted lips. Iona wonders what it would be like to touch her in other more sensitive places. Will their already enhanced pleasure be doubled? Iona does not know if she could withstand such intense sensations.

"We can explore that together, love," Ariadne says with a crooked smile.

Iona blushes deep red and takes her hand back.

"Your satyric thoughts will be a new amusement for me," Ariadne grins, "Your thoughts and your feelings."

Your body is mine too, nymph, and I intend to worship it now and forevermore, Ariadne thinks.

Iona's breathing deepens as she is coaxed onto Ariadne's lap. When they kiss, Iona can feel their combined perception of their soft lips moving together. Ariadne's fingers were always prophetic, seeming to know exactly where to touch her and when. Now they are nearly omnipotent, roaming over Iona's bare skin until she is dying for more.

Ariadne slips her hand between Iona's spread legs. Iona moans when Ariadne strokes her center, which is already soaked with her arousal. Ariadne moans with her, as if she was stroking herself. In a way, she was.

"Ariadne," Iona whimpers.

"You are so sensitive," Ariadne moans, her face contorting in response to Iona's pleasure, "How can you stand it?"

"Now you cannot tease me without torturing yourself too," Iona grins.

"My abnegation has always been stronger than yours," Ariadne pants, but Iona can see her resolve slipping and feel her desire growing.

Iona slips her own hand between Ariadne's legs and moans when she feels Ariadne's wetness sliding against her fingertips. They stroke each other fervently until their cries echo through the trees.

"Say it again," Ariadne begs.

"I love you," Iona says breathlessly, then moans when Ariadne pushes two fingers inside of her and curls them into her flesh.

When their pleasure overflows, they scream from the intensity of it. Iona is lightheaded when both her and Ariadne's pleasure washes over her. Tears stream down her face and her entire body trembles. Ariadne kisses the tears away and whispers her love to her, though she does not need to. Iona can feel her love, her fears, her desires, her regrets, her pain, everything that Ariadne is. The spell removes all boundaries, all pretense, and all doubt. A spell that binds them to each other for all time.

23 - ARIADNE

Ariadne is ever hesitant to believe that the worst may be over, though the malefician has not attacked in weeks. Ariadne's protective charms have prevented any blood magic spells that may have been attempted. She is overjoyed to be so useful in Iona's defense after months of feeling weak and powerless. Now that Iona's mind is linked to her own, if the malefician would try to attack one of them, the other would know immediately.

After the initial novelty of their joined thoughts wore off, Ariadne has been able to make Iona's thoughts blend into the background, like breathing or blinking. She only attunes to Iona's thoughts when it suits her, like when Iona is beneath her in their bed.

Iona clears her throat and Ariadne suppresses a grin. Perhaps she should be paying attention to Professor Salum's lecture rather than daydreaming of last night when Iona's body writhed as Ariadne slid her tongue inside her.

Iona sighs with frustration and Ariadne grins. She can feel Iona's blush as is spreads across her cheeks without needing to turn in her seat to look.

"A wand helps to minimize the toll a spell will take on your stores of magic, but for those with magic to spare, it is possible to cast spells without one. It takes a great deal of concentration, manifestation, and power to achieve but for some of you, it may be possible to perform simple spells with just your thoughts," Professor Salum says, "Today, we will be testing your skills with simple levitation on small objects. Please do not be frustrated if you are unable to perform this level of advanced magic yet. It takes practice and patience."

Ariadne has never tried to cast a spell without her wand. She had thought she would need to be at least a decade older before attempting it.

If anyone could do it, you can, Iona thinks.

Ariadne rolls her eyes, but inwardly she appreciates the encouragement. Iona's faith in her abilities emboldens her.

"Shall we?" Crescentia asks.

Ariadne is distracted from her and Iona's thoughts. She glances at Crescentia, then nods stiffly. Ariadne conjures two apples, one for each of them to levitate. Then she places her wand to the side and stares at her apple. She would normally incant "Kuelea" with a wave of her wand but now the magic must come from thought alone.

Ariadne notices her apple shift slightly to the left. She holds her breath and leans forward in her chair. She doubles her efforts to will the apple to float. The apple shifts again, then lifts off the table until it is at eye level. It rotates in the air until it falls back down. Ariadne exhales and pants, the levitation taking a considerable amount of energy to achieve. Crescentia watches the feat and is visibly impressed. Her apple stays flat on the table, not moving even a little.

"Very good, Ariadne," Professor Salum praises.

"Thank you, Professor," Ariadne says.

Showoff, Iona thinks.

Ariadne smirks, *Go on then, Iona.*

Iona had conjured her own apple. She stares at it with determination, but it will not move. Ksenia is struggling as well, though she does not speak. She had the good sense to stop her bullying after Iona made a fool of her in conjuration class. The witches still gossip about Ksenia being knocked down and humiliated.

When Iona does make her apple float, she smiles with pride. It hovers a foot off the desk and remains there. Ksenia shifts in her seat angrily.

Make Ksenia's float too, Ariadne thinks.

Iona suppresses a smile, then focuses on Ksenia's apple. In time, it also floats next to Iona's.

"I can do it myself," Ksenia hisses.

"Can you?" Iona asks, raising an eyebrow.

Ksenia stews in her discontent but has no response. Iona lets the apples drift back down to the desk before too much of her energy is diminished.

Then Crescentia's apple shifts slightly. Ariadne leaves Iona's mind and watches Crescentia manage to lift the apple only barely for a few seconds.

"What a marvel," Crescentia grins, picking up her apple and admiring its flawless red skin.

Crescentia smiles at Ariadne, and Ariadne forces a polite smile. Crescentia can sense Ariadne's coldness and looks away nervously. Ariadne can barely stand the sight of Crescentia nowadays, not since Iona's suspicions matched her own.

Ariadne has been observing Crescentia closely before and after their classes. She uses the invisibility spell to spy on her at times, but so far, she has not caught Crescentia in any wrongdoing. Iona avoids her altogether, too frightened to say more than a few words to her.

On the spring equinox, the students have picnics in the courtyard before their ritual. They all wear pastel-colored dresses and chaplets of spring flowers on their heads. The grass and trees are green again and the midday sun provides renewed warmth on their backs. They eat ham pies, boiled eggs, and lavender tea with fresh honey.

Iona is a dream in her purple silk dress that is reminiscent of her Samhain ball gown. Ariadne runs her fingers through Iona's soft red hair. She knows from Iona's thoughts that fingers scratching her scalp are a comfort to her. Iona's mother used to do this whenever Iona was upset.

"I wish you could have met my mother," Iona says, in response to Ariadne's thought.

"She would not have liked me," Ariadne says.

Iona turns to look at Ariadne.

"Why would you say that?" Iona asks.

I represent everything she despised. The sempiterna bloodline, the reputation for ruthlessness, the aristocratic magical family. She hid from the world to avoid people like me, Ariadne thinks.

"You are not your family," Iona says.

"I was," Ariadne says, "Not long ago."

"Not anymore," Iona says.

Now you are intrinsically tied to me, not them, Iona thinks.

Ariadne grins, then has a thought.

"Did your mother ever teach you about the spring equinox?" Ariadne asks.

"No," Iona shakes her head, "Is it different from other rituals?"

"The spring equinox is a time of rebirth and renewal. Fertility and balance. It is a time to conceive a child, either through sex or, in our case, through conjuration," Ariadne says.

Iona's eyebrows raise in surprise.

"If that was something you wanted one day, we could create a child with magic," Ariadne says, "Part of you and part of me."

Ariadne pictures a little girl with her red eyes and curls, and Iona's red hair and freckles. Iona sees the child in Ariadne's mind and smiles.

"I did not think that could be possible for us," Iona muses, her thoughts drifting to a beggar girl she had once given coins to in Cornwall and the prospect of adopting a lost child who needs a home.

"With magic as strong as ours, almost anything is possible," Ariadne says, leaning in to kiss Iona's cheek, "Though adoption is always a noble option as well."

Iona turns her head at the last second and kisses Ariadne's

mouth instead. The kiss lingers, tender and gentle, until Ariadne finally leans back.

"Someday," Iona says.

"Someday," Ariadne agrees, "We will have much to occupy our time when one of us claims the pendant."

Ariadne conjures a purple violet and tucks it behind Iona's ear.

"Will we?" Iona asks.

"My grandmother held gatherings on days such as these. Magic users from around the world would travel to attend because the pendant is a conduit for abundant magic. A ritual with a pendant-wearer makes all who attend stronger," Ariadne says.

"And your grandmother only invited witches and warlocks from sempiterna bloodlines," Iona says, seeing it in Ariadne's mind.

"She hoarded magic, only giving it to those who she deemed worthy. But if you or I owned the pendant and we invited all to attend, imagine the difference that would make," Ariadne says.

The trials are less than two months away. If they make it just a little while longer, they could start a new era of magic, in spite of what Ariadne's family has done for more than a hundred years.

After the spring equinox ritual, Ariadne and Iona walk back to campus hand in hand. Iona is talking about what she recently read in one of her astronomy books. There is an upcoming blood moon that should occur right before the end of Spring term. As they emerge from the trees, Ariadne wonders whether all these celestial events occurring so close together is a good omen or bad one.

Ariadne stops dead in her tracks right as Aster's ears go back in distress. Iona startles and looks around for what caused Ariadne's fear, then sees the woman standing in the courtyard. She wears a pristine white dress, a red fringed shawl around her arms, and a glittering ruby necklace. Her raven hair is piled high on top of her head.

"What is your mother doing here?" Iona asks, seeing the many images of Cintia Zerynthos in Ariadne's thoughts.

"I haven't the faintest idea," Ariadne says.

Ariadne's mother notices Iona and Ariadne's joined hands and does not mask her displeasure.

"She is even more frightening in person," Iona whispers.

"Not the most comforting statement for me to hear at present, Iona," Ariadne says.

"Sorry," Iona says, but Ariadne can sense her apprehension.

Ariadne notices Elise exiting the woods not far from them.

"Go to Elise. I shall find out what my mother wants," Ariadne says.

"Are you certain? I will need to meet her eventually, now that we are bonded," Iona says.

"Eventually, but not now," Ariadne says, "Trust me."

Iona looks into her eyes and her mind and sees that this is what must be.

"Come and find me when you are ready," Iona says, "Your mind will be your own until then."

Iona approaches Elise and asks if she would like to practice elemental magic. Ariadne walks over to her waiting mother and steels herself.

"Good afternoon, mother," Ariadne says, her tone polite, "To what do I owe the pleasure of your visit?"

"Come, my pet," her mother says.

Her mother walks to an empty patch of grass at the edge of the trees. With a wave of her hand, she conjures a wrought iron glass gazebo that rises from the ground. She opens the door and enters, leaving it open for Ariadne. The door closes on its own as soon as Ariadne steps inside and when she looks back, the door has disappeared and is replaced by another pane of glass. Then the once translucent walls blur until they are opaque. Ariadne feels instantly claustrophobic in the confined space.

Ariadne turns to face her mother, who is twirling an

oleander flower between her fingers, uncaring of its poison touching her skin. The walls of the greenhouse have shelves filled with flowers that are all in simultaneous bloom. The colors and scents are overwhelming to Ariadne when normally such redolence would calm her.

"You appear rather bloated, Ariadne. You haven't been overindulging, have you?" her mother asks, looking Ariadne up and down with distaste, "And your hair... did you not bother to tame your curls? I hope your professors did not see you in such a state."

Ariadne flushes with embarrassment, and smooths out her hair self-consciously, "Did you travel all this way to comment on my appearance?"

Her mother chuckles and looks back down at her flower.

"No, it was simply an observation. My visit is due to a much more serious issue," her mother says.

Her mother lifts the oleander flower to her nose and breathes in deeply. Ariadne picks at her cuticles.

"I was confused when you stopped returning my letters," her mother says, "I wondered what I must have done to deserve such callous disregard from my only child. Perhaps her studies were so rigorous that she could not spare the time to write. Perhaps she was sick, or simply distracted."

Her mother begins to pick the petals of the oleander, letting them fall onto the greenhouse floor.

"Then I received a rather disturbing letter from Ksenia," her mother says, "She claims that you admitted quite plainly that you no longer want the pendant. That you never did."

"She never should have..." Ariadne trails off, then wonders what else Ksenia had reported to her mother over the years.

"I was so despondent over Ksenia's letter that I decided to perform a ritual at your grandmother's grave to request an audience with her," her mother says, her eyes still on the oleander as she plucks the petals one by one.

Ariadne's blood runs cold. Her mother plucks the last petal, then tosses away the stem.

"Imagine my surprise when I heard of your acrimonious conversation on Samhain," her mother says, looking up at Ariadne and stepping closer to her, "Your grandmother is very, *very* cross with you."

"Let her be. She is as vile in death as she was in life," Ariadne says angrily.

Ariadne did not even have a chance to flinch. Her mother's hand slaps across her face with barbaric force, making her stumble backwards as her cheek stings horridly. Ariadne almost brings her hand to her face to soothe the pain, but she refrains. She glares at her mother, who glares right back at her.

"Never disrespect your grandmother in my presence. She is a better witch than you could ever hope to be," her mother spits.

"Why are you here, mother?" Ariadne asks.

"I am here to reiterate your grandmother's sentiments. You must win the pendant, or your father and I will never let you in our house again. I do not care what flirtation you are entertaining with the Lysander girl; it changes nothing."

"It is not a flirtation," Ariadne says.

"It is another hollow act of defiance that I had thought you'd outgrown, but it seems you are still the same foolish child who plays with dolls for her own amusement," her mother scoffs, "She is far beneath you, and you very well know it."

"She is not beneath me," Ariadne says through gritted teeth, "And her name is Iona."

"I do not need to know her name," her mother scoffs, "She will be gone before I could bother to remember it, just like all the other strumpets you cavort with."

"Not this time," Ariadne flushes, "I thought you wanted me to ally myself with a Lysander."

"A true born Lysander," her mother clarifies, "Not some illicit love child with no standing in high society."

Her mother sighs and rubs her forehead.

"I see Samaira's hand in this," her mother says.

"Samaira has nothing to do with," Ariadne tries to say but

her mother puts up a finger to stop her.

"I should never have allowed you to befriend one such as her. She has been a terrible influence from the start. She may be considered highborn where she is from," her mother's lip curls, "But here in civilized society, we conduct ourselves differently."

Ariadne's blood boils at her mother's bigotry, though it comes as no surprise. How she was able to stomach this sort of hatred for her entire childhood, Ariadne does not know.

"Samaira is the most civilized, wise woman I know," Ariadne seethes.

Her mother glowers but continues on.

"I was willing to acquiesce to your choice of companions after Vivien's attack, only because Samaira was the sole person who could calm you enough to speak or leave your rooms," her mother says, showing only a brief trace of concern for Ariadne's wellbeing, "But you are an adult now, Ariadne. Pull yourself together and move on. You must leave behind such weaknesses and prioritize more valuable alliances with those like Ksenia, a proper young lady."

"Ksenia has no further interest in an alliance with me," Ariadne says, but her mother talks over her.

"You are associating with the wrong sort of witches, and I shall not let it go on any longer," her mother insists, "Upon my word, you will break it off with the Lysander girl and focus on your studies like we planned."

"I shall do no such thing! And you cannot make me," Ariadne protests.

"I will not tolerate the continued whispers of the Zerynthos whore taking up with yet another damsel! You will do as I say, or I shall take you home this very minute and you can return to college when your father and I decide it is time. I should have made you wait another year as it is..." her mother rubs her temples and sighs, "But you were so insistent that you were ready. I see now that my instincts were correct, and I should have heeded them. The trials should be your only concern, your only purpose, and if you have lost sight of that, then you must come home."

"Even if you were to drag me home by my hair, it would not matter. Iona and I are bonded," Ariadne snaps, then immediately regrets the admonition when she sees the fury on her mother's face. All of the flowers around them wilt until the once colorful greenhouse turns brown and desolate.

"Bonded! You bonded with another witch without consulting me?!" her mother screeches, making Ariadne jump.

"It is my decision to make. I do not require your permission," Ariadne says, straightening her spine.

Her mother tries to slap her again, but Ariadne catches her wrist in midair and pulls her mother closer to glare directly into her eyes.

"If you ever try to put your hands on me again, I will do to you what I did to Vivien," Ariadne says menacingly.

At first, her mother's eyes betray palpable fear. Ariadne hates the slight satisfaction it gives her to witness her mother's rare loss of control. Then her mother smiles darkly.

"There is the Zerynthos witch in you. I feared that she was gone forever," her mother says.

Ariadne flinches away from her mother and releases her wrist.

"I am not a Zerynthos witch. Not anymore," Ariadne says, "I have renounced the family, as I am sure Grandmother told you."

"Your name and history are an everlasting part of you. It is not for you to shed away on a whim. I thought I had taught you that," her mother says, "You were conceived for one singular purpose; to serve your bloodline and its interests. Without that purpose, you are worthless."

"And this is the love of a mother?" Ariadne asks, her voice breaking despite her best efforts, but she holds back her tears.

"I am not your mother anymore, or did you not renounce your family name?" Her mother narrows her eyes.

One tear escapes and Ariadne angrily wipes it away. Her

mother rolls her eyes and scoffs.

"Power is wasted on the likes of you," her mother says.

"Yes, it should have gone to you, considering how blatantly you covet it," Ariadne retorts, "You resent me for my power, that which has cursed me with murderous friends and wicked, selfish family. But I am stronger now. You cannot manipulate me anymore."

"Can't I?" her mother asks.

Her mother regards her critically, and Ariadne can see her mind working to divert the conversation back in her favor.

"If I cannot appeal to your loyalty, or lack thereof, perhaps I can give you a new impetus," her mother says.

Ariadne's curiosity is peaked but she does not let it show.

"The one who claims the pendant shall have power enough to do what the average witch cannot. Even, perhaps, heal a broken mind," her mother says.

Ariadne's reality shifts irreversibly and her mother smirks when she knows she's hit her mark.

"You were so distraught about Vivien, the little would-be murderess. Her fate was deserved many times over for what she attempted to do to you, but if you are so convinced that she deserves a second chance, then win the pendant, and heal her," her mother says, "Morgan's powers of healing were legendary. I am sure a pendant of her own making would be capable of such a task."

Ariadne's heart beats manically in her chest as her composure fractures despite her best efforts.

"If the Lysander girl has somehow become your competition for the pendant, perhaps your shared bond could aid you in defeating her in the trials," her mother suggests.

"I will not manipulate the one I love for personal gain," Ariadne says, "If Iona won the pendant, I could ask her to heal Vivien for me."

"I suppose that is possible, but if you do not take the trials seriously and Iona is not as strong as you think her to be, then you will both end up with nothing. Then Ksenia, or whomever else wins the pendant, might not be so accommodating. Or perhaps no one will win this year, and the trials will continue on. Either way, you will be left to live with your regret for the rest of your life," her mother says.

Ariadne lowers her eyes, not wanting to internalize her mother's venomous words. Her mother presses her sharp nail under Ariadne's chin, forcing her to make eye contact.

"Win the pendant and you will have the power to heal the wound that you inflicted," her mother says.

Ariadne does not know what to say. The prospect of healing Vivien after all these years seems too good to be true.

"Do not disappoint me, pet," her mother says, "I did not create you to be a failure."

The gazebo disappears and so does her mother. All that remains is a pink dianthus flower discarded in the grass. Ariadne is left more conflicted about the pendant than ever before.

24 – IONA

Iona did not watch Ariadne's private conversation with her mother, nor did she ask about it when Ariadne returned to her. Ariadne concealed her distress expertly, but never enough to fool Iona.

The pure fear that Iona had felt when Ariadne saw her mother had made her think the malefician herself had stood before them. It was an alarming reaction to the mere sight of one's family. Iona did not want to press the matter and would only listen if Ariadne did decide to discuss it one day.

All Ariadne did say was that Ksenia had been the one to summon her mother to try and take her home. Ariadne is certain that Ksenia did so to try and separate her from Iona, therefore leaving Iona more vulnerable. Ariadne hasn't forgotten her suspicions of Crescentia, but now agrees with Iona that Ksenia cannot be underestimated.

Their classes were becoming more rigorous as Morgan's trials approach. Iona and Ariadne are holding their own, but by the end of each day, they are exhausted. Ariadne bestows protection magic onto Iona every morning and evening like clockwork and the spells seem to be enough to deter the malefician's blood magic.

"Védeni," Ariadne whispers over Iona, bringing her back to the present moment.

They are studying together on Ariadne's balcony,

surrounded by Spring flowers. Iona feels Ariadne's protective magic covering her like rain and giving her at least the semblance of safety. Ariadne takes Iona's hand and kisses it, then goes to sit beside her again and study her illusion grimoire.

"It seems to be working," Iona says.

"It must," Ariadne says, unable to hide the worry in her voice.

"Of course," Iona says, "It will work. Do not fret."

Ariadne smiles at her but it does not meet her tired eyes.

"I was hoping to speak to you about our plans for after college," Ariadne says, "I know your plan to spend part of the summer at the Lysanders, but what would you like to do when summer ends?"

Iona has not thought that far ahead. She closes her book and thinks for a moment.

"Would you like to go back to your home in Cornwall?" Ariadne asks.

"Only to gather some personal items that I had left behind," Iona says, "I would not like to live there anymore."

"And I do not want to live with my family anymore either," Ariadne says, "Where should we go?"

Iona looks up at the endless sky and the world suddenly seems unimaginably vast.

"We could go anywhere. Rome, Barcelona, Cairo, Constantinople, London, the Americas, or perhaps a tiny island in the middle of the ocean, away from everything and everyone," Ariadne says with a twinkle in her eye.

Iona smiles fondly at the memory of swimming with Ariadne as a mermaid. Ariadne reaches out and takes Iona's hand in hers.

"You do not need to decide right this minute. I only wanted to remind you that when this mess is behind us, we will have an entire world to explore together," Ariadne says.

Iona sees the hope in Ariadne's garnet eyes. They are so close to having everything they've ever wanted, a home of their very own.

"Do you have a preference?" Iona asks.

"In where we live?" Ariadne asks, "Not particularly. As long as it is not Thessaly, I will be happy with whatever you choose."

A thought emerges in Iona's mind, and subsequently in Ariadne's. Iona's mother's family had originally come from Brazil, and she wonders what such a place is like. Perhaps they could visit there after summer's end.

"I have never been to Brazil either," Ariadne says, "A fine choice indeed."

"Really?" Iona smiles and Ariadne's eyes light up at the sight.

"As soon as fate will allow," Ariadne promises as she reopens her grimoire.

Ariadne and Iona study together every day, sometimes with Elise or Samaira, but never with Crescentia. Iona misses her terribly but is also terrified of her. Anytime she sees Crescentia walking in her direction, Iona diverts her path and avoids her. Iona still hopes that Ksenia is the one she should fear but cannot risk being wrong.

One day, however, Crescentia practically corners Iona in the hallway.

"Good afternoon, Iona," Crescentia says.

"Good afternoon, Crescentia," Iona says, forcing a smile.

When an awkward silence drags on, Crescentia frowns and walks away with such a look of dejection, Iona's heart breaks for her. Even though her doubt tells her not to, Iona runs after Crescentia.

"Crescentia, wait," Iona says.

"What did I ever do to deserve such exile? I was your only friend when you arrived here and now you cannot even look me in the eye," Crescentia says, "Do you think yourself too lofty to be friends with such a common witch now that you are a Lysander?"

"No, of course not!" Iona says, disgusted by the prospect.

"Then why will you not deign to speak to me?" Crescentia asks.

"Crescentia, I... I cannot tell you why," Iona says, though she yearns to tell her everything.

"Are you in trouble?" Crescentia asks with concern, "Is someone harming you?"

Iona averts her gaze and looks around to see if anyone is watching them. Though she doesn't see anyone in the hallway, she cannot trust her eyes.

"Is this to do with the sirens?" Crescentia asks.

When Iona meets Crescentia's gaze, she searches for any sign of darkness. All Iona sees are Crescentia's warm amber eyes filled with care for her.

"I see Ariadne watching you like a dragon watches its treasure," Crescentia says, taking steps closer to Iona, "And Ksenia is a perpetual storm cloud after your spat with her."

Iona chuckles in spite of herself, "That was a mistake."

"A delightful mistake," Crescentia grins.

Iona's smile fades and her uncertainty makes her feel sick. Merlin's warning repeats in her mind.

"I am always here, Iona," Crescentia says, "Good day."

Iona watches as Crescentia walks down the hall.

"Stay away from the forest," Iona calls after her.

Crescentia looks back with an unreadable expression, then turns and walks away.

"Time is an illusory construct. There are some who will one day consider if time is happening all at once and we are only trapped within this one moment by our perception of it," Professor Pari says, "We can use magic to expand our perception of time to review the past and, with practice, see glimpses of our future in the form of prophecies."

Professor Pari picks up a moonstone slab and holds it up for her students to see. All her students have their own moonstone tablets on their desks as well.

"We use these enchanted tablets of moonstone to gaze into the past or the future," Professor Pari explains.

"Professor, why is the moonstone flat? Should it not

be spherical?" Phoebe Kimball asks, voicing the collective confusion of the other students in class.

"Some witches use spheres instead, but I have broken so many... They are quite slippery and difficult to store, so I use tablets instead," Professor Pari shrugs her shoulders, "The shape is not of importance. The magic of the stone is the same either way."

Iona suppresses a grin and admires her piece of moonstone. It glistens in the light with mesmerizing gleams of blue and purple.

"Today, please try to gaze into the past. It is easier to pick a memory that you can clearly envision," Pari says, "Simply look into your tablet and meditate on that memory."

Iona picks a memory in her mind. She wants to see her mother and does not want to wait until the next Samhain to do so. Iona decides on a day when she and her mother had walked on the beach when she was nine.

Iona gazes into the smooth, iridescent surface of the moonstone. The longer she looks, the more that everything around the moonstone goes blurry until it disappears entirely. Iona blinks and when she opens her eyes, her surroundings are completely changed.

When Iona looks down at herself, she is in her favorite amber dress. She is sitting on her bed in her old room. She expected to see herself as a child, but she does not look much different than she normally does. It seems she is not in the memory that she had chosen.

"Iona, your cake is ready!" Iona's mother calls.

Iona smiles wide at the sound of her mother's gentle voice.

"Coming, mother!" Iona says.

Iona runs from her room and into the kitchen. When she sees her mother's face, it takes everything she has to keep from crying. This was before her mother's illness had manifested, when she still had her tranquil beauty and enduring warmth. Her mother is finishing the icing on Iona's birthday cake. Iona runs over and embraces her tightly. Her mother laughs in surprise and hugs her back.

"Are you alright, darling?" her mother asks.

"Yes!" Iona says quickly, "All is well."

Iona pulls away and sits at the kitchen table to wait for her mother to bring the cake to the table.

"Your favorite, with strawberry icing," her mother says with pride, "Only the best for your eighteenth birthday."

"It looks truly delectable," Iona says.

Her mother cuts a piece of cake for both of them, putting a plate in front of Iona. Iona takes a bite and closes her eyes. The icing has just the right amount of sweetness, and the cake is perfectly moist.

When Iona opens her eyes, her mother has placed a small, wrapped package in front of her.

"Happy birthday, dear," her mother smiles.

Iona excitedly takes the present and rips open the wrapping. Inside is a silver bell. The slim handle is imprinted with a pixie's wing and the waist of the bell is decorated with tiny flying pixies.

"Your father made this for you when you were a baby. He wanted you to have it on your eighteenth birthday," her mother says, "He said it holds hidden secrets."

Iona's mother smiles fondly at the memory. Iona rings the bell. It chimes prettily and the sound resonates louder than Iona would expect from such a small bell. Then Iona has a dawning realization that she does not remember the bell. She has never seen it before. How could that be if she is in her own memory?

Iona's mother looks at her, really looks at her, and Iona shrinks down in her chair. Her mother's stare is unnerving as she reaches for her wand.

"Who are you?" her mother asks, "An illusion? A changeling?"

"No, no," Iona reassures her, "I am your daughter."

Her mother looks her up and down with wide eyes.

"You are not of this time," she realizes.

"No. I come from 1802," Iona says.

"My word," her mother breathes, "But why?"

"I wanted to see you again," Iona says, "I do not know how..."

Her mother's expression softens, and Iona realizes her mistake.

"I am dead in your time," her mother says softly.

"Yes," Iona says. It would not do to lie now. "I am so sorry."

"Do not be... Death is a sacred part of life, and it is not the end," her mother says with a wistful smile, "You are at Lysander College?"

"Yes, I am in my Spring term," Iona says.

"Was I right to send you there?" her mother asks.

Iona hasn't the faintest idea how to answer that question. Her ongoing clash with the malefician has grieved her for so long, but her love for Ariadne is worth more to her than silver or gold. Iona also does not want her mother's final two years of life to be consumed with worry for her.

"Yes, you were right to send me here, but it is complicated. There is such strife surrounding the trials for Morgan's pendant. There are some who believe I am a true contender and though I know my magic is strong, I still doubt that I am worthy of such a burden," Iona says.

"You will prevail, I know it. You are strong, just like your father," her mother says.

An unexpected bout of anger falls over Iona.

"Why did you lie to me all these years? Why did you leave me in ignorance to learn about father's family on my own?" Iona asks.

"I do not tell you?" Her mother says with slight confusion.

"No, you send me off without a word on the matter. I had to discover it on my own because you beg Samuel not to tell me," Iona says, her words spilling out in a rush.

Iona's mother looks away. She does not look guilty, or even conflicted. She only looks sad.

"I am grateful for all the sacrifices you made to care for me. I only wish that I could have known who I was before I was sent to the wolves," Iona says.

"You do know who you are. You are not, nor have you ever been a 'Lysander witch'. You are a witch in your own right," her mother says vehemently.

"That may be, but you benefited from my ignorance. Do not deny it," Iona insists.

Her mother purses her lips, stands, and goes to the kitchen. Iona watches her open a cabinet drawer and empty it. She lifts a false bottom from the drawer and pulls out a bottle of brandy. Her mother takes two glasses and goes back to the table.

She sits and pours one glass of brandy, then looks to Iona in question. Iona nods and her mother pours a second glass and hands it to her. Iona takes a sip while her mother drinks her brandy in one gulp and pours another glass.

"As far as what I will tell Samuel one day, you have sealed that fate on your own. I had planned on telling you today since you are of age. Now I know I must wait and tell Samuel to keep your relation a secret, or risk tangling the threads of time," her mother says, "I am not entirely sure how or why you have traveled here but I do know the rules. You cannot change the past or the future. Time can only be resolved."

Iona's eyes widen, now wishing she had held her tongue, though she does not want to break time for her own benefit. Iona's mother gazes out the window at the ocean and takes a moment before continuing.

"When your father died, I was lost. I did not know how to carry on," her mother says, "We had left everything behind to be together only for him to be taken from me so soon. It was a cruel joke."

Her mother swirls her brandy in her glass and holds back tears.

"It may have been selfish. It may have been wrong. I do not know anymore… but I did not want you to be taken from me too. If I had brought you back to society, the Lysanders would have assimilated you into their world. Samuel would have protected you as much as he could, but your grandparents would not be impeded forever. You would have been a pawn in their game of power and ambition. You do not know the lengths these families will go to control and exploit their children. They are ruthless," her mother says.

But Iona did know. It is what happened to Ariadne, Vivien, Ksenia, and all the others.

"Your grandparents tried and failed to control your father. They undervalued Samuel. If they saw how strong you were, even as a child, they would have snatched you up and sent me away. I would have been powerless to stop them," her mother says, "I would not let them take my baby from me. I would not survive it even now, but especially not then, when I had just lost your father."

Iona thinks of Ariadne and how broken she would be if she died suddenly in their youth. To live the rest of her life alone would be unbearable after knowing such love and devotion. She hopes never to know the pain of such unimaginable grief.

"I hope one day you will have a love so true as what I had with your father," her mother says.

"I do," Iona says, her voice breaking with emotion.

"You do?" her mother asks, a smile spreading across her face, "What is their name?"

"Ariadne... Zerynthos," Iona says, bracing herself for her mother's disappointment.

Her mother is shocked, but not disheartened, "A Zerynthos? Please forgive my surprise. I went to college with Cintia Zerynthos. Awful woman."

"She is Ariadne's mother," Iona says.

"Goodness, that poor child," her mother says, "I hope Ariadne has not inherited her mother's rancor."

"Not when I was through with her," Iona smiles to herself.

Her mother sees something in Iona that renews her tears.

"You do love her. I can see it," her mother says, "Hold fast to it. Live with compassion as I have always taught you."

"I shall, I promise," Iona says.

Her mother nods, then a far-off look crosses her wearied

face.

"I am the most fortunate of mothers to see her child grow into such an honorable woman. You are the best I have done with my life. Despite both of our struggles, your kindness and hope have persisted. I am glad that I do not have to wait much longer to be reunited with Victor. He has been waiting for me all this time," her mother says, her tears falling down her cheeks.

"Mother," Iona says, jumping to her feet and rushing to her mother's side to embrace her.

"I love you more than words can say, my dear girl," her mother says.

Iona gasps as she is brought back to her own time. She bursts into tears and Ariadne rushes over to her.

How extraordinary, Ariadne thinks as she kneels next to Iona's chair and takes her hand in hers, seeing what had happened through Iona's thoughts.

Professor Pari approaches the table, her mouth agape and her eyes wild with excitement. She inspects Iona's moonstone tablet, unable to believe what she sees.

"You are a praephora," Pari says reverently.

"A what?" Iona asks as she presses her hand to her chest to slow her breathing.

"A witch that can travel into her past," Pari says, "You do not simply observe past events, you can actively interact with them."

"I have never heard of such a thing," Ariadne says.

"That is because they are exceedingly rare," Pari says, "Iona is the first praephora I have ever taught."

"You could not control your past self?" Iona asks Ariadne.

"No, I watched the past happen with perfect clarity but could not alter the event," Ariadne says.

"Do you remember the memory you just inhabited?" Pari asks.

"I do now but I did not beforehand," Iona says, "How is that possible? How can I not remember something that has already happened?"

"It is possible because you traveled to the past, rather than observing what once was. You have just created your own memory," Pari says.

Iona's head spins as she looks warily at her moonstone tablet.

"Time is woven with care. It cannot be altered, only resolved," Pari says, "If you ever find yourself struggling to recollect a memory that others swear has occurred, it may be because you haven't experienced it yet."

Ariadne squeezes Iona's hand and she finds solace in Ariadne's warm red eyes.

Now who is the showoff? Ariadne thinks.

Iona suppresses a giggle and takes a deep breath. The ordeal sapped almost all her magic and energy away, but it was more than worth the effort. She will treasure that memory with her mother for the rest of her days. She understands now why her mother did what she did. She can forgive her and move forward.

25 – ARIADNE

The blooming wildflowers of May bring with it the promise that soon, this whole ugly mess will be behind them. The trials are less than two weeks away, and the malefician has gone silent. Ariadne would rather face the infernal witch with the pendant than without, but the prolonged reprieve is tinged with malaise.

Professor Salvador had begun instruction on how to resist illusions. Salvador made a collective illusion of grey smoke and challenged the witches to see beyond it. Not a single witch in class was able to resist successfully, even while knowing that what they saw was not real. Ariadne had no idea how they were meant to see past illusions that were not as obvious.

Iona and Ariadne decided to practice after class in the incantation chamber. Iona creates a simple illusion of a blue butterfly that flits around Ariadne in playful circles.

"Relax," Iona says softly.

Ariadne takes a deep breath in and out.

"Do not try to force it. The hardest part is already done. You know the butterfly is not there, now see beyond it," Iona says.

Ariadne nods and watches the butterfly float through the air. When she concentrates very hard, the butterfly will blur until it is only a blue streak but when she cannot focus any longer, the butterfly returns and her head pounds from the effort.

"I must rest for a moment," Ariadne says, rubbing her forehead.

The butterfly disappears and Iona puts her wand away. She takes Ariadne's hand and smiles.

"You are getting better," Iona says, rubbing her forehead as well.

"We have very little time to master it," Ariadne says.

"But we will master it," Iona says, "We shall practice every day until we get it right."

Ariadne feels Iona's hope and it bolsters her.

"Let us go to the parlor and rest for a while," Iona says, taking Ariadne's arm.

Iona leads Ariadne outside and they stroll towards the student's parlor, with their familiars following behind them.

"Have you any inclination as to what we should expect from the trials?" Iona asks.

"No, they are a mystery. Morgan erases the memory of any witch who attempts the trials and fails," Ariadne says, "That is why we are tutored on all forms of magic. We must be prepared for anything."

"Crescentia mentioned that... I suppose it would be too easy if we knew exactly what to expect," Iona says as they near the edge of the trees.

"The secrecy surrounding the trials has always intrigued and infuriated me. It makes me wonder what exactly Morgan is looking for," Ariadne says.

"I hope it is not some sort of gladiator tournament where we must pick each other off one by one," Iona mutters as Ariadne lifts a branch for her to step beneath.

"I do not think that is Morgan's approach. I would expect riddles and puzzles that test our magic," Ariadne says.

"I am much more amenable to that," Iona says.

"As am I," Ariadne says, lifting her skirts to avoid a puddle in the pine needles.

Then Iona stops dead in her tracks. Ariadne continues walking until she realizes that Iona is no longer beside her.

Ariadne looks back and notices Iona's distress.

"Ariadne," Iona whispers with fear.

"What is it?" Ariadne asks, looking around at the dense forest for any sign of danger.

"How did we get into the forest?" Iona whispers.

"We aren't in the forest, we're..." Ariadne says, but then she registers what her eyes are telling her.

They had only just been crossing the safe courtyard together, but now they are in the midst of tall pine trees with yellow pollen dusting the ground.

"We need to run," Ariadne starts to say, but just as she does, the ground opens up and swallows them whole.

Ariadne awakens with a gasp and when she touches her forehead, she winces. She feels a split in her skin and wetness that could be blood, possibly from hitting her head on a rock when she fell. It is impossible to tell because she is laying within the earth in pitch darkness. Ariadne grasps for her wand and is relieved to find that it is still there in her pocket.

"Fotiá," Ariadne whispers.

A ball of light fills her hand and illuminates the dirt tunnel that she has fallen into. Ariadne had not meant to use the Greek version of the spell, but in her state of terror she can barely remember any spells at all. The light she holds now is tinged blue and shimmers differently but is not any less bright.

Ariadne's skirt has been ripped up to her knees and her cloak is shredded in three pieces. The ground is cold and damp beneath her. When she looks at her fingers, they are coated in her own blood from the gash in her forehead.

"Iona!" Ariadne yells, looking everywhere but she is nowhere to be found. Ariadne reaches out for Iona's mind but cannot feel her. Perhaps she is still asleep like Ariadne had been.

Ariadne stands and looks at the dark abyss to her right, and the same darkness to her left. She considers using the earth spell to break through the walls, but she does not want to risk a cave in. She does not know how deep the tunnels are in the earth or if they may be beneath a body of water. Then she remembers the spell that Samuel had used after Iona's duel. Perhaps she could use it to find her way.

"Meydana çıkarmak," Ariadne whispers.

She gasps when she is entirely surrounded by black and blue strands of maleficium. The air is saturated with it. When Samuel had used the spell, there had only been slight traces. Ariadne's ball of light is barely enough to see through the swirling mist of malignance.

"Iona!" Ariadne calls again. There is no answer.

Ariadne undoes the spell so she can see, then picks a direction and starts walking. Iona had not been very far from her when the ground opened up. Perhaps she can find her close by.

The labyrinthine tunnels twist and turn erratically with no discernable pattern. Her footsteps splash against the wet dirt as she frantically searches for Iona. The walls of earth trigger Ariadne's claustrophobia and she feels her chest tighten with anxiety. No matter how far she runs, there is no end of the tunnels to be found and no sign of Iona or the malefician.

Then Ariadne doubles over and screams. It feels almost as if razors are dragging themselves over Ariadne's brain. Then she realizes it is not her brain, it is Iona's. The pain suddenly stops and Ariadne sobs with relief at the respite.

"Ariadne!" Iona screams.

Ariadne tenses with panic, unable to determine which direction Iona's voice was coming from. She groans again from new excruciating agony coming from her wand arm. She looks down in alarm, but her forearm is perfectly fine. She is experiencing Iona's pain again, but this pain persists.

"Iona!" Ariadne screams back, "Where are you?"

"Ariadne!" Iona yells, then only screams with terror.

Ariadne runs. No matter which direction she goes, it sounds as if Iona's screams are getting farther away. She calls Iona's name over and over again. She can sense Iona's fear but wherever she is, there is no light.

Then Ariadne feels the ground give way beneath her feet as she falls into a pit. Ariadne screeches when she feels thousands of insects crawling over her. Her ball of light falls into the pit and as it sinks, Ariadne can make out the creeping bodies of centipedes the size of birds. Their poisonous legs prickle over Ariadne's skin as they swarm her.

"Pyrkagiá!" Ariadne screams.

The centipedes scatter away from Ariadne's flames. She throws fire every which way until the centipedes burrow into the earth. Ariadne climbs out of the pit and brushes any remaining vermin off of her before running away. The skin of Ariadne's arms and legs are covered in pricks of red. Iona's screams persist, echoing down the never-ending tunnels.

Ariadne creates another ball of light and sprints away from the pit. She does not get far before she falls to her knees when agonizing pain emanates from within her skull again. It lasts longer this time, then stops.

Ariadne forces herself back onto her feet and tries to run, but something grabs her ankle, and she falls heavily into the mud. She looks back and screams. A skeletal hand has broken through the dirt and is gripping Ariadne's leg. Ariadne tries to kick it off but another hand bursts through the dirt floor and holds Ariadne's other ankle. The skeleton rises from the mud, using Ariadne as an anchor to pull themselves up. Ariadne twists and turns, tries to use the cutting spell to break the bones away, but the skeleton holds on.

Other skeletons emerge from the walls and ceiling, falling onto the ground around her. Ariadne panics and struggles to get free, almost losing hold of her wand. The skeletons descend, grabbing, and groping at her to hold her down. They pull at her hair until chunks get ripped out of her scalp.

Their cavernous skulls with empty eye sockets still seem to stare at her as she cries from fear. Pairs of skeletal arms rise from the dirt around Ariadne's body and wrap themselves around her. They pull her down into the dirt, their boney fingers digging into the flesh of her torso and legs, attempting to bury her alive.

"Gíinos!" Ariadne cries, no longer caring if the walls may be unstable.

Ariadne throws rocks and mounds of dirt at the skeletons to push them off of her. The arms wrapped around her from below still try to pull her down, but Ariadne shifts the mud until she rises upwards and the skeletons beneath her are pushed father down. She struggles and kicks until she is finally free and runs away. The skeletons chase after her with their arms outstretched.

"Gíinos!" Ariadne yells again, and the tunnel caves in on top of the skeletons. Ariadne coughs and dashes away before the dirt can collapse on her too.

Ariadne runs as skeletal hands burst through the dirt to try and restrain her again. She steps around them and stays in the center of the tunnel out of reach of the arms grasping at air along the walls.

"Help, please!" Iona sobs.

Ariadne turns a corner and there she finds Iona. She is on the ground and fights against tree roots that shamble around her. Iona's wand arm is broken in two places from her fall and induces debilitating pain. Iona has her wand in her left hand and tries to cut at the roots, but they keep reaching for her, trying to pull her up toward the surface.

"Ariadne!" Iona cries, relief filling her at the sight of Ariadne running to her aid with light in her hand.

"Use fire!" Ariadne says.

"Pyrkagiá!" Iona yells.

Her spell is not as strong as usual but still has the desired effect. The roots cower away from the flames, but they catch fire and burn away. Smoke collects within the confined space and makes Iona and Ariadne cough violently.

Ariadne crawls beneath the roots. When she has her arms around Iona, her panic is lessened.

"She was here," Iona cries, "I could not see her."

"Hold on to me," Ariadne orders.

Iona wraps her undamaged arm around Ariadne's neck and winces as she curls her broken one against her chest.

Ariadne looks to her right and sees the skeletons racing towards them.

"Démolir!" Ariadne screams.

An explosive force emits from the tip of her wand. It hits the skeletons and blasts them backwards, the tunnel collapsing on top of them. Then Ariadne sees a glimpse of sunlight through the dirt.

"Gíinos!" Ariadne yells, her magic nearing its limit as she pulls them up from the ground and shifts the earth above them.

When they break through to the surface, Ariadne scans their surroundings for any sign of the malefician. The trees rustle menacingly, and Ariadne decides that they are in no fit state to duel anyhow. They must run.

Iona leans on Ariadne as they sprint through the forest. The trees are alive around them, their branches reaching down to rip at their dresses and scratch their arms and legs. They almost get separated as the branches attempt to pull them apart but Ariadne throws fire spells until the trees let them go.

Ariadne is doubly disturbed when she notices the ground is littered with the carcasses of dead birds, all bloody and missing their eyes. Carved into the bark of the trees are those same wretched symbols. A distressed howl makes Ariadne pause.

"Look!" Iona says, pointing with the arm that is around Ariadne's neck.

Aster and Wisp are trapped inside a cage of branches that are sinking into the earth. Ariadne runs to them and cuts at the tangled wood with frenzied spells until she makes a hole big enough to free the wolf and fox.

The familiars run ahead of Ariadne and Iona to lead the way out of the forest. When they break through the trees, the branches reach for them, but they crawl away beyond their reach.

Iona is sobbing uncontrollably beside Ariadne. Ariadne is livid as she glares back into the trees, now barely lit by the crepuscular glow of twilight. Then the sky has the audacity to open up and let a torrential downpour fall upon them.

They are both covered in cuts and scratches from the branches of the trees. Iona's broken arm is bright red and swollen. Ariadne forces herself to stand and fight against her weariness. Her magic is nearly depleted after all her fire spells against the trees. She cannot heal Iona's arm herself and needs to find help. She uses what remains of her strength to lift Iona into her arms and carry her to the staff apartments. She bursts through the door and out of the freezing rain.

"Professor Lysander! Help, please!" Ariadne yells.

Ariadne collapses onto the wood floor and holds Iona in her lap. Aster and Wisp bark loudly to get Lysander's attention. A door slams above them and they hear footsteps running across the ceiling. Professor Yun comes running down the stairs with her wand drawn. She gasps when she sees the state of Ariadne and Iona on the floor. Salum and Pari follow right behind her.

"What happened?" Yun asks with wide eyes.

"Her arm, it is broken," Ariadne pants.

"Your forehead," Yun says.

"Fix her arm!" Ariadne yells, uncaring if her skull has caved in if Iona is in pain.

"Take them to the sitting room. I shall get my cauldron," Yun tells Pari and Salum, "And call the others back to campus."

The professors help Ariadne carry Iona into the sitting room to their left. They place Iona onto a chaise by the fire. Ariadne sits by Iona's head and brushes her hair back out of her face. Wisp jumps onto Iona's torso and rests her head on her chest. Iona holds tightly to Ariadne's hand, her sobs subsiding as the professors work around her.

"Iona, this will hurt only for a moment," Pari says calmly.

Iona nods and squeezes her eyes shut.

"Philisa," Pari incants.

Iona goes rigid as her bones snap back into place, then she

slumps into the cushions when the spell is finished. Ariadne clenches her fist to keep from showing Iona's pain manifesting in her. New tears fall down Iona's cheeks, but Ariadne feels her pain become dull until it is almost completely gone.

"Shhh," Ariadne strokes Iona's hair until her breathing slows.

Lysander and Salvador burst through the front doors. They are both covered in rain and scratches but are otherwise unharmed.

"Iona?" Lysander calls.

"She is here," Ariadne says.

Lysander rushes to her side, searching for any serious injuries with the worry of a father.

"You all look like you've escaped the underworld," Salum says.

"They have, in a way," Pari says knowingly.

Ariadne glances at Pari, then focuses back on Iona, who looks to be on the verge of fainting as the adrenaline leaves her system.

"What happened?" Lysander asks firmly.

Ariadne hesitates to answer with the other professors present.

"They know," Lysander says.

Ariadne looks at him indignantly.

"You told them?" Ariadne asks.

"I had to. If the malefician tries to attack the college head on, we must be prepared to protect our students," Lysander says.

Ariadne sighs but understands. Iona is the one who wanted all this secrecy, at the behest of her ghost. Perhaps it was for the best.

"We have been watching over you as best we can but you both disappeared without a trace this afternoon," Lysander says, "Salvador and I went looking for you but there was a border of living trees that we could not permeate."

Ariadne is grateful for Lysander and Salvador's bravery, even if they hadn't been able to reach her and Iona.

"The witch lured us into the wood with a powerful illusion. We did not realize we had left the courtyard until it was too late. Then the ground swallowed us up. There is a network of tunnels in the earth that seems to have no end. It must have taken weeks, maybe months to build," Ariadne says.

Yun rushes downstairs with her potions materials and sets them on a table against the wall.

"Ariadne," Yun beckons her over.

Ariadne is reluctant to leave the side of the now sleeping Iona.

"Your head is injured, and you could be bleeding internally. You cannot help her if you're dead," Yun says bluntly.

Ariadne reluctantly releases Iona's hand and goes to sit near Yun to be examined. When Yun gently presses her fingers along Ariadne's forehead, a piercing pain shoots through her and she flinches away. Iona groans and shifts restlessly on the chaise but does not awaken. The professors notice the reaction.

"You are bonded?" Yun asks.

"That is very reckless," Salvador chides.

"What do you know of it?" Ariadne snaps, her patience nonexistent, "I did what was necessary to protect Iona. The malefician has her blood."

"You told them to do this?" Salvador asks Professor Lysander, who shakes his head no.

Ariadne and Iona had never told Professor Lysander explicitly about their bond, but his lack of surprise indicates that he suspected what they had done. It was truly the only option.

"Merlin told us to do it," Ariadne says, letting Yun inspect the gashes in her arms.

"Merlin spoke to you?" Pari asks, putting her hand over her mouth in shock.

"He spoke to Iona," Ariadne says.

"I told you," Pari says to Salvador, who stills seems agitated but does not say anything more.

Yun brews a healing potion while Ariadne tells the

professors more about the tunnels. The memory of reanimated skeletons attacking her and pulling her into the mud makes her tremble with fear, but she puts on a brave face. Ariadne mentions the dead birds and the infernal symbols carved into the trees.

"She is becoming too strong," Lysander muses.

"Drink this," Yun says, handing Ariadne a cup of potion.

Ariadne chugs it down, ignoring the dubious taste. The pounding in her head dissipates and the cuts all over her body close up until all that is left are traces of blood. Iona sighs contentedly in her sleep, then blinks slowly as she awakens again.

"Can you heal her cuts too?" Ariadne asks Yun.

Yun nods resolutely. Ariadne rushes back to Iona's side.

"I am alright," Iona says, trying to sit up but Ariadne gently pushes her back down.

"Do you have any other broken bones or pains anywhere apart from the cuts?" Ariadne asks.

Iona shakes her head no. Ariadne takes Iona's hand again.

"She was right there," Iona whispers, "It was too dark, and the pain was too great. I tried to make light but... she cursed me..."

Iona's fear prevents her from speaking further. Ariadne looks into Iona's mind. The feeling of razors against Iona's brain had come from the curse.

"She stole my power," Iona whispers as a single tear falls down her cheek.

Dread fills Ariadne when she realizes what had happened.

"A leeching curse," Salum says gravely, "Did she manage to take it all?"

"No... but she stole enough," Iona says, looking at her hands with dejection, "I feel weaker."

"She cast the curse twice. I felt it too," Ariadne says.

"You did?" Iona looks at her with wide, regretful eyes.

"It was almost certainly the malefician's first attempt at the spell. She is not able to leech the magic easily... yet," Salum says, "You are fortunate that Ariadne was able to get to you in time. If she had not reached you soon enough, your magic would have been taken forever."

Iona reaches for Ariadne. Ariadne holds her gently, afraid of irritating any remaining wounds.

"You have power left. With time you can renew it with rituals," Lysander says in an effort to comfort Iona.

"What about the trials?" Ariadne asks.

When Ariadne turns to look back at Lysander, he cannot meet her gaze. The other professors are silent as well. Yun approaches Iona with a new potion meant to heal her cuts and bruises. Ariadne takes it and helps Iona drink it all. Only when Iona's skin is fully healed does Ariadne feel herself relax, her fatigue rushing over her until she can barely keep her eyes open.

"This was the malefician's desperate effort to attack before the trials. It will have taken a great deal of energy to attack in such a grandiose manner. We must hope that she is enervated enough from this that she will be unable to attack again for some time," Lysander says.

"In the meantime, we must be vigilant. We cannot allow this to go on any longer," Yun says with vehemence.

"What do you suggest we do? Corner and interrogate every student until they confess and attack?" Salvador asks, "That will only lead to a battle with substantial bloodshed."

"She has been careful thus far to avoid suspicion," Pari says, "It must be very important to her to remain anonymous."

"Can you not look into the future and see who it is?" Ariadne asks Pari.

Pari shakes her head with regret, "The future is not always clear, and I cannot summon it on command. It is not like the past which can be traversed freely. If Iona's ghost is adamant that she must find and confront the culprit on her own, I cannot help."

Ariadne suppresses her frustration and notices Iona is fighting back sleep.

"We must retire," Ariadne says, coaxing Iona to stand, "We will need time to recover."

"I shall escort you," Lysander says.

"Thank you," Ariadne says as she puts Iona's arm over her neck to support her.

"Thank you for all your help," Iona says to the professors, "I am so... I am so sorry for all of this."

"It is not your fault," Ariadne says.

"She is right. This witch is responsible for the devastation she has caused. Do not shoulder guilt that belongs to her," Pari says.

Iona nods but Ariadne knows that she is still filled with regret. Ariadne helps her walk to the dormitories. Lysander takes his leave when they arrive at Iona's room, letting them know that a professor will be stationed in the dormitories overnight until the trials are over.

Ariadne undresses Iona and helps her into the bath to wash off all the filth and blood. Iona reaches for her, so she undresses too and joins her. The water turns black from all the dirt until the tub's sponges scrub all the filth away. Iona leans back against Ariadne's chest with her eyes closed.

Before the blood is washed away, it marks every place where Iona had been hurt. Ariadne shoulders her own guilt for not being strong enough to protect Iona from this attack. Ariadne has to carry Iona to bed, and as soon as her own head hits the pillow, she falls into a deep sleep.

The final week before the trials goes by agonizingly slow. It rains every day after the maze attack, the patter of water on the roof a constant reminder of the malefician lying in wait.

Ariadne is also aware of the professors silently watching them and all of the other students. Iona practically runs between the lyceum and the dormitories, still afraid that she will be lured back into the forest again. Ariadne accompanies Iona in her room in complete isolation and as safe as they can be.

Iona has taken to meditation to help with her anxiety. She feels empty with part of her magic missing. The deficit is enough to weaken her spells and it hurts both of them to see it. Iona's control over the elements, her ability to conjure, even her illusions are not as adept as they once were. Ariadne was so sure Iona would be the one to take the pendant but now, in Iona's weakened state, Ariadne is altogether unsure.

Their paranoia grows in the few days before the trials, which will be held on a Monday night. Ariadne reminds Iona that once one of them claims the pendant, they will be better protected. Iona does not seem comforted by this and that scares Ariadne.

Though Ariadne had agreed not to search Iona's mind for the identity of her ghost, she regrets that promise now more than ever. Ariadne wants to see what warnings the ghost had given Iona about what might happen after the pendant is theirs. The malefician should not be capable of taking the pendant away once it is claimed. That is at least what Ariadne tells herself. She hopes against hope that she is right.

Ariadne calls Iona into her dream the night before the trials. They find themselves back in the glade and sitting among the red flowers. Iona picks one and lifts it to her nose, looking more like a nymph than ever.

"When was the last time I reminded you of your enchanting beauty beyond compare?" Ariadne asks.

Iona flushes and Ariadne's heart stutters when Iona's smile only further enhances her devastating beauty.

"Far too long ago. I expect such passionate flattery every day," Iona jokes.

Ariadne moves closer to her and takes the flower from Iona's hand to put it in her hair. Then she leans in closer to Iona until their lips almost touch.

"I love you," Ariadne whispers fervently.

"I love you," Iona whispers back, closing the distance and kissing Ariadne softly.

Ariadne has Iona lay across her lap and plays with her hair to soothe her.

"I want to talk about the pendant," Ariadne says, "I want to clear the air so we can be aligned in our understanding."

"I want that, too," Iona says.

"Whichever of us wins, we cannot let that come between us. You are all that matters to me now. You are everything, all I want, all I will ever need," Ariadne says.

Iona sits up and embraces Ariadne tightly.

"I feel the same," Iona says, her voice thick with emotion.

Ariadne is relieved to hear it.

"One of us must win the pendant, though. It is imperative that we do," Iona says as she pulls away.

"I think it will be you," Ariadne says.

"I think it will be you," Iona says.

They grin at each other, then Iona looks away.

"Without my full power, I do not know if I am strong enough anymore," Iona says, her eyes remorseful.

Ariadne is also unsure but feels in her bones that Iona still has a chance. Her skill, her ingenuity, and her virtue are just as strong now as they were before the malefician stole part of her power.

"I hope it goes to you," Iona says.

"Why?" Ariadne asks.

"You deserve it after all the work you have done and the sacrifices you made. You are the strongest witch I know," Iona says.

"And you are the strongest witch I know," Ariadne says, "Morgan would be fortunate to have either of us as her pendant bearer."

Iona nods absentmindedly.

"Whatever happens tomorrow, you must know that I have already won. With you, I have all that I desire," Ariadne whispers, kissing Iona again.

They cling to each other and Ariadne lays Iona down on the soft grass. With a thought, Ariadne makes their clothes disappear. The feeling of Iona's bare skin against hers is rejuvenative. They stay in the glade for an unknowable amount of time, bringing their pleasure to new heights, until the dream ends, and they are forced to face the morning and all its uncertainties.

26 – IONA

The witches are all gathered in the courtyard and wait for Professor Pari to commence the trials. A sense of calm has fallen over Iona since she woke up in Ariadne's warm embrace that morning. At around midday, the rain finally stopped. Iona meditated the afternoon away until Ariadne had kissed her forehead and told her it was time.

Iona gazes up at the waning gibbous moon. It's bright light makes the clouds blue and grey. Then Iona sees a new, brighter light that she does not immediately recognize. She pulls on Ariadne's sleeve and points up.

"Look," Iona says, "The great conjunction has occurred. Jupiter and Saturn."

Ariadne looks and smiles at the sight.

"A blessed omen indeed," Ariadne muses.

Then Professor Pari emerges from the belltower with a somber expression. Ariadne squeezes Iona's hand.

"Follow me all who are ready to take Morgan's trials," Pari says formally.

She turns and leads the witches into the belltower. The inside of the tower is mostly comprised of wooden scaffolding that leads to the silver bell at the top. Pari whispers a spell and the ground shifts downwards, revealing a spiral staircase that descends into the earth. Pari leads the way down.

The hidden staircase goes deeper and deeper until

they reach a cavern. Golden candelabras illuminate the subterranean space and on the far wall stands a pedestal carved from the stone. The carving depicts three women holding a slab of rock over their heads upon which sits Morgan Le Fay's pendant. The large opal glitters in the light of the candles.

Iona can sense Ariadne going rigid next to her at the sight of the pendant. Iona looks to Ariadne and can see how affected she is in the presence of power. Ksenia, Samaira, Elise, Crescentia, and the other twenty or so witches in attendance share a similar look of awe and yearning. Iona looks at the pendant warily but steels herself. Whatever magic she may have lost cannot be undone now. She will do what is necessary to succeed in the trials while helping Ariadne to advance as well. One of them must win.

"Take a cup," Pari instructs, gesturing to a small table that has enough golden cups for all of them.

The witches pass the cups around, then Pari lifts a bucket filled with green potion that has the consistency of wine. She uses a ladle to fill all the witch's bowls with the liquid, then sets the bucket aside and stands before them with her hands clasped in front of her.

"A final warning. These trials are not for the faint of heart. If any of you would like to turn back, you may do so now without judgement," Pari says.

None of the witches leave but their apprehension grows.

"Drink," Pari says.

Iona closes her eyes, lifts the cup to her lips, and drinks the potion. It tastes like apples and a mixture of herbs. When Iona opens her eyes again, the cavern is gone and in its place is a marsh, the same marsh where Morgan had spoken with Iona on Samhain.

"What now?" Kokuro asks.

Iona looks up and notices that the waltz of birds that once graced the sky are now but one that circles above them. The raven flies down and the women all make way for it, except for

Iona and Ariadne. Iona puts out her arm and the raven lands on it and croaks. Iona hesitantly strokes its feathers.

"Do you not have enough pets?" Ksenia sneers.

Iona ignores her. The raven takes flight again and Iona watches where it goes.

"Look!" Crescentia says, pointing out into the distance.

The witches all look in the direction of her pointed finger. At the other end of the marsh is a pedestal with the pendant glittering tantalizingly at them.

"That is where we ought to go," Kokuro says.

Kokuro and six other witches walk into the marsh towards the pendant.

"Wait, I am not sure..." Crescentia says, then gasps.

The seven witches all sink into the marsh. They scream and claw at the mud and grass but soon they are all gone in mere seconds.

"What the blazes..." Crescentia says, putting her hand on her forehead in surprise.

"This is only an illusion," Ksenia says, "They have all woken up in the cavern. Serves them right for being so hasty."

"Where are we meant to step?" Samaira asks.

The witches look amongst themselves, but no one knows what to do. Iona looks back up at the raven. It flies through the air above the marsh and seems to be indicating a path through the dark pools of water.

Iona takes a step forward experimentally and does not sink. She takes another step, and another, while holding Ariadne's hand and pulling her along. The raven flies deeper into the marsh and croaks again. Iona's heart beats loudly in her ears.

The raven falls through the air and dives into a pool of water. It does not resurface. Iona and Ariadne peer into the water warily.

"It could be another trick," Ariadne says.

"I do not think it is," Iona says, then starts shedding her dress.

Ariadne follows suit so they are both in only their stays and chemises. The other witches take the path that Iona had tested for them.

"But the pendant is right there," Gisela says, pointing to the pedestal not far from them.

"You are free to try and claim it," Ariadne says wryly.

Iona holds onto her wand and looks to Ariadne, who seems to be stifling her nerves as she gazes down into the dark water.

"Together?" Ariadne asks.

Iona nods. She tries to send a comforting thought to Ariadne, then realizes that their bond is missing. Iona's mind is only her own.

They jump into the water and swim down. The pool is black as ink and freezing cold. Iona struggles to swim, no longer able to discern where the surface was. She panics when her air begins to run out, then inhales deeply when her head breaks through the surface of water on the other side.

Iona looks around as she treads water. She is in the middle of a vast ocean at night. The stars twinkle above her but there is no moon. Iona waits for Ariadne to surface next to her, but she does not. Iona wonders for a moment if Ariadne had drowned, then puts the thought out of her mind. There is no land in any direction but there must be a destination.

Iona floats onto her back so her legs can rest. She watches the sky, then notices a shooting star that flits across the darkness. Then it happens again, going in the same direction. Iona watches the shooting stars that seem to be pointing to something.

"Havfrue," Iona says, turning herself into a mermaid.

Iona swims across the open sea in the direction the stars are pointing to. She jumps up from the water to check that she is still going in the right direction. Then the sun begins to rise in the east and the shooting stars become less visible.

Iona sees the hint of land in the distance right as the stars turn to blue sky. She swims as fast as she can until she makes it to the shore of a green island. She undoes the mermaid spell and climbs onto the white beach. She welcomes the pleasant warmth as she leaves the cool water behind. There is a metal fence that separates the island from the beach. She traverses the sand until she finds witches gathering by a golden gate.

"Iona," Ariadne calls behind her.

Iona spins around and is filled with relief when she sees Ariadne approach. She runs and embraces her, accidentally throwing them back into the sand.

"Unhand me, nymph, before you get us both disqualified," Ariadne giggles.

"I am glad you are alright," Iona says fervently.

"I am fine, love," Ariadne says as she stands and helps Iona onto her feet, "Your instincts were true."

With Ariadne at her side, they approach the remaining witches. Iona counts fourteen left, including her and Ariadne's friends, and Ksenia.

"Visitors. How lovely," an aged, gravelly voice rasps.

An old woman wearing a simple red dress approaches the gate. She opens it and allows the witches to enter.

"Follow me, dears," the crone says.

They climb up a hill to an orchard filled with ripe multicolored apples. The trees are planted in rows and all look slightly different from one another. One even has golden apples that shine in the morning light.

"Pick one apple and take a bite," the crone says, "Choose wisely."

"How are we meant to pick?" Elise asks.

The crone only stares sagely at her. Ksenia steps forward first and inspects the apples carefully. Ariadne takes Iona's hand and leads her down a different row of trees.

"How are we meant to know the right one?" Iona asks.

"I think we are meant to find the apple that is set apart from the rest," Ariadne says, "Have you been studying your phytology book?"

"Yes, but these all look ordinary to me," Iona says, "Except for the golden ones."

Ariadne shakes her head, "That feels too obvious."

"I agree," Iona says.

They inspect the trees meticulously alongside the other witches. Some have already chosen to bite the golden apples and when they do, they disappear. Some took that as a good sign while others hesitate.

Iona struggles to find some hidden clue within the leaves of the apple trees. Then she pauses and approaches what looks to her to be a yew tree.

"Yew trees do not grow apples," Iona whispers to Ariadne, "They grow berries."

"That is right," Ariadne says, "Good eye."

Iona looks up at the apples hanging from the yew tree despite the impossibility of such a thing. The apples are perfectly round and bright red.

"I think this might be it," Ariadne says.

"So do I," Iona says.

They each pick an apple and face each other.

"If this is how we fail, I will be very angry," Ariadne jokes before they each take a bite.

Iona almost chokes on the piece of apple as she laughs. They are instantly transported to a frozen lake on an overcast day. The lake is surrounded by dense, dark forest. Iona curls into herself and wraps her arms around her torso as she shivers. She is still only wearing her underclothes and her hair is wet from her swim in the ocean. Ariadne is not far from her but when Iona tries to take a step, she can hear the ice crack. Ariadne puts up her hand to stop her. Iona and Ariadne both tense when they hear menacing growls in the distance.

Other witches appear around them, scattered across the ice, including Ksenia, then Elise, then Crescentia, then Samaira. There are only twelve witches left already. A pack of large black wolves run across the ice towards the remaining witches. They circle them slowly, their jowls dripping with drool and blood from a recent kill.

"Izrezati!" Yoselin yells, cutting deep into a wolf's side. It snarls and charges at her. Yoselin tries to fight it off, but it wraps its jaws around her neck, and she disappears.

"Pyrkagiá!" Gisela incants, but the flames only melt the ice beneath her and makes her sink into the freezing water before Nenet can grab her.

The wolves all attack at once and it is chaos. Spells are thrown this way and that until witches drop like flies. Iona even sees Ksenia push Yuka, the witch from Greenland, into a gap in the ice so she will be eliminated. Then she uses the invisibility spell. Iona sees her footsteps across the ice as she leaves the other witches behind.

"Iona!" Crescentia cries as a wolf gnaws at her leg.

"Izrezati!" Iona yells before she can think it through. The wolf leaves Crescentia's leg and charges towards Iona.

"Diminuir!" Ariadne yells, making the wolf shrink down until it is much smaller.

The tiny wolf whines and runs away. Then Iona hears cracking in the ice when Crescentia tries to stand. She falls into the water and disappears. Iona does not have time to lament. She turns away and has an idea.

"Megálo!" Iona yells, making one wolf grow in size until it cracks through the ice and into the water below.

Iona and Ariadne now stand apart from the other wolves still attacking the remaining witches.

"I have an idea," Iona says to Ariadne.

"What?" Ariadne asks.

"Diminuir," Iona says, making Ariadne shrink down until she is only about three feet tall.

Ariadne casts the spell on Iona too. They gather their skirts to keep from tripping and run away holding their now overly large wands in their fists. Now that they are small, the ice no longer cracks beneath their feet.

When they are far enough away from the wolves, they conjure ice skates and skate across the lake towards the woods on the other side. When Iona turns back, she sees Elise, Nenet and Samaira not far behind them, but no others.

When they reach land, they make themselves their normal

size again and conjure warmer clothes for themselves. Elise and Samaira catch up to them and do the same. Ksenia is nowhere to be seen.

They enter a barren, rocky landscape and find Ksenia at the edge of a pit within the rock. She has a worried look but composes herself when the other witches approach.

"We have a problem," Ksenia says, then points to a pit in the rock.

There lying in the pit is a dragon. Its four legs are tucked beneath him, and his head is resting on the ground, his eyes closed in sleep. Glossy black scales cover his body, and his wings are folded against his back. The dragon is guarding a portal. Its body is curved around it, its long tail partially covering the spherical doorway to the next world they are meant to travel to.

"We must sneak past it," Samaira whispers, "To fight a dragon that large would not be wise."

"I will start," Nenet says.

Nenet uses an invisibility spell and makes her way down into the pit. The only hints to her whereabouts are small puffs of dust that mark her footprints.

"If only Gisela had not lost so soon. Nenet could have used her as bait," Ksenia smirks.

"Do not give me any ideas," Ariadne retorts, and Ksenia frowns.

Nenet makes small, calculated steps, and Iona thinks she may make it through until she steps on a small rock that shifts under her weight. She trips and falls in the dirt.

The dragon's black eyes open and he growls at the sound. Opening his impressive wings, he looks for the source of the noise. A cloud of dust surrounds the place where Nenet had fallen. The dragon narrows his eyes and breathes in. Nenet tries to get up and run, but the spray of the dragon's fire reaches her too soon. Before she burns, she screams until her voice cuts off as she disappears.

"Well, that will not work," Ksenia mutters, "And now the

bloody beast is awake."

Iona glances at Ksenia, then looks around. Elise is gone too. Iona searches the pit for her and finds the little puffs of dust as invisible Elise avoids the dragon's tail and enters the portal while he is still distracted by Nenet. Elise undoes the invisibility spell when she makes it through, then traverses deeper into the portal.

"She took my advice," Ksenia chuckles when she notices what happened, "Smart, but cowardly."

Ksenia approaches the dragon next and pulls out her wand.

"Gíinos," Ksenia says.

Iona's mouth falls open when a giant boulder breaks off the side of the pit. Ksenia hovers it over the dragon and right as he notices her, she drops the stone onto his outstretched wing. The dragon roars in pain as the rock pins him to the ground. Ksenia makes a run for the portal. The dragon is too distracted to attack and tries to pull his wing free, but it only rips his skin. Ksenia makes it through the portal.

"That is cruel," Iona says with contempt.

"We need a plan," Ariadne says.

"We must help him," Iona says, pointing to the dragon's wing.

"But if we get anywhere near him, he will attack us," Samaira says.

"We cannot leave him here like this. If he is pinned down and cannot fly, he will not be able to find food. He will starve," Iona says.

"Iona... this is likely only an illusion. He may not be real," Ariadne says.

"I do not care. We must help," Iona says adamantly.

Ariadne sighs, "How?"

After explaining her plan, Iona climbs down into the pit. Ariadne and Samaira follow with hesitation. The dragon is making such pitiful sounds as he tries to free his wing.

"Gíinos," they incant and lift the massive rock up and off the dragon's wing. The dragon grunts and pants with agitation as he sniffs at his wound.

"It may not work," Ariadne says.

"You must try. My magic… I might heal it improperly. It is skin and tendons, you can manage that," Iona says.

Ariadne steels herself and steps a bit closer to the giant reptile.

"Philisa," Ariadne says, attempting to heal the dragon's wing.

It takes a few minutes but eventually, the tear in the dragon's wing is mended. By now, the dragon has noticed Iona, Samaira, and Ariadne in the pit with him, but he makes no move to attack. When Ariadne is done healing the injury, the dragon opens and closes his wing experimentally, then looks down at them with intelligent eyes.

The dragon moves away from the portal and curls up in the corner of the pit. Ariadne eyes him warily, but Iona beckons her and Samaira forward. The dragon does not attack, only watches them disinterestedly, then closes his eyes to sleep. Ariadne exhales with relief when they make it through the portal unscathed.

"It is a shame that he is not real, or we would have made an interesting friend," Iona smiles.

Ariadne grins and takes Iona's hand. Then they turn away from the portal and walk into a wide-open field of grass. Three moonstone archways stand before them, ominous and imposing.

"I think these may be portals as well," Ariadne says.

"To where?" Samaira asks.

"I am not sure," Ariadne says.

"How are we meant to choose?" Iona asks.

They look between the three identical arches. Ksenia and Elise are nowhere in sight. Iona assumes they chose an arch and disappeared.

"I see no rhyme or reason to them," Ariadne says, "I think we should pick one on our own and walk through."

Iona nods and looks at the archways again. Iona focuses on

the one on the right and goes to it. Iona glances back at Ariadne and Samaira, who are still choosing, then turns and walks through the first arch.

Iona enters a grand party in a room that is foreign to her in many ways. The first anomaly she notices are the lights. There are no candles or lanterns burning, only oddly shaped orbs that emanate light from within.

A crowd of people inhabit the space, and they are all dancing wildly and obscenely. The women have short hair and even shorter, fringed skirts. The men wear suits in many vibrant colors. Beautiful, lively music in a style Iona has never heard is being played by a band of handsome black men. They have a piano, horns, and a collection of drums that are played so fast, Iona can barely comprehend what she hears.

The party is so loud and thrilling that Iona is overwhelmed. Iona looks down at herself and sees that she is wearing a sleeveless pale green beaded dress with long fringe that sways when she moves. She feels so exposed among these strangers, but they do not notice anything beyond their own enjoyment.

Iona finds her way through the dancing couples. The air around them is saturated in white smoke that makes Iona cough if she breathes too deeply. She finds a window and opens it to get a breath of clean air. Then she notices that right outside the window there is a metal platform fixed to the side of the building. She ducks through the window to watch the party from afar until she determines what she is meant to do.

The metal platform has stairs going up and down, and through the slates of the metal Iona can see that she is very high off the ground. Iona looks out in astonishment at the vast expanse of buildings that light up the night as if it might be day.

"You okay doll?" a woman says from behind her.

Iona jumps and turns around. There leaning against the building and holding a burnt cigarette is a beautiful black woman who looks to be in her early thirties. She wears a floor-length red dress covered in fringe and flat beads. Her lips match her bright dress, and her hair is slicked down to her head. Iona cannot see the woman's eyes as they are covered in shadow.

"What are you deaf? Drunk? Lost? Never mind. I can't care about your problems too. This fire escape is taken, honey," the woman sniffles, "Find somewhere else to hide."

She takes a step closer to Iona and the light reaches her brown eyes, which are red from tears. She puts out her cigarette on a brick and throws it over the side of the metal platform.

"I apologize for the intrusion," Iona stutters.

"Aren't you an odd bird," the woman says, looking Iona up and down.

Iona does not say anything, then tenses when the woman approaches her and extends her hand.

"Delia Glaspie," the woman says.

Iona looks at her hand, unsure of what she should do with it. She hesitantly extends her own hand and Delia takes it, shakes it once, then gives it back.

"Iona Evora Lysander," Iona says.

"Lysander?" Delia raises an eyebrow.

"Do you know the Lysanders?" Iona asks curiously.

Delia looks Iona up and down again with suspicion.

"Are you a witch?" Delia whispers.

"Are you a witch?" Iona asks, unsure if she should admit such a thing to a stranger.

Delia grins at Iona, "That I am."

"So am I," Iona says.

"I thought I knew all the witches on this godforsaken island," Delia says.

"I do not reside here," Iona says.

"Where are you from?" Delia asks.

"Cornwall," Iona says.

"Where is that? Long Island?" Delia asks.

"No, it is in England," Iona says.

"Oh, that's where the accent is from, huh?" Delia muses,

"What is an English witch doing in Manhattan?"

"I am not sure yet... I do not know if I should say, but I am not from this time. I am from 1802," Iona says.

Delia's eyes go wide, and she regards Iona with renewed interest.

"What year is this?" Iona asks.

"1925," Delia says.

Iona's mouth falls open as she looks around with wonder and trepidation.

"Why are you here, Iona?" Delia asks curiously.

"I am visiting. I do not know for how long or for what purpose. I am taking Morgan Le Fay's trials. Do you know of them?" Iona asks.

"I know about her pendant, sure. Every witch worth her salt knows about that trinket," Delia says.

Delia goes to a windowsill to take a bottle of liquor that Iona hadn't noticed was set there. Delia takes a long drink and Iona watches with concern.

"Listen, I do not mean to be rude, Iona, but I am having a real shitty night. Is there anything in particular that I can do for you?" Delia asks.

"I am not sure..." Iona hesitates, "Are you well, Delia?"

Delia averts her eyes and seems to be holding back tears.

"Not really, no. I thought I could handle a party. My brother, the trumpet player in there, convinced me that I was ready but... I'm not," Delia says, tears falling down her cheeks, "It's strange that you showed up here now of all nights."

"Why are you crying? If you do not mind my asking," Iona says.

Delia wipes her tears away with the back of her hand, "My sister died last week. Spanish flu."

"My deepest condolences for your loss," Iona says.

Delia nods and looks away.

"Have you ever lost someone you loved with all your heart?" Delia whispers.

"Yes, I lost my mother last autumn," Iona says.

Delia looks to Iona with such sorrowful eyes.

"Then you know how I feel," Delia says.

"I have some notion," Iona says.

"What did you do to numb the pain?" Delia asks.

Iona is taken aback by the question.

"I have tried everything I can think of. Booze, pills, powder... meditation, potions, rituals... nothing helps," Delia says.

Delia throws away her second cigarette with a flourish and it falls down to the dark street below.

"I did not numb my pain. I wallowed in it," Iona admits, "Until my beloved comforted me and made me feel whole again."

Delia smiles wistfully.

"Sometimes I wish I had a fella but knowing me I would get stuck with a useless sap. Men are messy as hell," Delia shakes her head, "But I do love 'em."

"I have little knowledge of men," Iona grins, "But I hope one day soon you may meet your prince."

Delia takes another long swig from her bottle, then offers it to Iona. Iona takes a sip and coughs. The liquid is like fire as it goes down her throat.

"The purest love I have ever felt was for my dear sister, my best friend. We healed our neighborhood together one person at a time. Friends, family, strangers, all of the sorry souls who are treated like dirt in this world. They came to us for help, and we obliged them. And now she has gone to the other side when there was so much more for us to do. I cannot do this all alone," Delia relents, "The world is only getting worse in new ways."

Iona is filled with sympathy for Delia but in the back of her mind, she senses danger.

"I could bring her back," Delia murmurs, so low that Iona barely hears her over the music from the party.

Iona's heart stutters in her chest.

"No... such magic is unnatural," Iona says.

"One spell won't hurt, will it? Only one, not for myself but for someone else," Delia says, "How dark could it really be, if the spell is cast with love?"

"It would still be maleficium, no matter the intention," Iona says.

"But my sister would understand, and we could be together again," Delia says.

"It would not be your sister. Not truly," Iona says.

Delia blinks away her tears.

"I think this is why I am here," Iona says, putting her hand on Delia's shoulder, but she flinches away.

"Who are you to judge me in how I use my magic?" Delia snaps.

"I am not judging you," Iona says, "I do not know your mind, your past, or your sister. I know so little, except that you can do great things with the time that you have left. Do not give in to despair. Do not corrupt yourself. Is that what your sister would want for you?"

Delia looks away but Iona can tell she is getting through to her.

"We will all be reunited one day in the hereafter. Imagine how proud your sister will be of you when she sees all the good you have done for others," Iona says.

"I miss her so much," Delia says, dissolving into sobs.

Iona embraces her and comforts her while she cries. The woman smells like alcohol and wisteria. When Delia pulls away, she fusses with her makeup.

"I wish you did not meet me at my weakest moment," Delia says with embarrassment.

"Grief is not weakness, nor is our love for those we have lost," Iona says.

Delia smiles and her eyes soften.

"You know... I have studied the history of witches," Delia says, "I know who wins the pendant in your time. Would you like to know?"

Iona's eyes widen at the prospect, but she shakes her head no.

"I do not think I should know. Not yet," Iona says.

"Fair enough," Delia says, "I am glad to have met you, Iona. I really needed a friend. I think I know what I must do now…"

"I wish you peace and success in your endeavors," Iona says.

"Same to you, darling," Delia smiles with tired eyes, "Now get a wiggle on."

Delia gestures for Iona to go back inside to the party. Iona steps through the window and finds herself back in the wide-open field with the three stone archways. No one else is there waiting for her. She turns to look at the arches again and decides to take the left one this time.

Iona enters a dark, dirty cell lit by a single candle that sits next to a cot of straw. On the cot lays an emaciated middle-aged woman. Her dark hair is matted and oily. Her skin is sallow and sunken. She looks half dead and has bruises on any skin not covered by her thin white dress. The woman's eyes open and she gasps when she sees Iona standing there at the foot of her cot.

"You need not fear me," Iona says, putting up her hands, "I mean you no harm."

"Am I dead?" the woman whimpers.

"No," Iona says softly.

The woman nods and seems almost disappointed.

"What is your name?" Iona asks.

"Lucretia," the woman says, "Why have you visited me?"

"Truthfully, I am not sure," Iona says, "What year is it? Where are we?"

"Triora, Italy. It is 1597… I believe. I am not sure anymore. I have been here for so long," Lucretia says.

Iona stifles her surprise, not wanting to alarm the other woman.

"Why are you imprisoned?" Iona asks, taking a step closer to her.

"I aided the wrong person, and they accused me of witchcraft. Villagers ambushed me in the night, stole my wand, and imprisoned me here, poisoned and starved me for weeks. I am so… sick. So tired. I could not manage a single spell, even if I did have my wand," Lucretia whispers, a single tear falling from her eye. She can barely lift her head to speak, and her lips are covered in dead, cracked skin.

Iona immediately reaches for her wand, but the black dress she wears has no pocket to hold it. Iona wonders if she could unlock the door with only her mind, using a substantial quantity of magic, but then what? There would likely be guards stationed outside and they would only apprehend them and drag them back to the cell. Or worse.

"Do not think of escape," Lucretia says, "That is not why you are here."

Iona nods, though she wishes more than anything that she could help.

"What do you need from me, Lucretia?" Iona asks.

Lucretia thinks for a moment, then says, "Comfort."

Iona goes to her and kneels by the side of her cot, gingerly taking one of Lucretia's hands in hers. Lucretia's hand is like ice. Iona puts her other hand over hers to try and warm it.

"What sort of help were you providing before you were imprisoned here?" Iona asks.

"I helped with fertility, childbirth, and provided care for women who did not want to be with child, to end their condition before anyone would notice," Lucretia says.

"Very noble work," Iona says.

"I brought countless babes into this world and saved many women from undue persecution. That will be the legacy I leave behind. I only wish I had more time," Lucretia says with a bittersweet smile.

"Is there no way to find your wand or send a message for help?" Iona asks, still not ready to abandon hope.

Lucretia shakes her head, "I have a strong suspicion that if you are here with me from wherever it is you came from, this is my final night on this Earth."

Lucretia seems resigned to the inevitability of her death. It reminds Iona of when she'd said goodbye to her mother before going to college.

Iona spends the rest of the night asking questions about Lucretia's life, her favorite places in the world, her favorite foods, and her lover, Ilario, who passed away two years ago.

"He used to conjure me a butterfly every morning before he left to work in the fields. He put it inside of a glass jar and when I woke, I would set it free in our garden," Lucretia smiles.

"He was a farmer?" Iona asks.

"Yes, he used his modest magic to help the crops grow and provide abundance to the town. When he died, the food would not grow, and the townspeople were angered. I tried to continue his work, but he was always the one that plants listened to. The villagers came to believe that witches were what made their bounties turn to dust, but really, we only wanted to help," Lucretia sighs, "The famine led to unrest and inevitably to my own demise."

"That is so unfair..." Iona laments.

"Life is but a series of tragedies with brief, renewing respites," Lucretia says, "Love makes it easier to bear."

Iona cannot dispute her description of life, though Iona would argue that the respites are not always so brief. But of course, some people are luckier than others in that regard.

"What time are you from?" Lucretia asks.

"1802," Iona says.

"My word," Lucretia's eyes widen in shock, "Is the future a kinder place?"

"In some ways, yes, it is. In others... it is the same," Iona says, "There is still tragedy, but the world is becoming smaller."

"I would like to hope that one day it will be better. What use is magic to us if it cannot heal the world?" Lucretia whispers.

Iona and Lucretia jump when they hear the sound of a key rattling in the lock of the wooden cell door. Lucretia's breathing quickens and Iona stands, ready to fend off anyone who would try to hurt the poor woman.

"They will not see you," Lucretia says, "Please do not forget me."

"Lucretia," Iona cries but she is cut off when the cell door opens, and two burly men enter.

They grab Lucretia by her arms and drag her from the cell. Lucretia cries and struggles weakly, and Iona tries to hold her back, but her hands go straight through the awful men as if she were a ghost.

"Lucretia!" Iona cries, running through the door after her.

Iona is transported back to the empty field. Iona falls to her knees and sobs. She wants to go back to the cell and save Lucretia's life, but she knows that Lucretia is already dead. At least Iona was there to console her in her final hours.

There is one archway left, the one in the center. Iona is scared to enter it but knows she must. When she has shed all her tears and finds the strength to stand, she enters the third archway.

Iona steps into a clearing within a dense forest. In the center of the clearing sits a two-story house that appears grey in the light of the moon. The windows are dark.

Iona searches for any sign of where she should go or who she should talk to. She goes up to the house but when she tries to open the front door, it is locked, and her wand is nowhere to be found. Instead, she notices a dirt road that leads away from the house and decides to follow it.

Iona rubs her arms to warm herself, then stops walking abruptly when she sees a dark figure ahead of her. It is a teenaged girl with her back turned to Iona. She wears a pair of trousers, a knitted shirt, and boots. Her dark hair is tied in a messy knot at the crown of her head. She is carrying a large knapsack on her back that seems rather heavy. The girl suddenly turns around and puts her hand over her mouth to stifle her scream of fright.

"I mean you no harm," Iona says, putting her arms up.

"Who are you? What do you want?" the girl asks, in an accent that is similar to Phoebe Kimball's.

"My sincerest apologies for startling you. My name is Iona. What is your name?" Iona asks.

The girl looks her up and down with suspicion.

"What are you wearing?" the girl asks.

Iona looks down at her simple black dress.

"I have pepper spray in my bag," the girl warns.

Iona does not want to know what that means and takes a step back.

"I am sorry. I did not intend to frighten you," Iona stutters.

The girl scrutinizes Iona's face and clothes.

"Are you a ghost?" the girl asks.

"No," Iona says.

Iona glances at the knapsack on the girl's back and she stiffens.

"You can't make me stay," the girl says.

"Stay?" Iona asks.

"I'm leaving," the girl says fiercely.

"Why? Are you in trouble?" Iona glances back at the dark house in the clearing.

"I don't know why I'm even talking to you. Just leave me alone. I don't want to be a witch, and no one's gonna change my mind," the girl says, turning on her heel and stomping away.

Iona's eyes widen and she runs to catch up with the girl.

"Why do you not want to be a witch?" Iona asks.

"Why do you care?" the girl retorts, imitating Iona's accent.

Iona narrows her eyes, "What are you so afraid of that you are running away."

The girl stops walking to turn and glare at her.

"I'm not running away! I'm… escaping. I'm liberating myself," the girl says.

"You seem rather young to be escaping your home," Iona observes, "How old are you?"

"I'm sixteen," the girl says, straightening her spine, "But I've been told I look older."

"If your parents have magic, they will be able to find you wherever you go," Iona points out.

The girl pouts and looks at the ground, "Maybe… but even if I'm only gone for a day, I'd at least have time to think without them smothering me."

The girl looks back at the dark house with a forlorn expression.

"I will not try to stop you," Iona decides, "But might I at least accompany you? To ensure your safety."

"I don't know you," the girl says.

"There will be strangers out there too," Iona points out, "It could be dangerous to be walking alone at night."

The girl sighs and says, "Fine."

They walk together in silence for a while and Iona considers what she is meant to do here.

"Might I ask what year it is?" Iona asks.

"1986," the girl says, giving Iona an odd look, "You're not from here. I can tell."

"I'm from 1802," Iona says.

"Jesus H. Christ," the girl mutters, "No wonder you're dressed like a grandmother."

"I am not," Iona protests, smoothing out her skirts self-consciously.

"Yeah, you're right. You're more like a great grandmother," the girl says, "Can't you conjure some normal clothes, so people don't give us weird looks?"

"My wand did not travel with me," Iona says.

"Typical," the girl rolls her eyes, "What are you doing here anyway?"

"I have traveled through time twice before now and met women who needed to discuss something important with me," Iona says, "Is there anything you would like to talk about?"

"With you? No," the girl says.

"Alright," Iona says.

Another silence stretches on.

"What would I talk to you about... hypothetically," the girl asks.

"Whatever you would like," Iona says, "Is there anything on your mind?"

The girl deliberates, then asks, "If I talk to you, will you go away?"

"That is what happened with the other two women," Iona says.

"Fine... I found my wand last week. My parents are wigging out about it. They want me to drop out of school to practice magic all day so they can send me to some college in Europe when I'm eighteen. I don't want to leave all my friends because of something I didn't choose. I never wanted this..." the girl says.

"Could you not remain in school and practice magic when you are at home?" Iona asks.

"I asked and they said no," the girl says.

Iona understands the girl's frustration. Could her parents not try to compromise at least?

"And why exactly do you not want to be a witch?" Iona asks.

The girl frowns and looks down at her feet as she thinks.

"Magic is dangerous," the girl says softly, "I don't want to, like, make a mistake and hurt someone, or hurt myself with it."

Iona nods, understanding now.

"I just want to be normal," the girl says.

"But not all magic is dangerous. You choose how you use it. If you practice, you can learn how to use it safely," Iona says, "If living a life without magic is truly what you want, you should pursue that. I only wonder if you are letting your fear rule you."

Iona thinks of her own fear, that which was only shed away when she'd grown confident in her magic.

"Magic can be quite beautiful in the right hands. If you would prefer not to practice dangerous magic that might hurt others, you may excel in healing magic," Iona says, "Advanced healing is difficult and takes years of study, but it would make a great difference in the world."

"Healing magic?" the girl muses, "But I would have to go to college to do that, right?"

"Yes," Iona says, "If your magic was only used to help others, would it be worth the effort?"

The girl thinks for a moment, then nods slowly, "I guess so. My parents would need some convincing, but maybe they'd be willing to listen if I agree to study."

The girl stops walking right before the end of the dirt road, which opens into a wide black road that stretches far in both directions.

"I never did ask, where exactly are we?" Iona asks.

"Ontario," the girl says, "It's in Canada."

Iona nods absentmindedly.

"And my name is Vanessa, by the way," Vanessa says.

"Happy to make your acquaintance, Vanessa," Iona smiles.

Vanessa returns the smile, then looks out at the road in front of her.

"You don't want me to go, do you?" Vanessa asks with an exasperated sigh.

"I would prefer you did not," Iona says.

"A 200-year-old ghost is telling me not to run away from home," Vanessa scoffs, "I didn't sign up for any of this shit."

Vanessa turns and walks back the way they came.

"Come on," Vanessa says, gesturing for Iona to follow.

They walk down the long dirt road until they approach the dark house again.

"How long are you staying?" Vanessa asks.

"Until I am brought back," Iona shrugs.

"Do you want some hot chocolate while you wait?" Vanessa asks.

"If it would be no trouble," Iona says as they walk up the steps to the front door.

Vanessa takes out a ring of keys and opens the door.

"Do you like marshmallows?" Vanessa asks.

Iona is about to answer when she steps through the door, and everything goes black.

"Come back to me," Ariadne whispers.

Iona's eyes open and she is lying on hard stone. Her head is resting in Ariadne's lap, who is playing with Iona's hair while she waits for her to wake up. Ariadne leans down and kisses Iona's forehead. Iona smiles and takes Ariadne's hand as she sits up and stands.

When Iona looks to her left, there is a sheet of billowing clouds below that surround the peak of a tall mountain. She looks to her right and sees Samaira is there too, sitting and meditating on a boulder.

"Elise? Ksenia?" Iona asks.

Samaira opens her eyes, then shakes her head. So, it was only the three of them.

"These trials were not what I thought they would be," Samaira says, "They were quite invigorating."

"I am glad they met your approval, Samaira."

The three witches turn to see the old crone from the apple orchard. On a raised piece of rock in front of the crone is the pendant, which shimmers ever brighter in the light of the sun. The witches stand in a line before the crone, who regards them all critically.

"I must praise you all for making it this far," the crone says, "Your presence here is a commendation of your acumen."

The crone's white hair blows wildly in the tumultuous wind.

"Why do you believe that you deserve this pendant?" the crone asks Samaira.

"I abdicate any claim to the pendant," Samaira says.

"What?" Ariadne and Iona both say in unison.

The crone only smiles fondly at Samaira and with a wave of her hand, Samaira disappears. Then the crone focuses on Ariadne, who clears her throat nervously, still thrown by Samaira's decision to abstain.

"Why do you believe that you deserve this pendant?" the crone asks again.

"I deserve it because I would respect it. I know what power can do if it is used without thought or care. I know the devastation it can cause. I do not want another witch to use the pendant recklessly or with ill intent," Ariadne says with conviction, "And I would use the power to right a wrong that I have caused."

Iona looks to Ariadne in surprise. Iona can guess the wrong that Ariadne is referring to, but she had not mentioned it until now.

"Why do you believe that you deserve this pendant?" the crone asks a final time.

"I... do not deserve it. Such immense power is not owed to me, nor do I think that I am the only one that could use it well," Iona says candidly, "I could wield it though... I know that now. I am strong enough. And if I did possess it, I would treasure it and share its magic with all who need it."

The crone nods thoughtfully, her faded green eyes flitting between Iona and Ariadne. They both knew it would be between them, in the end. Their fate was written in the stars and contained within their hearts. Iona knows without doubt that whatever happens, she will be content. The malefician, whoever she is, is not among them. Iona has fulfilled her obligation to Morgan.

The piece of rock that carries the pendant moves forward until it stands closer to where Iona and Ariadne are standing.

"You must decide," the crone says, a twinkle in her eye.

Iona's eyes widen and she looks to Ariadne, who seems similarly shocked.

"You are letting us choose?" Ariadne asks.

The crone nods and clasps her hands in front of her. Iona looks down at the glittering necklace. By standing this close to it, Iona can feel the power radiating off of the pendant's stones.

"You should take it," Iona says.

Ariadne glances at her, "Should I?"

"Yes," Iona says, with slight disbelief at her hesitance, "This is what you have been working toward your entire life! Of course, you should take it."

Ariadne steps forwards and gingerly picks up the pendant by its golden chain. Iona watches intently, expecting Ariadne to put it around her neck and fulfill her lifelong quest once and for all. But Ariadne turns and steps in front of Iona. Before Iona can protest or step away, Ariadne places the pendant around Iona's neck.

Iona's knees buckle and she cries out as soon as the opal touches her skin. Iona feels as if she is burning from the inside out as pure magic courses through her all at once. The magic is so potent that it makes her glow. Ariadne holds her up until the overwhelming feeling finally passes. Iona breathes heavily as she looks at Ariadne with awed confusion.

"What did you do?" Iona asks, "This is yours, not mine."

Ariadne only shakes her head and smiles.

"You can still take it back," Iona says, though she is not sure if that is true.

"We both know that this is what was always meant to be. I fought against it at first, tried and failed to hinder you, but I could not change fate. No one could," Ariadne says.

"But you studied and practiced for so long," Iona says.

"I did. But I never wanted the pendant, not really. My family did, but I renounce them. What I always needed was you and now I have you forever," Ariadne says, "The malefician is still out there. You need the pendant's magic to protect you when I cannot. Now I know you are safe, and I am content."

Iona's sight blurs from her tears, which Ariadne wipes away. Ariadne leans down and kisses her softly. Iona closes her eyes and wraps her arms around Ariadne's neck. Then the wind from the mountain abruptly stops and Iona's eyes open.

They are back in the orchard. The sweet smell of apples lingers in the air around them. The crone walks between the trees until she passes into another row and transforms into Morgan Le Fay.

Ariadne gasps at the sight of the enchantress, while Iona only smiles.

"It is good to see you again, Iona," Morgan smiles back.

"Again?" Ariadne asks, then it dawns on her, "Morgan was your ghost?"

"You did not look after all," Iona says, "I was not sure if you would be able to resist the temptation."

"Your woman is as loyal as she is stubborn," Morgan says with a musical laugh.

Ariadne blushes deep red and Iona giggles.

"Congratulations, both of you. Iona, you have done beautifully. Your doubt persisted, but in the end, it was your love for another that stayed your hand, not insecurity," Morgan says, then looks to Ariadne, "Ariadne, there are very few witches who would relinquish power the way you did. You must know that even now, you are worthy of the pendant as much as Iona, or the pendant's magic would have burned you when you touched it. Let go of your guilt, your shame, and know that you are an honorable woman, better than those who came before you."

"Thank you," Ariadne says solemnly.

"Walk with me," Morgan says, beckoning them closer.

Iona and Ariadne walk beside Morgan between the many rows of apple trees.

"In years past, my pendant was won by strength alone, but I have come to realize that skill is not sufficient enough to justify such a bequeathal. The time has come for a new age of witches who value compassion over greed. Only those from within the previous hierarchy can effectively dismantle the rampant corruption and make the changes necessary to foster new strains of magic. That is my delegation to you both," Morgan says.

Iona looks to Ariadne, the weight of a new, much more complicated mandate falling upon their shoulders.

"One of my deepest regrets was my choice to give the pendant to Katrin Zerynthos. She was skilled, ambitious, and regal, all traits that I believed would make her a strong leader, but the pendant's power twisted her into a cruel old woman who became obsessed with dominance and superiority," Morgan says, then looks to Ariadne, "What were you told of your ancestry?"

"My mother told me that we were descended from Hecate," Ariadne says, but Morgan shakes her head.

"The Zerynthos are indeed a sempiterna bloodline, but they are not descended from a goddess. Your ancestors worshiped Hecate in antiquity but there is no further connection. They fought for generations to maintain the illusion of divinity. Your red eyes are due to a simple coloring charm cast long ago by your ancestors and passed all the way down to you," Morgan says.

Iona is even more shocked than Ariadne to hear such a historic deception come to light.

"This does not make you any less of a marvel, Ariadne," Morgan clarifies, "I hope this truth is a comfort to you. Any expectation enforced on you to be perfect because you are 'descended from gods' is unfounded and harmful."

Ariadne nods slowly, her brow furrowed.

"I think I knew that, somehow," Ariadne muses, "I am glad to know the truth. Such vain and false pretensions only served to alienate me from others."

Morgan gives her a sympathetic smile.

"We are not gods. We are guardians of nature and preservers of life. I hope both of you will see your powers as an opportunity to create wonders and maintain balance. Use my magic to protect the innocent, advise those who are lost, and fight evil in all its forms," Morgan says.

Iona blinks, then she, Ariadne, and Morgan are back in the cavern where all the other witches are waiting for them. Pari smiles brilliantly when she sees Iona wearing the pendant, then gasps when she notices Morgan standing regally beside her.

"Witches, young and old, witness the start of a new age. Iona Evora Lysander is my conduit and my champion, from now until her death. Please go in peace with your memories of my trials and know that this is my will, and no one may oppose it," Morgan says with complete authority.

Morgan glances one final time at Ariadne before she disappears.

27 – IONA

"**G**íinos," Iona says.

The earth rumbles, then a section of dirt that is the size of a house and shaped in a perfect cube lifts up from the ground and hovers in the air. Iona does not feel even slightly winded by the spell, despite the fact that she is not using her wand. Ariadne, Samuel, and Elise watch the feat of magic with awe.

"Incredible," Ariadne says with a wide grin, "How do you feel?"

Iona struggles to put her emotions into words, "I feel... powerful."

Iona puts the cube of dirt back where it was, then says "Neró."

A stream of water materializes before her. She manipulates it into a dome that surrounds all four of them. Ariadne reaches out to run her fingers through the water, her smile never wavering.

"Such unfathomable magic..." Samuel says reverently.

Iona looks back at her uncle who smiles at her. Elise mirrors her father's reverence and gazes up at the glittering water in astonishment.

Ariadne approaches Iona and caresses her cheek.

"You did it," Ariadne smiles.

"We did," Iona clarifies and cannot help but smile, though

she is still growing accustomed to this new reality.

Ariadne had impressed upon Iona that she is sincerely happy with how events unfolded. Ariadne has not heard from her mother yet but undoubtedly the news had reached her family. She is slightly worried about her mother's reaction but does not regret her decision.

Ariadne is adamant that the pendant was never meant for her. Iona cannot argue it because she can tell that Ariadne's thoughts are lighter than they ever have been. By letting the pendant go, and it being her choice to do so, she feels completely renewed.

"I always knew you were special," Elise says softly as she stands next to Iona and looks up at the water.

"That is very kind," Iona says bashfully, "Apparently everyone did except for me."

"Who could blame you for doubting. This was all thrust upon you at once without preamble," Elise says.

"I suppose you're right," Iona says, "But do not discredit yourself. You made it farther in the trials than most of your critics. That is no small feat."

"No, I suppose it isn't," Elise smiles, "I will be glad when I leave this school behind and can start anew."

"I feel the same way," Iona says, "After I visit your family for the summer, of course."

"Of course," Elise says.

"With that in mind, I shall take my leave. I have some packing to do," Samuel says.

Iona makes the water turn to mist and disappear. Samuel smiles to himself and walks towards the staff apartments, "Good evening."

"Good evening," Iona and Ariadne say.

"I must retire also. I will see you at the ritual tomorrow," Elise says with a wave, "Enjoy the day!"

Iona and Ariadne walk through the courtyard. Iona hasn't spent much time outside of late because of the malefician, but now that she has the pendant, she is not as afraid as she once was.

"I will eventually need to face my family again," Ariadne muses, "Or they will come and find me at an inopportune moment."

"Would you prefer to visit before we stay with the Lysanders?" Iona asks, "You may not be able to enjoy your summer if the threat of conflict looms over you."

"I shall think on it. We still have a few days to decide," Ariadne says, "I do not know if they will desire to see me anyhow."

"I hope they can come to realize that with or without the pendant, you are still their daughter, and they are fortunate to have one so extraordinary as you," Iona says, caressing Ariadne's cheek.

Iona leans her head on Ariadne's shoulder as they walk. Ariadne reaches into her dress pocket and hands Iona a single white flower with pointed petals and yellow in its center. Iona takes it and smiles.

"Which flower is this?" Iona asks.

"Edelweiss," Ariadne says, "In Austrian and Swiss tradition, it symbolizes eternal love. Suitors often climb to the tops of mountains to pick the flowers and give them to the ones they admire as an act of devotion to them."

"Soon you will have conjured every flower of love known to man," Iona grins.

"I did not conjure this one," Ariadne says, "I flew to the mountains this morning and picked it myself. Otherwise, it would not hold the same meaning."

"Oh... that is so thoughtful. Thank you, love," Iona says, kissing Ariadne first on the cheek, then on the lips.

The flower would soon whither as all natural flowers do, but the fact that Ariadne had taken the time to pick it for her personally made it special. It is because of this that Iona takes the flower from the vase the next day and pins it in her hair.

There will be a blood moon ritual tonight, the last ritual of the year before the term officially ends. The other witches at college expect for the ritual to be special because now, Iona will be wearing the pendant. All who attend shall be rewarded with even more magic than they would at normal rituals. Iona is admittedly nervous to lead a ritual for the first time. Knowing that Ariadne's flower will be in her hair gives her comfort.

"You look beautiful as always," Ariadne says, sensing Iona's nerves.

Iona smiles shyly and looks down at her red flowing dress with moons and stars embroidered in gold. She'd conjured it to reflect the style of witches and warlocks of old that she'd seen in grimoires and on the stained-glass windows of the lyceum. Normally red was Ariadne's color but since it is a blood moon ceremony, Iona thought it was only fitting.

Ariadne is ravishing in a dark royal purple gown with gold trim on the bodice. Her curls are loose and wild across her back. She holds her obsidian wand tightly in her hand as they enter the forest to find the ritual site.

Did you talk to Samaira about the trials? Iona asks Ariadne through their bond.

I attempted to discuss it with her, but she said that it was not time, Ariadne thinks, shaking her head incredulously, *I haven't the faintest idea why she would take part in the trials if she did not want the pendant. I knew she did not desire it as much as I once did, but to leave it behind like that…*

I am sure she walked away from it for a good reason, Iona thinks.

A branch snaps ahead of them and Ariadne grabs Iona's arm. They wait, but no one emerges. Ariadne cautiously beckons Iona forward, holding tightly to her hand.

Do you sense anything? Ariadne thinks.

Do I sense her, you mean? Iona thinks.

Yes, I wondered if you could now that you have the pendant, Ariadne thinks.

I had hoped that I could too, but she is concealing herself well, Iona replies.

Perhaps she has given up. There are only days left in Spring term, she already failed the trials, and there has been no sign of her, Ariadne thinks.

Iona wants to believe it could be true but is not convinced. She does not know if it would be preferable for an anonymous malefician to be let loose on the world to do who knows what.

Though she cannot sense the presence of the malefician anywhere, she does have a persistent feeling of foreboding that will not subside. As wind moves the clouds overhead, the blood moon bathes the forest in red light.

"Iona!" Crescentia calls from ahead of them.

Crescentia runs to meet them in a beautiful black velvet gown.

"I thought I heard you approach. May I walk with you?" Crescentia asks, "These woods are so unnerving of late."

Iona looks to Ariadne, who is tense with apprehension.

"Yes, I have been avoiding the forest since you misplaced your herb basket," Iona says.

"As have I, but I suppose it is worth the risk for the last ritual at college," Crescentia shrugs.

Iona stares at Crescentia as her smile wavers. Iona inspects the woman's mannerisms, the way she shifts on her feet, and her smile that does not reach her eyes.

"What is wrong?" Crescentia asks, her eyes flitting between Iona and Ariadne.

"Crescentia, please forgive me but I have forgotten the name of your beau. Would you remind me?" Iona asks, covertly shifting to stand between Ariadne and Crescentia.

"My beau?" Crescentia asks, tilting her head to the side.

"Yes, the one you spoke of months ago. What was his name again?" Iona asks.

Crescentia forces a smile, but her eyes are vacant.

"Do you not remember?" Iona asks, her voice unsteady.

Then suddenly the forest goes quiet. The owls stop hooting, the insects stop chirping, all of nature becomes deathly still until Iona's breath seems too loud in her own ears. Ariadne slowly raises her wand at Crescentia.

"Iona! Ariadne!" Crescentia calls from behind them, her voice echoing in the void of silence.

They both look back as Crescentia runs towards them with a look of terror. There is blood seeping from a cut in her arm and she looks like she can barely stand.

"Elise just attacked…" Crescentia starts to say, then gapes at the identical imposter standing across from her.

When Iona looks forward again, the illusion falls away like smoke. Elise stands before them where Crescentia once stood, her posture slumped and off balance. Her long hair is a mess of tangles, and she has dark circles under her eyes. Her blue dress is stained with mud and traces of blood, Crescentia's blood.

Iona's crippling fear keeps her tears at bay as she regards her cousin with spurning contempt. Elise only has eyes for the pendant that sits on Iona's chest.

Wisp and Aster growl menacingly in unison, making Iona jump. The familiars growl and snap their teeth until their barks sound more like chthonian screeches that no earthly animal could create. The familiars' fur bristles as they grow in size, their nails transforming to sharp claws and their jaws extending to fit multiple rows of teeth. They fall back on their hind legs and stand as tall as men, snarling at Elise with glowing red and orange eyes.

When Iona manages to tear her eyes away from the transforming familiars, she gasps and puts her hand over her mouth. The familiars had been reacting to Elise's now exposed aura, which is dripping with infernal darkness and corruption.

"Crescentia, run!" Iona screams.

"What is wrong with her?" Crescentia cries, taking steps back.

"Wrong with me?" Elise scoffs, her voice unusually low and minacious.

"You have lost, Elise," Ariadne says, pushing Iona behind her, "The pendant is already claimed. You should go now before the professors arrive and apprehend you."

"Be silent, Ariadne!" Elise says, spitting her name as if it was poisonous, "I have heard enough from you to last a lifetime. You will sing a different song when I am through with you."

Iona has no inclination of what that could mean but does not like the way Elise leers at Ariadne.

"Why?" Iona asks Elise, her tears finally forming as she processes this betrayal, "Why would you try to hurt me? I helped you with your magic. I was only ever kind to you. We are family!"

A blast of midnight blue maleficium explodes from Elise and pushes the three witches onto their backs.

"We are not family!" Elise screams.

Iona struggles to breathe with the wind knocked out of her lungs. She looks to Ariadne, who is gasping for air next to her.

"You are tainted with inferior blood. You were never meant to exist. I am a true born Lysander witch! It was meant to be me!" Elise screams.

The trees creak and groan as strong winds pick up in a spiral. Iona pushes herself up to standing and searches for Crescentia, who lays in a motionless heap on the ground.

"You loved how weak I once was compared to you. You relished in my struggles, watched me barely manage to cast spells that were effortless for you," Elise sneers, "I was never fooled by your so-called kindness. It was only a cunning ploy to manipulate me and take everything I was owed."

Iona looks over at Crescentia, still sprawled in the dirt but her chest is moving.

"What did you do to Crescentia?" Iona asks.

"I stole some of her magic. She has no real use for it anyhow. She is only common, and I can use it better," Elise says with an unhinged smile, "I did the same to you in the tunnels, and yet Morgan still gave the pendant to you... it does not make sense! Her judgement is flawed, so I will make matters right in my own way."

Ariadne stands and runs to Iona. She tries to shield Iona with her body, but Iona holds her back. Wisp and Aster stand between Elise and their masters, snapping their large jaws angrily.

"Do you know what I thought when I saw your witch's mark? All those months ago... at the blue comet ritual," Elise says, pacing as she speaks, "You stole my magic. It was always you, hiding under a rock in Cornwall, a cowardly, gluttonous miscreant too stupid to know what you had. I knew then that maleficium was my only hope to take back what was always meant to be mine."

Elise's eyes never leave Iona. A calm, disconcerting smile returns to Elise's lips.

"Once I drain you of every drop of magic you possess and rip that pendant from your cold, dead neck, the whole world shall know of my renascence," Elise says, her eyes darkening with every word.

"Your father would be ashamed of who you have become," Iona says.

"My father is weak," Elise spits, "My grandparents were ashamed of him, though not as ashamed as they were of your wretched father. I am their one hope to preserve their legacy."

"Even if you do kill me, Morgan would never let you wield the pendant," Iona says, "This is a fool's errand."

Elise glowers but her resolve does not slip.

"A wraith then... to bear the pendant and do my bidding until my last breath," Elise says, "It is just as well. I will enjoy watching you rot."

Iona steps back in fear and Ariadne grasps her arm tightly. Iona cannot let herself become that dead thing with black eyes and sharp teeth. Elise lifts her hand to cast a spell but before she can, another voice rings out over the howl of the wind.

"Pyrkagiá!" Crescentia cries, throwing a ball of flame at Elise's head.

Elise lifts her hand, and the flames die in midair. Iona is relieved to see that Crescentia is okay. Then she panics when Elise's attention centers on Crescentia instead.

"Wait!" Iona cries.

"Hirudovis!" Elise incants.

Crescentia's blood curdling scream pierces the air as Elise uses a leeching spell to devour Crescentia's remaining magic away.

"Ánemos!" Iona yells.

A blast of air that should have knocked Elise to the ground is stopped with a single wave of her hand, just as she had done with the fire.

"Démolir!" Ariadne cries.

An explosive force hits an invisible field of protection around Elise but does not affect her.

Crescentia's screams suddenly stop as the final traces of magic are ripped from her soul. Her eyes are wide with terror as she crawls away from Elise. With a lazy wave of her hand, Elise tosses Crescentia's body through the air until she slams into the trunk of a tree, and she collapses to the ground.

"No!" Iona cries.

Elise runs her hands through her hair and laughs maniacally, drunk off of the power she had just stolen. Iona runs to Crescentia's side to see if she is still breathing. Before Iona can reach her, Elise's laughter dissipates, and she takes a step towards Iona. Wisp lunges at Elise and gnaws at her arm until she breaks through the skin. Elise roars as she tries to pull her arm back. Elise pushes the malformed fox away and throws her backwards. Wisp flies through the air, breaking straight through multiple tree trunks, before falling heavily to the forest floor. Trees fall around Wisp's body but fortunately do not fall on top of her.

"Wisp!" Iona cries.

"We have to run," Ariadne says, "Aster!"

Iona tries to run to Wisp but Ariadne pulls at her waist and drags Iona away. Aster runs to find Wisp within the pile of fallen trees.

"I shall be the Lysander witch of our age," Elise says to herself in a shaky voice, "No one will take my legacy from me. No one. It is my destiny."

Elise's eyes are mad with reckless power when she chants an

incantation in a language that makes Iona's ears ring painfully. Black sludge falls from Elise's mouth and drips onto her dress and the ground below her.

Iona is pulled towards Elise and would have flown through the air if Ariadne hadn't grasped her arms and held her back. Iona screams and clings to Ariadne, but her hands are slipping.

"Izrezati!" Ariadne screams.

Ariadne's powerful cutting spell breaks straight through the trunk of a tree, which almost falls onto Elise. Elise pauses her spell to evade the tree while Ariadne pulls Iona up, and they run.

"This forest answers to me now. You cannot hide," Elise's voice echoes in the night.

The trees shift around them, the ground quaking and birds flying away from the fight. Iona screams when they sink to their waists into a bog of mud and moss. Ariadne tries to pull Iona along, but the black water is too thick and murky. When Iona looks behind her, Elise is sprinting towards them on top of the water, then levitates off the ground with her arm outstretched.

Ariadne tries to keep Iona out of her reach but Elise grabs Iona by the throat and pulls her up out of the muck. Elise's hand burns Iona's skin with poison that makes her skin bubble underneath. Iona cries and struggles but Elise only clenches her hand tighter and laughs. Elise rips the edelweiss flower from Iona's hair and sets it aflame in the palm of her hand until its ashes blow away in the wind.

"Your death was not meant to be so grievous. I tried to have the sirens kill you pleasantly. I tried to shrink you and keep you in a jar until after the trials were over. But you kept defying me. Ariadne kept interfering. Now, all that's left is suffering," Elise says as her blue eyes decay and sink into her skull.

Iona screams as Elise's nails pierce her throat, her skin burning from Elise's acidic touch. Then Iona falls as Elise snarls angrily. Ariadne had conjured wings, flown up to them, and uses an earth spell to throw a giant clump of mud into

Elise before she can block it. Ariadne catches Iona in midair and flies above the cover of the trees.

"She is lost to insanity," Iona cries.

"We must find help," Ariadne says, "None of our spells will hinder her and we will not be able to elude her for long."

The forest shifts ominously below them, making it impossible to determine where the ritual site is.

"We should go back to the college," Iona says, "We will not find anyone from up here."

Ariadne screams when she spots a boulder shooting up from the trees in their direction. She only barely manages to evade it, then almost gets hit by another boulder, and another, until one clips her wing, and they plummet down. Ariadne uses her remaining wing to try and control their descent, but they crash through branches and slam to the ground heavily.

Ariadne takes the brunt of it when she shields Iona from the impact. Ariadne groans and curls into herself from the pain. Iona reaches for her but Elise floats towards them and lands nearby. With effort, Iona stands and positions herself between Elise and Ariadne. Iona throws fireballs at Elise but she dodges the flames and approaches with a crazed look in her eye.

"You were always meant to die Iona. You can only avoid the inevitable for so long," Elise says.

"Gíinos," Iona yells, making a rift in the earth that separates her and Ariadne from Elise.

Elise watches the earth shift and crumble, then smiles. Iona's stomach turns at the sight. Elise whispers a spell while gazing down the crack in the earth. Hot orange magma bubbles up from the ground and burns everything in its wake. Iona grabs Ariadne's arm and pulls her backwards away from the lava. They cast water spells to try and cool the magma as it flows closer and closer, then give up and run away before the lava can overtake them.

As they run, lightning strikes make bright flashes of white light as they hit the ground and split trees in half. The thunder is deafening and the debris flying in the wind cuts their face and arms. Ariadne pulls Iona out of the way of a falling tree, then throws water at a trail of lava that almost traps them within a cage of thick branches and tree trunks.

Iona screams when she feels Elise's fingers grasping at her hair and lifting her up. Ariadne tries to pull her down, but Elise kicks her in the face and Iona hears and feels the crunch of Ariadne's nose. Ariadne falls to her knees with her hands on her face.

"Ariadne!" Iona cries, trying to unlatch Elise's fingers from her hair.

Elise pulls Iona up, turns her about, and wraps her hand over Iona's throat again. Her lips and chin are stained black from the bile that spews from her mouth with every spell. Her eyes are now cavernous black spots in her face. Iona cries and tries to think of something, anything that could save her. She kicks and struggles but she is not strong enough to break free. Elise grins at whatever helpless expression is displayed on Iona's face.

A roar emanates from Iona's chest. Elise and Iona both look down at the pendant as it shines like the birth of a star. Elise lets Iona fall back to the ground as a figure made completely of fire is unleashed from within the glowing opal of Morgan's pendant.

Iona is about to hit the ground, until she hears Ariadne cast a floating spell on her. Iona safely lands in the dirt, she runs to Ariadne's side. The fire is still emanating from the pendant until a sphere of flame floats in the air above them.

The fire builds until it forms wings and a tail. Another roar shakes the ground as a dragon spreads its wings wide and glares furiously down at Elise, whose mouth has fallen open in shock. When Iona looks at the dragon's face, she recognizes the same dragon that she and Ariadne helped during Morgan's trials. Iona crawls over to Ariadne, who is still holding her bleeding nose.

"Philisa," Iona says with her hand over Ariadne's nose.

Ariadne cries out in pain as the nose snaps back into place, but the bleeding stops, and her breathing slows as the pain subsides.

Iona and Ariadne look up as the dragon spits fire at Elise, who dodges the flames and tries throwing water at the beast, but it does hardly anything to fight the flames. The dragon swipes Elise with its claws and she only barely manages to evade it. Ariadne takes Iona's hand and they run even deeper into the forest, away from the scorched earth of the dragon's clash with Elise.

"My magic is waning," Ariadne warns and Iona's stomach drops, "I have a few spells left in me."

"We must find Samuel," Iona cries.

The earth suddenly roils beneath their feet as the forest groans, as if in pain. The trees bend and break as they are pushed away to reveal a winding river. Elise is forcing the forest to change, rather than letting it shift naturally on its own. Ariadne starts to hyperventilate, her eyes wide with fear.

"What is it?" Iona asks.

Iona sees in Ariadne's mind that this is the same river from Elise's dreadful illusion. The fire dragon bursts through the trees behind them with a roar. Elise throws blasts of water at the dragon, trying to back it into the river to smother the flames.

"Pyrkagiá!" Iona screams, throwing fire at the dragon to try and strengthen it.

The dragon spits fire and Elise puts up her hand to shield herself. Elise screams when some of the fire permeates her spell and burns her hand until the skin blisters.

Elise bellows as she reaches out towards the river. The water trembles as Elise creates a tidal wave that crashes onto the dragon, Ariadne, and Iona, while Elise flies above it.

Iona and Ariadne are swept away in the water, only barely able to hold each other's hands, though the tide tries to pull them apart. The wave disperses through the trees and Iona is finally able to lift her head above the water. She inhales sharply, and her lungs burn in protest.

"Iona, get up!" Ariadne cries, trying to pull Iona back to her feet.

Iona groans in pain, then coughs violently until Ariadne practically carries her away. Iona catches her breath, spitting water from her lungs, then runs alongside Ariadne, though she is beginning to wonder if this is futile. Even with the pendant, Iona is no match for Elise. None of her spells work and they can only hope to evade Elise for so long. Perhaps if she let Elise have her, she would let Ariadne go.

"NO! You are not allowed to die. Do not even think it!" Ariadne yells, dragging Iona further into the trees.

Iona cringes when Elise's macabre laughter echoes around them. She is getting closer and seems to be toying with them now. With the dragon slain, she has regained the upper hand.

"We will survive this. We will. I just need to think," Ariadne says, her panicked voice bringing tears to Iona's eyes.

"I love you," Iona says through her tears.

"No! Stop," Ariadne yells.

"She is too strong. I can hold her off for as long as I can, but you must go and find the others," Iona says.

"Iona, be quiet and let me think!" Ariadne snaps.

Iona looks behind them and sees the shadow of Elise in the air with the blood moon shining behind her.

"I love you," Iona says again.

"I love you too," Ariadne says, her voice breaking, "But we must keep going. Do not give up!"

They run aimlessly through the trees and scream when Elise throws flaring blasts of fire from above, the explosions raining dirt and rocks down upon them. Ariadne pulls Iona along, narrowly missing the blasts as they try to flee.

They stumble on their hands and knees into a glade with red wildflowers. Pixies with purple wings dance above them, seemingly unaware of the terror that is approaching. Iona recognizes the glade from somewhere and when she looks to Ariadne, she is staring at the towering oak tree in utter disbelief.

"Wait," Ariadne says, looking around, "I dreamt this."

Ariadne helps Iona to stand, right as Elise enters the glade behind them and incants, "Dominari somnia."

28 – ARIADNE

"**N**o, no, no, no," Ariadne says over and over.

Iona's hand is still in hers and Ariadne clenches it tightly until it turns to smoke and disappears. The glade expands into a vast valley of red flowers with a mighty oak tree that looms so tall, its branches touch the clouds.

"Elise!" Ariadne screams, "If you touch a hair on her head, I will rip you to shreds!"

Elise's taunting laugh reverberates across the valley. Ariadne screams when the red wildflowers spring up from the ground and wrap their stems around Ariadne's limbs, pulling her onto her back in the grass. Ariadne struggles against the tethers that hold her immobile.

"You're a filthy coward!" Ariadne cries, then winces when the stems dig into the flesh of her arms and legs.

Elise appears, looking down on Ariadne with a self-satisfied smirk. In the illusion, Elise looks normal again, her blue eyes gleaming and her reddish-brown hair falling in perfect waves down her back. Ariadne holds back tears and tries to break free, but she cannot move a muscle.

"Let me go," Ariadne screams.

"No," Elise says, "Did you think it was only Iona I was after?"

"Free her," Ariadne begs, "You can have me. I will do whatever you want. Just please, do not harm her."

"I will have you," Elise says with eerie calmness, "Did you know that maleficians can brew love potions? I always thought it to be a human's invention, some silly fantasy for those who wished their affection would be requited. But in my new grimoires, I found the recipe. All I required was your hair, your tears, and your blood, which the skeletons kindly gathered for me when you were trapped underground. The potion is already brewed, I only need to fetch it once I am done with Iona."

Ariadne's heart beats erratically in her chest as Elise's eyes roam over her with barely restrained lust that makes her skin crawl.

"I admit, initially I did want to murder you, painfully and slowly, for using me only to break my heart. I almost succeeded, but in time I decided that killing you would be rash and shortsighted. Why destroy you when I can have you as I always wanted? You will soon see my devotion to you is stronger than Iona's could ever be," Elise says.

"Iona would never force me to love her," Ariadne says.

"No, she would only manipulate you into abandoning your family to be with her," Elise says.

"That was my choice," Ariadne says.

"It was also my uncle's choice to abandon us to be with his whore, taking his magic with him. I will not let you make the same horrible mistake, no matter how... severe your mother may have been. She was only inciting you to be better, to be worthy of your name, like my grandparents did to me. Would it not be worth all the pain, the hidden scars, if we could craft a new empire of our own and rule as we see fit?" Elise says, "We could be free together."

"It would not be freedom if it was at the expense of others," Ariadne says, "If you know what it means to suffer, why would you wish that for anyone else?"

"If we are in power, no one will ever be able to hurt us again," Elise argues, her frustration beginning to show, "And no one need suffer if they surrender to our greatness."

"It is wrong, Elise," Ariadne insists, "Let Iona go."

Elise's expression hardens at the mention of Iona, and she sits back on her heels.

"Soon it will be your choice to be with me the way it always should have been, and we will be happy," Elise says.

"Elise, please," Ariadne sobs, "What you speak of is twisted limerence. Would you not want to be with someone who truly loves you?"

Elise ignores the question and stands.

"I am afraid I must depart. Iona will soon wake as a wraith, and I am eager to watch her kill for me. I will be back with the love potion soon. Then we can begin our lives together," Elise smiles menacingly, "I shall skin Iona's little rodent and make a nice fox fur scarf for you."

Elise chuckles to herself, her voice unhinged, then disappears. Ariadne whimpers and pulls at her bindings. She reminds herself that none of this is real. She is not truly being restrained in a valley of flowers, that is Elise's sick fantasy being projected onto her.

Ariadne pulls at her right arm to try to break through. The stems will not budge but Ariadne keeps trying. Then Ariadne hears Iona's voice, her cries and screams of pain from Elise's spell. Ariadne can feel fractions of her anguish through their bond, then sobs when she senses their bond breaking as Iona's life slips away.

"No, no please," Ariadne cries, thrashing around desperately to no avail.

Ariadne Iona's thought is but a whisper.

Ariadne lets loose a thunderous, guttural roar as she pulls her wrist free. Her arm slips through the vines as if they are not even there. She pulls her other arm free, then one leg, then the other, then rips the stems around her neck until she is free. She pushes herself up to her feet, evading the slithering flowers as they try to pull her back down. Ariadne breathes in and out, in and out.

It is not real. It is not real. IT IS NOT REAL!

Ariadne opens her eyes, and she is back in the glade. Before her, Elise floats above Iona's nearly lifeless body.

"Servus immortui," Elise incants, "Servus immortui."

With every word, Iona's cheeks lose their color, her red hair turns dull, her bones protrude through her skin, and her nails grow sharp like claws. Even the pendant seems to lose its perpetual glow. Ariadne is running out of time to stop this, and she does not know what to do.

Then Elise's voice warps, slowing more and more until it stops altogether. The pixies that fly away from Elise in fear are also frozen overhead. All time has stopped.

Ariadne stands, though her limbs feel heavy as lead. She stares up at the oak tree behind Elise and Iona and senses the magic that extravasates from it. She approaches the tree, wondering if this is another of Elise's illusions.

As Ariadne stands before the oak, still mighty at its natural height, the roots shift within the earth like snakes. They twist and lift off the ground, until they form the shape of a staff with a single labradorite stone that shimmers blue, yellow, and green. Ariadne reaches out and takes it, falling to her knees when power courses through her, revitalizing her magic and filling her with vitality.

Ariadne breaks the staff free of the roots, knowing without a shadow of doubt that she now holds the lost staff of Merlin in her grasp. She turns to face Elise again, her rage making way for resolution. She knows what she must do.

"Servus immortui," Elise whispers as time starts again.

Elise gasps in surprise when she sees Ariadne standing in front of the tree when to her, Ariadne had just been laying asleep in the grass.

"How did you get there?" Elise asks, her surprise turning to rage, "What is that in your hand?"

"Let her go," Ariadne orders, and the stone on her staff glows in warning.

"Whatever new trinket you have found is no match for me," Elise warns.

"I will never love you," Ariadne says, in an attempt to bate

Elise into recklessness, "I will only love Iona. I do not care what potion you may have brewed. You cannot have me, and I will not let you have her."

Elise snarls angrily and raises her hand to cast a spell. Ariadne braces herself. If this is her final stand, she will proudly die for loving Iona.

"Hirudovis!" Elise screams.

"Zárolt!" Ariadne counters, knowing that if this does not work, Elise will leech her power and surely kill her.

Elise's spell hits a protective field coming from the staff. It blocks the maleficium, something that Ariadne thought was impossible until now. Even Morgan's pendant cannot block dark magic.

To her further surprise, the staff is strong enough to revert the spell back at Elise. It hits her square in the chest and throws her onto her back. Ariadne gasps as Elise's power fills her in a rush until Elise looks down at her hands in horror.

"No!" Elise screeches, realizing her mistake too late. By her own hand, her power is gone forever.

"Dominari Somnia," Ariadne says, lowering her head.

Ariadne enters Elise's mind and puts her in an endless void of inescapable darkness. Elise screams and curses Ariadne and Iona's names, swearing that she will make them pay for what they have done to her. Her crazed, hateful voice fades away as Ariadne leaves her mind. The staff glows as it maintains the illusion. Elise's blue eyes return in her sockets, though any life in them is gone.

"Halat," Ariadne says, conjuring ropes to tie Elise's wrists and ankles together so she cannot blindly hurt herself or anyone else.

Then Ariadne runs to Iona's side and sets the staff down in the grass. Iona's skin and hair already show signs of life. Ariadne holds onto hope as she shakes Iona's shoulders.

"Iona, please wake up," Ariadne begs, tears streaming down her cheeks as she lifts Iona's torso into her arms.

The seconds tick by agonizingly before Iona stirs, opens her hazel eyes, and stares up at Ariadne.

"Are we dead?" Iona asks, lifting her hand to stroke Ariadne's cheek.

"No," Ariadne shakes her head and smiles, "You are safe, love. I stopped her."

"How did you…" Iona says, then sees Merlin's staff lying in the grass and her eyes widen.

"Merlin's staff…" Iona whispers.

"It is not lost after all," Ariadne says.

"No, it is not," Merlin says.

Iona and Ariadne look to see Merlin's ghost smiling down at them with kind eyes. Ariadne recognizes him from the image within Iona's mind. He wears a blue robe, and his falcon sits on his shoulder.

"You have done well, Ariadne," Merlin says, "I knew I chose correctly."

"You always did have a gift for choosing champions," Morgan says wryly as she materializes next to Merlin, then faces Iona and Ariadne, "You have vanquished evil this night. The world owes you a great debt for your bravery."

"Is it over?" Iona asks, her voice still frail.

"Yes, sweet Iona, it is over," Morgan says.

Iona relaxes into Ariadne's arms, the weight of her troubles lifting away.

"Ariadne, I must impress upon you my deepest pride and gratitude. Only an entirely selfless witch or warlock could have conjured the staff back into existence. All who have sought the staff before did so in the pursuit of power to fuel their egos and facilitate their own conquests. You sought to protect your love from harm, to save her from a horrible fate. Your love for Iona has redeemed you and made you worthy of this artifact," Merlin says, "Use it well. It has the power to right past wrongs and take you wherever you wish to go."

Ariadne nods respectfully, her emotions too high for her to manage speech.

"May your love be a beacon for all magic users in this

world for generations to come. You will be the most powerful coupling in centuries with a bond that is unbreakable," Morgan professes.

Ariadne and Iona look to each other with devotion and gratitude.

"Thank you both for your guidance," Iona says as she sits up, her strength returning.

"Thank you for listening," Morgan says, "Until we meet again."

Merlin and Morgan smile at them as they disappear into mist. As soon as their figures evaporate in air, it begins to rain. Ariadne sighs.

"Iona? Ariadne?" Samuel calls in the distance.

Iona stiffens at the sound. She and Ariadne both look to Elise, still tied and motionless in the grass, then to each other.

"I cannot… I do not have the heart to tell him," Iona says, her tears renewed.

Ariadne nods, and stands, "Stay here."

When Ariadne tells Samuel what his daughter has done, what Crescentia had already told him when he found her collapsed in the forest, he weeps with regret and shame.

"Where is she?" Samuel barely whispers through his tears.

"I shall take you to her," Ariadne says, then leads Samuel to the glade.

Samuel sinks to his knees and pushes Elise's hair out of her face, though her unseeing eyes are vacant and glassy.

"I can release her from the illusion," Ariadne offers.

"No, you mustn't yet," Samuel says, "I will take her back to the college first. I must talk to the other professors about what we should do with her."

Ariadne nods.

"Samuel," Iona says, "I am so, terribly sorry."

"As am I," Samuel says, his shoulders slumped, "I will never forgive myself. I thought… I did not raise her to harbor such enmity. I did not realize how strong my parents' influence had been on her. I should not have let them near her. I should not have let this cycle of misplaced supremacy continue. It is my failing as much as hers."

"I do not blame you," Iona says vehemently.

"You are too kind as always, Iona," Samuel says.

Samuel lifts his daughter into his arms and walks away with his head hung low.

When Ariadne and Iona emerge from the forest, they find their classmates and professors gathered in the courtyard and whispering nervously amongst themselves. When the witches notice Ariadne and Iona approaching, they murmur and exclaim their surprise.

"Where is Crescentia?" Iona calls to them.

"I am here," Crescentia calls from behind the crowd.

Iona runs over to her, and Ariadne follows. Iona sighs with relief when she sees Wisp and Aster lying next to Crescentia. Professor Yun is attending to Crescentia's wounds with a grave expression.

"Wisp," Iona says, opening her arms for her beloved familiar to jump into.

Wisp barks and licks Iona's face. Ariadne had sensed that Wisp was alive through her bond with Iona and though the fox is bruised and has a slight limp on her back leg, she is otherwise unharmed.

"Philisa," Iona whispers with her hand resting gently on Wisp's leg, healing it and the bruises in seconds. Iona kisses Wisp on the head in gratitude for her loyalty.

Ariadne had ordered Aster to stay behind, guard Crescentia's body, and howl for help, which must have been how Samuel was able to find her. Aster runs up to Ariadne and she scratches his ears lovingly.

Iona sets Wisp on the ground and refocuses on Crescentia. Her smile falls away as she takes Crescentia's hand, "Crescentia... I do not know what to say. I never should have doubted you. Elise was cruel to use your face for such terrible deeds."

"I am alright, Iona. She tricked us all," Crescentia says with a weak smile, "The trouble now is, I cannot feel my legs. Professor Yun is trying to heal them."

Iona puts her hand over her mouth. Ariadne meets Yun's gaze, and, in her eyes, Ariadne can tell that she does not know if the injury can be healed with potions.

"Is that Merlin's staff?" Crescentia asks, her joy at the sight making Ariadne's heart break for her.

"It is," Ariadne says with a tired smile, "I am sorry too, for doubting you."

Iona looks to Ariadne and extends her hand. Ariadne takes it and kneels next to her. Iona guides both of their hands to Crescentia's forehead.

"Philisa," Iona whispers.

They incant the spell continuously in unison. Crescentia watches them with hope that spurs them both on. Then Iona grunts and squeezes her eyes shut as magic is siphoned from her and into Crescentia. Iona does not let go, even when it causes her pain. When Iona's eyes open again, she removes their hands and regards Crescentia nervously.

"Can you feel your legs?" Iona asks.

Crescentia tries to move them, and she smiles through her tears when they bend and straighten as normal.

"Thank you," Crescentia cries.

"Oh, thank goodness," Yun says, the stoic professor giving way to tears.

"What about your magic?" Iona asks.

Crescentia's smile falters, "That can never be repaired. My family will be devastated but…"

"Try to cast a spell," Iona insists as she stands and motions for Ariadne to take a few steps back.

Crescentia regards Iona quizzically, then takes out her wand.

"Neró," Crescentia says reluctantly.

The blast of water that shoots out of Crescentia's wand has enough force to push her backwards onto the grass. Crescentia quickly ends the spell before she accidentally creates a flood. Then she stares at her wand in amazement.

"It cannot be," Crescentia says.

Yun only gapes at Crescentia in disbelief. Crescentia gasps again when she looks down at the inside of her left wrist. There is a newly made witch's mark in the shape of a wreath of oak and laurel, a mark for a new line of witches. Crescentia jumps up and embraces Iona.

"Thank you, thank you, thank you," Crescentia sobs.

Iona holds her friend close, so happy that she is okay. Then she almost collapses but Crescentia holds her up.

"Iona?" Crescentia exclaims.

"Kuelea," Ariadne incants, so Iona's body floats instead of falling to the ground.

Ariadne releases Merlin's staff, which stands upright on its own against gravity, and rushes to Iona's side. Ariadne takes Iona from Crescentia and cradles her in her arms. Aster takes Merlin's staff gently between his teeth and runs with Wisp to their witches' sides.

"She is just drained," Ariadne says to quell Crescentia's concern, "I should put her to bed so we can both rest."

"Of course," Crescentia says, "Thank you, Ariadne. For everything."

"Here take these," Yun says, handing Ariadne two vials with healing potion, "This should help with any surface cuts, burns, and bruises. If you need more healing than that, please come and find me."

"I will. Thank you, Professor," Ariadne says.

"Classes are over, Ariadne. Please call me Corella," Corella says with a proud smile.

Ariadne smiles back and nods respectfully. She carries Iona to the dormitories and careful walks up the stairs to Iona's room. Ariadne strips them both down to check for serious wounds and helps Iona drink her healing potion. After they've bathed, they fall into bed, too exhausted to even speak. Iona curls up against Ariadne and they fall into a dreamless, peaceful slumber.

"Ariadne," Iona whispers.

Ariadne jerks awake, "What? What is it?"

"Hush," Iona says softly, caressing Ariadne's cheek, "We have slept clear into the afternoon."

Ariadne looks out the window and sees that Iona is right. The sun is far too high in the sky for it to still be morning. Ariadne groans and rubs her face. She is still tired but not as exhausted as she had been the previous night.

"How are you feeling?" Ariadne asks.

"As well as can be expected," Iona says, tracing Ariadne's witch's mark with her finger.

Iona is lost in thought. Ariadne could look into her mind for more insight, but she remains patient, allowing Iona to express herself in her own time.

"I should have known it was her," Iona whispers.

"How could you have? She concealed herself well enough that her own father did not suspect her," Ariadne says.

"He did not see her for the same reason I did not," Iona's eyes are distant, "Our hearts blinded us."

Ariadne sees a glimpse of Merlin in Iona's mind.

"For Elise, it was never about the pendant, not really. It was about her resentment towards me and my mother," Iona says, "And I never thought to watch Elise or question her because she was my family, and she took advantage of that."

Iona rubs the sleep from her eyes and sighs.

"My mother was right to hide me from the Lysanders the way she did. The only one worth knowing is Samuel. And now his only daughter will be taken from him... Elise..." Iona's voice breaks, "If I had discovered her sooner, confronted her before the maleficium destroyed her, perhaps she could have been saved."

"Don't," Ariadne says, "Elise's undoing is her own fault. She tried to kill you. And she almost..."

Iona jerks and shifts to look down at Ariadne with dismay.

Ariadne had been careful not to think of what Elise had threatened to do to her because she knew it would upset Iona, but she could not hide it indefinitely. Ariadne lets her thoughts recount Elise's speech about the love potion she had brewed and watches any residual sympathy Iona had for Elise melt away.

"Oh..." Iona says, "How evil... How completely reprehensible."

"Do not waste your guilt on such a person. You do not owe her anything. Samuel knows that. He is a good man. How Elise came from him, I will never understand," Ariadne says.

Iona wraps her arms around Ariadne's neck and burrows her face into her neck. Ariadne closes her eyes and enjoys the feeling of their magic coiling between them and warming them up.

"I love you," Iona whispers in Ariadne's ear.

"I love you too," Ariadne says, then grins "How many times is that?"

"Is what?" Iona asks.

"How many times have I saved your life," Ariadne clarifies, ghosting her fingers down Iona's spine.

"Oh, are we keeping score?" Iona asks sardonically.

"If we are, then I am winning," Ariadne says, digging her fingers into Iona's ribs and making her squeal with giggles until Ariadne flips them over so Iona is beneath her.

Iona looks at Ariadne lovingly and reaches up to trace Ariadne's lips with her fingers. Ariadne kisses the center of Iona's palm, then leans down to capture Iona's lips with hers.

I am hers and she is mine. We have nothing to fear anymore. To love her is my fate and I will thank the stars every night for their intervention, Iona thinks to herself.

Ariadne smiles and kisses along Iona's jaw before sucking at Iona's neck until she moans softly. She lets her hand slide down Iona's side to grasp at her leg and hitch it over her hips. Iona locks her ankles around Ariadne's waist and lightly runs her nails down the smooth plains of Ariadne's back.

Ariadne knows they have much to do today, so much to explain to so many people, but she almost lost Iona. She cannot imagine life without her sweet smile, her quiet strength, and her unparallel beauty, both inside and out. Ariadne cannot leave this bed without giving Iona pleasure at least once, maybe twice.

Ariadne lays on her side, puts an arm along Iona's back, and her other hand between Iona's spread legs to slide fingers along her growing wetness. Iona kisses Ariadne until her breathing is too labored to manage it. Ariadne sucks on Iona's neck, her collarbone, her nipple, all while thrusting two, then three fingers inside Iona's wet heat. Ariadne feels her own pleasure grow alongside Iona's.

"You are mine," Ariadne growls as she quickens the pace of her fingers, "Your lips are mine, your cunt, your heart, your storm-touched soul. All mine."

"All yours," Iona agrees, grinding her hips as her moans grow louder and more impatient.

Ariadne moans, licking along the pulsing vein on Iona's neck.

"Say my name," Ariadne demands.

"Ariadne," Iona barely chokes out as her pleasure builds.

Ariadne hooks one of her legs over Iona's to keep her thighs spread wide, though Iona instinctively tries to close them around Ariadne's thrusting fingers.

"Say you love me," Ariadne whispers in Iona's ear.

"I love you. I love you so much," Iona whimpers.

Iona's back arches so rigidly that it looks almost painful. Ariadne kisses along her ribs and upon every freckle. Iona moans when Ariadne moves over her most sensitive spot over and over, then slows her fingers just before she can climax. Iona whimpers and Ariadne grins against her flushed skin. She loves to watch Iona lose all control, her timidity fading away, replaced by primal need that only Ariadne can satisfy.

"Please," Iona begs.

"Please what?" Ariadne asks, grinning down at her as she

squirms.

"Does our bond not render this game meaningless?" Iona whines.

The bond only serves as further amusement for Ariadne, to see Iona's conflicted thoughts as she decides between holding onto her pride or begging Ariadne to stroke her harder. It thrills Iona to be toyed with this way, though she would never admit it out loud.

"You know I could keep you like this forever if I desire it," Ariadne says against Iona's breast.

Iona sighs heavily, trying to thrust her hips into Ariadne's hand, "You are insufferable."

"I know, nymph," Ariadne coddles, "But you love it."

Iona flushes with indignance but does not deny it. She knows it would be a lie. Ariadne strokes her in earnest again, then pulls back, and Iona whimpers with disappointment. Ariadne presses soft, gentle kisses on Iona's neck as she waits for Iona to give in.

"You know that I would die for you, kill for you, live only for you. All you need do," Ariadne slides her fingers in deeper, "is ask."

Iona suddenly lets out a frenzied moan when Ariadne strokes her in a devastatingly sensitive spot, and the pleasure brings tears to her eyes.

"Please, fuck me harder," Iona pleads, her voice cracking, "Please... Please... Ariadne... I need you..."

Ariadne moans at the desperation in Iona's voice, then quickens her fingers until Iona falls apart. Though Iona barely touched her, Ariadne loses herself too, their pleasure mixing together in the confines of their minds until she cannot tell where she ends, and Iona begins. Ariadne kisses the salty tears from Iona's cheeks as she strokes her through her pleasure, then presses their foreheads together as they catch their breath, and their heartbeats slow.

"I cannot wait to spend an eternity with you in my arms," Ariadne whispers.

Iona only smiles contentedly and pulls Ariadne closer for a kiss.

"I feel so powerful," Crescentia giggles, "It is euphoric, is it not?"

"It is," Iona agrees.

They are both playing with water magic to test the bounds of their new power. The mostly empty courtyard is now covered in puddles. Iona creates a water horse that canters around them, his mane flowing as he rears his head and whinnies happily. Wisp and Aster chase the horse around as Iona and Crescentia laugh together.

"Do you remember when we used to take such simple joy from magic?" Samaira asks softly, "Before it became an obligation rather than a wonderment."

Ariadne looks away from Iona and Crescentia and into Samaira's curious gaze.

"I thought I had lost that feeling forever, until Iona reignited it," Ariadne says.

Samaira looks between Ariadne and Iona, a smile forming across her lips.

"You love her," Samaira says, a statement rather than a question.

"I do," Ariadne says, flushing slightly, "She is everything to me now."

"You protected her valiantly," Samaira praises, "She would be dead if it were not for you."

"A fact I will be sure to remind her of anytime I'd like to win an argument," Ariadne jokes.

Samaira laughs with her, then Ariadne clears her throat.

"I am waiting in suspense for your explanation about the trials," Ariadne prompts.

Samaira fiddles with her ring, the sapphire sparkling in the sun.

"I have not been entirely honest with you," Samaira says.

Samaira conjures two chairs and gestures for Ariadne to

sit. She does so and folds her hands in her lap to keep from fidgeting.

"Do you remember when I told you that there were other artifacts in this world, apart from the pendant, that were worth pursuing?" Samaira asks.

"Yes, I remember," Ariadne says.

Samaira extends her hand, showing the ring to Ariadne, who admires it with new eyes.

"This is a sapphire ring of unknown origin. No one forged it or acquired it. It always was. It is a blessed artifact of Nepal," Samaira says, "One that many Nepali witches and warlocks compete for, similarly to the trials of Morgan. I won the ring and now wield its magic."

Samaira smiles wide as Ariadne takes her hand and inspects the ring. Ariadne goes to touch the stone out of curiosity but pulls her hand away when she senses the power within that would surely burn her.

"But... how did I not notice?" Ariadne asks, "Why did you not tell me?"

"As fall term approached, you were in rare form. I have never seen you so agitated, so easily provoked, due to your anxiety about the pendant. I decided that when I won this sacred artifact last summer, I would wait until the proper moment to reveal it to you," Samaira says.

"I... I am sorry you thought it was necessary to hide something so monumental from me," Ariadne says with regret.

"But you are not that person anymore. I knew you would not be. I know a great deal more these days," Samaira says, "The ring gives me visions and heightened intuition. I am not omniscient, more of an oracle. I have visions and can sometimes perceive the threads of fate connecting us all."

Ariadne stares at the sapphire ring in awe.

"What visions have you had?" Ariadne asks.

"I did know before fall term began that you would not win the pendant. Iona would," Samaira says, then cringes when

Ariadne gapes at her, "Please do not be cross with me!"

"Samaira... why did you not say anything about it?" Ariadne asks, trying not to snap at her.

"If I had told you definitively that you would not win the pendant before you were ready, how do you think you would have reacted?" Samaira asks, "I know you, Ari. You would have had a conniption!"

Ariadne pouts but cannot dispute her.

"After I had the vision, I saw it as my purpose to assist in the peaceful transference of the pendant to its rightful owner. Part of that quest was to help you in what little ways I could to accept that the pendant was never yours, that you did not truly want it, so you could let it go on your own," Samaira says, "It was the best way."

"Did you know Iona was a Lysander?" Ariadne asks.

"I knew she was very powerful and saw threads connecting her to Professor Lysander and Elise, but I did not know they were family," Samaira says, "I also saw that a strong thread of fate connected the two of you, but I did not know why."

"Did you know about Merlin's staff?" Ariadne asks.

"I had a vision of you holding the staff the day before Morgan's trials," Samaira says.

Ariadne's mood darkens and she narrows her eyes, "Did you know about Elise?"

"No," Samaira says, "I would have warned you; I swear. Elise hid herself completely, even from me. You and Iona were fated to discover her at a specific point in time."

"But then... why enter into the trials at all if you did not need to?" Ariadne asks,

"I entered the trials for fun," Samaira shrugs.

Samaira giggles at Ariadne's confusion.

"I wanted to see how far I could get," Samaira says, "When I saw the end of the trials was nigh, I took my leave. I was happy to meet Morgan and test my own strength. I trusted you to make the right decision."

Ariadne sits back in her chair and rubs her forehead, unable to believe it all.

"You watched me make such a fool of myself," Ariadne groans.

"I only laughed about it occasionally," Samaira grins, "It can be quite entertaining to know important pieces of information before anyone else. You only have yourself to blame for your petulance, Ari. I hope you will be less impulsive in future."

Ariadne sighs and Samaira takes her hands in hers.

"Are you cross with me?" Samaira asks.

"No," Ariadne says, "A tad annoyed, but I understand your position."

"I knew you would understand," Samaira grins, then her eyes drift to Merlin's staff in Ariadne's grasp, "Now that you have all this magic, what shall you do with it?"

"I imagine I shall have many opportunities to use the magic for noble purposes... but I am sure you can surmise what I will try first," Ariadne says.

"I suspected as much," Samaira says with tender eyes.

"For so long, everyone was frightened of me... I was frightened of myself. No longer," Ariadne says, "I want to be known for something better."

"And so, you shall," Samaira says with knowing eyes.

Ariadne stands and takes a few steps away from where they were sitting. She admires Merlin's staff, the way the labradorite shimmers blue and yellow in the afternoon sun, then closes her eyes, and centers herself. She imagines Mount Pelion, a mountain near her home that she would often fly to when she wanted to be alone. When she opens her eyes, her suspicions are proven correct. Merlin had told her that the staff could take her where she needed to go. Before them stands a portal to the peak of Mount Pelion, just as Ariadne had pictured.

"Extraordinary," Samaira says softly, "Imagine what more it can do that you haven't yet discovered."

"How did you do that?" Crescentia asks, running over to them and pulling Iona along with her.

"The staff," Ariadne lifts the staff and shrugs.

"You will never need to buy a train ticket again," Crescentia says to Iona as she comes to stand next to her, "You can visit me whenever you please! Promise you will! I want you to meet my family, and Erik, and all of my friends."

Iona seems a bit overwhelmed by Crescentia's excitement, but she cannot help but smile.

"If Ariadne does not mind," Iona says.

Crescentia hugs her and gushes about all the places to see in France and how she wants to invite Iona and Ariadne to her wedding. Once Erik proposes, of course.

"You and Iona should come and visit me too. Nepal is a vision in summer, I am sure you remember," Samaira says, "Or you could visit in autumn to avoid the rain."

"I would prefer to visit sooner than later. I think Iona will love it, too," Ariadne says, "There are many forests she would enjoy exploring."

"Splendid," Samaira smiles.

Then Ariadne spies Samuel approaching. Ariadne quickly closes the portal and glances at Iona, who turns around to see her uncle walking towards her with his hands in his pockets.

"We shall take our leave," Samaira says, taking Crescentia by the arm, "Crescentia, let me see your witch's mark. Have you told your family yet?"

"No, I haven't. I am waiting to surprise them," Crescentia grins.

Samaira and Crescentia chatter away as they walk to the dining hall. Iona makes all the leftover water evaporate so the mud will not soil anyone's shoes or hems.

"Good day, Iona," Samuel says.

"Good day, Samuel. How are you?" Iona asks gently.

"I am... Well, I am quite awful, in fact. I am still in a bit of shock," Samuel admits.

Iona goes to him and pulls him into an embrace. Samuel is hesitant at first, but he returns the embrace and looks to be holding back tears. When Iona pulls away, Samuel composes himself.

"When we searched Elise's room, we found her maleficium grimoires and burned them, though no matter how many times us warlocks and witches burn those books, they always seem to resurface somewhere else," Samuel says, "We also disposed of the love potion she made."

Ariadne is relieved to hear it.

"Where is Elise now?" Iona asks.

"In my apartments. Salvador has remolded her illusion to make her more comfortable. The professors and I agree that for now, until we are certain that she has no magic left and no way to regain it, she should remain in the illusion. She will need to be tried and punished for her crimes," Samuel says.

"I am so sorry," Iona says again.

"If there is anything we can do, please let us know," Ariadne says.

"Of course," Samuel says, "Thank you for not… hurting her. Anyone else would have made her suffer when she lost her powers and became vulnerable to attacks. I am unsure of what life she could possibly lead now, but at least if she is alive, she may be reformed."

Iona nods, her expression darkening as she considers what Elise had tried to do to Ariadne. Iona will never forgive Elise for that, or for what she'd tried to do to Crescentia.

"I come with sad news that I hope you can understand," Samuel says, "Violet and I are unable to host you this summer. We require time to heal from this awful ordeal. When all of this mess is officially resolved as best as it can be, I would still very much like for you and Ariadne to visit, though I would understand if you were uncomfortable," Samuel says.

"Whenever you and your wife are ready, we would be honored to visit your home," Iona says.

Ariadne nods in agreement and Samuel seems relieved to hear it.

"Thank you," Samuel says.

"Of course," Iona says.

"Until then," Samuel says, with a melancholy smile.

Ariadne watches Samuel walking away. To her own eyes, he looks like a broken man that may never recover. Through Iona's eyes, she sees a man who is unfairly suffering for the sins of his family.

"Are you okay, love?" Ariadne asks, taking Iona's hand and kissing her knuckles.

"Yes," Iona says with a small smile.

"I require your help with something," Ariadne says.

Iona looks into Ariadne's mind and sees her plan.

"Will you come with me?" Ariadne asks.

"Most certainly," Iona says, her eyes filled with compassion.

As the thought enters Ariadne's mind, a portal appears before them. On the other side is a house that looks similar to Zerynthos Manor but not as grand. Iona creates necklaces with communication charms, then Ariadne steps through the portal first and offers her hand to help Iona step through too. Once their familiars jump across, the portal disappears.

They are surrounded by Thessaly's beauty. A looming ridge of brown rock stands before them with grass that is impossibly green. Olive trees are planted in a line down the front path, and behind them, in the distance, a peaceful river stretches on into the horizon.

"Is that where..." Iona whispers.

"Yes," Ariadne says, unable to turn and look at it, but she can still hear the sound of the river's water, where her life had almost been taken.

Iona takes Ariadne's hand, the warmth of her palm a simple comfort to her. Ariadne takes a deep breath as they approach the front door of the manor. Ariadne knocks three times. When a servant answers the door, Ariadne tells them that she is here to visit Vivien Nicolo. The servant allows them to wait in the courtyard while she informs the Nicolos of their arrival.

"How dare you show your face here again," an angry woman shouts as she descends the staircase.

Ariadne recognizes the woman, though she looks older now all these years later. She is wearing a black dress and her hair is peppered with grey.

"Mrs. Nicolo," Ariadne starts to say, but she is interrupted.

"I would never allow you to be within ten paces of my daughter. Never again," Mrs. Nicolo says.

Then when Mrs. Nicolo notices Merlin's staff, she loses all her words.

"Mrs. Nicolo, I would like to help Vivien if you would let me," Ariadne says, trying to remain polite.

"If you desired to help her, you would not have done what you did in the first place," Mrs. Nicolo hisses.

"I was protecting myself from your daughter," Ariadne says, "Do not pretend to have the moral high ground in this matter."

Mrs. Nicolo glowers at Ariadne, then glances at Iona.

"And who might you be?" Mrs. Nicolo asks.

"Iona Evora Lysander," Iona says with a polite curtsy.

"A Lysander and a Zerynthos?" Mrs. Nicolo asks, "What an odd pairing. I would not-"

Mrs. Nicolo stops midsentence when she notices Morgan's pendant shimmering on Iona's chest.

"Please, we only wish to help," Iona says.

Mrs. Nicolo looks between them with suspicion in her eyes.

"If you allow me to see your daughter for fifteen minutes, I give you my word that you will never see me again," Ariadne says.

Mrs. Nicolo's frown never wavers but a glimmer of hope brightens her eyes.

"Very well," Mrs. Nicolo says.

Mrs. Nicolo turns on her heels and walks back towards the staircase. They follow her up the stairs and down the hall until they stop at the last door.

"Do not make me regret this," Mrs. Nicolo says.

Ariadne does not even acknowledge her as she opens the door and steps inside. The room is dim and musty. The windows are covered, and the weak fire barely provides any light or warmth. There on the bed lays a young woman wearing a white nightgown. She has light brown hair and long eyelashes.

At first it looked as if she was sleeping but when Ariadne steps closer, Vivien's blue eyes are open, cloudy, and unseeing. Ariadne chokes on a sob at the sight of the woman who was once her closest friend. Iona closes the door behind them, then rushes over to Ariadne to comfort her.

To be alive inside but unable to move or speak is a tortuous plight fit for the pit of Tarturus. Ariadne had pictured what Vivien would look like but seeing her before her very eyes is so much worse than Ariadne had imagined. Ariadne steps closer and sits on the edge of Vivien's bed.

"I am here," Iona whispers.

Ariadne takes Iona's hand and like they did with Crescentia, they place their palms against Vivien's forehead and chant the healing spell. The stone on Merlin's staff glows until it illuminates the entire room. Ariadne grits her teeth as magic spills from her and into Vivien. She closes her eyes and bears the pain until finally the staff dims and the spell is finished. When Ariadne moves her and Iona's hands away, Vivien looks up at them with wide, childlike eyes.

"Ariadne?" Vivien asks, "But... I thought I..."

"You tried to," Ariadne says, unable to suppress her bitterness.

Vivien looks down in shame, then tenses when she sees her body.

"You have been catatonic for seven years," Ariadne says, her voice barely a whisper, "When you tried to drown me, I used illusion magic to make you stop. I broke your mind, and no one could mend it. Not until now."

Vivien starts to cry and reaches for Ariadne's hands, "I am so, so sorry. My father made me do it. I tried to tell him you were my friend, but he insisted that you were my enemy. He said if you aged much more, I would have no chance at claiming the pendant. Please forgive me. Please, please!"

"Vivien..." Ariadne takes a deep breath and pulls her hands away, "I understand that it is like no time has passed for you but for me, it has been seven long years."

"No, I was awake the entire time," Vivien says, "I only forgot how the fight ended. I did not know if I had killed you or not. I do not remember any of the illusions you made. I think my mind has suppressed it."

"Good," Ariadne says, unable to think of the illusions she'd made without shuddering.

"You have the pendant," Vivien says with admiration when she notices Iona standing behind Ariadne.

"Yes," Iona says, stepping closer to the bed, "How do you do. My name is Iona."

Vivien reaches out to touch the opal with the tips of her fingers. She takes her hand back with a wince when the magic burns her.

"I am glad the pendant is taken," Vivien says, "It was poisoning everyone against each other."

Vivien sighs and shifts in bed to test her atrophied muscles.

"Would you like us to fetch your mother?" Iona asks, "She is right outside the door."

"Wait a moment," Vivien says, "Please, I do not know what I will say to her."

"She is very protective of you," Iona says.

"She stood by while my father forced me to try and kill my friend," Vivien says, "Now that I have a second chance, I do not think I can stomach such toxicity any longer."

Ariadne nods and stands up.

"We can leave from here," Ariadne says, taking the staff and making a portal back to Lysander College.

Vivien's eyebrows raise in shock when she sees the portal, but when Ariadne walks away, she quickly says, "Thank you for healing me. You did not need to, but you did anyway. I will be in your debt for the rest of my life."

Ariadne hesitates before she steps through the portal.

"I cannot be friends with you any longer, but I hope you find peace in your new life," Ariadne says.

Vivien nods, tears forming in her eyes again, "Farewell,

Ariadne."

Ariadne turns away and steps through the portal, leaving all thoughts of Vivien behind in that room.

29 – IONA

"**G**oodbye," Crescentia says as she hugs Iona so tightly, she can barely breathe.

"Goodbye," Iona wheezes, "I shall see you very soon."

"Not soon enough," Crescentia says when she pulls away.

Iona already misses her, her first true friend in the world.

"Crescentia..." Iona says.

"If you apologize again, I will wring your pretty little neck, then Ariadne will murder me, and the world will go back to the chaos it was before," Crescentia warns.

Iona chuckles, "I only meant to say that I am grateful for your friendship and forgiveness."

"There was nothing to forgive," Crescentia insists.

"I avoided you for weeks without telling you why," Iona argues.

Crescentia sighs and puts both her hands on Iona's shoulders.

"The illusion of me quite literally led you to your doom, dragged you into the forest, and even when your eyes told you it was me, what did you do?" Crescentia asks.

"I still knew it was not you," Iona admits.

"Precisely. And you told me that you only doubted whether it was me when Merlin told you the malefician was someone close to you," Crescentia says.

"Yes, that is true too," Iona says.

"All I hear are copious examples of your fondness for me. And who could blame you? I am quite spectacular," Crescentia grins.

Iona giggles. Crescentia moves her hands from Iona's shoulders to hold Iona's hands in hers.

"Only a true friend would still believe my innocence even when a force of pure evil tried to convince you otherwise," Crescentia says, "You never need to apologize. I only wish I could have been more of a comfort to you in such a tumultuous time."

"You were," Iona says, "You were kind to me before I was a Lysander. Before anyone knew I was powerful."

"Then let us leave this unfortunate business in the past where it belongs," Crescentia says.

"Alright," Iona agrees.

Crescentia brings Iona into another warm hug. Iona smiles and takes solace in knowing that only a few weeks from now, she will see Crescentia again. Iona never thought she would visit Brazil, France, and Nepal all in one summer, but fortunately with an artifact like Merlin's staff, travel is but a thought away.

Ariadne is saying her goodbyes to Samaira across the courtyard. They are less maudlin than Iona and Crescentia, likely because they have been friends for so many years and know they will see each other again as they always have. Samaira is holding her orange kitten, which appears almost fully grown, while Ariadne scratches under its chin.

"Write to me. I want to hear all about your salacious adventures under the Brazilian sun," Crescentia waggles her eyebrows, "No details spared."

"I promise I will... when I have the time," Iona blushes.

Crescentia teases her a bit more before taking her leave. Iona watches her step inside the carriage that will take her down from the mountains to the train station, since Crescentia despises traveling by broom. Iona looks around at the Lysander

College grounds, not knowing if she will ever return here again.

So much has changed in her since the first day she'd arrived here. She has learned a great deal about magic, found family she did not know she had, found everlasting love with her once bitter rival, and suffered for months at the hand of her own cousin. Saying goodbye to this place is bittersweet.

"You have your work cut out for you, you know," Ksenia says from behind Iona.

Iona turns and sees Ksenia watching her intently. Iona has not spoken to Ksenia since she had lost the trials. She wears a light grey dress that makes her intuitive sky-blue eyes even more prominent.

"Why do you say that?" Iona asks.

"Whatever truce we may have here on these grounds will not be found out there. Magic folk will always be vying for influence, control, power... Those from sempiterna bloodlines may not be so quick to accept an orphaned Lysander witch with only a circumstantial tie to their world. They will almost certainly not trust a Zerynthos witch after everything Katrin did in her time. Countless witches and warlocks were betrayed and exploited by her. They will see Ariadne as her ghost," Ksenia warns.

Iona glances at Ariadne, who is still talking with Samaira.

"Ariadne is entirely different from her grandmother," Iona says.

"So, she says," Ksenia mutters, "Words mean little."

"She is," Iona insists.

Ksenia shrugs and Iona glowers at her. Iona knows Ariadne's mind better than Ksenia ever could. Nevertheless, she might be right about Ariadne's reputation preceding her. And Iona's lack of any reputation could also be a challenge.

"You intend to share the pendant's magic with all witches," Ksenia guesses.

"Yes, and I shall," Iona says.

"You will be challenging a century of tradition. Be sure that you are ready for such a debacle," Ksenia says.

"Why are you suddenly concerned with my success, Ksenia?" Iona asks, tilting her head with curiosity, "What did Morgan show you within the moonstone arches?"

Ksenia narrows her eyes and ignores Iona's question.

"I only want to warn you," Ksenia says again, "All the magic in the world cannot fix such deeply intrenched sovereignty."

Iona nods, confused by Ksenia's decision to tell her this. She did not think Ksenia cared what happened to her.

"I may not be able to reform every mind. I can only lead by example and help those in need," Iona says, "That is my intention with whatever time I have."

Ksenia regards her critically, but her hatred is not as overt as it once was. Iona is not entirely sure, but she thinks she may have finally earned Ksenia's respect.

"Fair enough," Ksenia says, "Goodbye, Iona Evora."

"Ready?" Ariadne asks.

"Yes," Iona says.

Ariadne searches Iona mind for an image of her home on the cliff. The portal opens up and Iona gasps softly at the sight of the white cottage. The windows are dirty from months of sea weather without being cleaned. They step through the portal and Ariadne goes to close it again.

"Wait," Iona says, turning to peer through the portal and look at Lysander College one last time.

The belltower chimes twelve and Iona listens to the sound with a bittersweet smile, a feeling of enouement giving her goosebumps. Wisp comes to sit next to Iona and licks her hand. Iona reaches down and pets the black fur on her cheeks and ears.

"Will you miss it?" Ariadne asks.

"Yes, I believe I will," Iona says, "Not the bad parts, of course, but it was not all bad. Will you miss it?"

"No," Ariadne says, "I am glad to leave, if I'm honest. I could never be fully content in a place where you were in danger."

Iona nods and gives the college one final look, then glances at Ariadne, who closes the portal. Iona approaches the cottage and opens the door. Every surface of the furniture is covered in a layer of dust. Pieces of the dust float through the air, made visible by the rays of light streaming through the clouded windows.

Iona does not remember the cottage being so tiny. Before, it and the beach had been her entire world. Now, after living at the college with its many grand rooms, the cottage seems quaint and meager.

Iona has a flash of memory, remembering her and her mother eating beef stew at the kitchen table and laughing together. She does not remember the joke, only that she'd felt safe and loved. A tear escapes from Iona's eye and she quickly wipes it away.

Ariadne appraises the cottage with a sober expression. Aster runs around the space and sniffs anything he can find with rapt curiosity until he sneezes from the dust going up his nose. Wisp follows Iona and does not seem interested in the cottage at all, as if the fox had been here before.

Iona steps into her mother's old room. Moths have made their home in her mother's bed sheets and flit here and there across the white fabric. Iona takes a trunk from her mother's wardrobe and set it onto the bed, startling the moths and making a cloud of dust. Iona coughs and waves the dust away, then opens the trunk.

Iona looks through her mothers' room for any drawings, jewelry, books, and clothes that she would like to keep in remembrance. Iona passes by a basket of pearls that her mother kept by her bedside. Sometimes her mother had trouble sleeping and she would conjure pearls until she drifted off. Iona runs her fingers through the lustrous spheres, lifts her hand up, and shifts her palm around until only one pearl is left. Iona wraps the pearl in a handkerchief and places it in the trunk.

Iona also finds a small drawing in her mother's papers. It is of a beautiful beach with clear blue water and mountains along the coastline. The words "São Paulo, Brazil" are written in the corner in her mother's elegant script. Iona puts it in her pocket.

Iona goes to her own room next and places the trunk onto her bed. She packs her favorite books, shells, and stones from the beach that she'd found when she was a child, and any clothing that she had left behind. When she is finished, she closes the clasps on the trunk and holds it by the handle. Ariadne goes to her and takes the trunk to set it with their other luggage.

Iona is about to leave the cottage when she sees a flash of silver in the corner of her eye. Iona looks back to her mother's room and there is something shiny on the bed that was not there before. When Iona approaches, she recognizes the bell that she'd gotten for her eighteenth birthday. Next to the bell is a piece of paper with her mother's handwriting that says, "Our bodies are our gardens, and our wills are our gardeners."

Iona recognizes the quote from the Shakespeare play, *Othello*. Her mother used to read Shakespeare to her on occasion, though this particular line had not held significance to Iona until now. Iona picks up the silver trinket, remembering her mother telling her that the bell had secrets that her father had not disclosed.

"What is that?" Ariadne asks from the doorway.

"It was a birthday gift," Iona says, "My father made it for me before he died."

Ariadne steps closer to admire the silver bell, "It is beautiful."

Iona smiles and says, "Would you mind terribly if I took a moment alone on the beach? I should not be too long."

"Of course not, take as much time as you need. I shall wait for you here," Ariadne says, kissing Iona on the cheek.

Iona takes Wisp with her as they make their way down the many steps along the cliffside. When Iona's boots touch the shifting sand, she breathes in the salty air and feels ten years younger. The air is warm, at least for Cornwall, as summer takes its hold again. Wisp runs ahead of her and digs holes into the sand.

As Iona walks along the edge of the waves, she spins the silver bell between her fingers. She feels the magic locked inside.

Iona holds the bell out in front of her and lets it ring. The bell's chime is clear and bright and penetrating. Iona senses magic swirling around her, then watches as a ghost materializes before her, a tall man with reddish-brown hair and freckles. He wears a three-piece brown suit and a hat that he removes when his soft blue eyes meet Iona's. Iona recognizes the man when he smiles jubilantly at her, the way he used to when she was young.

"Father," Iona whispers, then runs across the sand, "Father!"

When Iona wraps her arms around her father's neck, and he spins her around.

"Iona," her father says, "I thought this day would never come."

Iona hugs him close and cries into his shoulder. Then she pulls away and laughs through her tears. She cannot believe he is here.

"Look at you," her father says fondly, "You have grown into the woman I always hoped you would be."

Iona beams and beckons Wisp to meet her father.

"And Wisp, the bravest fox to ever live," her father grins as he scratches the fox's ear.

"I would have rung the bell sooner, but I did not know I had it," Iona says.

"I am happy to see you now, with your troubles far behind you," her father says, "I only have a short while before I will go back to the other side. Your mother sends her love."

"Please tell her I love her too. I miss her terribly every day," Iona says.

"I will tell her," he promises.

Iona's cheeks hurt from smiling. She is relieved to know that her mother is not alone in death.

"Shall we, my dear?" her father asks, offering his arm.

Iona takes it and they walk along the beach. The sun breaks through the clouds and makes the water sparkle.

"I would like to apologize for my family. Not Samuel of course. He is the best of us all. But the others..." her father trails off.

"You do not need to apologize," Iona says, and she means it. She has no resentment left regarding the secret of her parentage.

"I hope that my name does not burden you," he says, "I believe that you will redefine the name of Lysander and I cannot wait to see it from the beyond."

"I am proud to have your name, as I am also proud of mother's," Iona says.

"As you should be. Your mother is the strongest, most resilient creature I have ever known," her father says, then chuckles, "She found me in the afterlife not long ago and said I have a great deal to make up for since I had the audacity to die so much earlier than her."

"'Tis shameful behavior," Iona grins.

"I have an eternity to atone," her father says with mock sincerity, "And now I hear you have your own bond with Ariadne Zerynthos."

"I do," Iona says.

"Do inform me if she ever causes you trouble. I would not be averse to some innocuous haunting if she ever vexes you," her father says mischievously.

Iona laughs, "I think the poor girl deserves some peace for a while, but I shall keep that in mind."

"Of course. She has been quite loyal. A lesser witch would have abandoned you in the face of such malevolent magic," her father says.

"Would you like to meet her?" Iona asks.

"No, not today," he says, "I am sure I will become acquainted with her in time. For now, I would like to stroll with my daughter. I almost forgot the beauty of this beach."

They both look out at the sea as the sun dances off the waves.

"What does the other side look like for you and mother?" Iona asks, "For Morgan, it was a marsh. For Merlin, an island."

"How casually you mention such powerful magic users," her father chuckles, "Our new home is a forest with tall trees, sweet water, gentle animals, and bright stars."

"How lovely," Iona says, "I hope to visit this year for Samhain, if you would both have me."

"We look forward to welcoming you," her father says.

They walk for about ten more minutes in comfortable silence. Iona rests her head on her father's shoulder and remembers when she was small, and her tiny hand had been dwarfed by his when he ran around the beach with her.

"Did you ever regret leaving home?" Iona asks.

Her father looks down at her and considers her question, "Sometimes I did, but only partly. I missed having all of my power. It took so much magic to hide us away. I am still impressed that your mother was able to sustain the illusion when I was gone. There were days when I wished life was simpler and I could see my brother again. It was worth it to protect you."

"Samuel missed you too," Iona says.

"In retrospect, I believe I should have brought him with us. Forced him to, if necessary," her father muses, "I offered, of course, but he'd decided to stay behind to be with Violet. He was able to take over the Lysander estate when our parents passed on. He was able to be a mentor to you when I could not. He is his own man, as valiant as ever."

"He did not deserve what Elise did," Iona says, "She had a father and mother who loved her, and she could only wallow in discontent."

"Elise idolized the wrong members of our family. My parents, her grandparents, made her so many promises, filled her head with such delusions of grandeur, that when she learned she was not superior like she was led to believe, it drove her to madness," her father says, "They attempted to do the same to me and Samuel in our youth. We would look to Leona, your mother, and not see how we could ever be inherently superior to someone as lovely and clever as her. It strains credulity."

Her father clears his throat of emotion.

"My love for your mother was worth more than any accolades or power. Those things all seemed trivial to me the older I became and the more in love I was. I saw the beauty of the world in her eyes and that was all I needed," her father says, "Then you came into this world, and my love only grew."

Her father suddenly stops walking and Iona's heart sinks.

"It is almost time for me to say goodbye," her father says.

Iona hugs him close, not wanting him to leave.

"What is past cannot be undone now," he says, "This year was a time for you to unravel mysteries long forgotten, but now I wish for you to also look to the future and treasure the present."

"Yes, father," Iona whispers.

"I love you," her father says.

Iona loses her balance and falls forwards when her father suddenly disappears. Iona lands on her hands and knees in the sand, then sits back on her feet and sighs.

"I love you too," Iona whispers.

When Iona does make it back up all the stairs to the cliff, her tears have dried, and she is lost in thought. Ariadne had conjured a picnic for them and is drinking a cup of tea. She sets her cup and saucer aside when she sees Iona approach.

"I saw my father," Iona says.

"Just now?" Ariadne asks, "How is that possible?"

"This was a talisman," Iona says, handing Ariadne the silver bell, "A very powerful one."

"Ah, I see," Ariadne says, admiring the silver trinket.

Iona kneels beside Ariadne and guides her chin up to press a kiss on her lips. It is sweet and gentle, and when Iona pulls away, Ariadne sighs contentedly.

"Your hair looks beautiful in this light," Ariadne observes as she takes a strand of Iona's hair between her fingers.

Iona smiles shyly, picks a sandwich from Ariadne's picnic, and takes a bite. It is filled with cucumber and cream cheese. Then she notices that pieces of food have been arranged in a line across the blanket they are sitting on. Iona looks at Ariadne in question.

"I was mapping time," Ariadne says.

"Oh, of course," Iona says.

Ariadne chuckles, "Look."

Ariadne points to a sandwich at the beginning of the line.

"That is when you spoke to your mother in the past. You told her that she will make Samuel swear not to tell you that he is your uncle," Ariadne says, "And so she knew she must do so, to resolve time."

Iona frowns, still kicking herself for letting that slip.

"It was meant to be," Ariadne says.

"Yes, I know. It would break time irreparably if my mother did not tell him," Iona says.

"No, beyond that," Ariadne says.

Ariadne points to an apple in the middle of the line.

"This is when you discovered you were a Lysander and spoke with Samuel in his office," Ariadne says, then she picks up the apple and moves it to the front of the line, "If he had told you at the very beginning, then Elise would have known sooner too. Samuel would have told her, or perhaps you would have."

Ariadne drags her finger along the timeline of food as she speaks.

"Elise began practicing maleficium when she learned who you were, when she saw your witch's mark at the blue comet ritual. If she knew earlier, she may have begun practicing dark magic much sooner and would have attacked when you barely knew any spells at all. Far before you had confidence in your power," Ariadne says, "And when was our transmundane magnetism activated? At the blue comet ritual. The same day, the same exact moment that Elise discovered your witch's mark, which ensured that we would be connected even more strongly before Elise decided to attack."

Iona's eyes widen at that, and she begins to see what Ariadne sees.

"You learned you were a Lysander at the exact right moment. As did Elise, because once fate connected us, we were far too entangled for her to attack you without me noticing," Ariadne says, moving the apple back to its proper place in the timeline.

"Goodness," Iona whispers.

"If I am right about this, fate has been very kind to us. In odd ways, but still," Ariadne says.

"This praephora business is only going to make matters more complicated," Iona gripes.

"If it protects you, it is worth it," Ariadne says.

Ariadne takes Iona's hand. They both look at the line of food, lost in thought for a moment.

"What did your father tell you?" Ariadne asks.

"He told me to let go of the past. I should treasure the present and look towards the future," Iona says, "He also said that I will redefine the Lysander name."

"I think you will too," Ariadne says, conjuring a pink peony and handing it to Iona.

"Always so charming when you want to be," Iona says, lifting the flower to her nose.

"Only for you," Ariadne says, kissing Iona on the cheek.

Iona grins and looks out over the cliff's edge at the roiling ocean waves. There was a time when this was all she knew, and it was beautiful. Now, she is ready to leave it behind.

Iona stands and approaches the white cottage. Iona checks that Wisp and Aster are not inside, then closes her eyes. She hears the breaking of glass, the impact of cracking bricks, the clatter of metal, quieter and quieter until there is no sound left. When Iona opens her eyes, the house is gone.

Ariadne approaches and takes Iona's hand. Looking to her for permission, Iona nods. The labradorite stone on her staff glows as blooms of sea campion flowers grow from the dirt patch where the cottage's foundation once stood. At the center of the flowers, an oak tree and yew tree grow, their trunks twisting around each other until their branches create a single canopy over the small white flowers.

"There," Ariadne says, "Now you have something to visit if you ever decide to return."

"It is perfect," Iona says, putting her arm around Ariadne's waist.

They admire the trees for only a moment, then Iona decides she is ready to leave. A Brazilian beach is awaiting them.

"Shall we?" Ariadne asks.

"We shall," Iona says, handing Ariadne the drawing that she'd found in her mother's room, "Can you take us here?"

Ariadne takes the drawing and studies it. Then she centers herself and creates a portal to another beach that is bathed in bright sunshine and has crystal-clear blue water. Wisp and Aster jump straight through and run down the beach. Then Ariadne takes Iona's hand, and they step across together. Iona does not look back.

BOOKS BY THIS AUTHOR

Her Paramour

In 16th century Spain, Liliana Ruiz is a lowly maid in the household of a powerful Lord. Liliana finds herself at the beck and call of his spoiled, beautiful daughter. When Liliana's attraction to the Lord's daughter is revealed under devastating circumstances, Liliana is sent away in disgrace and imprisoned.

Heartbroken by betrayal, Liliana thinks all is lost until she is unexpectedly rescued by two mysterious and beautiful noblewomen, Duchess Violante Martin and her closest friend Elena Moreno. The Duchess will erase Liliana's past if she agrees to be Elena's paramour while Violante is away advising the Queen of Spain. By day, Liliana would act as Elena's dutiful handmaiden. By night, she would satisfy Elena's every need and desire...

Liliana must decide whether she will walk away and take her chances on her own or will she dare to explore her desires with the alluring Elena. Contains mature themes.

Pretty Little Pledge

Wild parties, cruel games, and an unexpected romance of sapphic proportions.

Nicole knows that pledging to the most exclusive sorority on campus means every boundary she has will be pushed to its limit, she will be debased and humiliated on a daily basis, and she'll have to endure all this suffering in silence because hazing isn't technically allowed.

What she doesn't expect is to fall for her sorority big sister, Christina, a beautiful blonde bombshell who enjoys toying with her a little too much.

Christina is a star soccer player with a killer smile and a mysterious secret. Nicole becomes Christina's assigned pledge, shares a room with her, and spends every waking minute with her. The line between pledge and member blurs until they're forced to admit their attraction to each other.

When pledging evolves from humiliating mind games, to blackmail, to an unprecedented campus controversy, Nicole and Christina must decide where their loyalties lie.

Pretty Little Pledge is a standalone F/F sorority bully romance novel that contains scenes and references to hazing, abuse, assault, and detailed sex. Suitable for readers 18+.

Gemma

Growing up, Gemma Evans was always aware of her attraction to other girls but never acted on it out of fear of her parent's disapproval. When she starts her freshman year at the University of St. Maria's, a women's college full of devout Catholic students and faculty, she continues to suppress her sexuality to avoid judgment from her pious classmates.

That is until she meets Cole...

Gemma's roommate, Collette Khloros, tests Gemma's resolve

for the first time and Gemma finds herself finally giving in to her desires. The more Gemma connects with Cole, the more difficult it is for Gemma to justify hiding her sexuality. Cole wants to take that step, but Gemma isn't ready.

When things go wrong, Gemma has to choose between the life that she's expected to accept and the one person who loves her for who she really is. Contains mature themes.

Printed in Great Britain
by Amazon

49924811R00274